Pedro Calderón de la Barca, Denis Florence MacCarthy

Calderon's Dramas

Pedro Calderón de la Barca, Denis Florence MacCarthy

Calderon's Dramas

ISBN/EAN: 9783337375461

Printed in Europe, USA, Canada, Australia, Japan

Cover: Foto ©Andreas Hilbeck / pixelio.de

More available books at **www.hansebooks.com**

CALDERON'S DRAMAS.

THE WONDER-WORKING MAGICIAN:
LIFE IS A DREAM:
THE PURGATORY OF SAINT PATRICK.

NOW FIRST TRANSLATED FULLY FROM THE SPANISH IN THE METRE
OF THE ORIGINAL.

BY

DENIS FLORENCE MAC-CARTHY.

LONDON: HENRY S. KING & CO.,
65 CORNHILL, AND 12, PATERNOSTER ROW.
1873.

CONTENTS.

INTRODUCTION.

Two of the dramas contained in this volume are the most celebrated of all Calderon's writings. The first, *La Vida es Sueño*, has been translated into many languages and performed with success on almost every stage in Europe but that of England. So late as the winter of 1866-7, in a Russian version, it drew crowded houses to the great theatre of Moscow; while a few years earlier, as if to give a signal proof of the reality of its title, and that Life was indeed a Dream, the Queen of Sweden expired in the theatre of Stockholm during the performance of *La Vida es Sueño*. In England the play has been much studied for its literary value and the exceeding beauty and lyrical sweetness of some passages ; but with the exception of a version by John Oxenford published in *The Monthly Magazine* for 1842, which being in blank verse does not represent the form of the original, no complete translation into English has been attempted. Some scenes translated with considerable elegance in the metre of the original were published by Archbishop Trench in 1856 ; but these comprised only a portion of the graver division of the drama. The present version of the entire play has been made with the advantages which the author's long experience in the study and interpretation of Calderon has enabled him to apply to this master-piece of the great Spanish poet. All the forms of verse have been preserved ; while the closeness of the translation may be inferred from the fact, that not only the whole play but every speech and fragment of a speech are represented in English in the exact number of lines of the original, without the sacrifice, it is to be hoped, of one important idea.

A note by Hartzenbusch in the last edition of the drama published at Madrid (1872), tells that *La Vida es Sueño,* is founded on a story which turns out to be substantially the same as that with which English students are familiar as the foundation of the famous Induction to the *Taming of the Shrew.* Calderon found it however in a different work from that in which Shakespeare met with it, or rather his predecessor, the anonymous author of *The Taming of a Shrew,* whose work supplied to Shakespeare the materials of his own comedy.

On this subject Malone thus writes. " The circumstance on which the Induction to the anonymous play, as well as to the present Comedy [Shakespeare's *Taming of the Shrew*], is founded, is related (as Langbaine has observed) by Heuterus, *Rerum Burgund.* lib. iv. The earliest English original of this story in prose that I have met with is the following, which is found in Goulart's *Admirable and Memorable Histories,* translated by E. Grimstone, quarto, 1607 ; but this tale (which Goulart translated from Heuterus) had undoubtedly appeared in English, in some other shape, before 1594 :

" Philip called the good Duke of *Burgundy,* in the memory of our ancestors, being at Bruxelles with his Court, and walking one night after supper through the streets, accompanied by some of his favourites, he found lying upon the stones a certaine artisan that was very dronke, and that slept soundly. It pleased the prince in this artisan to make trial of the vanity of our life,

whereof he had before discoursed with his familiar friends.
He therefore caused this sleeper to be taken up, and
carried into his palace; he commands him to be layed
in one of the richest beds; a riche night-cap to be given
him; his foule shirt to be taken off, and to have another
put on him of fine holland. When as this dronkard had
digested his wine, and began to awake, behold there
comes about his bed Pages and Groomes of the Duke's
Chamber, who drawe the curteines, make many
courtesies, and being bare-headed, aske him if it please
him to rise, and what apparell it would please him to
put on that day. They bring him rich apparell. This
new *Monsieur* amazed at such courtesie, and doubting
whether he dreamt* or waked, suffered himselfe to be
drest, and led out of the chamber. There came noble-
men which saluted him with all honour, and conduct him
to the Masse, where with great ceremonie they give him
the booke of the Gospell, and the Pixe to kisse, as they
did usually to the Duke. From the Masse they bring him
back unto the pallace; he washes his hands, and sittes
down at the table well furnished. After dinner, the
Great Chamberlain commands cards to be brought with
a great summe of money. This Duke in imagination
playes with the chief of the Court. Then they carry
him to walke in the gardein, and to hunt the hare, and to
hawke. They bring him back into the pallace, where he
sups in state. Candles being light the musitions begin
to play; and the tables taken away, the gentlemen and
gentlewomen fell to dancing. Then they played a
pleasant comedie, after which followed a Banket,
whereat they had presently store of Ipocras and pretious
wine, with all sorts of confitures, to this prince of the
new impression; so as he was dronke, and fell soundlie
asleepe. Hereupon the Duke commanded that he

should be disrobed of all his riche attire. He was put into his old ragges, and carried into the same place, where he had been found the night before; where he spent that night. Being awake in the morning, he began to remember what had happened before; he knewe not whether it were true indeede, or a dream that had troubled his braine. But in the end, after many discourses, he concludes that ALL WAS BUT A DREAME that had happened unto him; and so entertained his wife, his children, and his neighbours, without any other apprehension."

It is curious to find that the same anecdote which formed the Induction to the original *Taming of a Shrew*, and which, from a comic point of view, Shakspeare so wonderfully developed in his own comedy, Calderon invested with such solemn and sublime dignity in *La Vida es Sueño*. He found it, as Señor Hartzenbusch points out in the edition of 1872 already quoted, in the very amusing *Viage Entretenido* of Augustin de Rojas, which was first published in 1603. Hartzenbusch refers to the modern edition of Rojas, Madrid, 1793, tomo 1, pp. 261, 262, 263, but in a copy of the Lerida edition of 1615, in my own possession, I find the anecdote at folios 118, 119, 120. There are some slight differences between the version of Rojas and that of Goulart, but the incidents and the persons are the same. The conclusion to which the artizan arrived at, in the version of Goulart, that all had been a dream, is expressed more strongly by the Duke himself in the story as told by Rojas.

"Y dijo entónces el Duque : 'veis aqui, amigos, *Lo que es el Mundo : Todo es un Sueño*, pues esto verdaderamente ha pasado por éste, como habéis visto, y le parece que lo ha soñado.' "—

The story in all probability came originally from the

East. Mr. Lane in his translation of the Thousand and One Nights gives a very interesting narrative which he believes to be founded on an historical fact in which Haroun Al Raschid plays the part of the good Duke of Burgundy, and Abu-l-Hasan the original of Christopher Sly. The gravity of the treatment and certain incidents in this Oriental story recall more strongly Calderon's drama than the Induction to the *Taming of the Shrew*. *La Vida es Sueño* was first published either at the end of 1635 or beginning of 1636.

The *Aprobacion* for its publication along with eleven other dramas (not nine as Archbishop Trench has stated), was signed on the 6th of November in the former year by the official licenser, Juan Bautista de Sossa. The volume was edited by the poet's brother, Don Joseph Calderon. So scarce has this first authorised collection of any of Calderon's dramas become, that a Spanish writer Don Vicente Garcia de la Huerta, in his *Teatro Español* (Parte Segunda, tomo 3°), denies the existence of this volume of 1635, and states that it did not appear until 1640. As if to corroborate this view, Barrera in his *Catálogo del Teatro antiguo Español*, gives the date 1640 to the *Primera parte de comedias de Calderon* edited by his brother Joseph.

There can be no doubt, however, that the volume appeared in 1635 or 1636 as stated. In 1637 Don Joseph Calderon published the *Second Part* of his brother's dramas containing like the former volume twelve plays.* In his dedication of this volume to D. Rodrigo de Mendoza, Joseph Calderon expressly

---

* In the library of the British Museum there is a fine copy of this *Segunda Parte de Comedias de Don Pedro Calderon de la Barca*. Madrid, 1637. Mr. Ticknor mentions (1863) that he too had a copy of this interesting volume.

alludes to the First Part of his brother's comedies which he had "printed." "En la primera Parte, Excellentissimo Señor, de las comedias que imprimi de Don Pedro Calderon de La Barca, mi hermano," etc. This of course settles the fact of the prior publication of the first Part. It is singular, however, to find that the most famous of all Calderon's dramas should have been frequently ascribed to Lope de Vega. So late as 1857 it is given in an Italian version by Giovanni La Cecilia, under the title of *La Vita è un Sogno*, as a drama of Lope de Vega, with the date 1628. This of course is a mistake, but Señor Hartzenbusch, who makes no allusion to this circumstance, admits that two dramas of Lope de Vega, which it is presumed preceded the composition of Calderon's play turn on very nearly the same incidents as those of *La Vida es Sueño*. These are *Lo que ha de ser*, and *Barlan y Josafá*. He gives a passage from each of these dramas which seem to be the germ of the fine lament of Sigismund, which the reader will find translated at pp. 11 and 12 of the present volume.

Señor Hartzenbusch, in the edition of Calderon's *La Vida es Sueño*, already referred to (Madrid, 1872), prints the passages from Lope de Vega's two dramas, but in neither of them, he justly remarks, can we find anything that at all corresponds to the "grandioso carácter de Segismundo."

The second drama in this volume, *The Wonderful Magician*, is perhaps better known to poetical students in England than even the first, from the spirited fragment Shelley has left us in his "Scenes from Calderon." The preoccupation of a subject by a great master throws immense difficulties in the way of any one who ventures to follow in the same path : but as Shelley allowed himself great licence in his versification, and either from carelessness or an imperfect knowledge of Spanish is occasionally unfaithful to the meaning of his author, it may be hoped in my own version that strict fidelity both as to the form as well as substance of the original may be some compensation for the absence of those higher poetical harmonies to which many of my readers will have been accustomed.

El Magico Prodigioso appeared for the first time in the same volume as *La Vida es Sueño*, prepared for publication in 1635 by Don Joseph Calderon. The translation is comprised in the same number of lines as the original, and all the preceding remarks on *Life is a Dream*, whether in reference to the period of the first publication of the drama in Spain, or the principles I kept in view while attempting this version may be applied to it. As in the Case of *Life is a Dream*, *The Wonderful Magician* has previously been translated entire by an English writer, (*Justina*, by J. H. 1848); but as Archbishop Trench truly observes, "the writer did not possess that command of the resources of the English language, which none more than Calderon requires."

The Legend on which Calderon founded *El Magico Prodigioso* will be found in Surius, *De probatis Sanctorum historiis*, t. V. (Col. Agr. 1574), p. 351 : *Vita et Martyrium SS. Cypriani et Justinae, autore Simeone Metaphraste*, and in Chapter cxlii. of the *Legenda Aurea* of Jacobus de Voragine *De Sancta Justina virgine*.

The martyrdom of the Saints took place in the year 290, and their festival is celebrated by the Church on the 26th of September.

Mr. Ticknor in his History of Spanish Literature, 1863, volume ii. p. 369, says that the Wonder-working Magician is founded on "the same legend on which

Milman has founded his 'Martyr of Antioch.'" This is a mistake of the learned writer. " The Martyr of Antioch " is founded not on the history of St. Justina but of Saint Margaret, as Milman himself expressly states. Chapter xciii., *De Sancta Margareta*, in the *Legenda Aurea* of Jacobus de Voragine contains her story.

The third translation in this volume is that of *The Purgatory of St. Patrick*. This, though perhaps not so famous as the two preceding dramas, is intended to be given by Don P. De la Escosura, in a selection of Calderon's finest *comedias*, now being edited by him for the Spanish Academy, as the representative piece of its class—namely, the mystical drama founded on the lives of Saints. Mr. Ticknor prefers it to the more celebrated " Devotion of the Cross," and says that it " is commonly ranked among the best religious plays of the Spanish theatre in the seventeenth century."

In all that relates to the famous cave known through the middle ages as the *Purgatory of Saint Patrick*, as well as the Story of Luis Enius—the Owain Miles of Ancient English poetry—Calderon was entirely indebted to the little volume published at Madrid, in 1627, by Juan Perez de Montalvan, entitled *Vida y Purgatorio de San Patricio*. This singular work met with immense success. It went through innumerable editions, and continues to be reprinted in Spain as a chap-book, down to the present day. I have the fifth impression " improved and en-larged by the author himself," Madrid, 1628, the year after its first appearance : also a later edition, Madrid, 1664. As early as 1637 a French translation appeared at Brussels by " F. A. S. Chartreux, à Bruxelles." In 1642 a second French translation was published at Troyes, by " R. P. François Bouillon, de l'Ordre de S.

François, et Bachelier de Théologie." Mr. Thomas Wright in his " Essay on St. Patrick's Purgatory," London, 1844, makes the singular mistake of supposing that Bouillon's " Histoire de la Vie et Purgatoire de S. Patrice " was founded on the drama of Calderon, it being simply a translation of Montalvan's " Vida y Purgatorio," from which, like itself, Calderon's play was derived. Among other translations of Montalvan's work may be mentioned one in Dutch (Brussels, 1668) and one in Portuguese (Lisbon, 1738). It was also translated into German and Italian, but I find no mention of an English version. For this reason I have thought that a few extracts might be interesting, as showing how closely Calderon adhered even to the language of his predecessor.

In all that relates to the Purgatory, Montalvan's work is itself chiefly compiled from the " Florilegium Insulæ Sanctorum, seu vitæ et Actæ sanctorum Hiberniæ," Paris, 1624, fol. This work, which has now become scarce, was written by Thomas Messingham, an Irish priest, the Superior of the Irish Seminary in Paris. No complete English version appears to have been made of it, but a small tract in English containing everything in the original work that referred to St. Patrick's Purgatory was published at Paris in 1718. As this tract is perhaps more scarce than even the Florilegium itself, the account of the Purgatory as given by Messingham from the MS. of Henry of Saltrey is reprinted in the notes to this drama in the quaint language of the anonymous translator. Of this tract, " printed at *Paris* in 1718 " without the name of author, publisher or printer, I have not been able to trace another copy. In other points of interest connected with Calderon's drama, particularly to the clearing up of the difficulty hitherto felt as to the confused list of authorities at the end, the reader is also referred to the notes.

The present version of *The Purgatory of Saint Patrick* is, with the exception of a few unimportant lines, an entirely new translation. It is made with the utmost care, imitating all the measures and contained, like the two preceding dramas, in the exact number of lines of the original. One passage of the translation which I published in 1853 is retained in the notes, as a tribute of respect to the memory of the late John Rutter Chorley, it having been mentioned with praise by that eminent Spanish scholar in an elaborate review of my earlier translations from Calderon, which appeared in the *Athenæum*, Nov. 19 and Nov. 26, 1853.

It only remains to add that the text I have followed is that of Hartzenbusch in his edition of Calderon's *Come-dias*, Madrid, 1856 (*Biblioteca de Autores Españoles*). His arrangement of the scenes has been followed throughout, thus enabling the reader in a moment to verify for himself the exactness of the translation by a reference to the original, a crucial test which I rather invite than decline.

CLAPHAM PARK, *Easter*, 1873.

LIFE IS A DREAM.

TO

DON JUAN EUGENIO HARTZENBUSCH,

POET, DRAMATIST, NOVELIST, AND CRITIC,

THE MOST ILLUSTRIOUS OF LIVING SPANISH WRITERS,

THIS TRANSLATION

INTO ENGLISH IMITATIVE VERSE

OF

CALDERON'S MOST FAMOUS DRAMA,

Is Inscribed,

WITH THE ESTEEM AND REGARD

OF

THE AUTHOR.

PERSONS.

BASILIUS, *King of Poland.*
SIGISMUND, *his Son.*
ASTOLFO, *Duke of Muscovy.*
CLOTALDO, *a Nobleman.*
ESTRELLA, *a Princess.*
ROSAURA, *a Lady.*
CLARIN, *her Servant.*

Soldiers.
Guards.
Musicians.
Attendants.
Ladies.
Servants.

The Scene is in the Court of Poland, in a fortress at some distance, and in the open field.

LIFE IS A DREAM.

ACT THE FIRST.

At one side a craggy mountain, at the other a tower, the lower part
of which serves as the prison of Sigismund. The door facing
the spectators is half open. The action commences at nightfall.

Scene I.

Rosaura, Clarin.

Rosaura *in man's attire appears on the rocky heights and
descends to the plain. She is followed by* Clarin.

Rosaura.   Wild hippogriff swift speeding,
Thou that dost run, the wingéd winds exceeding,
Bolt which no flash illumes,
Fish without scales, bird without shifting plumes,
And brute awhile bereft
Of natural instinct, why to this wild cleft,
This labyrinth of naked rocks, dost sweep
Unreined, uncurbed, to plunge thee down the steep?
Stay in this mountain wold,
And let the beasts their Phaëton behold.
For I, without a guide,
Save what the laws of destiny decide,
Benighted, desperate, blind,

Take any path whatever that doth wind
Down this rough mountain to its base,
Whose wrinkled brow in heaven frowns in the sun's
    bright face.
Ah, Poland ! in ill mood
Hast thou received a stranger, since in blood
The name thou writest on thy sands
Of her who hardly here fares hardly at thy hands.
My fate may well say so :—
But where shall one poor wretch find pity in her woe ?
    CLARIN.   Say two, if you please ;
Don't leave me out when making plaints like these.
For if we are the two
Who left our native country with the view
Of seeking strange adventures, if we be
The two who, madly and in misery,
Have got so far as this, and if we still
Are the same two who tumbled down this hill,
Does it not plainly to a wrong amount,
To put me in the pain and not in the account ?
    ROSAURA.   I do not wish to impart,
Clarin, to thee, the sorrows of my heart ;
Mourning for thee would spoil the consolation
Of making for thyself thy lamentation ;
For there is such a pleasure in complaining,
That a philosopher I've heard maintaining
One ought to seek a sorrow and be vain of it,
In order to be privileged to complain of it.
    CLARIN.   That same philosopher
Was an old drunken fool, unless I err :
Oh, that I could a thousand thumps present him,
In order for complaining to content him !
But what, my lady, say,
Are we to do, on foot, alone, our way
Lost in the shades of night ?
For see, the sun descends another sphere to light.

ROSAURA.   So strange a misadventure who has seen?
But if my sight deceives me not, between
These rugged rocks, half-lit by the moon's ray
And the declining day,
It seems, or is it fancy? that I see
A human dwelling?
    CLARIN.   So it seems to me,
Unless my wish the longed-for lodging mocks.
    ROSAURA.   A rustic little palace 'mid the rocks
Uplifts its lowly roof,
Scarce seen by the far sun that shines aloof.
Of such a rude device
Is the whole structure of this edifice,
That lying at the feet
Of these gigantic crags that rise to greet
The sun's first beams of gold,
It seems a rock that down the mountain rolled.
    CLARIN.   Let us approach more near,
For long enough we've looked at it from here ;
Then better we shall see
If those who dwell therein will generously
A welcome give us.
    ROSAURA.   See an open door
(Funereal mouth 'twere best the name it bore),
From which as from a womb
The night is born, engendered in its gloom.
                    [*The sound of chains is heard within.*
    CLARIN.   Heavens ! what is this I hear ?
    ROSAURA.   Half ice, half fire, I stand transfixed with
        fear.
    CLARIN.   A sound of chains, is it not ?
Some galley-slave his sentence here hath got ;
My fear may well suggest it so may be.

SCENE II.

SIGISMUND, *in the tower.* ROSAURA, CLARIN.

SIGISMUND (*within*). Alas! Ah, wretched me! Ah,
    wretched me!
ROSAURA. Oh what a mournful wail!
Again my pains, again my fears prevail.
    CLARIN. Again with fear I die.
    ROSAURA. Clarin!
    CLARIN.   My lady!
    ROSAURA.   Let us turn and fly
The risks of this enchanted tower.
    CLARIN.   For one,
I scarce have strength to stand, much less to run.
    ROSAURA. Is not that glimmer there afar—
That dying exhalation—that pale star—
A tiny taper, which, with trembling blaze
Flickering 'twixt struggling flames and dying rays,
With ineffectual spark
Makes the dark dwelling place appear more dark?
Yes, for its distant light,
Reflected dimly, brings before my sight
A dungeon's awful gloom,
Say rather of a living corse, a living tomb;
And to increase my terror and surprise,
Drest in the skins of beasts a man there lies:
A piteous sight,
Chained, and his sole companion this poor light.
Since then we cannot fly,
Let us attentive to his words draw nigh,
Whatever they may be.
        [*The doors of the tower open wide, and* SIGISMUND
           is discovered in chains and clad in the skins
           of beasts. The light in the tower increases.

SIGISMUND.   Alas! Ah, wretched me! Ah, wretched
   me !
Heaven, here lying all forlorn,
I desire from thee to know,
Since thou thus dost treat me so,
Why have I provoked thy scorn
By the crime of being born ?—
Though for being born I feel
Heaven with me must harshly deal,
Since man's greatest crime on earth
Is the fatal fact of birth—
Sin supreme without appeal.
This alone I ponder o'er,
My strange mystery to pierce through ;
Leaving wholly out of view
Germs my hapless birthday bore,
How have I offended more,
That the more you punish me ?
Must not other creatures be
Born ?   If born, what privilege
Can they over me allege
Of which I should not be free ?
Birds are born, the bird that sings,
Richly robed by Nature's dower,
Scarcely floats—a feathered flower,
Or a bunch of blooms with wings —
When to heaven's high halls it springs,
Cuts the blue air fast and free,
And no longer bound will be
By the nest's secure control :—
And with so much more of soul,
Must I have less liberty ?
Beasts are born, the beast whose skin
Dappled o'er with beauteous spots,
As when the great pencil dots
Heaven with stars, doth scarce begin

From its impulses within—
Nature's stern necessity,
To be schooled in cruelty,—
Monster, waging ruthless war :—
And with instincts better far
Must I have less liberty?
Fish are born, the spawn that breeds
Where the oozy sea-weeds float,
Scarce perceives itself a boat,
Scaled and plated for its needs,
When from wave to wave it speeds,
Measuring all the mighty sea,
Testing its profundity
To its depths so dark and chill :—
And with so much freer will,
Must I have less liberty?
Streams are born, a coiled-up snake
When its path the streamlet finds,
Scarce a silver serpent winds
'Mong the flowers it must forsake,
But a song of praise doth wake,
Mournful though its music be,
To the plain that courteously
Opes a path through which it flies :—
And with life that never dies,
Must I have less liberty?
When I think of this I start,
Ætna-like in wild unrest
I would pluck from out my breast
Bit by bit my burning heart :—
For what law can so depart
From all right, as to deny
One lone man that liberty—
That sweet gift which God bestows
On the crystal stream that flows,
Birds and fish that float or fly?

ROSAURA. Fear and deepest sympathy
Do I feel at every word.
    SIGISMUND. Who my sad lament has heard ?
What !   Clotaldo !
    CLARIN (*aside to his mistress*).   Say 'tis he.
    ROSAURA. No, 'tis but a wretch (ah, me !)
Who in these dark caves and cold
Hears the tale your lips unfold.
    SIGISMUND. Then you'll die for listening so,
That you may not know I know
That you know the tale I told.   [*Seizes her.*
Yes, you'll die for loitering near :
In these strong arms gaunt and grim
I will tear you limb from limb.
    CLARIN. I am deaf and couldn't hear :—
No !
    ROSAURA.   If human heart you bear,
'Tis enough that I prostrate me.
At thy feet, to liberate me !
    SIGISMUND. Strange thy voice can so unbend me,
Strange thy sight can so suspend me,
And respect so penetrate me !
Who art thou ? for though I see
Little from this lonely room,
This, my cradle and my tomb,
Being all the world to me,
And if birthday it could be,
Since my birthday I have known
But this desert wild and lone,
Where throughout my life's sad course
I have lived, a breathing corse,
I have moved, a skeleton ;
And though I address or see
Never but one man alone,
Who my sorrows all hath known,
And through whom have come to me

Notions of earth, sky, and sea ;
And though harrowing thee again,
Since thou'lt call me in this den,
Monster fit for bestial feasts,
I'm a man among wild beasts,
And a wild beast amongst men.
But though round me has been wrought
All this woe, from beasts I've learned
Polity, the same discerned
Heeding what the birds had taught,
And have measured in my thought
The fair orbits of the spheres ;
You alone, 'midst doubts and fears,
Wake my wonder and surprise—
Give amazement to my eyes,
Admiration to my ears.
Every time your face I see
You produce a new amaze :
After the most steadfast gaze,
I again would gazer be.
I believe some hydropsy
Must affect my sight, I think
Death must hover on the brink
Of those wells of light, your eyes,
For I look with fresh surprise,
And though death result, I drink.
Let me see and die : forgive me ;
For I do not know, in faith,
If to see you gives me death,
What to see you not would give me ;
Something worse than death would grieve me,
Anger, rage, corroding care,
Death, but double death it were,
Death with tenfold terrors rife,
Since what gives the wretched life,
Gives the happy death, despair !

ROSAURA.   Thee to see wakes such dismay,
Thee to hear I so admire,
That I'm powerless to inquire,
That I know not what to say :
Only this, that I to-day,
Guided by a wiser will,
Have here come to cure my ill,
Here consoled my grief to see,
If a wretch consoled can be
Seeing one more wretched still.
Of a sage, who roamed dejected,
Poor, and wretched, it is said,
That one day, his wants being fed
By the herbs which he collected,
" Is there one " (he thus reflected)
" Poorer than I am to-day ? "
Turning round him to survey,
He his answer got, detecting
A still poorer sage collecting
Even the leaves he threw away.
Thus complaining to excess,
Mourning fate, my life I led,
And when thoughtlessly I said
To myself, " Does earth possess
One more steeped in wretchedness ? "
I in thee the answer find.
Since revolving in my mind,
I perceive that all my pains
To become thy joyful gains
Thou hast gathered and entwined.
And if haply some slight solace
By these pains may be imparted,*
Hear attentively the story

---

* The metre changes here to the vocal *asonante* in *a—e*, and continues to the end of the Fourth Scene.

Of my life's supreme disasters.
I am . . . .

SCENE III.

CLOTALDO, Soldiers, SIGISMUND, ROSAURA, CLARIN.

CLOTALDO (*within*).   Warders of this tower,
Who, or sleeping or faint-hearted,
Give an entrance to two persons
Who herein have burst a passage . . . .
ROSAURA.   New confusion now I suffer.
SIGISMUND.   'Tis Clotaldo, who here guards me ;
Are not yet my miseries ended ?
CLOTALDO (*within*).   Hasten   hither,   quick !   be
active !
And before they can defend them,
Kill them on the spot, or capture !
(*Voices within.*)   Treason !
CLARIN.   Watchguards of this tower,
Who politely let us pass here,
Since you have the choice of killing
Or of capturing, choose the latter.
[*Enter* CLOTALDO *and* Soldiers ; *he with a pistol,
and all with their faces covered.*
CLOTALDO (*aside to the* Soldiers).   Keep your faces
all well covered,
For it is a vital matter
That we should be known by no one,
While I question these two stragglers.
CLARIN.   Are there masqueraders here ?
CLOTALDO.   Ye who in your ignorant rashness
Have passed through the bounds and limits
Of this interdicted valley,

'Gainst the edict of the King,
Who has publicly commanded
None should dare descry the wonder
That among these rocks is guarded,
Yield at once your arms and lives,
Or this pistol, this cold aspic
Formed of steel, the penetrating
Poison of two balls will scatter,
The report and fire of which
Will the air astound and startle.

   SIGISMUND.   Ere you wound them, ere you hurt
      them,
Will my life, O tyrant master,
Be the miserable victim
Of these wretched chains that clasp me;
Since in them, I vow to God,
I will tear myself to fragments
With my hands, and with my teeth,
In these rocks here, in these caverns,
Ere I yield to their misfortunes,
Or lament their sad disaster.

   CLOTALDO.   If you know that your misfortunes,
Sigismund, are unexampled,
Since before being born you died
By Heaven's mystical enactment;
If you know these fetters are
Of your furies oft so rampant
But the bridle that detains them,
But the circle that contracts them.
Why these idle boasts?   The door   [*To the* Soldiers.
Of this narrow prison fasten;
Leave him there secured.

   SIGISMUND.   Ah, heavens,
It is wise of you to snatch me
Thus from freedom ! since my rage
'Gainst you had become Titanic,

Since to break the glass and crystal
Gold-gates of the sun, my anger
On the firm-fixed rocks' foundations
Would have mountains piled of marble.
    CLOTALDO.   'Tis that you should not so pile them
That perhaps these ills have happened,
        [*Some of the* SOLDIERS *lead* SIGISMUND *into his
          prison, the doors of which are closed upon him.*

SCENE IV.

ROSAURA, CLOTALDO, CLARIN, Soldiers.

    ROSAURA.   Since I now have seen how pride
Can offend thee, I were hardened
Sure in folly not here humbly
At thy feet for life to ask thee ;
Then to me extend thy pity,
Since it were a special harshness
If humility and pride,
Both alike were disregarded.
    CLARIN.   If Humility and Pride
Those two figures who have acted
Many and many a thousand times
In the *autos sacramentales,*
Do not move you, I, who am neither
Proud nor humble, but a sandwich
Partly mixed of both, entreat you
To extend to us your pardon.
    CLOTALDO.   Ho !
    SOLDIERS.   My lord ?
    CLOTALDO.   Disarm the two,
And their eyes securely bandage,

So that they may not be able
To see whither they are carried.

    Rosaura.   This is, sir, my sword ; to thee
Only would I wish to hand it,
Since in fine of all the others
Thou art chief, and I could hardly
Yield it unto one less noble.

    Clarin.   Mine I'll give the greatest rascal
Of your troop : so take it, you.   [*To a* Soldier.

    Rosaura.   And if I must die, to thank thee
For thy pity, I would leave thee
This as pledge, which has its value
From the owner who once wore it ;
That thou guard it well, I charge thee,
For although I do not know
What strange secret it may carry,
This I know, that some great mystery
Lies within this golden scabbard,
Since relying but on it
I to Poland here have travelled
To revenge a wrong.

    Clotaldo (*aside.*)   Just heavens !
What is this ?   Still graver, darker,
Grow my doubts and my confusion,
My anxieties and my anguish.—
Speak, who gave you this ?

    Rosaura.   A woman.

    Clotaldo.   And her name ?

    Rosaura.   To that my answer
Must be silence.

    Clotaldo.   But from what
Do you now infer, or fancy,
That this sword involves a secret ?

    Rosaura.   She who gave it said : " Depart hence
Into Poland, and by study,
Stratagem, and skill so manage

That this sword may be inspected
By the nobles and the magnates
Of that land, for you, I know,
Will by one of them be guarded,"—
But his name, lest he was dead,
Was not then to me imparted.

    CLOTALDO. (*aside*).   Bless me, Heaven! what's this
        I hear?

For so strangely has this happened,
That I cannot yet determine
If 'tis real or imagined.
This is the same sword that I
Left with beauteous Violante,
As a pledge unto its wearer,
Who might seek me out thereafter,
As a son that I would love him,
And protect him as a father.
What is to be done (ah, me!)
In confusion so entangled,
If he who for safety bore it
Bears it now but to dispatch him,
Since condemned to death he cometh
To my feet?   How strange a marvel!
What a lamentable fortune!
How unstable! how unhappy!
This must be my son—the tokens
All declare it, superadded .
To the flutter of the heart,
That to see him loudly rappeth
At the breast, and not being able
With its throbs to burst its chamber,
Does as one in prison, who,
Hearing tumult in the alley,
Strives to look from out the window;
Thus, not knowing what here passes
Save the noise, the heart uprusheth

To the eyes the cause to examine—
They the windows of the heart,
Out through which in tears it glances.
What is to be done?   (O Heavens!)
What is to be done?   To drag him
Now before the King were death;
But to hide him from my master,
That I cannot do, according
To my duty as a vassal.
Thus my loyalty and self-love
Upon either side attack me;
Each would win.   But wherefore doubt?
Is not loyalty a grander,
Nobler thing than life, than honour?
Then let loyalty live, no matter
That he die; besides, he told me,
If I well recall his language,
That he came to revenge a wrong,
But a wronged man is a lazar,—
No, he cannot be my son,
Not the son of noble fathers.
But if some great chance, which no one
Can be free from, should have happened,
Since the delicate sense of honour
Is a thing so fine, so fragile,
That the slightest touch may break it,
Or the faintest breath may tarnish,
What could he do more, do more,
He whose cheek the blue blood mantles,
But at many risks to have come here
It again to re-establish?
Yes, he is my son, my blood,
Since he shows himself so manly.
And thus then betwixt two doubts
A mid course alone is granted:
'Tis to seek the King, and tell him

Who he is, let what will happen.
A desire to save my honour
May appease my royal master ;
Should he spare his life, I then
Will assist him in demanding
His revenge ; but if the King
Should, persisting in his anger,
Give him death, then he will die
Without knowing I'm his father.—
Come, then, come then with me, strangers.

[To Rosaura and Clarin.

Do not fear in your disasters
That you will not have companions
In misfortune ; for so balanced
Are the gains of life or death,
That I know not which are larger.   [Exeunt.

Scene V.

A HALL IN THE ROYAL PALACE.

Enter at one side Astolfo *and* Soldiers, *and at the other the* Infanta Estrella *and her* Ladies. *Military music and salutes within.*

Astolfo. Struck at once with admiration
At thy starry eyes outshining,
Mingle many a salutation,
Drums and trumpet-notes combining,
Founts and birds in alternation ;
Wondering here to see thee pass,
Music in grand chorus gathers
All her notes from grove and grass :

Here are trumpets formed of feathers,
There are birds that breathe in brass.
All salute thee, fair Señora,
Ordnance as their Queen proclaim thee,
Beauteous birds as their Aurora,
As their Pallas trumpets name thee,
And the sweet flowers as their Flora ;
For Aurora sure thou art,
Bright as day that conquers night—
Thine is Flora's peaceful part,
Thou art Pallas in thy might,
And as Queen thou rul'st my heart.

    ESTRELLA.   If the human voice obeying
Should with human action pair,
Then you have said ill in saying
All these flattering words and fair,
Since in truth they are gainsaying
This parade of victory,
'Gainst which I my standard rear,
Since they say, it seems to me,
Not the flatteries that I hear,
But the rigours that I see.
Think, too, what a base invention
From a wild beast's treachery sprung,—
Fraudful mother of dissension—
Is to flatter with the tongue,
And to kill with the intention.

    ASTOLFO.   Ill informed you must have been,
Fair Estrella, thus to throw
Doubt on my respectful mien :
Let your ear attentive lean
While the cause I strive show.
King Eustorgius the Fair,
Third so called, died, leaving two
Daughters, and Basilius heir ;
Of his sisters I and you

Are the children—I forbear
To recall a single scene
Save what's needful.   Clorilene,
Your good mother and my aunt,
Who is now a habitant
Of a sphere of sunnier sheen,
Was the elder, of whom you
Are the daughter; Recisunda,
Whom God guard a thousand years,
Her fair sister (Rosamunda
Were she called if names were true)
Wed in Muscovy, of whom
I was born.   'Tis needful now
The commencement to resume.
King Basilius, who doth bow
'Neath the weight of years, the doom
Age imposes, more inclined
To the studies of the mind
Than to women, wifeless, lone,
Without sons, to fill his throne
I and you our way would find.
You, the elder's child, averred,
That the crown you stood more nigh :
I, maintaining that you erred,
Held, though born of the younger, I,
Being a man, should be preferred.
Thus our mutual pretension
To our uncle we related,
Who replied that he would mention
Here, and on this day he stated,
What might settle the dissension.
With this end, from Muscovy
I set out, and with that view,
I to-day fair Poland see,
And not making war on you,
Wait till war you make on me.

Would to love—that God so wise—
That the crowd may be a sure
Astrologue to read the skies,
And this festive truce secure
Both to you and me the prize,
Making you a Queen, but Queen
By my will, our uncle leaving
You the throne we'll share between—
And my love a realm receiving
Dearer than a King's demesne.
   ESTRELLA.   Well, I must be generous too,
For a gallantry so fine ;
This imperial realm you view,
If I wish it to be mine
'Tis to give it unto you.
Though if I the truth confessed,
I must fear your love may fail—
Flattering words are words at best,
For perhaps a truer tale
Tells that portrait on your breast.
   ASTOLFO. On that point complete content
Will I give your mind, not here,
For each sounding instrument   [*Drums are heard.*
Tells us that the King is near,
With his Court and Parliament

SCENE VI.

The KING BASILIUS, *with his retinue.* — ASTOLFO,
    ESTRELLA, Ladies, Soldiers.

   ESTRELLA. Learned Euclid . . .
   ASTOLFO.   Thales wise . .
   ESTRELLA. The vast Zodiac . . .

ASTOLFA.   The star spaces . . .
ESTRELLA. Who dost soar to . . .
ASTOLFO.   Who dost rise . . .
ESTRELLA. The sun's orbit . . .
ASTOLFO.   The stars' places . . .
ESTRELLA. To describe . . .
ASTOLFO.   To map the skies . . .
ESTRELLA. Let me humbly interlacing . . .
ASTOLFO. Let me lovingly embracing . . .
ESTRELLA. Be the tendril of thy tree.
ASTOLFO. Bend respectfully my knee.
BASILIUS. Children, that dear word displacing
Colder names, my arms here bless;
And be sure, since you assented
To my plan, my love's excess
Will leave neither discontented,
Or give either more or less.
And though I from being old
Slowly may the facts unfold,
Hear in silence my narration,
Keep reserved your admiration,
Till the wondrous tale is told.
You already know—I pray you
Be attentive, dearest children,*
Great, illustrious Court of Poland,
Faithful vassals, friends and kinsmen,
You already know—my studies
Have throughout the whole world given me
The high title of " the learnéd,"
Since 'gainst time and time's oblivion
The rich pencils of Timanthes,
The bright marbles of Lysippus,
Universally proclaim me

---

* The metre changes here to the *asonante* in *i—c*, or their vocal
equivalents, and is kept up for the remainder of the Act.

Through earth's bounds the great Basilius.
You already know the sciences
That I feel my mind most given to
Are the subtle mathematics,
By whose means my clear prevision
Takes from rumour its slow office,
Takes from time its jurisdiction
Of, each day, new facts disclosing ;
Since in algebraic symbols
When the fate of future ages
On my tablets I see written,
I anticipate time in telling
What my science hath predicted.
All those circles of pure snow,
All those canopies of crystal,
Which the sun with rays illumines,
Which the moon cuts in its circles,
All those orbs of twinkling diamond,
All those crystal globes that glisten,
All that azure field of stars
Where the zodiac signs are pictured,
Are the study of my life,
Are the books where heaven has written
Upon diamond-dotted paper,
Upon leaves by sapphires tinted,
With light luminous lines of gold,
In clear characters distinctly
All the events of human life,
Whether adverse or benignant.
These so rapidly I read
That I follow with the quickness
Of my thoughts the swiftest movements
Of their orbits and their circles.
Would to heaven, that ere my mind
To those mystic books addicted
Was the comment of their margins

And of all their leaves the index,
Would to heaven, I say, my life
Had been offered the first victim
Of its anger, that my death-stroke
Had in this way have been given me,
Since the unhappy find even merit
Is the fatal knife that kills them,
And his own self-murderer
Is the man whom knowledge injures !—
I may say so, but my story
So will say with more distinctness,
And to win your admiration
Once again I pray you listen.—
Clorilene, my wife, a son
Bore me, so by fate afflicted
That on his unhappy birthday
All Heaven's prodigies assisted.
Nay, ere yet to life's sweet light
Gave him forth her womb, that living
Sepulchre (for death and life
Have like ending and beginning),
Many a time his mother saw
In her dreams' delirious dimness
From her side a monster break,
Fashioned like a man, but sprinkled
With her blood, who gave her death,
By that human viper bitten.
Round his birthday came at last,
All its auguries fulfilling
(For the presages of evil
Seldom fail or even linger) :
Came with such a horoscope,
That the sun rushed blood-red tinted
Into a terrific combat
With the dark moon that resisted ;
Earth its mighty lists outspread

As with lessening lights diminished
Strove the twin-lamps of the sky.
'Twas of all the sun's eclipses
The most dreadful that it suffered
Since the hour its bloody visage
Wept the awful death of Christ.
For o'erwhelmed in glowing cinders
The great orb appeared to suffer
Nature's final paroxysm.
Gloom the glowing noontide darkened,
Earthquake shook the mightiest buildings,
Stones the angry clouds rained down,
And with blood ran red the rivers.
In this frenzy of the sun,
In its madness and delirium,
Sigismund was born, thus early
Giving proofs of his condition,
Since his birth his mother slew,
Just as if these words had killed her,
" I am a man, since good with evil
I repay here from the beginning,"—
I, applying to my studies,
Saw in them as 'twere forewritten
This, that Sigismund would be
The most cruel of all princes,
Of all men the most audacious,
Of all monarchs the most wicked ;
That his kingdom through his means
Would be broken and partitioned,
The academy of the vices,
And the high school of sedition ;
And that he himself, borne onward
By his crimes' wild course resistless,
Would even place his feet on me :
For I saw myself down-stricken,
Lying on the ground before him

(To say this what shame it gives me !)
While his feet on my white hairs
As a carpet were imprinted.
Who discredits threatened ill,
Specially an ill previsioned
By one's study, when self-love
Makes it his peculiar business ?—
Thus then crediting the fates
Which far off my science witnessed,
All these fatal auguries
Seen though dimly in the distance,
I resolved to chain the monster
That unhappily life was given to,
To find out if yet the stars
Owned the wise man's weird dominion.
It was publicly proclaimed
That the sad ill-omened infant
Was stillborn.   I then a tower
Caused by forethought to be builded
'Mid the rocks of these wild mountains
Where the sunlight scarce can gild it,
Its glad entrance being barred
By these rude shafts obeliscal.
All the laws of which you know,
All the edicts that prohibit
Anyone on pain of death
That secluded part to visit
Of the mountain, were occasioned
By this cause, so long well hidden.
There still lives Prince Sigismund,
Miserable, poor, in prison.
Him alone Clotaldo sees,
Only tends to and speaks with him ;
He the sciences has taught him,
He the Catholic religion
Has imparted to him, being

Of his miseries the sole witness.
Here there are three things : the first
I rate highest, since my wishes
Are, O Poland, thee to save
From the oppression, the affliction
Of a tyrant King, because
Of his country and his kingdom
He were no benignant father
Who to such a risk could give it.
Secondly, the thought occurs
That to take from mine own issue
The plain right that every law
Human and divine hath given him
Is not Christian charity ;
For by no law am I bidden
To prevent another proving,
Say, a tyrant, or a villain,
To be one myself : supposing
Even my son should be so guilty,
That he should not crimes commit
I myself should first commit them.
Then the third and last point is,
That perhaps I erred in giving
Too implicit a belief
To the facts foreseen so dimly ;
For although his inclination
Well might find its precipices,
He might possibly escape them :
For the fate the most fastidious,
For the impulse the most powerful,
Even the planets most malicious
Only make free will incline,
But can force not human wishes.
And thus 'twixt these different causes
Vacillating and unfixèd,
I a remedy have thought of

Which will with new wonder fill you.
I to-morrow morning purpose,
Without letting it be hinted
That he is my son, and therefore
Your true King, at once to fix him
As King Sigismund (for the name
Still he bears that first was given him)
'Neath my canopy, on my throne,
And in fine in my position,
There to govern and command you,
Where in dutiful submission
You will swear to him allegiance.
My resources thus are triple,
As the causes of disquiet
Were which I revealed this instant.
The first is ; that he being prudent,
Careful, cautious, and benignant,
Falsifying the wild actions
That of him had been predicted,
You'll enjoy your natural prince,
He who has so long been living
Holding court amid these mountains,
With the wild beasts for his circle.
Then my next resource is this :
If he, daring, wild, and wicked,
Proudly runs with loosened rein
O'er the broad plain of the vicious,
I will have fulfilled the duty
Of my natural love and pity ;
Then his righteous deposition
Will but prove my royal firmness,
Chastisement and not revenge
Leading him once more to prison.
My third course is this : the Prince
Being what my words have pictured,
From the love I owe you, vassals,

I will give you other princes
Worthier of the crown and sceptre ;
Namely, my two sisters' children,
Who their separate pretensions
Having happily commingled
By the holy bonds of marriage,
Will then fill their fit position.
This is what a king commands you,
This is what a father bids you,
This is what a sage entreats you,
This is what an old man wishes ;
And as Seneca, the Spaniard,
Says, a king for all his riches
Is but slave of his Republic,
This is what a slave petitions.

    ASTOLFO.   If on me devolves the answer,
As being in this weighty business
The most interested party,
I, of all, express the opinion :—
Let Prince Sigismund appear ;
He's thy son, that's all-sufficient.

    ALL.   Give to us our natural prince,
We proclaim him king this instant !

    BASILIUS.   Vassals, from my heart I thank you
For this deference to my wishes :—
Go, conduct to their apartments
These two columns of my kingdom,
On to-morrow you shall see him.

    ALL.   Live, long live great King Basilius !

        [*Exeunt all, accompanying* ESTRELLA *and*
        ASTOLFO ; The King *remains.*

SCENE VII.

CLOTALDO, ROSAURA, CLARIN, *and* BASILIUS.

CLOTALDO.   May I speak to you, sire?
BASILIUS.   Clotaldo,
You are always welcome with me.
    CLOTALDO.   Although coming to your feet
Shows how freely I'm admitted,
Still, your majesty, this once,
Fate as mournful as malicious
Takes from privilege its due right,
And from custom its permission.
    BASILIUS.   What has happened?
    CLOTALDO.   A misfortune,
Sire, which has my heart afflicted
At the moment when all joy
Should have overflown and filled it.
    BASILIUS.   Pray proceed.
    CLOTALDO.   This handsome youth here,
Inadvertently, or driven
By his daring, pierced the tower,
And the Prince discovered in it.
Nay . . . .
    BASILIUS.   Clotaldo, be not troubled
At this act, which if committed
At another time had grieved me,
But the secret so long hidden
Having myself told, his knowledge
Of the fact but matters little.
See me presently, for I
Much must speak upon this business,
And for me you much must do
For a part will be committed
To you in the strangest drama

That perhaps the world e'er witnessed.
As for these, that you may know
That I mean not your remissness
To chastise, I grant their pardon.   [*Exit.*
    CLOTALDO.   Myriad years to my lord be given!

SCENE VIII.

CLOTALDO, ROSAURA, *and* CLARIN.

    CLOTALDO (*aside*).   Heaven has sent a happier fate;
Since I need not now admit it,
I'll not say he is my son.—
Strangers who have wandered hither,
You are free.
    ROSAURA.   I give your feet
A thousand kisses.
    CLARIN.   I say misses,
For a letter more or less
'Twixt two friends is not considered.
    ROSAURA.   You have given me life, my lord,
And since by your act I'm living,
I eternally will own me
As your slave.
    CLOTALDO.   The life I've given
Is not really your true life,
For a man by birth uplifted
If he suffers an affront
Actually no longer liveth;
And supposing you have come here
For revenge as you have hinted,
I have not then given you life,
Since you have not brought it with you,

For no life disgraced is life.—
('This I say to arouse his spirit.)   [*Aside.*

 ROSAURA. I confess I have it not,
Though by you it has been given me;
But revenge being wreaked, my honour
I will leave so pure and limpid,
All its perils overcome,
That my life may then with fitness
Seem to be a gift of yours.

 CLOTALDO. Take this burnished sword which hither
You brought with you; for I know,
To revenge you, 'tis sufficient,
In your enemy's blood bathed red;
For a sword that once was girded
Round me (I say this the while
That to me it was committed),
Will know how to right you.

 ROSAURA.   Thus
In your name once more I gird it,
And on it my vengeance swear,
Though the enemy who afflicts me
Were more powerful.

 CLOTALDO.   Is he so?
 ROSAURA. Yes; so powerful, I am hindered
Saying who he is, not doubting
Even for greater things your wisdom
And calm prudence, but through fear
Lest against me your prized pity
Might be turned.

 CLOTALDO.   'Twill rather be,
By declaring it, more kindled;
Otherwise you bar the passage
'Gainst your foe of my assistance.—
(Would that I but knew his name!)   [*Aside.*

 ROSAURA. Not to think I set so little
Value on such confidence,

Know my enemy and my victim
Is no less than Prince Astolfo,
Duke of Muscovy.
    CLOTALDO (*aside*).   Resistance
Badly can my grief supply
Since 'tis heavier than I figured.
Let us sift the matter deeper.—
If a Muscovite by birth, then
He who is your natural lord
Could not 'gainst you have committed
Any wrong ; reseek your country,
And abandon the wild impulse
That has driven you here.
    ROSAURA.   I know,
Though a prince, he has committed
'Gainst me a great wrong.
    CLOTALDO.   He could not,
Even although your face was stricken
By his angry hand.   (Oh, heavens !)   [*Aside*.
    ROSAURA.   Mine's a wrong more deep and bitter.
    CLOTALDO.   Tell it, then ; it cannot be
Worse than what my fancy pictures.
    ROSAURA.   I will tell it ; though I know not,
With the respect your presence gives me,
With the affection you awaken,
With the esteem your worth elicits,
How with bold face here to tell you
That this outer dress is simply
An enigma, since it is not
What it seems   And from this hint, then,
If I'm not what I appear,
And Astolfo with this princess
Comes to wed, judge how by him
I was wronged : I've said sufficient.
          [*Exeunt* ROSAURA *and* CLARIN.
    CLOTALDO.   Listen ! hear me ! wait ! oh, stay !

What a labyrinthine thicket
Is all this, where reason gives
Not a thread whereby to issue?
My own honour here is wronged,
Powerful is my foe's position,
I a vassal, she a woman;
Heaven reveal some way in pity,
Though I doubt it has the power;
When in such confused abysses,
Heaven is all one fearful presage,
And the world itself a riddle.

ACT THE SECOND.

A HALL IN THE ROYAL PALACE.

—◆—

SCENE I.

BASILIUS *and* CLOTALDO.

CLOTALDO.   Everything has been effected
As you ordered.
    BASILIUS.   How all happened *
Let me know, my good Clotaldo.
    CLOTALDO.   It was done, sire, in this manner.
With the tranquillising draught,
Which was made, as you commanded,
Of confections duly mixed
With some herbs, whose juice extracted
Has a strange tyrannic power,
Has some secret force imparted,
Which all human sense and speech
Robs, deprives, and counteracteth,
And as 'twere a living corpse
Leaves the man whose lips have quaffed it
So asleep that all his senses,
All his powers are overmastered. . . .
—No need have we to discuss
That this fact can really happen,

---

* The metre of this and the following scene is the *asonante* in *a—e*.

Since, my lord, experience gives us
Many a clear and proved example ;
Certain 'tis that Nature's secrets
May by medicine be extracted,
And that not an animal,
Not a stone, or herb that's planted,
But some special quality
Doth possess : for if the malice
Of man's heart, a thousand poisons
That give death, hath power to examine,
Is it then so great a wonder
That, their venom being abstracted,
If, as death by some is given,
Sleep by others is imparted ?
Putting, then, aside the doubt
That 'tis possible this should happen,
A thing proved beyond all question
Both by reason and example . . . .
—With the sleeping draught, in fine,
Made of opium superadded
To the poppy and the henbane,
I to Sigismund's apartment—
Cell, in fact—went down, and with him
Spoke awhile upon the grammar
Of the sciences, those first studies
Which mute Nature's gentle masters,
Silent skies and hills, had taught him ;
In which school divine and ample,
The bird's song, the wild beast's roar,
Were a lesson and a language.
Then to raise his spirit more
To the high design you planned here,
I discoursed on, as my theme,
The swift flight, the stare undazzled
Of a pride-plumed eagle bold,
Which with back-averted talons,

Scorning the tame fields of air,
Seeks the sphere of fire, and passes
Through its flame a flash of feathers,
Or a comet's hair untangled.
I extolled its soaring flight,
Saying, " Thou at last art master
Of thy house, thou'rt king of birds,
It is right thou should'st surpass them."
He who needed nothing more
Than to touch upon the matter
Of high royalty, with a bearing
As became him, boldly answered ;
For in truth his princely blood
Moves, excites, inflames his ardour
To attempt great things : he said,
" In the restless realm of atoms
Given to birds, that even one
Should swear fealty as a vassal !
I, reflecting upon this,
Am consoled by my disasters,
For, at least, if I obey,
I obey through force : untrammelled,
Free to act, I ne'er will own
Any man on earth my master."—
This, his usual theme of grief,
Having roused him nigh to madness,
I occasion took to proffer
The drugged draught : he drank, but hardly
Had the liquor from the vessel
Passed into his breast, when fastest
Sleep his senses seized, a sweat,
Cold as ice, the life-blood hardened
In his veins, his limbs grew stiff,
So that, knew I not 'twas acted,
Death was there, feigned death, his life
I could doubt not had departed.

Then those, to whose care you trust
This experiment, in a carriage
Brought him here, where all things fitting
The high majesty and the grandeur
Of his person are provided.
In the bed of your state chamber
They have placed him, where the stupor
Having spent its force and vanished,
They, as 'twere yourself, my lord,
Him will serve as you commanded:
And if my obedient service
Seems to merit some slight largess,
I would ask but this alone
(My presumption you will pardon),
That you tell me, with what object
Have you, in this secret manner,
To your palace brought him here?
  BASILIUS. Good Clotaldo, what you ask me
Is so just, to you alone
I would give full satisfaction.
Sigismund, my son, the hard
Influence of his hostile planet
(As you know) doth threat a thousand
Dreadful tragedies and disasters;
I desire to test if Heaven
(An impossible thing to happen)
Could have lied—if having given us
Proofs unnumbered, countless samples
Of his evil disposition,
He might prove more mild, more guarded
At the least, and self-subdued
By his prudence and true valour
Change his character; for 'tis man
That alone controls the planets.
This it is I wish to test,
Having brought him to this palace,

Where he'll learn he is my son,
And display his natural talents.
If he nobly hath subdued him,
He will reign ; but if his manners
Show him tyrannous and cruel,
Then his chains once more shall clasp him.
But for this experiment,
Now you probably will ask me
Of what moment was 't to bring him
Thus asleep and in this manner ?
And I wish to satisfy you,
Giving all your doubts an answer.
If to-day he learns that he
Is my son, and some hours after
Finds himself once more restored
To his misery and his shackles,
Certain 'tis that from his temper
Blank despair may end in madness—
But once knowing who he is,
Can he be consoled thereafter ?
Yes, and thus I wish to leave
One door open, one free passage,
By declaring all he saw
Was a dream.　With this advantage
We attain two ends.　The first
Is to put beyond all cavil
His condition, for on waking
He will show his thoughts, his fancies :
To console him is the second ;
Since, although obeyed and flattered,
He beholds himself awhile,
And then back in prison shackled
Finds him, he will think he dreamed.
And he rightly so may fancy,
For, Clotaldo, in this world
All who live but dream they act here. .

CLOTALDO.　Reasons fail me not to show
That the experiment may not answer;
But there is no remedy now,
For a sign from the apartment
Tells me that he hath awoken
And even hitherward advances.

BASILIUS.　It is best that I retire;
But do you, so long his master,
Near him stand; the wild confusions,
That his waking sense may darken,
Dissipate by simple truth.

CLOTALDO.　Then your licence you have granted
That I may declare it?

. BASILIUS.　　　　　Yes;
For it possibly may happen
That admonished of his danger
He may conquer his worst passions.　　　　[*Exit.*

SCENE II.

CLARIN *and* CLOTALDO.

CLARIN (*aside*).　Four good blows are all it cost me
To come here, inflicted smartly
By a red-robed halberdier,
With a beard to match his jacket,
At that price I see the show,
For no window's half so handy
As that which, without entreating
Tickets of the ticket-master,
A man carries with himself;
Since for all the feasts and galas
Cool effrontery is the window
Whence at ease he gazes at them.

CLOTALDO (*aside*).   This is Clarin, heavens ! of
    her,
Yes, I say, of her the valet,
She, who dealing in misfortunes,
Has my pain to Poland carried ;—
Any news, friend Clarin ?
    CLARIN.   News ?
Yes, sir, since your great compassion
Is disposed Rosaura's outrage
To revenge, she has changed her habit,
And resumed her proper dress.
    CLOTALDO.   'Tis quite right, lest possible scandal
Might arise.
    CLARIN.   More news : her name
Having changed and wisely bartered
For your niece's name, she now
So in honour has advanced her,
That among Estrella's ladies
She here with her in the palace
Lives.
    CLOTALDO.   'Tis right that I once more
Should her honour re-establish.
    CLARIN.   News ; that anxiously she waiteth
For that very thing to happen,
When you may have time to try it.
    CLOTALDO.   Most discreetly has she acted ;
Soon the time will come, believe me,
Happily to end this matter.
    CLARIN.   News, too ; that she's well regaled,
Feasted like a queen, and flattered
On the strength of being your niece.
And the last news, and the saddest,
Is that I who here came with her
Am with hunger almost famished.
None remember me, or think
I am Clarin, clarion rather,

And that if that clarion sounded,
All the Court would know what passes.
For there are two things, to wit,
A brass clarion and a lackey,
That are bad at keeping secrets ;
And it so may chance, if haply
I am forced to break my silence,
They of me may sing this passage :
" Never, when the day is near,
Does clarion sound more clear." *

　　CLOTALDO.　　Your complaint is too well-founded ;
I will get you satisfaction,
Meanwhile you may wait on me.

　　CLARIN.　　See, sir, Sigismund advances.

SCENE III.

Music and song. SIGISMUND *enters, lost in amazement.*
　　Servants *minister to him, presenting costly robes.—*
　　CLOTALDO, *and* CLARIN.

　　SIGISMUND.　　Help me, Heaven, what's this I see !
Help me, Heaven, what's this I view !
Things I scarce believe are true,
But, if true, which fright not me.
I in palaces of state ?
I 'neath silks and cloth of gold ?
I, around me, to behold

---

* " *Clarin, que rompe el albor,*
　　　No suena mejor."—

This is a quotation by Calderon from his own drama, " *En esta
vida todo es verdad y todo mentira.*"—Act 2, sc. x.

Rich-robed servants watch and wait ?
I so soft a bed to press
While sweet sleep my senses bowed ?
I to wake in such a crowd,
Who assist me even to dress ?
'Twere deceit to say I dream,
Waking I recall my lot,
I am Sigismund, am I not ?
Heaven make plain what dark doth seem !
Tell me, what has phantasy—
Wild, misleading, dream-adept—
So effected while I slept,
That I still the phantoms see ?
But let that be as it may,
Why perplex myself and brood.?
Better taste the present good,
Come what will some other day.

FIRST SERVANT (*aside to the* Second Servant, *and to*
CLARIN).   What a sadness doth oppress him !

SECOND SERVANT.   Who in such-like case would be
Less surprised and sad than he ?

CLARIN.   I for one.

SECOND SERVANT (*to the* First).   You had best address
    him.

FIRST SERVANT (*to* SIGISMUND).   May they sing
    again ?

SIGISMUND.   No, no ;
I don't care to hear them sing.

SECOND SERVANT.   I conceived the song might bring
To your thought some ease.

SIGISMUND.   Not so ;
Voices that but charm the ear
Cannot soothe my sorrow's pain ;
Tis the soldier's martial strain
That alone I love to hear.

CLOTALDO.   May your Highness, mighty Prince,

Deign to let me kiss your hand,
I would first of all this land
My profound respect evince.
    SIGISMUND (*aside*).   'Tis my gaoler ! how can he
Change his harshness and neglect
To this language of respect ?
What can have occurred to me ?
    CLOTALDO.   The new state in which I find you
Must create a vague surprise,
Doubts unnumbered must arise
To bewilder and to blind you ;
I would make your prospect fair,
Through the maze a path would show,
Thus, my lord, 'tis right you know
That you are the prince and heir
Of this Polish realm : if late
You lay hidden and concealed
'Twas that we were forced to yield
To the stern decrees of fate,
Which strange ills, I know not how,
Threatened on this land to bring
Should the laurel of a king
Ever crown thy princely brow.
Still relying on the power
Of your will the stars to bind,
For a man of resolute mind
Can them bind how dark they lower ;
To this palace from your cell
In your life-long turret keep
They have borne you while dull sleep
Held your spirit in its spell.
Soon to see you and embrace
Comes the King, your father, here—
He will make the rest all clear.
    SIGISMUND.   Why, thou traitor vile and base,
What need I to know the rest,

Since it is enough to know
Who I am my power to show,
And the pride that fills my breast ?
Why this treason brought to light
Hast thou to thy country done,
As to hide from the King's son,
'Gainst all reason and all right,
This his rank ?

 CLOTALDO. Oh, destiny !

 SIGISMUND. Thou the traitor's part hast played
'Gainst the law; the King betrayed,
And done cruel wrong to me ;
Thus for each distinct offence
Have the law, the King, and I
Thee condemned this day to die
By my hands.

 SECOND SERVANT. Prince . . . .

 SIGISMUND   No pretence
Shall undo the debt I owe you.
Catiff, hence ! By Heaven ! I say,
If you dare to stop my way
From the window I will throw you.

 SECOND SERVANT. Fly, Clotaldo !

 CLOTALDO.   Woe to thee,
In thy pride so powerful seeming,
Without knowing thou art dreaming !   [*Exit.*

 SECOND SERVANT.   Think . . . .

 SIGISMUND.   Away ! don't trouble me.

 SECOND SERVANT. He could not the King deny.

 SIGISMUND. Bade to do a wrongful thing
He should have refused the King ;
And, besides, his prince was I.

 SECOND SERVANT. 'Twas not his affair to try
If the act was wrong or right.

 SIGISMUND. You're indifferent, black or white,
Since so pertly you reply.

CLARIN.   What the Prince says is quite true,
What you do is wrong, I say.
  SECOND SERVANT.   Who gave you this licence, pray?
  CLARIN.   No one gave; I took it.
  SIGISMUND.   Who
Art thou, speak?
  CLARIN.   A meddling fellow,
Prating, prying, fond of scrapes,
General of all jackanapes,
And most merry when most mellow.
  SIGISMUND.   You alone in this new sphere
Have amused me.
  CLARIN.   That's quite true, sir,
For I am the great amuser
Of all Sigismunds who are here.

SCENE IV.

ASTOLFO, SIGISMUND, CLARIN, Servants, *and*
Musicians.

  ASTOLFO.   Thousand times be blest the day,
Prince, that gives thee to our sight,
Sun of Poland, whose glad light
Makes this whole horizon gay,
As when from the rosy fountains
Of the dawn the stream-rays run,
Since thou issuest like the sun
From the bosom of the mountains!
And though late do not defer
With thy sovran light to shine;
Round thy brow the laurel twine—
Deathless crown.
  SIGISMUND.   God guard thee, sir.

ASTOLFO.   In not knowing me I o'erlook,
But alone for this defect,
This response that lacks respect,
And due honour.   Muscovy's Duke
Am I, and your cousin born,
Thus my equal I regard thee.
 SIGISMUND.   Did there, when I said " God guard thee,"
Lie concealed some latent scorn?—
Then if so, now having got
Thy big name, and seeing thee vexed,
When thou com'st to see me next
I will say God guard thee not.
 SECOND SERVANT (*to* ASTOLFO).   Think, your High-
  ness, if he errs
Thus, his mountain birth's at fault,
Every word is an assault.

          [*To* SIGISMUND.

Duke Astolfo, sir, prefers . . . .
 SIGISMUND.   Tut ! his talk became a bore,
Nay his act was worse than that,
He presumed to wear his hat.
 SECOND SERVANT.   As grandee.
 SIGISMUND.   But I am more.
 SECOND SERVANT.   Nevertheless respect should be
Much more marked betwixt ye two
Than 'twixt others.
 SIGISMUND.   And pray who
Asked your meddling thus with me ?

SCENE V.

ESTRELLA.—THE SAME.

 ESTRELLA.   Welcome may your Highness be,
Welcomed oft to this thy throne,

Which long longing for its own
Finds at length its joy in thee ;
Where, in spite of bygone fears,
May your reign be great and bright,
And your life in its long flight
Count by ages, not by years.

  SIGISMUND (*to* CLARIN). Tell me, thou, say, who can be
    can be
This supreme of loveliness—
Goddess in a woman's dress—
At whose feet divine we see
Heaven its choicest gifts doth lay ?—
This sweet maid ?   Her name declare.

  CLARIN.   'Tis your star-named* cousin fair.

  SIGISMUND.   Nay, the sun, 'twere best to say.—
Though thy sweet felicitation   [*To* ESTRELLA.
Adds new splendour to my throne,
'Tis for seeing thee alone
That I merit gratulation ;
Therefore I a prize have drawn
That I scarce deserved to win,
And am doubly blessed therein :—
Star, that in the rosy dawn
Dimmest with transcendent ray
Orbs that brightest gem the blue,
What is left the sun to do,
When thou risest with the day ?—
Give me then thy hand to kiss,
In whose cup of snowy whiteness
Drinks the day delicious brightness.

  ESTRELLA.   What a courtly speech is this ?

  ASTOLFO (*aside*).   If he takes her hand I feel
I am lost.

  SECOND SERVANT (*aside*).   Astolfo's grief

---

   * *Estrella*, which means star in Spanish.

I perceive, and bring relief :—
Think, my lord, excuse my zeal,
That perhaps this is too free,
Since Astolfo . . . .
    SIGISMUND.   Did I say
Woe to him that stops my way ?—
    SECOND SERVANT.   What I said was just.
    SIGISMUND.   To me
This is tiresome and absurd.
Nought is just, or good or ill,
In my sight that balks my will.
    SECOND SERVANT.   Why, my lord, yourself I
      heard
Say in any righteous thing
It was proper to obey.
    SIGISMUND.   You must, too, have heard me say
Him I would from window throw
Who should tease me or defy ?
    SECOND SERVANT.   Men like me perhaps might
      show
That could not be done, sir.
    SIGISMUND.   No ?
Then, by Heaven, at least, I'll try !
        [He seizes him in his arms and rushes to the side.
          All follow, and return immediately.
    ASTOLFO.   What is this I see ?   Oh, woe !
    ESTRELLA.   Oh, prevent him ! Follow me !   *[Exit.*
    SIGISMUND. (*returning*).   From the window into the
      sea
He has fallen ; I told him so.
    ASTOLFO.   These strange bursts of savage malice
You should regulate, if you can ;
Wild beasts are to civilised man
As rude mountains to a palace.
    SIGISMUND.   Take a bit of advice for that:
Pause ere such bold words are said,

Lest you may not have a head
Upon which to hang your hat.   [*Exit* ASTOLFO.

SCENE VI.

BASILIUS, SIGISMUND, *and* CLARIN.

BASILIUS.   What's all this?
SIGISMUND.   A trifling thing :
One who teased and thwarted me
I have just thrown into the sea.
  CLARIN (*to* SIGISMUND).   Know, my lord, it is the
    King.
  BASILIUS.   Ere the first day's sun hath set,
Has thy coming cost a life?
  SIGISMUND.   Why he dared me to the strife,
And I only won the bet.
  BASILIUS.   Prince, my grief, indeed is great,
Coming here when I had thought
That admonished thou wert taught
To o'ercome the stars and fate,
Still to see such rage abide
In the heart I hoped was free,
That thy first sad act should be
A most fearful homicide.
How could I, by love conducted,
Trust me to thine arms' embracing,
When their haughty interlacing,
Has already been instructed
How to kill?   For who could see,
Say, some dagger bare and bloody,
By some wretch's heart made ruddy,
But would fear it?   Who is he,
Who may happen to behold

On the ground the gory stain
Where another man was slain
But must shudder?   The most bold
Yields at once to Nature's laws;
Thus I, seeing in your arms
The dread weapon that alarms,
And the stain, must fain withdraw;
And though in embraces dear
I would press you to my heart,
I without them must depart,
For, alas! your arms I fear.

SIGISMUND.   Well, without them I must stay,
As I've staid for many a year,
For a father so severe,
Who could treat me in this way,
Whose unfeeling heart could tear me
From his side even when a child,
Who, a denizen of the wild,
As a monster there could rear me,
And by many an artful plan
Sought my death, it cannot grieve me
Much his arms will not receive me
Who has scarcely left me man.

BASILIUS.   Would to God it had not been
Act of mine that name conferred,
Then thy voice I ne'er had heard,
Then thy boldness ne'er had seen.

SIGISMUND.   Did you manhood's right retain,
I would then have nought to say,
But to give and take away
Gives me reason to complain;
For although to give with grace
Is the noblest act 'mongst men,
To take back the gift again
Is the basest of the base.

BASILIUS.   This then is thy grateful mood

For my changing thy sad lot
To a prince's!
    SIGISMUND.   And for what
Should I show my gratitude!
Tyrant of my will o'erthrown,
If thou hoary art and gray,
Dying, what do'st give me? Say,
Do'st thou give what's not mine own?
Thou'rt my father and my King,
Then the pomp these walls present
Comes to me by due descent
As a simple, natural thing.
Yes, this sunshine pleaseth me,
But 'tis not through thee I bask ;
Nay, a reckoning I might ask
For the life, love, liberty
That through thee I've lost so long :
Thine 'tis rather to thank me,
That I do not claim from thee
Compensation for my wrong.
    BASILIUS.   Still untamed and uncontrolled ;—
Heaven fulfils its word I feel,
I to that same court appeal
'Gainst thy taunts, thou vain and bold,
But although the truth thou'st heard,
And now know'st thy name and race,
And do'st see thee in this place,
Where to all thou art preferred,
Yet be warned, and on thee take
Ways more mild and more beseeming,
For perhaps thou art but dreaming,
When it seems that thou'rt awake.   [*Exit.*
    SIGISMUND.   Is this, then, a phantom scene?—
Do I wake in seeming show?—
No, I dream not, since I know
What I am and what I've been.

And although thou should'st repent thee,
Remedy is now too late.
Who I am I know, and fate,
Howsoe'er thou should'st lament thee,
Cannot take from me my right
Of being born this kingdom's heir.
If I saw myself erewhile
Prisoned, bound, kept out of sight,
'Twas that never on my mind
Dawned the truth; but now I know
Who I am—a mingled show
Of the man and beast combined.

Scene VII.

ROSAURA, *in female attire;* SIGISMUND, CLARIN, *and*
Servants.

ROSAURA (*aside*). To wait upon Estrella I come
 here,
And lest I meet Astolfo tremble with much fear;
Clotaldo's wishes are
The Duke should know me not, and from afar
See me, if see he must.
My honour is at stake, he says; my trust
Is in Clotaldo's truth.
He will protect my honour and my youth.
 CLARIN (*to* SIGISMUND). Of all this palace here can
 boast,
All that you yet have seen, say which has pleased you
 most?
 SIGISMUND. Nothing surprised me, nothing scared,
Because for everything I was prepared;
But if I felt for aught, or more or less

Of admiration, 'twas the loveliness
Of woman ; I have read
Somewhere in books on which my spirit fed,
That which caused God the greatest care to plan,
Because in him a little world he formed, was man ;
But this were truer said, unless I err,
Of woman, for a little heaven he made in her ;
She who in beauty from her birth
Surpasses man as heaven surpasseth earth ;
Nay, more, the one I see.

    ROSAURA ·(*aside*).   The Prince is here ; I must this
        instant flee.

    SIGISMUND.   Hear, woman ! stay ;
Nor wed the western with the orient ray,
Flying with rapid tread ;
For joined the orient rose and western red,
The light and the cold gloom,
The day will sink untimely to its tomb.
But who is this I see ?

    ROSAURA (*aside*).   I doubt and yet believe that it is
        he.

    SIGISMUND (*aside*).   This beauty I have seen
Some other time.

    ROSAURA (*aside*).   This proud, majestic mien,
This form I once saw bound
Within a narrow cell.

    SIGISMUND (*aside.*)   My life I have found.—
Woman, the sweetest name   [*Aloud.*
That man can breathe, or flattering language frame,
Who art thou ? for before
I see thee, I believe and I adore ;
Faith makes my love sublime,
Persuading me we've met some other time.
Fair woman, speak ; my will must be obeyed.

    ROSAURA.   In bright Estrella's train a hapless maid.—
He must not know my name.   [*Aside.*

SIGISMUND.   The sun, say rather, of that star whose
    flame,
However bright its blaze
Is but the pale reflection of thy rays.
In the fair land of flowers,
The realm of sweets that lies in odorous bowers,
The goddess rose I have seen
By right divine of beauty reign as queen.
I have seen where brightest shine
Gems, the assembled glories of the mine,
The brilliant throng elect the diamond king
For the superior splendour it doth fling.
Amid the halls of light,
Where the unresting star-crowds meet at night,
I have seen fair Hesper rise
And take the foremost place of all the skies.
And in that higher zone
Where the sun calls the planets round his throne,
I have seen, with sovereign sway,
That he presides the oracle of the day.
How, then, 'mid flowers of earth or stars of air,
'Mid stones or suns, if that which is most fair
The preference gains, canst thou
Before a lesser beauty bend and bow,
When thine own charms compose
Something more bright than sun, stone, star, or rose ?

SCENE VIII.

CLOTALDO, *who remains at the side-scene ;* SIGISMUND,
CLARIN, *and* Servants.

CLOTALDO (*aside*). To calm Prince Sigismund devolves
    on me,
Because 'twas I who reared him :—What do I see ?

ROSAURA.   Thy favour, sir, I prize ;
To thee the silence of my speech replies ;
For when the reason's dull, the mind depressed,
He best doth speak who keeps his silence best.
   SIGISMUND.   You must not leave me.   Stay :
What ! would you rob my senses of the ray
Your beauteous presence gave ?
   ROSAURA.   That licence, from your Highness, I must
       crave.
   SIGISMUND.   The violent efforts that you make
Show that you do not ask the leave you take.
   ROSAURA.   I hope to take it, if it is not given.
   SIGISMUND.   You rouse my courtesy to rage, by
       heaven !—
In me resistance, as it were, distils
A cruel poison that my patience kills.
   ROSAURA.   Then though that poison may be strong,
The source of fury, violence, and wrong,
Potent thy patience to subdue,
It dare not the respect to me that's due.
   SIGISMUND.   As if to show I may,
You take the terror of your charms away.
For I am but too prone
To attempt the impossible ; I to-day have thrown
Out of this window one who said, like you,
I dare not do the thing I said I would do.
Now just to show I can,
I may throw out your honour, as the man.
   CLOTALDO (*aside*).   More obstinate doth he grow;
What course to take, O heavens ! I do not know,
When wild desire, nay, crime,
Perils my honour for the second time.
   ROSAURA.   Not vainly, as I see,
This hapless land was warned thy tyranny
In fearful scandals would eventuate,
In wrath and wrong, in treachery, rage and hate.

But who in truth could claim
Aught from a man who is but a man in name,
Audacious, cruel, cold,
Inhuman, proud, tyrannical and bold,
'Mong beasts a wild beast born ?—

SIGISMUND. It was to save me from such words of scorn
So courteously I spoke,
Thinking to bind you by a gentler yoke;
But if I am in aught what you have said,
Then, as God lives, I will be all you dread.
Ho, there ! here leave us. See to it at your cost,
The door be locked ; let no one in.

[Exeunt CLARIN *and the attendants.*

ROSAURA. I'm lost !
Consider . . . .

SIGISMUND. I'm a despot, and 'tis vain
You strive to move me, or my will restrain.

CLOTALDO (*aside*). Oh, what a moment ! what an
agony !
I will go forth and stop him though I die. [*He advances.*
My lord, consider, stay . . . .

SIGISMUND. A second time you dare to cross my way,
Old dotard : do you hold
My rage in such slight awe you are so bold ?
What brought you hither ? Speak !

CLOTALDO. The accents of this voice, however weak,
To tell you to restrain
Your passions, if as King you wish to reign,—
Not to be cruel, though you deem
Yourself the lord of all, for all may be a dream.

SIGISMUND. You but provoke my rage
By these old saws, the unwelcome light of age,
In killing you, at least I'll see
If 'tis a dream or truth.

[*As he is about to draw his dagger* CLOTALDO
detains it, and throws himself on his knees.

CLOTALDO.   Sole hope for me
To save my life is thus to humbly kneel.
  SIGISMUND.   Take your audacious hand from off my
      steel.
  CLOTALDO.   Till some kind aid be sent,
Till some one come who may your rage prevent,
I will not loose my hold.
  ROSAURA.   Oh, Heaven !
  SIGISMUND.   I say,
Loose it, old dotard, grim and gaunt and gray,
Or by another death   [*They struggle.*
I'll crush you in my arms while you have breath.
  ROSAURA.   Quick ! quick ! they slay
Clotaldo, help ! oh, help !   [*Exit.*
          [ASTOLFO *enters at this moment, and* CLOTALDO
              falls at his feet ; he stands between them.
  ASTOLFO.   This strange affray,
What can it mean, magnanimous Prince? would you
So bright a blade imbrue
In blood that age already doth congeal?
Back to its sheath return the shining steel.
  SIGISMUND.   Yes, when it is bathed red
In his base blood.
  ASTOLFO.   This threatened life hath fled
For sanctuary to my feet ;
I must protect it in that poor retreat.
  SIGISMUND.   Protect your own life, then, for in this
      way,
Striking at it, I will the grudge repay
I owe you for the past.
  ASTOLFO.   I thus defend
My life ; but majesty will not offend.
          [ASTOLFO *draws his sword and they fight.*
  CLOTALDO.   Oh ! wound him not, my lord.

SCENE IX.

BASILIUS, ESTRELLA *and* Attendants, SIGISMUND,
ASTOLFO, *and* CLOTALDO.

BASILIUS.   Swords flashing here !—

ESTRELLA (*aside*).   Astolfo is engaged :—Oh, pain
   severe !

BASILIUS.   What caused this quarrel? Speak, say
   why ?

ASTOLFO.   'Tis nothing now, my lord, since thou
   art by.

SIGISMUND.   'Tis much, although thou now art by,
   my lord.

I wished to kill this old man with my sword.

   BASILIUS.   Did you not then respect

These snow-white hairs ?

   CLOTALDO.   My lord will recollect

They scarce deserved it, being mine.

   SIGISMUND.   Who dares

To ask of me do I respect white hairs ?

Your own some day

My feet may trample in the public way,

For I have not as yet revenged my wrong,

Your treatment so unjust and my sad state so long.

[Exit.

   BASILIUS.   But ere that dawn doth break,

You must return to sleep, where when you wake

All that hath happened here will seem—

As is the glory of the world—a dream.

      [*Exeunt* The King, CLOTALDO, *and* Attendants.

SCENE X.

ESTRELLA *and* ASTOLFO.

ASTOLFO.   Ah, how rarely fate doth lie
When it some misfortune threatens ! *
Dubious when 'tis good that's promised,
When 'tis evil, ah, too certain !—
What a good astrologer
Would he be, whose art foretelleth
Only cruel things ; for, doubtless,
They would turn out true for ever !
This in Sigismund and me
Is exemplified, Estrella,
Since between our separate fortunes
Such a difference is presented.
In his case had been foreseen
Murders, miseries, and excesses,
And in all they turned out true,
Since all happened as expected.
But in mine, here seeing, lady,
Rays so rare and so resplendent
That the sun is but their shadow.
And even heaven a faint resemblance,
When fate promised me good fortune,
Trophies, praises, and all blessings,
It spoke ill and it spoke well ;
For it was of both expressive,
When it held out hopes of favour,
But disdain alone effected.
  ESTRELLA.   Oh, I doubt not these fine speeches
Are quite true, although intended

---

* The vocal asonante in *e—e* here commences, and continues to
the end of the Sixteenth Scene.

Doubtless for that other lady,
She whose portrait was suspended
From your neck, when first, Astolfo,
At this Court here you addressed me.
This being so, 'tis she alone
Who these compliments deserveth.
Go and pay them to herself,
For like bills that are protested
In the counting-house of love,
Are those flatteries and finesses
Which to other kings and ladies
Have been previously presented.

Scene XI.

ROSAURA, *who remains at the side ;* ESTRELLA, *and*
ASTOLFO.

ROSAURA (*aside*).   Well, thank God, my miseries
Have attained their lowest level,
Since by her who sees this sight
Nothing worse can be expected.
  ASTOLFO.   Then that portrait from my breast
Shall be taken, that thy perfect
Beauty there may reign instead.
For where bright Estrella enters
Shadow cannot be, or star
Where the sun ; I go to fetch it.—
Pardon, beautiful Rosaura,   [*Aside.*
This offence ; the absent never,
Man or woman, as this shows,
Faith or plighted vows remember.   [*Exit.*
          (ROSAURA *comes forward.*)
  ROSAURA (*aside*).   Not a single word I heard,
Being afraid they might observe me.

ESTRELLA.   Oh, Astrea !
ROSAURA.   My good lady!
ESTRELLA.   Nothing could have pleased me better
Than your timely coming here.
I have something confidential
To entrust you with.
ROSAURA.   You honour
Far too much my humble service.
ESTRELLA.   Brief as is the time, Astrea,
I have known you, you already
Of my heart possess the keys.
'Tis for this and your own merits
That I venture to entrust you
With what oft I have attempted
From myself to hide.
ROSAURA.   Your slave !
ESTRELLA.   Then concisely to express it,
Know, Astolfo, my first cousin
('Tis enough that word to mention,
For some things may best be said
When not spoken but suggested),
Soon expects to wed with me,
If my fate so far relenteth,
As that by one single bliss
All past sorrows may be lessened.
I was troubled, the first day
That we met, to see suspended
From his neck a lady's portrait.
On the point I urged him gently,
He so courteous and polite
Went immediately to get it,
And will bring it here.   From him
I should feel quite disconcerted
To receive it.   You here stay,
And request him to present it
Unto you.   I say no more.

You are beautiful and clever,
You must know too what is love.   [*Exit.*

SCENE XII.

ROSAURA.   Would I knew it not! O help me
Now, kind heaven! for who could be
So prudential, so collected,
As to know how best to act
In so painful a dilemma?
Is there in the world a being,
Is there one a more inclement
Heaven has marked with more misfortunes,
Has 'mid more of sorrow centred?—
What, bewildered, shall I do,
When 'tis vain to be expected
That my reason can console me,
Or consoling be my helper?
From my earliest misfortune
Everything that I've attempted
Has been but one misery more—
Each the other's sad successor,
All inheritors of themselves.
Thus, the Phœnix they resemble,
One is from the other born,
New life springs where old life endeth,
And the young are warmly cradled
By the ashes of the elder.
Once a wise man called them cowards,
Seeing that misfortunes never
Have been seen to come alone.
But I call them brave, intrepid,
Who go straight unto their end,
And ne'er turn their backs in terror:—

By the man who brings them with him
Everthing may be attempted,
Since he need on no occasion
Have the fear of being deserted.
I may say so, since at all times,
Whatsoever life presented,
I, without them, never saw me,
Nor will they grow weary ever,
Till they see me in death's arms,
Wounded by fate's final weapon.
Woe is me ! but what to-day
Shall I do in this emergence ?—
If I tell my name, Clotaldo,
Unto whom I am indebted
For my very life and honour,
May be with me much offended ;
Since he said my reparation
Must in silence be expected.
If I tell not to Astolfo
Who I am, and he detects me
How can I dissemble then ?
For although a feigned resemblance
Eyes and voice and tongue might try,
Ah, the truthful heart would tremble,
And expose the lie.   But wherefore
Study what to do ?   'Tis certain
That however I may study,
Think beforehand how to nerve me,
When at last the occasion comes,
Then alone what grief suggesteth
I will do, for no one holds
In his power the heart's distresses.
And thus what to say or do
As my soul cannot determine,
Grief must only reach to-day
Its last limit, pain be ended,

And at last an exit make
From the doubts that so perplex me
How to act : but until then
Help me, heaven, oh, deign to help me !

Scene XIII.

Astolfo, *with the portrait; and* Rosaura.

Astolfo.   Here then is the portrait, Princess :
But, good God !
Rosaura.   Your Highness trembles ;
What has startled, what surprised you ?
Astolfo.   Thee, Rosaura, to see present.
Rosaura.   I Rosaura ?   Oh, your Highness
Is deceived by some resemblance
Doubtless to some other lady;
I'm Astrea, one who merits
Not the glory of producing
An emotion so excessive.
Astolfo.   Ah, Rosaura thou mayst feign,
But the soul bears no deception,
And though seeing thee as Astrea,
As Rosaura it must serve thee.
Rosaura.   I, not knowing what your Highness
Speaks of, am of course prevented
From replying aught but this,
That Estrella (the bright Hesper
Of this sphere) was pleased to order
That I here should wait expectant
For that portrait, which to me
She desires you give at present :
For some reason she prefers

It through me should be presented—
So Estrella—say, my star—
Wishes—so a fate relentless
Wills—in things that bring me loss—
So Estrella now expecteth.

   ASTOLFO.   Though such efforts you attempt,
Still how badly you dissemble,
My Rosaura !   Tell the eyes
In their music to keep better
Concert with the voice, because
Any instrument whatever
Would be out of tune that sought
To combine and blend together
The true feelings of the heart
With the false words speech expresses.

   ROSAURA.   I wait only, as I said,
For the portrait.

   ASTOLFO.   Since you're bent then
To the end to keep this tone,
I adopt it, and dissemble.
Tell the Princess, then, Astrea,
That I so esteem her message,
That to send to her a copy
Seems to me so slight a present,
How so highly it is valued
By myself, I think it better
To present the original,
And you easily may present it,
Since, in point of fact, you bring it
With you in your own sweet person.

   ROSAURA.   When it has been undertaken
By a man, bold, brave, determined,
To obtain a certain object,
Though he get perhaps a better,
Still not bringing back the first
He returns despised : I beg, then.

That your highness give the portrait ;
I, without it, dare not venture.
    Astolfo.   How, then, if I do not give it
Will you get it?
Rosaura.   I will get it
Thus, ungrateful.   *[She attempts to snatch it.*
    Astolfo.   'Tis in vain.
    Rosaura.   It must ne'er be seen, no, never
In another woman's hands.
    Astolfo.   Thou art dreadful.
    Rosaura.   Thou deceptive.
    Astolfo.   Oh, enough, Rosaura mine.
    Rosaura.   Thine !   Thou liest, base deserter.
               [Both struggle for the portrait.

Scene XIV.

Estrella, Rosaura, *and* Astolfo.

Estrella.   Prince ! Astrea ! What is this?
Astolfo (*aside*).   Heavens ! Estrella !
Rosaura (*aside*).   Love befriend me ;
Give me wit enough my portrait
To regain :—If thou would'st learn then *[To* Estrella.
What the matter is, my lady,
I will tell thee.
    Astolfo (*aside to* Rosaura.) Would'st o'erwhelm
      me ?
    Rosaura.   You commanded me to wait here
For the Prince, and, representing
You, to get from him a portrait.
I remained alone, expecting,
And, as often by one thought

Is some other thought suggested,
Seeing that you spoke of portraits,
I, reminded thus, remembered
That I had one of myself
In my sleeve : I wished to inspect it,
For a person quite alone
Even by trifles is diverted.
From my hand I let it fall
On the ground ; the Prince, who entered
With the other lady's portrait,
Raised up mine, but so rebellious
Was he to what you had asked him
That, instead of his presenting
One, he wished to keep the other.
Since he mine will not surrender
To my prayers and my entreaties :
Angry at this ill-timed jesting
I endeavoured to regain it,
That which in his hand is held there
Is my portrait, if you see it ;
You can judge of the resemblance.

    ESTRELLA.   Duke, at once, give up the portrait.
[She takes it from his hand.

    ASTOLFO.   Princess . . . .
    ESTRELLA.   Well, the tints were blended
By no cruel hand, methinks.
    ROSAURA.   Is it like me ?
    ESTRELLA.   Like ! 'Tis perfect.
    ROSAURA.   Now demand from him the other.
    ESTRELLA.   Take your own, and leave our presence.
    ROSAURA (*aside*).   I have got my portrait back :
Come what may I am contented.   [*Exit.*

Scene XV.

Estrella *and* Astolfo.

Estrella.   Give me now the other portrait ;
For—although perhaps I never
May again address or see you—
I desire not, no, to let it
In your hands remain, if only
For my folly in requesting
You to give it.
    Astolfo (*aside*).   How escape
From this singular dilemma ?—
Though I wish, most beauteous Princess,
To obey thee and to serve thee,
Still I cannot give the portrait
Thou dost ask for, since . . . .
    Estrella.   A wretched
And false-hearted lover art thou.
Now I wish it not presented,
So to give thee no pretext
For reminding me that ever
I had asked it at thy hands.   [*Exit.*
    Astolfo.   Hear me ! listen ! wait ! remember !—
God, what hast thou done, Rosaura ?
Why, or wherefore, on what errand,
To destroy thyself and me
Hast thou Poland rashly entered ?   [*Exit.*

SCENE XVI.

PRISON OF THE PRINCE IN THE TOWER.

SIGISMUND, *as at the commencement, clothed in skins, chained, and lying on the ground;* CLOTALDO, Two Servants, *and* CLARIN.

CLOTALDO.　Leave him here on the ground,
Where his day,—its pride being o'er,—
Finds its end too.
　　A SERVANT.　　　　　As before
With the chain his feet are bound.
　　CLARIN.　Never from that sleep profound
Wake, O Sigismund, or rise,
To behold with wondering eyes
All thy glorious life o'erthrown,
Like a shadow that hath flown,
Like a bright brief flame that dies!
　　CLOTALDO.　One who can so wisely make
Such reflections on this case
Should have ample time and space,
Even for the Solon's sake,
To discuss it; him you'll take　　　[*To the* Servant.
To this cell here, and keep bound.
　　　　　　　　　　[*Pointing to an adjoining room.*
　　CLARIN.　But why me?
　　CLOTALDO.　　　　　Because 'tis found
Safe, when clarions secrets know,
Clarions to lock up, that so
They may not have power to sound.
　　CLARIN.　Did I, since you treat me thus,
Try to kill my father?　No.
Did I from the window throw
That unlucky Icarus?

Is my drink somniferous?
Do I dream?   Then why be pent?
   CLOTALDO.   'Tis a clarion's punishment.
   CLARIN.   Then a horn of low degree,
Yea, a cornet I will be,
A safe, silent instrument.
    [*They take him away, and* CLOTALDO *remains alone.*

SCENE XVII.

BASILIUS, *disguised ;* CLOTALDO, *and* SIGISMUND, *asleep.*

   BASILIUS.   Hark, Clotaldo !
   CLOTALDO.   My lord here?
Thus disguised, your majesty ?
   BASILIUS.   Foolish curiosity
Leads me in this lowly gear
To find out, ah, me ! with fear,
How the sudden change he bore.
   CLOTALDO.   There behold him as before
In his miserable state.
   BASILIUS.   Wretched Prince ! unhappy fate !
Birth by baneful stars watched o'er !—
Go and wake him cautiously,
Now that strength and force lie chained
By the opiate he hath drained.
   CLOTALDO.   Muttering something restlessly,
See he lies.
   BASILIUS.   Let's listen ; he
May some few clear words repeat.
   SIGISMUND.   [*Speaking in his sleep.*
Perfect Prince is he whose heat
Smites the tyrant where he stands,

Yes, Clotaldo dies by my hands,
Yes, my sire shall kiss my feet.
    CLOTALDO.   Death he threatens in his rage.
    BASILIUS.   Outrage vile he doth intend.
    CLOTALDO.   He my life has sworn to end.
    BASILIUS.   He has vowed to insult my age.
    SIGISMUND (*still sleeping*).   On the mighty world's
      great stage,
'Mid the admiring nations' cheer,
Valour mine, that has no peer,
Enter thou : the slave so shunned
Now shall reign Prince Sigismund,
And his sire his wrath shall fear.—   [*He awakes.*
But, ah me ! Where am I ? Oh !—
    BASILIUS.   Me I must not let him see.
                     [*To* CLOTALDO.
Listening I close by will be,
What you have to do you know.   [*He retires.*
    SIGISMUND.   Can it possibly be so ?
Is the truth not what it seemed ?
Am I chained and unredeemed ?
Art not thou my lifelong tomb,
Dark old tower ? Yes ! What a doom !
God ! what wondrous things I've dreamed !
    CLOTALDO.   Now in this delusive play
Must my special part be taken :—
Is it not full time to waken ?
    SIGISMUND.   Yes, to waken well it may.
    CLOTALDO.   Wilt thou sleep the livelong day ? —
Since we gazing from below
Saw the eagle sailing slow,
Soaring through the azure sphere,
All the time thou waited here,
Didst thou never waken ?
    SIGISMUND.   No,
Nor even now am I awake,

Since such thoughts my memory fill,
That it seems I'm dreaming still :
Nor is this a great mistake ;
Since if dreams could phantoms make
Things of actual substance seen,
I things seen may phantoms deem.
Thus a double harvest reaping,
I can see when I am sleeping,
And when waking I can dream.
    CLOTALDO.   What you may have dreamed of, say.
    SIGISMUND.   If I thought it only seemed.
I would tell not what I dreamed,
But what I beheld, I may.
I awoke, and lo ! I lay
(Cruel and delusive thing !)
In a bed whose covering,
Bright with blooms from rosy bowers,
Seemed a tapestry of flowers
Woven by the hand of Spring.
Then a crowd of nobles came,
Who addressed me by the name
Of their prince, presenting me
Gems and robes, on bended knee.
Calm soon left me, and my frame
Thrilled with joy to hear thee tell
Of the fate that me befell,
For though now in this dark den,
I was Prince of Poland then.
    CLOTALDO.   Doubtless you repaid me well ?
    SIGISMUND.   No, not well : for, calling thee
Traitor vile, in furious strife
Twice I strove to take thy life.
    CLOTALDO.   But why all this rage 'gainst me ?
    SIGISMUND.   I was master, and would be
Well revenged on foe and friend.
Love one woman could defend. . . . . .

That, at least, for truth I deem,
All else ended like a dream,
That alone can never end.   [*The* King *withdraws.*
  CLOTALDO (*aside*). From his place the King hath
    gone,
Touched by his pathetic words :—
Speaking of the king of birds   [*Aloud.*
Soaring to ascend his throne,
Thou didst fancy one thine own ;
But in dreams, however bright,
Thou shouldst still have kept in sight
How for years I tended thee,
For 'twere well, whoe'er we be,
Even in dreams to do what's right.   [*Exit.*

Scene XVIII.

  SIGISMUND.   That is true : then let's restrain
This wild rage, this fierce condition
Of the mind, this proud ambition,
Should we ever dream again :
And we'll do so, since 'tis plain,
In this world's uncertain gleam,
That to live is but to dream :
Man dreams what he is, and wakes
Only when upon him breaks
Death's mysterious morning beam.
The king dreams he is a king,
And in this delusive way
Lives and rules with sovereign sway ;
All the cheers that round him ring,
Born of air, on air take wing.
And in ashes (mournful fate !)

Death dissolves his pride and state :
Who would wish a crown to take,
Seeing that he must awake
In the dream beyond death's gate ?
And the rich man dreams of gold,
Gilding cares it scarce conceals,
And the poor man dreams he feels
Want and misery and cold.
Dreams he too who rank would. hold,
Dreams who bears toil's rough-ribbed hands,
Dreams who wrong for wrong demands,
And in fine, throughout the earth,
All men dream, whate'er their birth,
And yet no one understands.
'Tis a dream that I in sadness
Here am bound, the scorn of fate ;
'Twas a dream that once a state
I enjoyed of light and gladness.
What is life ?   'Tis but a madness.
What is life ?   A thing that seems,
A mirage that falsely gleams,
Phantom joy, delusive rest,
Since is life a dream at best,
And even dreams themselves are dreams.

ACT THE THIRD.

WITHIN THE TOWER.

SCENE I.

CLARIN.   In a strange enchanted tower,
I, for what I know, am prisoned ;*
How would ignorance be punished,
If for knowledge they would kill me?
What a thing to die of hunger,
For a man who loves good living !
I compassionate myself ;
All will say : " I well believe it " ;
And it well may be believed,
Because silence is a virtue
Incompatible with my name
Clarin, which of course forbids it.
In this place my sole companions,
It may safely be predicted,
Are the spiders and the mice :
What a pleasant nest of linnets !—
Owing to this last night's dream,
My poor head I feel quite dizzy
From a thousand clarionets,
Shawms, and seraphines and cymbals,
Crucifixes and processions,

---

* The *asonante* to the end of Scene IV. is in *i—e*, or their vocal
equivalents.

Flagellants who so well whipped them,
That as up and down they went,
Some even fainted as they witnessed
How the blood ran down the others.
I, if I the truth may whisper,
Simply fainted from not eating,
For I see me in this prison
All day wondering how this Poland
Such a *Hungary* look exhibits,
All night reading in the *Fasti*
By some half-starved poet written.*
In the calendar of saints,
If a new one is admitted,
Then St. Secret be my patron,
For I fast upon his vigil ;
Though it must be owned I suffer
Justly for the fault committed,
Since a servant to be silent
Is a sacrilege most sinful.

> [*A sound of drums and trumpets, with
> voices within.*

Scene II.

Soldiers *and* Clarin.

First Soldier (*within*). He is here within this
>   tower.
Dash the door from off its hinges ;
Enter all.

---

* These four lines are a paraphrase of the original. Clarin's jokes are different, and not much better. He says he spends his days studying philosophy in the works of *Nicomedes* (or *Not-eating*), and his nights perusing the decrees of the *Nicene* Council (Concilio *Niceno*, the Council of *No-Supper*).

CLARIN.   Good God ! 'tis certain
That 'tis me they seek so briskly,
Since they say that I am here.
What can they require ?
    FIRST SOLDIER (*within*).   Go in there.
                            [*Several* Soldiers *enter*.
    SECOND SOLDIER.   Here he is.
    CLARIN.   He's not.
    ALL THE SOLDIERS.   Great lord !
    CLARIN (*aside*).   Are the fellows mad or tipsy ?
    FIRST SOLDIER.   Thou art our own Prince, and we
Will not have, and won't admit of,
Any but our natural Prince ;
We no foreign Prince here wish for.
Let us kneel and kiss thy feet.
    THE SOLDIERS.   Live, long live our best of Princes !
    CLARIN (*aside.*) 'Gad ! the affair grows rather serious.
Is it usual in this kingdom
To take some one out each day,
Make him Prince, and then remit him
To this tower ? It must be so,
Since each day that sight I witness.
I must therefore play my part.
    SOLDIERS.   Thy feet give us !
    CLARIN.   I can't give them,
As I want them for myself.
For a prince to be a cripple
Would be rather a defect.
    SECOND SOLDIER.   We have all conveyed our wishes
To your father ; we have told him
You alone shall be our Prince here,
Not the Duke.
    CLARIN.   And were you guilty
'Gainst my sire, of disrespect ?
    FIRST SOLDIER.   'Twas the loyalty of our spirit.
    CLARIN.   If 'twas loyalty, I forgive you.

SECOND SOLDIER. Come, regain thy lost dominion.
Long live Sigismund!
    ALL.   Live the Prince.
    CLARIN (*aside*). Say they Sigismund? Good. Ad-
        mitted.
Sigismund must be the name
Given to all pretended princes.

SCENE III.

SIGISMUND, CLARIN, *and* Soldiers.

SIGISMUND. Who has named here Sigismund?
CLARIN (*aside.*) Ah, I'm but an addled prince,
    then!
FIRST SOLDIER. Who is Sigismund?
SIGISMUND.   Who? I.
SECOND SOLDIER (*to* CLARIN). How, then, didst thou,
    bold and silly,
Dare to make thee Sigismund?
    CLARIN. I a Sigismund? Thou fibbest;
It was you yourselves that thus
Sigismundized me and princed me:
All the silliness and the boldness
Have been by yourselves committed.
    FIRST SOLDIER. Great and brave Prince Sigismund
(For thy bearing doth convince us
Thou art he, although on faith
We proclaim thee as our prince here)..
King Basilius, thy father,.
Fearful of the Heavens fulfilling
A prediction, which declared
He would see himself submitted.
At thy victor feet, attempts

'To deprive thee of thy birthright,
And to give it to Astolfo,
Muscovy's duke.· For this his missives
Summoned all his court : the people
Understanding, by some instinct,
That they had a natural king,.
Did not wish a foreign princeling
To rule o'er them,   And 'tis thus,
That the fate for thee predicted
Treating with a noble scorn,.
They have sought thee where imprisoned
Thou dost live, that issuing forth,
By their powerful arms assisted,
From this tower, thy crown and sceptre
Thou shouldst thus regain, and quit them.
Of a stranger and a tyrant.,
Forth ! then ; for among these cliffs here
There is now a numerous army,
Formed of soldiers and banditti,·
That invoke thee : freedom waits thee ;
To the thousand voices listen.
    (*Voices within.*)   Long, long live Prince Sigismund !
    SIGISMUND. Once again, O Heaven ! wouldst wish me
Once again to dream of greatness
Which may vanish in an instant ?
Once again to see the glories,...
That a royal throne encircle,
Die in darkness and in gloom, ;
Like a flame the winds extinguish ?
Once again by sad experience
To be taught the dangerous limits
Human power may overleap, ں
At its birth and while it liveth ?
No, it must not, must not be :—
See me now once more submitted
To my fate ; and since I know

Life is but a dream, a vision,
Hence, ye phantoms, that assume
To my darkened sense the figure
And the voice of life—although
Neither voice nor form is in them.
I no longer now desire
A feigned majesty, a fictitious
And fantastic pomp—illusions
Which the slightest breath that ripples
The calm ether can destroy,
Even as in the early spring-time,
When the flowering almond tree
Unadvisedly exhibits
All its fleeting bloom of flowers,
The first blast their freshness withers,
And the ornament and grace
Of its rosy locks disfigures.
Now I know ye—know ye all,
And I know the same false glimmer
Cheats the eyes of all who sleep.
Me false shows no more bewilder ;
Disabused, I now know well
Life is but a dream—a vision.

    SECOND SOLDIER. If thou thinkest we deceive thee,
Turn thine eyes to those proud cliffs here,
See the crowds that wait there, willing,
Eager to obey thee.

    SIGISMUND.   Yet
Just as clearly and distinctly,
I have seen another time
The same things that now I witness,
And 'twas but a dream.

    SECOND SOLDIER. At all times
Great events, my lord, bring with them
Their own omens ; and thy dream
But the actual fact prefigured.

Sigismund.   You say well, it was an omen ;
But supposing the bright vision
Even were true, since life is short,
Let us dream, my soul, a little,
Once again, remembering now
With all forethought and prevision
That we must once more awake
At the better time not distant ;
That being known, the undeceiving,
When it comes, will be less bitter ;
For it takes the sting from evil
To anticipate its visit.
And with this conviction, too,
Even its certainty admitting,
That all power being only lent
Must return unto the Giver,
Let us boldly then dare all.—
For the loyalty you exhibit,
Thanks, my lieges.   See in me
One who will this land deliver
From a stranger's alien yoke.
Sound to arms ; you soon shall witness
What my valour can effect.
'Gainst my father I have lifted
Hostile arms, to see if Heaven
Has of me the truth predicted.
At my feet I am to see him . . .
But if I, from dreams delivered,   [*Aside.*
Wake ere then, and nothing happens,
Silence now were more befitting.
    All.   Long live Sigismund, our king !

SCENE IV.

CLOTALDO, SIGISMUND, CLARIN, *and* Soldiers.

CLOTALDO.   Ha ! what tumult, Heavens ! has risen ?
SIGISMUND.   Well, Clotaldo.
CLOTALDO.   Sire . . . . On me   [*Aside.*
Will his wrath now fall.
 CLARIN (*aside*).   He'll fling him
Headlong down the steep, I'll bet.   [*Exit.*
 CLOTALDO.   At your royal feet submitted
I know how to die.
 SIGISMUND.   My father,
Rise, I pray, from that position,
Since to you, my guide and polestar,
Are my future acts committed ;
All my past life owes you much
For your careful supervision.
Come, embrace me.
 CLOTALDO.   What do you say ?
 SIGISMUND.   That I dream, and that my wishes
Are to do what's right, since we
Even in dreams should do what's fitting.
 CLOTALDO.   Then, my prince, if you adopt
Acting rightly as your symbol,
You will pardon me for asking,
So to act, that you permit me.
No advice and no assistance
Can I give against my king.
Better that my lord should kill me
At his feet here.
 SIGISMUND.   Oh, ungrateful !
Villain ! wretch ! (*Aside.*) But, Heavens ! 'tis fitter
I restrain myself, not knowing
But all this may be a vision.—

The fidelity I envy
Must be honoured and admitted.
Go and serve your lord, the king.
Where the battle rages thickest
We shall meet.—To arms, my friends !
    CLOTALDO.   Thanks, most generous of princes. [*Exit.*
    SIGISMUND.   Fortune, we go forth to reign ;
Wake me not if this is vision,
Let me sleep not if 'tis true.
But whichever of them is it,
To act right is what imports me.
If 'tis true, because it is so ;
If 'tis not, that when I waken
Friends may welcome and forgive me.
                  [*Exeunt all, drums beating.*

SCENE V.

HALL IN THE ROYAL PALACE.

BASILIUS *and* ASTOLFO.

    BASILIUS.   Who can expect, Astolfo, to restrain
An untamed steed that wildly turns to flee?
Who can the current of a stream detain,
That swollen with pride sweeps down to seek the sea?
Who can prevent from tumbling to the plain
Some mighty peak the lightning's flash sets free ?
Yet each were easier in its separate way,
Than the rude mob's insensate rage to stay.
The several bands that throng each green retreat
This truth proclaim by their disparted cries ;
Astolfo here the echoing notes repeat,
While there 'tis *Sigismund* that rends the skies.

The place where late the land was glad to greet
The choice we made, a second venture tries ;
And soon will be, as Horror o'er it leans,
The fatal theatre of tragic scenes.

ASTOLFO.   My lord, let all this joy suspended be,
These plaudits cease, and to another day
Defer the rapture thou hast promised me ;
For if this Poland (which I hope to sway)
Resists to-day my right of sovereignty,
'Tis that by merit I should win my way.
Give me a steed ; to stem this wild revolt
My pride shall be the flash that bears the bolt.   [*Exit.*

BASILIUS.   Slight help there is for what is fixed by fate,
And much of danger to foresee the blow ;
If it must fall, defence is then too late,
And he who most forestalls doth most foreknow.
Hard law !   Stern rule !   Dire fact to contemplate !
That he who thinks to fly doth nearer go.
Thus by the very means that I employed,
My country and myself I have destroyed.

<hr>

SCENE VI.

ESTRELLA *and* BASILIUS.

ESTRELLA.   If, mighty lord, thy presence, which it
     braves,
The tumult of the crowd cannot defeat—
The frenzy of the multitude that raves
In hostile bands through every square and street,—
Thou'lt see thy kingdom swim in crimson waves,
A purple sea of blood shall round it beat ;
For even already in its dismal doom
All is disaster, tragedy, and gloom.

Such is thy kingdom's ruin, so severe
The hard and bloody trial fate hath sent,
Dazed is the eye, and terrified the ear;
Dark grows the sun, and every wind is spent;
Each stone a mournful obelisk doth rear,
And every flower erects a monument;
A grave seems every house, whence life is gone,—
Each soldier is a living skeleton.

SCENE VII.

CLOTALDO, BASILIUS, *and* ESTRELLA.

CLOTALDO.   Thanks be to God, I reach thy feet alive.
BASILIUS.   What news of Sigismund, Clotaldo, say?
CLOTALDO.   The crowd, whom frenzy and blind im-
        pulse drive,
Into the tower resistless burst their way,
Released the Prince, who seeing thus revive
The honour he had tasted for one day,
Looked brave, declaring, in a haughty tone,
The truth at last that heaven must now make known,
    BASILIUS.   Give me a horse!   In person forth I'll
        ride
To check the pride of this ungrateful son.
Where Science erred let now the sword decide;
By my own valour shall my throne be won!   [*Exit.*
    ESTRELLA.   Let me the glory of the fight divide—
A twinkling star beside that royal sun—
Bellona matched with Mars: for I would dare
To scale even heaven to rival Pallas there.
                    [*Exit, and they sound to arms.*

SCENE VIII.

ROSAURA, *who detains* CLOTALDO.

ROSAURA.   Though the trumpets from afar
Echo in thy valorous breast,
Hear me, list to my request,
For I know that all is war.
Well thou knowest that I came
Poor to Poland, sad, dejected;
And that graciously protected,
Thou thy pity let me claim.
It was thy command, ah, me!
I should live here thus disguised,
Striving, as thy words advised
(Hiding all my jealousy),
To avoid Astolfo's sight;
But he saw me, and though seeing,
With Estrella, he—false being!—
Converse holds this very night
In a garden bower. The key
I have taken, and will show
Where, by entering, with a blow
Thou canst end my misery.
Thus, then, daring, bold, and strong,
Thou my honour wilt restore;
Strike, and hesitate no more,
Let his death revenge my wrong.
CLOTALDO.   It is true, my inclination
Since thou first wert seen by me,
Was to strive and do for thee
(Be thy tears my attestation)
All my life could do to serve thee.
What I first was forced to press,
Was that thou should'st change thy dress,
Lest if chancing to observe thee

Masquerading like a page,
By appearances so strong
Led astray, the Duke might wrong
By a thought thy sex and age.
Meanwhile various projects held me
In suspense, oft pondering o'er
How thy honour to restore;
Though (thy honour so compelled me)
I Astolfo's life should take—
Wild design that soon took wing —
Yet, as he was not my king,
It no terror could awake.
I his death was seeking, when
Sigismund with vengeful aim
Sought for mine; Astolfo came,
And despising what most men
Would a desperate peril deem,
Stood in my defence; his bearing,
Nigh to rashness in its daring,
Showed a valour most extreme.
How then, think, could I, whose breath
Is his gift, in murderous strife,
For his giving me my life,
Strive in turn to give him death?
And thus, grateful, yet aggrieved,
By two opposite feelings driven,
Seeing it to thee have given,
And from him have it received,
Doubting this, and that believing,
Half revenging, half forgiving,
If to thee I'm drawn by giving,
I to him am by receiving;
Thus bewildered and beset,
Vainly seeks my love a way,
Since I have a debt to pay,
Where I must exact a debt.

ROSAURA.   It is settled, I believe,
As all men of spirit know,
That 'tis glorious to bestow,
But a meanness to receive.
Well, admitting this to be,
Then thy thanks should not be his,
Even supposing that he is
One who gave thy life to thee ;
As the gift of life was thine,
And from him the taking came,
In his case the act was shame,
And a glorious act in mine.
Thus by him thou art aggrieved,
And by me even complimented,
Since to me thou hast presented
What from him thou hast received :
Then all hesitation leaving,
Thou to guard my fame shouldst fly,
Since my honour is as high
As is giving to receiving.
    CLOTALDO.   Though it seems a generous fever
In a noble heart to give,
Still an equal fire may live
In the heart of the receiver.
Heartlessness is something hateful,
I would boast a liberal name ;
Thus I put my highest claim
In the fact of being grateful.
Then to me that title leave,—
Gentle birth breeds gentleness ;
For the honour is no less
To bestow than to receive.
    ROSAURA.   I received my life from thee,
But for thee I now were dead ;
Still it was thyself that said
No insulted life could be

Called a life : on that I stand ;
Nought have I received from thee,
For the life no life could be
That was given me by thy hand.
But if thou wouldst first be just
Ere being generous in this way
(As I heard thyself once say),
Thou wilt give me life I trust,
Which thou hast not yet ; and thus
Giving will enhance thee more,
For if liberal before,
Thou wilt then be generous.

  CLOTALDO. Conquered by thy argument,
Liberal I first will be.
I, Rosaura, will to thee
All my property present ;
In a convent live ; by me
Has the plan been weighed some time,
For escaping from a crime
Thou wilt there find sanctuary ;
For so many ills present them
Through the land on every side,
That being nobly born, my pride
Is to strive and not augment them.
By the choice that I have made,
Loyal to the land I'll be,
I am liberal with thee,
And Astolfo's debt is paid ;
Choose then, nay, let honour, rather,
Choose for thee, and for us two,
For, by Heaven ! I could not do
More for thee were I thy father !—

  ROSAURA. Were that supposition true,
I might strive and bear this blow ;
But not being my father, no.

  CLOTALDO. What then dost thou mean to do ?

ROSAURA. Kill the Duke.
CLOTALDO. A gentle dame,
Who no father's name doth know,
Can she so much valour show ?
ROSAURA. Yes.
CLOTALDO. What drives thee on ?
ROSAURA. My fame.
CLOTALDO. Think that in the Duke thou'lt see . . . .
ROSAURA. Honour all my wrath doth rouse.
CLOTALDO. Soon thy king—Estrella's spouse.
ROSAURA. No, by Heaven ! it must not be.
CLOTALDO. It is madness.
ROSAURA. Yes, I see it.
CLOTALDO. Conquer it.
ROSAURA. I can't o'erthrow it.
CLOTALDO. It will cost thee . . . .
ROSAURA. Yes, I know it.
CLOTALDO. Life and honour.
ROSAURA. Well, so be it.
CLOTALDO. What wouldst have ?
ROSAURA. My death.
CLOTALDO. Take care !
It is spite.
ROSAURA. 'Tis honour's cure.
CLOTALDO. ''Tis wild fire.
ROSAURA. That will endure.
CLOTALDO. It is frenzy.
ROSAURA. Rage, despair.
CLOTALDO. Can there then be nothing done
This blind rage to let pass by ?
ROSAURA. No.
CLOTALDO. And who will help thee ?
ROSAURA. I.
CLOTALDO Is there then no remedy ?
ROSAURA. None.
CLOTALDO. Think of other means whereby . . . .

ROSAURA.   Other means would seal my fate.   [*Exit.*
CLOTALDO.   If 'tis so, then, daughter, wait,
For together we shall die.   [*Exit.*

SCENE IX.

THE OPEN PLAIN.

SIGISMUND, *clothed in skins:* Soldiers *marching.*
CLARIN.   (*Drums are heard.*)

SIGISMUND.   If Rome could see me on this day
Amid the triumphs of its early sway,.
Oh, with what strange delight
It would have seen so singular a sight,
Its mighty armies led
By one who was a savage wild beast bred,
Whose courage soars so high,
That even an easy conquest seems the sky !
But let us lower our flight,
My spirit ; 'tis not thus we should invite
This doubtful dream to stay,
Lest when I wake and it has past away,
I learn to my sad cost,
A moment given, 'twas in a moment lost ;
Determined not to abuse it,
The less will be my sorrow should I lose it.
　　　　　　　　　　　[*A trumpet sounds.*
CLARIN.   Upon a rapid steed,
(Excuse my painting it ; I can't indeed
Resist the inspiration),
Which seems a moving mass of all creation,
Its body being the earth,
The fire the soul that in its heart hath birth,

Its foam the sea, its panting breath the air,
Chaos confused at which I stand and stare,
Since in its soul, foam, body, breath, to me
It is a monster made of fire, earth, air, and sea ;
Its colour dapple grey,
Speckled its skin, and flecked, as well it may,
By the impatient spur its flank that dyes,
For lo ! it doth not run, the meteor flies ;
As borne upon the wind,
A beauteous woman seeks thee.
  SIGISMUND.   I'm struck blind !
  CLARIN. Good God, it is Rosaura, oh, the pain !
             [Retires.

SIGISMUND. Heaven has restored her to my sight
  again.

SCENE X.

ROSAURA, *in a light corselet, with sword and dagger ;*
SIGISMUND, *and* Soldiers.

  ROSAURA. Noble-hearted Sigismund !
Thou whose hidden light heroic
Issues from its night of shadows
To the great deeds of its morning ;
And as heaven's sublimest planet
From the white arms of Aurora
Back restores their beauteous colour
To the wild flowers and the roses,
And upon the seas and mountains,
When endiademed with glory,
Scatters light, diffuses splendour,
Braids their foam, their hair makes golden ;
Thus thou dawnest on the world

Bright auspicious sun of Poland,
Who will help a hapless woman,
She who at thy feet doth throw her,
Help her, since she is unhappy,
And a woman; two good motives
Quite enough to move a man
Who of valour so doth boast him,
Though even one would be sufficient,
Though even one would be all potent.
Thou hast seen me thrice already,
Thrice thou hast not truly known me,
For each time by different dresses
Was I strangely metamorphosed.
First I seemed to thee a man,
When within thy sad and sombre
Cell thou sawest me, when thy life
Wiled from me mine own misfortunes.
As a woman next thou sawest me,
Where the splendours of thy throne-room
Vanished like a fleeting vision,
Vain, phantasmal and abortive.
The third time is now, when being
Something monstrous and abnormal,
In a woman's dress thou see'st me
With a warrior's arms adornéd.
And to pity and compassion
That thou may'st be moved more strongly,
Listen to the sad succession
Of my tragical misfortunes.
In the Court of Muscovy
I was born of a noble mother,
Who indeed must have been fair
Since unhappiness was her portion.
Fond and too persuading eyes
Fixed on her, a traitor lover,
Whom, not knowing, I don't name,

Though mine own worth hath informed me
What was his : for being his image,
I sometimes regret that fortune ·
Made me not a pagan born,
That I might, in my wild folly,
Think he must have been some god,
Such as he was, who in golden
Shower wooed Danae, or as swan
Leda loved, as bull, Europa.
When I thought to lengthen out,
Citing these perfidious stories,
My discourse, I find already
That I have succinctly told thee
How my mother, being persuaded
By the flatteries of love's homage,
Was as fair as any fair,
And unfortunate as all are.
That ridiculous excuse
Of a plighted husband's promise
So misled her, that even yet
The remembrance brings her sorrow.
For that traitor, that Æneas
Flying from his Troy, forgot there,
Or left after him his sword.
~~By this sheath its blade is covered,~~
~~But it shall be naked drawn~~
~~Ere this history is over.~~
From this loosely fastened knot
Which binds nothing, which ties nothing,
Call it marriage, call it crime,
Names its nature cannot alter,
I was born, a perfect image,
A true copy of my mother,
In her loveliness, ah, no !
In her miseries and misfortunes.
Therefore there is little need

To say how the hapless daughter,
Heiress of such scant good luck,
Had her own peculiar portion.
All that I will say to thee
Of myself is, that the robber
Of the trophies of my fame,
Of the sweet spoils of my honour,
Is Astolfo . . . . Ah! to name him
Stirs and rouses up the choler
Of the heart, a fitting effort
When an enemy's name is spoken,—
Yes, Astolfo was that traitor,
Who, forgetful of his promise
(For when love has passed away,
Even its memory is forgotten),
Came to Poland, hither called.
From so sweet so proud a conquest,
To be married to Estrella,
Of my setting sun the torch-light.
Who'll believe that when one star
Oft unites two happy lovers,
Now one star, Estrella, comes
Two to tear from one another?
I offended, I deceived,
Sad remained, remained astonished,
Mad, half dead, remained myself;
That's to say, in so much torment,
That my heart was like a Babel
Of confusion, hell, and horror:
I resolving to be mute,
(For there are some pains and sorrows
That by feelings are expressed,
Better than when words are spoken),
I by silence spoke my pain,
Till one day being with my mother
Violante, she (oh, heavens!)

Burst their prison ; like a torrent
Forth they rushed from out my breast,
Streaming wildly o'er each other.
No embarrassment it gave me
To relate them, for the knowing
That the person we confide to
A like weakness must acknowledge
Gives as 'twere to our confusion
A sweet soothing and a solace,
For at times a bad example
Has its use.   In fine, my sorrows
She with pity heard, relating
Even her own grief to console me :
When he has himself been guilty
With what ease the judge condoneth !
Knowing from her own experience
That 'twas idle, to slow-moving
Leisure, to swift-fleeting time,
To intrust one's injured honour.
She could not advise me better,
As the cure of my misfortunes,
Than to follow and compel him
By prodigious acts of boldness
To repay my honour's debt :
And that such attempt might cost me
Less, my fortune wished that I
Should a man's strange dress put on me.
She took down an ancient sword,
Which is this I bear : the moment
Now draws nigh I must unsheath it,
Since to her I gave that promise,
When confiding in its marks,
Thus she said, " Depart to Poland,
And so manage that this steel
Shall be seen by the chief nobles
Of that land, for I have hope

That there may be one among them
Who may prove to thee a friend, .
An adviser and consoler."
Well, in Poland I arrived ;
It is useless to inform thee
What thou knowest already, how
A wild steed resistless bore me
To thy caverned tower, wherein
Thou with wonder didst behold me.
Let us pass too, how Clotaldo
Passionately my cause supported,
How he asked my life of the king
Who to him that boon accorded ;
How discovering who I am
He persuaded me my proper
Dress to assume, and on Estrella
To attend as maid of honour,
So to thwart Astolfo's love
And prevent the marriage contract.
Let us, too, pass by, that here
Thou didst once again behold me
In a woman's dress, my form
Waking thus a twofold wonder,
And approach the time, Clotaldo
Being convinced it was important
That should wed and reign together
Fair Estrella and Astolfo,
'Gainst my honour, me advised
To forego my rightful project.
But, O valiant Sigismund,
Seeing that the moment cometh
For thy vengeance, since heaven wishes
Thee to-day to burst the portals
Of thy narrow rustic cell,
Where so long immured, thy body
Was to feeling a wild beast,

Was to sufferance what the rock is,
And that 'gainst thy sire and country
Thou hast gallantly revolted,
And ta'en arms, I come to assist thee,
Intermingling the bright corselet
Of Minerva with the trappings
Of Diana, thus enrobing
Silken stuff and shining steel
In a rare but rich adornment.
On, then, on, undaunted champion !
To us both it is important
To prevent and bring to nought
This engagement and betrothal ;
First to me, that he, my husband,
Should not falsely wed another.
Then to thee, that their two staffs
Being united, their joined forces
Should with overwhelming power
Leave our doubtful victory hopeless.
Woman, I come here to urge thee
To repair my injured honour,
And as man I come to rouse thee
Crown and sceptre to recover.
Woman I would wake thy pity
Since here at thy feet I throw me,
And as man, my sword and person
In thy service I devote thee.
But remember, if to-day
As a woman thou should'st court me,
I, as man, will give thee death
In the laudable upholding,
Of my honour, since I am
In this strife of love, this contest,
Woman my complaints to tell thee,
And a man to guard my honour.

    SIGISMUND (*aside*).   Heavens ! if it is true I dream,

Memory then suspend thy office,
For 'tis vain to hope remembrance
Could retain so many objects.
Help me, God ! or teach me how
All these numerous doubts to conquer,
Or to cease to think of any !—
Whoe'er tried such painful problems ?
If 'twas but a dream, my grandeur,
How then is it, at this moment,
That this woman can refer me
To some facts that are notorious ?
Then 'twas truth, and not a dream ;
But if it was truth (another
And no less confusion,) how
Can my life be called in proper
Speech a dream ? So like to dreams
Are then all the world's chief glories,
That the true are oft rejected
As the false, the false too often
Are mistaken for the true ?
Is there then 'twixt one and the other
Such slight difference, that a question
May arise at any moment
Which is true or which is false ?
Are the original and the copy
So alike, that which is which
Oft the doubtful mind must ponder ?
If 'tis so, and if must vanish,
As the shades of night at morning,
All of majesty and power,
All of grandeur and of glory,
Let us learn at least to turn
To our profit the brief moment
That is given us, since our joy
Lasteth while our dream lasts only.
In my power Rosaura stands,

Thou, my heart, her charms adoreth,
Let us seize then the occasion ;
Let love trample in its boldness
All the laws on which relying
She here at my feet has thrown her.
'Tis a dream ; and since 'tis so,
Let us dream of joys, the sorrows.
Will come soon enough hereafter.
But with mine own words just spoken,
Let me now confute myself !
If it is a dream that mocks me,
Who for human vanities
Would forego celestial glory ?
What past bliss is not a dream ?
Who has had his happy fortunes
Who hath said not to himself
As his memory ran o'er them,
" All I saw, beyond a doubt .
Was a dream."   If this exposeth
My delusion, if I know ,
That desire is but the glowing
Of a flame that turns to ashes .
At the softest wind that bloweth ;
Let us seek then the eternal,
The true fame that ne'er reposeth,
Where the bliss is not a dream,
Nor the crown a fleeting glory.
Without honour is Rosaura.
But it is a prince's province
To give honour, not to take it :
Then, by Heaven ! it is her honour
That for her I must win back,
Ere this kingdom I can conquer.
Let us fly then this temptation.
'Tis too strong : To arms ! March onward !

[To the Soldiers.

For to-day I must give battle,
Ere descending night, the golden
Sunbeams of expiring day
Buries in the dark green ocean.
    ROSAURA.   Dost thou thus, my lord, withdraw thee?
What! without a word being spoken?
Does my pain deserve no pity?
Does my grief so little move thee?
Can it be, my lord, thou wilt not
Deign to hear, to look upon me?
Dost thou even avert thy face?
    SIGISMUND.   Ah, Rosaura, 'tis thy honour
That requires this harshness now,
If my pity I would show thee.
Yes, my voice does not respond,
'Tis my honour that respondeth;
True I speak not, for I wish
That my actions should speak for me;
Thee I do not look on, no,
For, alas! it is of moment,
That he must not see thy beauty
Who is pledged to see thy honour.
[Exit, followed by the Soldiers.
    ROSAURA. What enigmas, O ye skies!
After many a sigh and tear,
Thus in doubt to leave me here
With equivocal replies!

SCENE XI.

CLARIN *and* ROSAURA.

    CLARIN.   Madam, is it visiting hour?
    ROSAURA.   Welcome, Clarin, where have you been?

CLARIN.   Only four stout walls between
In an old enchanted tower ;
Death was on the cards for me,
But amid the sudden strife
Ere the last trump came, my life
Won the trick and I got free.
I ne'er hoped to sound again.
  ROSAURA.   Why?
  CLARIN.   Because alone I know
Who you are : And this being so,
Learn, Clotaldo is . . . . . This strain
Puts me out.   [*Drums are heard.*
  ROSAURA.   What can it be?
  CLARIN.   From the citadel at hand,
Leagured round, an armed band
As to certain victory
Sallies forth with flags unfurled.
  ROSAURA.   'Gainst Prince Sigismund ! and I,
Coward that I am, not by
To surprise and awe the world,
When with so much cruelty
Each on each the two hosts spring !   [*Exit.*

SCENE XII.

CLARIN ; *and* Soldiers *within.*

Voices of some.   Live, long live our victor King !
Voices of others.   Live, long live our liberty !
  CLARIN.   Live, long live the two, I say !
Me it matters not a pin,
Which doth lose or which doth win,
If I can keep out of the way !—
So aside here I will go,

Acting like a prudent hero,
Even as the Emperor Nero
Took things coolly long ago.
Or if care I cannot shun,
Let it 'bout mine ownself be ;
Yes, here hidden I can see
All the fighting and the fun ;
What a cosy place I spy
Mid the rocks there ! so secure,
Death can't find me out I'm sure,
Then a fig for death I say !
> [*Conceals himself, drums beat and the sound
> of arms is heard.*

Scene XIII.

Basilius, Clotaldo, Astolfo, *flying.*—Clarin *concealed.*

Basilius. Hapless king ! disastrous reign !
Outraged father ! guilty son !
 Clotaldo. See thy vanquished forces run
In a panic o'er the plain !
 Astolfo. And the rebel conqueror's stay,
Proud, defiant.
 Basilius.   'Tis decreed
Those are loyal who succeed,
Rebels those who lose the day.
Let us then, Clotaldo, flee,
Since the victory he hath won,
From a proud and cruel son.
> [*Shots are fired within, and* Clarin *falls
> wounded from his hiding-place.*

 Clarin. Heaven protect me !
 Astolfo.   Who can be
This last victim of the fight,

Who struck down in the retreat,
Falls here bleeding at our feet ?
    CLARIN.   I am an unlucky wight,
Who to shun Death's fearful face
Found the thing I would forget :
Flying from him, him I've met.
For there is no secret place
Hid from death ; and therefore I
This conclusion hold as clear,
He 'scapes best who goes more near,
He dies first who first doth fly.
Then return, return and be
In the bloody conflict lost ;
Where the battle rages most,
There is more security
Than in hills how desolate,
Since no safety can there be
'Gainst the force of destiny,
And the inclemency of fate ;
Therefore 'tis in vain thou flyest
From the death thou draw'st more nigh,
Oh, take heed for thou must die
If it is God's will thou diest !   [*Falls within.*
    BASILIUS.   Oh, take heed for thou must die
If it is God's will thou diest !—
With what eloquence, O heaven !
Does this body that here lieth,
Through the red mouth of a wound
To profoundest thoughts entice us
From our ignorance and our error !
The red current as it glideth
Is a bloody tongue that teaches
All man's diligence is idle,
When against a greater power,
And a higher cause it striveth.
Thus with me, 'gainst strife and murder

When I thought I had provided,
I but brought upon my country
All the ills I would have hindered.
    CLOTALDO.   Though, my lord, fate knoweth well
Every path, and quickly findeth
Whom it seeks; yet still it strikes me
'Tis not christian-like to say
'Gainst its rage that nought suffices.
That is wrong, a prudent man
Even o'er fate victorious rises;
And if thou art not preserved
From the ills that have surprised thee,
From worse ills thyself preserve.
    ASTOLFO.   Sire, Clotaldo doth address thee
As a cautious, prudent man,
Whose experience time hath ripened.
I as a bold youth would speak :
Yonder, having lost its rider,
I behold a noble steed
Wandering reinless and unbridled,
Mount and fly with him while I
Guard the open path behind thee.
    BASILIUS.   If it is God's will I die,
Or if Death for me here lieth
As in ambush, face to face
I will meet it and defy it.

SCENE XIV.

SIGISMUND, ESTRELLA, ROSAURA, Soldiers, Attendants,
BASILIUS, ASTOLFO, *and* CLOTALDO.

    A SOLDIER.   'Mid the thickets of the mountain,
'Neath these dark boughs so united,
The King hides.
    SIGISMUND.   Pursue him then,

Leave no single shrub unrifled,
Nothing must escape your search,
Not a plant, and not a pine tree.
    CLOTALDO.   Fly, my lord!
    BASILIUS.   And wherefore fly?
    ASTOLFO.   Come!
    BASILIUS.   Astolfo, I'm decided.
    CLOTALDO.   What to do?
    BASILIUS.   To try, Clotaldo,
One sole remedy that surviveth.   [*To* SIGISMUND.
If 'tis me thou'rt seeking, Prince,
At thy feet behold me lying.   [*Kneeling.*
Let thy carpet be these hairs
Which the snows of age have whitened.
Tread upon my neck, and trample
On my crown; in base defilement
Treat me with all disrespect;
Let thy deadliest vengeance strike me
Through my honour; as thy slave
Make me serve thee, and in spite of
All precautions let fate be,
Let heaven keep the word it plighted.
    SIGISMUND.   Princes of the Court of Poland,
Who such numerous surprises
Have astonished seen, attend,
For it is your prince invites ye.
That which heaven has once determined,
That which God's eternal finger
Has upon the azure tablets
Of the sky sublimely written,
Those transparent sheets of sapphire
Superscribed with golden ciphers
Ne'er deceive, and never lie;
The deceiver and the liar
Is he who to use them badly
In a wrongful sense defines them.

Thus, my father, who is present,
To protect him from the wildness
Of my nature, made of me
A fierce brute, a human wild-beast ;
So that I, who from my birth,
From the noble blood that trickles
Through my veins, my generous nature,
And my liberal condition,
Might have proved a docile child,
And so grew, it was sufficient
By so strange an education,
By so wild a course of living,
To have made my manners wild ;—
What a method to refine them !
If to any man 'twas said,
" It is fated that some wild. beast
Will destroy you," would it be
Wise to wake a sleeping tiger
As the remedy of the ill?
If 'twere said, " this sword here hidden
In its sheath, which thou dost wear,
Is the one foredoomed to kill thee,"
Vain precaution it would be
To preserve the threatened victim,
Bare to point it at his breast.
If 'twere said, " these waves that ripple
Calmly here for thee will build
Foam-white sepulchres of silver,"
Wrong it were to trust the sea
When its haughty breast is lifted
Into mountain heights of snow,
Into hills of curling crystal.
Well, this very thing has happened
Unto him, who feared a wild-beast,
And awoke him while he slept ;
Or who drew a sharp sword hidden

Naked forth, or dared the sea
When 'twas roused by raging whirlwinds.
And though my fierce nature (hear me)
Was as 'twere the sleeping tiger,
A sheathed sword my innate rage,
And my wrath a quiet ripple,
Fate should not be forced by means
So unjust and so vindictive,
For they but excite it more ;
And thus he who would be victor
O'er his fortune, must succeed
By wise prudence and self-strictness.
Not before an evil cometh
Can it rightly be resisted
Even by him who hath foreseen it,
For although (the fact's admitted)
By an humble resignation
It is possible to diminish
Its effects, it first must happen,
And by no means can be hindered.
Let it serve as an example
This strange sight, this most surprising
Spectacle, this fear, this horror,
This great prodigy ; for none higher
E'er was worked than this we see,
After years of vain contriving,
Prostrate at my feet a father,
And a mighty king submitted.,
This the sentence of high heaven
Which he did his best to hinder
He could not prevent.   Can I,
Who in valour and in science,
Who in years am so inferior,
It avert? My lord, forgive me,   [*To the* King.
Rise, sir, let me clasp thy hand ;
For since heaven has now apprized thee

'That thy mode of counteracting
Its decree was wrong, a willing
Sacrifice to thy revenge
Let my prostrate neck be given.
    BASILIUS.   Son, this noble act of thine
In my heart of hearts reviveth
All my love, thou'rt there reborn.
Thou art Prince ; the bay that bindeth
Heroes' brows, the palm, be thine,
Let the crown thine own deeds give thee.
    ALL.   Long live Sigismund our King !
    SIGISMUND.   Though my sword must wait a little
Ere great victories it can gain,
I to-day will win the highest,
The most glorious, o'er myself.—
Give, Astolfo, give your plighted
Hand here to Rosaura, since
It is due and I require it.
    ASTOLFO.   Though 'tis true I owe the debt,
Still 'tis needful to consider
That she knows not who she is ;
It were infamous, a stigma
On my name to wed a woman . . . .
    CLOTALDO.   Stay, Astolfo, do not finish ;
For Rosaura is as noble
As yourself.   My sword will right her
In the field against the world :
She's my daughter, that's sufficient.
    ASTOLFO.   What do you say ?
    CLOTALDO.   Until I saw her
To a noble spouse united,
I her birth would not reveal.
It were now a long recital,
But the sum is, she's my child.
    ASTOLFO.   That being so, the word I've plighted
I will keep.

SIGISMUND.   And that Estrella
May not now be left afflicted,
Seeing she has lost a prince
Of such valour and distinction,
I propose from mine own hand
As a husband one to give her,
Who, if he does not exceed
Him in worth, perhaps may rival.
Give to me thy hand.
     ESTRELLA.   I gain
By an honour so distinguished.
     SIGISMUND.   To Clotaldo, who so truly
Served my father, I can give him
But these open arms wherein
He will find whate'er he wishes.
     A SOLDIER. If thou honorest those who serve thee,
Thus, to me the first beginner
Of the tumult through the land,
Who from out the tower, thy prison,
Drew thee forth, what wilt thou give ?
     SIGISMUND.   Just that tower : and that you issue
Never from it until death,
I will have you guarded strictly ;
For the traitor is not needed
Once the treason is committed.
     BASILIUS.   So much wisdom makes one wonder.
     ASTOLFO.   What a change in his condition !
     ROSAURA.   How discreet ! how calm ! how prudent !
     SIGISMUND.   Why this wonder, these surprises,
If my teacher was a dream,
And amid my new aspirings
I am fearful I may wake,
And once more a prisoner find me
In my cell ?   But should I not,
Even to dream it is sufficient :
For I thus have come to know

That at last all human blisses
Pass and vanish as a dream,
And the time that may be given me
I henceforth would turn to gain :
Asking for our faults forgiveness,
Since to generous, noble hearts
It is natural to forgive them.

THE
WONDER-WORKING MAGICIAN.

TO THE MEMORY OF

SHELLEY,

WHOSE ADMIRATION FOR

" THE LIGHT AND ODOUR OF THE FLOWERY AND STARRY AUTOS "

IS THE HIGHEST TRIBUTE TO THE BEAUTY OF
CALDERON'S POETRY,

This Drama

IS INSCRIBED.

PERSONS.

CYPRIAN.

THE DEMON.

LELIUS, *the Governor of Antioch's Son.*

FLORUS, *friend of* Lelius. '

MOSCON, }
CLARIN, } *Servants of* Cyprian.

THE GOVERNOR OF ANTIOCH.

FABIUS, *his Servant.*

LYSANDER, *the reputed Father of* Justina.

JUSTINA.

LIVIA, *her Maid.*

A Servant.

A Soldier.

Attendants, Soldiers, People.

SCENE—*Antioch and its environs.*

THE WONDER-WORKING MAGICIAN.

ACT THE FIRST.

SCENE I.

A WOOD NEAR ANTIOCH.

Enter CYPRIAN *in a Student's gown, followed by* CLARIN *and* MOSCON, *as poor Scholars, carrying books.*

CYPRIAN.   In the pleasant solitude
Of this tranquil spot, this thicket
Formed of interlacing boughs,
Buds, and flowers, and shrubs commingled,
You may leave me, leaving also,
As my best companions, with me,
(For I need none else) those books
Which I bade you to bring hither
From the house ; for while, to-day,
Antioch, the mighty city,
Celebrates with such rejoicing
The great temple newly finished
Unto Jupiter, the bearing
Thither, also, of his image
Publicly, in grand procession,
To its shrine to be uplifted ;—
I, escaping the confusion

Of the streets and squares, have flitted
Hitherward, to spend in study
What of daylight yet may glimmer.
Go, enjoy the festival,
Go to Antioch and mingle
In its various sports, returning
When the sun descending sinketh
To be buried in the waves,
Which, beneath the dark clouds' fringes,
Round the royal corse of gold,
Shine like sepulchres of silver.
Here you'll find me.

    MOSCON.   Sir, although
Most decidedly my wish is
To behold the sports, yet I
Cannot go without a whisper
Of some few five thousand words,
Which I'll give you in a jiffy.
Can it be that on a day
Of such free, such unrestricted
Revelry, and mirth, and fun,
You with your old books come hither
To this country place, rejecting
All the frolic of the city?

    CLARIN.   Well, I think my master's right;
For there's nothing more insipid
Than a grand procession day,
Half fandangos, priests, and fiddles.

    MOSCON.   Clarin, from the first to last,
All your life you've been a trickster,
A smart, temporizing toady,
A bold flatterer, a trimmer,
Since you praise the thoughts of others,
And ne'er speak your own.

    CLARIN.   The civil
Way to tell a man he lies

Is to say he's wrong :—you twig me,
Now I think I speak my mind.
  CYPRIAN.   Moscon, Clarin, both I bid ye
Cease this silly altercation.
It is ever thus betwixt ye,
Puffed up with your little knowledge
Each maintains his own opinion.
Go, and (as I've said) here seek me
When night falls, and with the thickness
Of its shadows veils from view
This most fair and wondrous system
Of the universe.
  MOSCON.   How comes it,
That although you have admitted
'Tis not right to see the feast,
Yet you go to see it?
  CLARIN.   Simple
Is the answer : no one follows
The advice which he has given
To another.
  MOSCON (*aside*).   To see Livia,
Would the gods that I were wingèd.   [*Exit.*
  CLARIN (*aside*). If the honest truth were told
Livia is the girl that gives me
Something worth the living for.
Even her very name has in it
This assurance : *Livia*, yes,
Minus *a*, I live for *Livi.**   [*Exit.*

---

* This, of course, is a paraphrase of the original, which, perhaps,
may be given as an explanation.

" llega, *Livia*,

Al *ma*, y sé, Livia, *liviana*."

SCENE II.

CYPRIAN.   Now I am alone, and may,
If my mind can be so lifted,
Study the great problem which
Keeps my soul disturbed, bewilder'd,
Since I read in Pliny's page
The mysterious words there written,
Which define a god; because
It doth seem beyond the limits
Of my intellect to find
One who all these signs exhibits.
This mysterious hidden truth
Must I seek for.   [*Reads.*

SCENE III.

Enter the DEMON, *in gala dress.*   CYPRIAN.

DEMON (*aside*). Though thou givest
All thy thoughts to the research,
Cyprian, thou must ever miss it,
Since I'll hide it from thy mind.
CYPRIAN.   There's a rustling in this thicket.
Who is there? who art thou?
DEMON.   Sir,
A mere stranger, who has ridden
All this morning up and down
These dark groves, not knowing whither,
Having lost my way, my horse,
To the emerald that encircles,
With a tapestry of green,
These lone hills, I've loosed, it gives him
At the same time food and rest.

I'm to Antioch bound, on business
Of importance, my companions
I have parted from ; through listless
Lapse of thought (a thing that happens
To the most of earthly pilgrims),
I have lost my way, and lost
Comrades, servants, and assistants.
    CYPRIAN.   I am much surprised to learn
That in view of the uplifted
Towers of Antioch, you thus
Lost your way.   There's not a single
Path that on this mountain side,
More or less by feet imprinted,
But doth lead unto its walls,
As to its one central limit.
By whatever path you take,
You'll go right.
    DEMON.   It is an instance
Of that ignorance which in sight
Even of truth the true goal misses.
And as it appears not wise
Thus to enter a strange city
Unattended and unknown,
Asking even my way, 'tis fitter
That 'till night doth conquer day,
Here while light doth last, to linger ;
By your dress and by these books
Round you, like a learned circle
Of wise friends, I see you are
A great student, and the instinct
Of my soul doth ever draw me
Unto men to books addicted.
    CYPRIAN.   Have you studied much ?
    DEMON.   Well, no ;
But I've knowledge quite sufficient
Not to be deemed ignorant.

CYPRIAN.   Then, what sciences know you ?
DEMON.   Many.
CYPRIAN.   Why, we cannot reach even one
After years of studious vigil,
And can you (what vanity !)
Without study know so many ?
DEMON.   Yes; for I am of a country
Where the most exalted science
Needs no study to be known.
CYPRIAN.   Would I were a happy inmate
Of that country !   Here our studies
Prove our ignorance more.
DEMON.   No figment
Is the fact that without study.
I had the superb ambition
For the first Professor's chair
To compete, and thought to win it,
Having very numerous votes.
And although I failed, sufficient
Glory is it to have tried.
For not always to the winner
Is the fame.   If this you doubt,
Name the subject of your study,
And then let us argue on it ;
I not knowing your opinion,
Even although it be the right,
Shall the opposite view insist on.
CYPRIAN.   I am greatly gratified
That you make this proposition.
Here in Plinius is a passage
Which much anxious thought doth give me
How to understand, to know
Who's the God of whom he has written.
DEMON.   'Tis that passage which declares
(Well I know the words) this dictum :
"God is one supremest good,

One pure essence, one existence,
Self-sustained, all sight, all hands."
    CYPRIAN.   Yes, 'tis true.
    DEMON.   And what is in it
So abstruse ?
    CYPRIAN.   I cannot find
Such a god as Plinius figures.
If he be the highest good,
Then is Jupiter deficient
In that attribute ; we see him
Acting like a mortal sinner
Many a time,—this, Danae,
This, Europa, too, doth witness.
Can then, by the Highest Good,
All whose actions, all whose instincts,
Should be sacred and divine,
Human frailty be committed ?
    DEMON.   These are fables which the learned
First made use of, to exhibit
Underneath the names of gods
What in truth was but a hidden
System of philosophy.
    CYPRIAN.   This reply is not sufficient,
Since such awe is due to God,
None should dare to Him attribute,
None should stain His name with sins.
Though these sins should be fictitious.
And considering well the case,
If the highest good is figured
By the gods, of course, they must
Will what is the best and fittest ;
How, then, can some gods wish one thing,
Some another ? This we witness
In the dubious responses
Which are by their statues given.
Here you cannot say I speak of

Learned abstractions of the ideal.
To two armies, if two shrines
Promise give of being victors,
One, of course, must lose the battle :
The conclusion is so simple,—
Need I say it ? that two wills,
Mutually antagonistic,
Cannot lead unto one end.
They being thus in opposition,
One we must consider good,
One as bad we must consider.
But an evil will in God
Would imply a contradiction :
Then the highest good can dwell not
Among gods who know division.

 DEMON. I deny your major, since
These responses may be given,
By the oracles, for ends
Which our intellectual vision
Cannot reach : 'tis providence.
Thus more good may have arisen
To the loser in that battle
Than its gain could bring the winner.

 CYPRIAN. Granted ; but that god ought not,
For the gods are not malicious,
To have promised victory ;—
It would have been quite sufficient,
Without this most false assurance,
The defeat to have permitted.
Then if God must be all sight,
Every god should see distinctly
With clear vision to the end ;
Seeing *that*, he erred in fixing
On a false conclusion ; then
Though the deity may with fitness
Be divided into persons,

Yet His essence must be single
In the smallest circumstance.
    DEMON.   It was needful for this business,
That the oracle should rouse
The two hosts alike.
    CYPRIAN.   If fitting,
There were genii that could rouse them
(Good and bad, as they're distinguished
By the learned), who are, in fact,
Spirits who among us mingle,
And who good and evil acts,
Evil thoughts, suggest and whisper,
A convincing argument
For the immortal soul's existence :
Of these ministers could God
Have made use, nor thus exhibit
He was capable of a lie
To effect his ends ?
    DEMON.   Consider,
That these seeming contradictions
Cannot our firm faith diminish
In the oneness of the gods,
If in things of higher import
They know naught of dissonance.
Take man's wondrous frame, for instance,
Surely that majestic structure
One conception doth exhibit.
    CYPRIAN.   If man's maker then were one
He some vantage must have given him
O'er the others ; and if they
All are equal,—'tis admitted
That they are so, from the fact
Of their mutual opposition
To each other,—when the thought
Of creating man was hinted
By one god, another could

Say, " No, no, I do not wish it."
Then if God must be all hands,
Time might come when they would differ,
One creating, one undoing,
Ere the other's work was finished,
Since the power of each was equal,
But unequal were their wishes.
Which of these two powers would conquer ?

   DEMON.   On impossible and false issues
There can be no argument ;—
But your premises admitting,
Say what then ?

   CYPRIAN.   That there must be
One sole God, all hands, all vision,
Good Supreme, supreme in grace,
One who cannot err, omniscient.
One the highest, none can equal,
Not beginning, yet the Beginner,
One pure essence, one sole substance,
One wise worker, one sole willer ;—
And though He in one or two
Or more persons be distinguished,
Yet the sovereign Deity
Must be one, sublime and single,
The first cause of every cause,
The first germ of all existence.

   DEMON. How can I deny so clear,   [*They rise.*
So conclusive a position ?

   CYPRIAN.   Do you feel it ?

   DEMON.   Who would not
Feel to find another quicker
In the rivalry of wit ?—
And though I am not deficient
In an answer, I restrain it,
Hearing steps approaching hither
Through the wood ; besides 'tis time

I proceeded to the city.
    CYPRIAN.   Go in peace.
    DEMON.   Remain in peace.—
So involved in study *is* he,   [*Aside.*
That I now must wean him from it,
Weaving round him the bewitchment
Of rare beauty. Since I have leave
To attempt my fires to kindle
In Justina's breast, one stroke,
Thus, two vengeances shall give me.   [*Exit.*
    CYPRIAN.   Never saw I such a man.
But since still my people linger,
I, the cause of so much doubt,
Will now strive to reconsider.
    [*He resumes his reading, without perceiving the
      approach of those who enter.*

SCENE IV.

Enter LELIUS *and* FLORUS.—CYPRIAN.

    LELIUS.   Further let us not proceed ;
For these rocks, these boughs so thickly
Interwoven, that the sun
Cannot even find admittance,
Shall be the sole witnesses
Of our duel.
    FLORUS.   Then, this instant
Draw your sword ; for here are deeds,
If in words elsewhere we've striven.
    LELIUS.   Yes, I know that in the field,
While the tongue is mute, the glitter
Of the sword speaks thus.   [*They fight.*
    CYPRIAN.   What's this?

Hold, good Florus !   Lelius, listen !—
Here until your rage is calmed,
Even unarmed I stand betwixt ye.
　　LELIUS.   Thus to interrupt my vengeance,
Whence, O Cyprian, have you risen
Like a spectre ?
　　FLORUS.　　　A wild wood-god,
Have you from these tree-trunks issued ?

SCENE V.

Enter MOSCON *and* CLARIN.

　　MOSCON.   Yonder, where we left our master,
I hear sword-strokes ; run, run quickly.
　　CLARIN.   Well, except to run away,
I am anything but nimble ;—
Truly a retiring person.
　　MOSCON *and* CLARIN.   Sir . . . .
　　CYPRIAN.　　No more : your gabble irks me.—
How ?   What's this ?   Two noble friends,
Who in blood, in birth, in lineage,
Are to-day of Antioch all
Its expectancy, the city's
Eye of fashion, one the son
Of the Governor, of the princely
House Colalto, one the heir,
Thus to peril, as of little
Value, two such precious lives
To their country and their kindred ?
　　LELIUS.   Cyprian, although respect
Which on many grounds I give thee,
Holds my sword suspended thus
In due deference for an instant,—

To the scabbard's calm repose
It hath got no power to win it.
Thou of science knowest more,
Than the duel, pretermitting
This, that when two nobles meet
In the field, no power can link them
Friends again, save this, that one
Must his life give as a victim.
  FLORUS.   This I also say, and ask thee,
With thy people, that thou quittest,
Leaving us to end our quarrel
Without any help or hindrance.
  CYPRIAN.   Though it seems to you my calling
Makes me know the laws but little
Of the duel—that strict code
Valour and vain pride have written,
You are wrong, for I was born
With the obligations fitting
Rank like yours, to know in truth
Infamy and honour's limits.
The devotion to my studies
Has my courage not diminished,
For they oftentimes shake hands
Arms and letters as though kinsmen.
If to meet here in the field
Was the quarrel's first condition,
Having met and fought, its lies
Calumny can never whisper.
And the cause you thus can tell me
Of the feud that brings you hither ;
For I promise, if, on hearing
What to me is thus committed,
I perceive that satisfaction
Must on either side be given,
Here to leave you both alone,
Unobserved by any witness.

LELIUS.   Then on this condition solely,
That you leave us, when the bitter
Truth is told, to end our quarrel,
I to tell the cause am willing.
I a certain lady love,
The same lady as his mistress
Florus also loves ; now see,
How incompatible are our wishes !—
Since betwixt two jealous nobles
No mediation is admitted.
    FLORUS.   I this lady love so much,
That the sunlight I would hinder
From beholding her sweet face.
Since then all interposition
Is in vain, pray stand aside,
And our quarrel let us finish.
    CYPRIAN.   Stay, for one more thing I'd know.
Tell me this of your fair mistress,
Is she possible to your hopes,
Or impossible to your wishes ?—
    LELIUS.   Oh : she is so good and wise,
That if even the sun enkindled
Jealousy in the heart of Florus,
It was jealousy pure and simple,
Without cause, for even the sun
Dare not look upon her visage.
    CYPRIAN.   Would you marry with her, then ?
    FLORUS.   This is all my heart's ambition.
    CYPRIAN.   And would you ?
    LELIUS.   Ah, would to heaven,
I were destined for such blisses !—
For although she's very poor,
Virtue dowers her with its riches.
    CYPRIAN.   If you both aspire to wed her,
Is it not an act most wicked,
Most unworthy, thus beforehand

Her unspotted fame to injure?
What will say the world, if one
Of you two shall marry with her
After having killed the other
For her sake?   The supposition
Is not probable in fact,
To imagine it is sufficient.
I by no means say you should
Each your chances try to win her
At one time, for I would blush
Such a craven proposition
Came from me, because the lover
Who could keep his jealousy hidden,
Would condone even shame thereafter,
Were the opportunity given;
But I say that you should learn
Which of you it is your mistress
Gives the preference to, then . . . .
    LELIUS.   Stay! –
For it were an act too timid,
Too faint-hearted thus to ask
Of a lady such admission
As the choosing him or me.
For if me she chose, more fixéd
Is my call for satisfaction;
For his fault has this addition,
He loves one who loves but me.
If to him the choice is given,
This intensifies my anger
All the more, that she, my mistress,
Whom I love, should love another.
Her selection could do little
In the matter, which at last
To our swords should be committed,—
The accepted for his honour,
The refused for his dismissal.

FLORUS.   I confess that I adopt
Altogether that opinion,
Still the privilege of selection
May to ladies be permitted ;
So to-day I mean to ask her
Of her father.   'Tis sufficient
To have come here to the field,
And my naked sword uplifted,
(Specially as one is by
Who the further fight resisteth,)
For my honour ;—so to sheathe,
Lelius, my sword I'm willing.

                            [Sheathes his sword.

  LELIUS.   By your argument and action,
Florus, you have half convinced me ;
I forego the remaining half—
True or false, I thus act with you.

                            [Sheathes his sword.

I to-day will seek her father.
  CYPRIAN.   On, of course, the supposition,
That this lady you pay court to
Suffers naught by the admission,
Since you both have spoken proudly
Of her virtue and her strictness,
Tell me who she is ; for I,
Who am held throughout the city
In esteem, would for you both
Speak to her at first a little,
That she thus may be prepared
When her father tells your wishes.
  LELIUS.   You are right.
  CYPRIAN.   Her name ?
  FLORUS.   Justina,
Daughter of Lysander.
  CYPRIAN.   Little,
Now that I have heard her name,

Seem the praises you have given her ;
She is virtuous as she's noble.
Instantly I'll pay my visit.
    FLORUS (*aside*). May heaven grant that in my favour
Her cold heart be moved to pity !   [*Exit.*
    LELIUS.   Love, my hopes with laurels crown
When they are to her submitted !   [*Exit.*
    CYPRIAN.   Further mischief or misfortune,
Grant me, heaven, that I may hinder !   [*Exit.*

SCENE VI.

MOSCON, CLARIN.

    MOSCON.   Has your worship heard our master
Now is gone to pay a visit
To Justina ?
    CLARIN.   Yes, my lord.
But what matter if he didn't ?
    MOSCON.   Matter quite enough, your worship ;
He has no business there.
    CLARIN.   Why, prithee ?
    MOSCON.   Why ? because I die for Livia,
Who is maid to this Justina,
And I wouldn't have even the sun
Get a glimpse of her through the window.
    CLARIN.   Well, that's good ; but, for a lady,
To contend were worse than silly,
Whom I mean to make my wife.
    MOSCON.   Excellent, faith ! the fancy tickles
Quite my fancy.   Let her say
Who it is that annoys or nicks her
To a nicety.   Let's go see her,
And she'll choose.

CLARIN.　　　A good idea!—
Though I fear she'll pitch on you.
　　MOSCON.　Have you then that wise suspicion?
　　CLARIN.　Yes; for always these same Livias
Choose the worst, th' ungrateful minxes.*　　[*Exeunt.*

SCENE VII.

A HALL IN THE HOUSE OF LYSANDER.

Enter JUSTINA *and* LYSANDER.

JUSTINA.　Consolation, sir, is vain,
After what I've seen to-day :
The whole city, madly gay,
Error-blinded and insane,
Consecrating shrine and fane
To an image, which, I know,
Cannot be a god, although
Some demoniac power may pass,
Making breathe the silent brass
As a proof that it is so.
　　LYSANDER.　Fair Justina, thou indeed,
Wert not who thou art, if thou
Didst not weep as thou dost now,
Didst not in thy pure heart bleed
For what Christ's divinest creed
Suffers on this sinful day.
　　JUSTINA.　Thus my lineage I display :—
For thy child I could not be,

---

* The *asonante* versification in *i-e,* which has been kept up through
these six scenes, ends here. The seventh scene commences in
rhymed five-line stanzas, which change to the *asonante* in *e-e,* at the
beginning of Lysander's long speech.

Could I without weeping see
This idolatrous display.
    LYSANDER.   Ah, my good, my gentle maid !
Thou art not my daughter, no,
'Twere too happy, if 'twere so.
But, O God ! what's this I've said ?—
My life's secret is betrayed !
'Twas my soul that spoke aloud.
    JUSTINA.   What do you say, sir ?
    LYSANDER.   Oh ! a crowd
Of old thoughts my heart hath stirred.
    JUSTINA.   Many times methought I heard
What but now you have avowed,
And yet never wished to hear,
At the risk perchance of paining,
A more accurate explaining
Of your sorrow and my fear ;
But since now it doth appear
Right that I should be possess'd
Of the whole truth half confess'd,
Let me say, though bold appearing,—
Trust your secret to my hearing,
Since it hath escaped your breast.
    LYSANDER.   Ah ! Justina, I have long
Kept this secret from your ears,
Fearing from your tender years
That the telling might be wrong ;
But now seeing you are strong,
Firm in thought, in action brave,
Seeing too, that with this stave,
I go creeping o'er the ground,
Rapping with a hollow sound
At the portals of the grave,
Knowing that my time is brief,
I would not here leave you, no,
In your ignorance ; I owe

My own peace, too, this relief :
Then attentive to my grief
Let your pleasure list.
    JUSTINA.   A fear
Struggles in my breast.
    LYSANDER.   Severe
Is the test my duty pays.
    JUSTINA.   From this most perplexing maze
Oh, sir, rescue me.
    LYSANDER.   Then hear.
I, most beautiful Justina,
Am Lysander . . . .   This commencement
With my name need not surprise you ;
For though known to you already,
It is right, for all that follows,
That it should be well remembered,
Since of me you know no more
Than what this my name presenteth.
Yes, I am Lysander, son
Of that city which on Seven
Hills a hydra seems of stone,
Since it seven proud heads erecteth ;
Of that city now the seat
Of the mighty Roman empire,
Cradle of·Christ's wider realm,—
Boon that Rome alone could merit.
There of poor and humble parents
I was born, if " poor " expresses
Well their rank who left behind them
Virtues, not vain earthly treasures.
Both of them by birth were Christians,
Joyful both to be descended
From brave sires who with their blood
Happily life's page had reddened,
Terminating the dull scroll
With death's bright emblazoned letters.

In the Christian faith well grounded
I grew up, and so well learnt it,
That I would, in its defence,
Even a thousand lives surrender.
I was young still, when to Rome,
In disguise and ill attended,
Came our good Pope Alexander,
Who then prudently directed
The high apostolic see,
Though its place there was not settled ;
For, as the despotic power
Of the stern and cruel gentiles
Satisfies its thirst with blood
From the martyrs' veins that shed it,
So must still the primitive church
Keep concealed its sons and servants ;
Not that they decline to die,
Not that marytrdom is dreaded
But that rebel rage should not,
At one stroke, one hour of vengeance,
Triumph o'er the ruined church,
So that no one should be left it
Who could preach and teach the word,
Who could catechise the gentile.
Alexander being in Rome,
I was secretly presented
To him there, and from his hand
Which was graciously extended,
With his blessing I received
Holy Orders, which the seraphs
Well might envy me, since man
Only such an honour merits.
Alexander, as my mission,
Unto Antioch then sent me,
Where the law of Christ in secret
I should preach.   With glad contentment

I obeyed, and at their mercy,
Through so many nations wending,
Came at length to Antioch ;
And when I, these hills ascending,
Saw beneath me in the valley
All its golden towers and temples,
The sun failed me, and down-sinking
Drew with him the day, presenting
For my solace a companion,
And a substitute for his presence
In the light of stars, a pledge
That he'd soon return to bless me.
With the sun I lost my way,
And then wandering dejected
Through the windings of the forest,
Found me in the dim recesses
Of a natural bower, wherein
Even the numerous rays that trembled
Downward from each living torch
Could in noways find an entrance,
For to black clouds turned the leaves
That by day were green with freshness.
Here arranging to await
The new sun's reviving presence,
Giving fancy that full scope,
That wide range which it possesses,
I in solitude indulged
Many and many a deep reflection.
Thus absorbed was I in thought
When there came to me the echo
Of a sigh half heard, for half
To its owner retroverted.
Then collecting in mine ear
All my senses joined together,
I again heard more distinctly
That weak cry, that faint expression,

That mute idiom of the sad,
Since by it they're comprehended.
From a woman came that groan
To whose sigh so low and gentle
Followed a man's deeper voice,
Who thus speaking low addressed her :
"Thou first stain of noblest blood
By my hands this moment perish,
Ere thou meetest with thy death
'Neath the hands of infamous headsmen."—
Then the hapless woman said
In a voice that sobbed and trembled,
" Ah, lament for thine own blood,
But for me do not lament thee ! "—
I attempted then to reach them,
That the stroke might be prevented,
But I could not, since the voices
At that moment ceased and ended,
And a horseman rode away
'Mong the tree-trunks undetected.
Loadstone of my deep compassion
Was that voice which still exerted
All its failing powers to speak
Amid groans and tears this sentence,—
" Dying innocent and a Christian
I a martyr's death may merit."—
Following the polar-star
Of the voice, I came directly
Where the gloom revealed a woman,
Though I could not well observe her,
Who in life's despairing struggle,
Hand to hand with death contended.
Scarcely was I heard, when she
Summoning up her strength addressed me,—
" Blood-stained murderer mine, come back,
Nor in this last hour desert me

Of my life."—"I am," said I,
"Only one whom chance hath sent here,
Guided it may be by heaven,
To assist you in this dreadful
Hour of trial."—"Vain," she said,
"Is the favour that your mercy
Offers to my life, for see,
Drop by drop the life-stream ebbeth,
Let this hapless one enjoy it,
Who it seems that heaven intendeth,
Being born upon my grave,
All my miseries should inherit."—
So she died, and then I . . .

Scene VIII.

Livia, Justina, *and* Lysander.

Enter Livia.

Livia.   Sir,
The same tradesman who so presses
To be paid, comes here to seek you,
By the magistrate attended.
That you were not in, I told him :
By that door you have an exit.
    Justina.   This untimely interruption
By their coming, how it frets me !
For upon your tragic story
Life, soul, reason, all depended !—
But retire, sir, lest the justice
Should here meet you, if he enters.
    Lysander.   Ah ! with what indignities
Poverty must be contented !   [*Exit.*

JUSTINA.   They are coming here, no doubt,
Outside I can hear some persons.
    LIVIA.   No, they are not they.   I see
It is Cyprian.
    JUSTINA.   How? what sendeth
Cyprian here?

SCENE IX.

Enter CYPRIAN, CLARIN, *and* MOSCON.

    CYPRIAN.   A wish to serve you
Is the sole cause of my presence.
For on seeing the officials
Issuing from your house, the friendship
Which I owe unto Lysander
Made me bold herein to enter;
But to know (*Aside.* Disturbed, bewildered
Am I.) if by chance (*Aside.* What gelid
Frost is freezing up my veins!)
I in any way could help you.
(*Aside.* Ah, how badly have I spoken!—
Fire not frost my blood possesses!)
    JUSTINA.   May heaven guard you many years,
Since in his more grave concernments,
Thus you honour my dear father
With your favours.
    CYPRIAN.   I shall ever
Be most gratified to serve you.
(*Aside.* What disturbs me, what unnerves me?)
    JUSTINA.   He is not just now at home.
    CYPRIAN.   Thus then, lady, I can better
Tell you what is the true cause
That doth bring me here at present;

For the cause that you have heard
Is not that which wholly led me
Here to see you.
    JUSTINA.   Then, what is it?
    CYPRIAN. This, which craves your brief attention.—
Fair Justina, beauty's shrine,*
To whose human loveliness
Nature, with a fond excess,
Adds such marks of the divine,
'Tis your rest that doth incline
Hither my desire to-day ;
But see what the tyrant sway
Of despotic fate can do,—
While I bring your rest to you,
You from me take mine away.
Lelius, of his passion proud,
(Never less was love to blame !)
Florus, burning with love's flame,
(Ne'er could flame be more allowed !)
Each of them by vows they vowed
Sought to kill his friend for you :
I for you disturbed the two,
(Woe is me !) but see the end ;
While from death I saved my friend,
You my own death give in lieu.
Lest the scandal-monger's hum
Should be buzzed about your name,
Here to speak with you I came,
(Would that I had never come !)
That your choice might strike it dumb,
Being the umpire in the cause,
Being the judge in love's sweet laws ;—
But behold what I endure,

---

* The five-lined rhymed stanza here recommences, and continues
to the end of the scene.

While I their sick hearts may cure,
Jealousy mine own heart gnaws.
Lady, I proposed to be
Their bold spokesman here, that you
Might decide betwixt the two
Which you would select (ah, me !)
That I might (oh, misery !)
·Ask you of your father : vain
This pretence.   No more I'll feign :—
For you see while I am speaking
About them, my heart is seeking
But a vent for its own pain.
    JUSTINA.   Half in wonder and dismay
At the vile address you make me,
Reason, speech, alike forsake me,
And I know not what to say.
Never in the slightest way
Have your clients had from me
Encouragement for this embassy—
Florus never—Lelius no :—
Of the scorn that I can show
Let then this a warning be.
    CYPRIAN.   If I, knowing that you loved
Some one else, would dare to seek
Your regard, my love were weak,
And could justly be reproved.
But here seeing you stand unmoved,
Like a rock mid raging seas,
No extraneous miseries
Make me say I love you now.
'Tis not for my friends I bow,
So your warning hear with ease.—
To Lelius what shall I say?
    JUSTINA.   That he
Well may trust the boding fears
Of his love of many years.

CYPRIAN.   To Florus?
JUSTINA.   Not my face to see.
CYPRIAN.   And to myself?
JUSTINA.   Your love should be
Not so bold.
CYPRIAN.   Though a god should woo?
JUSTINA.   Will a god do more for you
Than for those I have denied?
CYPRIAN.   Yes.
JUSTINA.   Well then, I have replied
To Lelius, Florus, and to you.
    [*Exeunt* JUSTINA *and* CYPRIAN *at opposite sides.*

SCENE X.

CLARIN, MOSCON, *and* LIVIA.

CLARIN.   Livia, heigh!
MOSCON.   And Livia, ho!—
List good lass.
CLARIN.   We're here, we two.
LIVIA.   Well, what *want* you, sir?   And *you*,
What do you want?
CLARIN.   We both would show,
If perchance you do not know,
That we love you to distraction.
On a murderous transaction
We came here, to kill each other :—
So to put an end to the bother,
Just choose one for satisfaction.
    LIVIA.   Why the thing that you're demanding
Is so great, it hath bereft me
Of my wits.   My grief hath left me
Without sense or understanding.

Choose but one !   My heart expanding,
Beats so hard a strait to shun !
I one only !   'Tis for fun
That you ask me so to do.
For with heart enough for two,
Why require that I choose one ?
    CLARIN.   Two at once would you have to woo ?
Would not two embarrass you, pray ?
    LIVIA.   No, we women have a way
To dispose of them two by two.
    MOSCON.   What's the way ? do tell us, do ;—
What is it ? speak.
    LIVIA.   You put one out !—
I would love them, do not doubt . . . .
    MOSCON.   How ?
    LIVIA.   *Alternatively.*
    CLARIN.   Eh,
What's *alternatively ?*
    LIVIA.   'Tis to say,
That I would love them day about.   [*Exit.*
    MOSCON.   Well, I choose to-day : good-bye.
    CLARIN.   I, to-morrow, the better part.
So I give it with all my heart.
    MOSCON.   Livia, in fine, for whom I die,
To-day loves me, and to-day love I.
Happy is he who so much can say.
    CLARIN.   Hearken, my friend : you know my way.
    MOSCON.   Why this speech ?   Does a threat lie
        in it ?
    CLARIN.   Mind, she is not yours a minute
After the clock strikes twelve to-day.   [*Exeunt.*

SCENE XI.

THE STREET BEFORE LYSANDER'S HOUSE : NIGHT.

Enter FLORUS *and* LELIUS *at opposite sides,
not seeing each other.*

LELIUS (*aside*). Scarcely has the darksome night
O'er the brow of heaven extended *
Its black veil, when I come hither
To adore this sacred threshold ;
For although at Cyprian's prayer,
I my sharp sword have suspended,
I have not my love, for love
Cannot be suspended ever.

FLORUS (*aside*). Here the dawn will find me waiting :—
Here, because 'tis force compels me
To go hence, for I, elsewhere,
Am away from my true centre.
Would to love the day had come,
And with it the dear, expected
Answer Cyprian may bring me,
Risking all upon that venture.

LELIUS (*aside*). I have surely in that window
Heard a noise.

FLORUS (*aside*). Some sound descends here
From that balcony.

------

* *Asonante* in *e—e,* to the end of the Act.

SCENE XII.

The Demon *appears at a window in the house of*
LYSANDER.

LELIUS (*aside*).   A figure
Issues from it, whose dim presence
I distinguish.
    FLORUS (*aside*).   Through the darkness
I can there perceive some person.
    DEMON (*aside*). For the many persecutions
O'er Justina's head impending,
Her pure honour to defame
Thus I make a bold commencement.
                    [*He descends by a ladder.*
    LELIUS (*aside*). But, O woe! what's this I witness!—
    FLORUS (*aside*). What do I see! Oh, wretched!
        wretched!—
    LELIUS (*aside*). From the balcony to the ground
The dark figure has descended.
    FLORUS (*aside*). From her house a man comes forth!—
Jealousy kill me not, preserve me,
'Till I discover who he is.
    LELIUS (*aside*). I will try to intercept him
And find out at once who thus
Tastes the bliss I've lost for ever.
        [*They advance with drawn swords to recognise
            the person who has descended.*
    DEMON (*aside*). Not alone Justina's fame
Do I by this act discredit,
But dissensions, perhaps murders,
Thus provoke.   Ope, earth's dark centre,
And receive me, leaving here
This confusion.   [*He disappears between* FLORUS *and*
                LELIUS, *who meet together.*

Scene XIII.

Florus *and* Lelius.

LELIUS.   Sir, whoever
You may be, it doth import me
To know who you are directly;
So at every risk I come here,
On this resolute quest determined.
Say who are you.
    FLORUS.   If the accident
Of my having been the observer
Of your secret love, compels you
To this valorous aggression,
More than it can you concern
Me to know, it doth concern me
To know you ; for to be curious
Is far less than to be jealous.
Yes, by Heaven ! for who is master
Of the house have I to learn here,
Who it is at such an hour,
By this balcony ascending,
Gaineth that which I lose weeping
At these gratings.
    LELIUS.   This excelleth,
Good, in faith, is it thus to dim
The clear light of my resentment,
By attributing to me
That which solely your offence is !—
Who you are I have to know,
Death to give to him who has left me
Dead with jealousy here, by coming
From this balcony.
    FLORUS.   How excessive,

How superfluous is this caution,
Proving what it would dissemble!
    Lelius.   Vainly would the tongue untangle
That which the keen sword can better
Thus cut through.
    Florus.   With it I answer. [*They fight.*
    Lelius. In this way I'll know for certain
Who is the admitted lover
Of Justina.
    Florus.   My intention
Is the same. I'll die or know you.

Scene XIV.

Enter Cyprian, Moscon, *and* Clarin.

    Cyprian.   Gentlemen, I pray you let me
Interpose in this your quarrel,
Since by accident I am present.
    Florus. You cannot oblige me more
Than by letting the fight be ended.
    Cyprian. Florus?
    Florus. Yes, for sword in hand,
I my name deny not ever
To who asks.
    Cyprian.   I'm at your side,
Death to him who would offend you.
    Lelius. You produce in me less fear,
Both of you thus joined together,
Than did he alone.
    Cyprian.   What! Lelius?
    Lelius. Yes.
    Cyprian.   I am prevented

Now from standing at your side,   [*To* FLORUS.
Since between you I present me.
How is this?   In one day twice
Have I your disputes to settle!—
    LELIUS.   Then this time will be the last,
. For we've settled them already;
Since in knowing who is he
Who Justina's heart possesses,
Now no more my hope remaineth,
Even the thought of it hath left me.
If you have not to Justina
Spoken yet, do not address her;
This I ask you in the name
Of my wrongs and my resentments,
Having seen her secret favours
Florus' happier fate deserveth.
From this balcony I saw him,
From my lost delight descending;
And my heart is not so base
As to meanly love, in presence
Of such jealousies so well proved,
Of disillusions, ah! so certain.   [*Exit.*
    FLORUS.   Stay.

SCENE XV.

    CYPRIAN.   You must not follow him,
(Oh, this news with death o'erwhelms me!) [*Aside.*
Since if he who is the loser
Of what you have gained, expressly
Says he would forget it, you
Should not try his patient temper.
    FLORUS.   Both by you and him at once
Has mine own been too well tested.

Speak not now unto Justina
About me ; for though full vengeance
I propose to take for being
Thus supplanted and rejected,
Every hope of her being mine
Now has ceased, for shameful were it,
In the face of such proved facts,
To persist in my addresses.   [*Exit.*

SCENE XVI.

CYPRIAN, MOSCON, *and* CLARIN.

CYPRIAN (*aside*).What is this, O heavens ! I hear?
Can it be the two are jealous
Of each other at one time ?
And I too of both together ?—
Doubtless from some strange delusion
The two suffer, which I welcome
With a sort of satisfaction,
For to it I am indebted
For the fact of their desisting
From their suit and their pretension.--
Moscon, have for me by morning
A rich court-suit ; sword and feathers,
Clarin, be thy care ; for love
In a certain airy splendour
Takes delight ; for now no longer
Books or studies give me pleasure ;—
Love they say doth murder mind,
Learning dies when he is present.   [*Exeunt.*

ACT THE SECOND.

SCENE I.

THE STREET IN FRONT OF LYSANDER'S HOUSE.

Enter CYPRIAN, MOSCON, *and* CLARIN, *in gala dresses.*

CYPRIAN (*aside*). Where, presumptuous thoughts, ah !
    where,
Would you lead me, whither go ?
If for certain now you know
That the high attempts you dare
Are delusive dreams of bliss,
Since you strive to scale heaven's wall,
But from that proud height to fall
Headlong down a dark abyss ?
I Justina saw . . . . . So near
Would to God I had not seen her,
Nor in her divine demeanour
All the light of heaven's fourth sphere.
Lovers twain for her contend,
Both being jealous each should woo,
And I, jealous of the two,
Know not which doth most offend.
All I know is, that suspicion,
Her disdain, my own desires,
Fill my heart with furious fires—
Drive me, ah ! to my perdition.
This I know, and know no more,
This I feel in all my strait ;
Heavens ! Justina is my fate !

Heavens ! Justina I adore !—
Moscon.
    MOSCON.   Sir.
    CYPRIAN.   Inquire, I pray,
If Lysander's in.
    MOSCON.   I fly.
    CLARIN. No, sir, no. On me rely,—
Moscon can't go there to-day.
    CYPRIAN. Ever wrangling in this way,
How ye both my patience try !
Why can he not go ? Say why ?
    CLARIN. Because to-day is not his day.
Mine it is, sir, to his sorrow.
So your message I will bear.
Moscon can't to-day go there ;
He will have his turn to-morrow.
    CYPRIAN. What new madness can this be
Which your usual feud doth show ?
But now neither of you go,
Since in all her brilliancy
Comes Justina.
    CLARIN.   From the street
To her house she goes.

SCENE II.

Enter JUSTINA *and* LIVIA, *veiled.*—CYPRIAN, MOSCON,
and CLARIN.

    JUSTINA.   Ah, me !
Cyprian's here. See, Livia, see !   [*Aside to her.*
    CYPRIAN (*aside*). I must strive and be discreet,
Feigning with a ready wit,
Till my jealousy I can prove.

I will only speak of love,
If my jealousy will permit.
Not in vain, señora sweet,—
Have I changed my student's dress,
The livery of thy loveliness,
As a servant at thy feet,
Thus I wear.   If sighs could move thee
I would labour to deserve thee ;
Give me leave at least to serve thee,
Since thou wilt not let me love thee.

    JUSTINA.   Slight effect, sir, as I see,
Have my words produced on you,
Since they have not brought . . . .
    CYPRIAN.·   Too true !
    JUSTINA.   A forgetfulness of me.
In what way must I explain
Clearer than I have done before,
That persistence at my door
Is and ever must be vain ?
If a day, a month, a year,
If for ages there you stay,
Naught but this that now I say
Ever can you hope to hear.
As it were my latest breath,
Let this sad assurance move thee,—
Fate forbids that I should love thee,
Cyprian, except in death.
                          [*She moves towards the house.*

    CYPRIAN.   At these words my hopes revive :—
Sad ! no, no, to joy they move me,
For if thou in death canst love me,
Soon for me will death arrive.
Be it so ; and since so nigh
Comes the hour your words to prove—
Ah ! even now begin to love,
Since I now begin to die.   [JUSTINA *enters.*

SCENE III.

CYPRIAN, MOSCON, CLARIN, *and* LIVIA.

CLARIN.   Livia, while my master yonder,
Like a living skeleton,
Life and motion being gone,
On his luckless love doth ponder,
Give me an embrace.
    LIVIA.   Stay, stay.
Patience, man ! until I see,
For I like my conscience free,
If to-day is your right day.—
Tuesday, yes, and Wednesday, no.
    CLARIN.   What are you counting there ?   Awake !
Moscon's mum.
    LIVIA.   He might mistake,
And I wish not to act so.
For, desiring to pursue
A just course betwixt you both,
Turn about, I would be loth
Not to give you each his due.
But I see that you are right,
'Tis your day.
    CLARIN.   Embrace me, then.
    LIVIA.   Yes, again, and yet again.
    MOSCON.   Hark to me, my lady bright,
May I from your ardour borrow
A good omen in my case ;
And as Clarin you embrace,
Moscon you'll embrace to-morrow ?
    LIVIA.   Your suspicion is, in fact,
Quite absurd ; on me rely.
Jupiter forbid that I
Should commit so bad an act

As to be cool in any way
To a friend.   I will to thee
Give an embrace in equity,
When it is your worship's day.   [*Exit.*

SCENE IV.

CYPRIAN, MOSCON, *and* CLARIN.

CLARIN.   Well, I'll not be by to see,
That's a comfort.
  MOSCON.   How? why so?
Need I be chagrined to know,
If the girl's not mine, that she
Thus to you her debt did pay.
  CLARIN.   No.
  MOSCON.   This makes my point more strong,
Since to me it were no wrong
If it chanced not on my day.
But our master yonder, see,
How absorbed he seems.
  CLARIN.   More near,
If he speaks I'd like to hear.
  MOSCON.   And I, too, would like.
  CYPRIAN.   Ah, me!
[*As* MOSCON *and* CLARIN *approach* CYPRIAN
    *from opposite sides, he gesticulates with his
    arms, and accidentally strikes both.*
Love, how great thy agonies!—
  CLARIN.   Ah! ah, me!
  MOSCON.   Ah, me! I bawl.
  CLARIN.   Well, I think that we may call
This the land of the *sigh-ah-mes!*
  CYPRIAN.   What! and have you both been here?
  CLARIN.   I, at least, was here, I'll swear.

MOSCON.   And I, also.
CYPRIAN.   O, despair
End at once my sad career !
Ah, what human heart to woe
Like to mine has given a home ?

SCENE V.

THE COUNTRY.

CYPRIAN, CLARIN, *and* MOSCON.

CLARIN.   Whither Moscon, do we roam ?
MOSCON.   When we've reached the end, we'll know.
Leagues behind us lies the town,
Still we go.
CLARIN.   A strange proceeding !—
Little time have we for reading,
Idly pacing up and down.
CYPRIAN.   Clarin, get thee home.
MOSCON.   And I ?
CLARIN.   Sly-boots, would you rather stay ?
CYPRIAN.   Go : here leave me both ; away !
CLARIN.   Mind, he tells us both to fly.
                    [*Exeunt* CLARIN *and* MOSCON.

SCENE VI.

CYPRIAN.   Memory of a maddened brain,
Do not with such strong control
Make me think another soul
Is what in my heart doth reign.
Blind idolator I have been—

Lost in love's ambitious flight,
Since such beauty met my sight,
Since a goddess I have seen.
Yet in such a maze of woe
Rigorous fate doth make me move,
That I know but whom I love,
And of whom I am jealous—no.
Yet this passion is so strong—
Ah, so sweet this fascination;
Driving my imagination
With resistless force along—
That I would (I know too well
How this madness doth degrade me)
To some devilish power to aid me,
Were it even to rise from hell,
Where some mightier power hath kept it,—
Sharing all its pains in common,—
I would, to possess this woman,
Give my soul.

Scene VII.

The Demon *and* Cyprian.

Demon (*within*).   And I accept it.
    [*A great tempest is heard, with thunder and
        lightning.*
Cyprian.   What's this, ye heavens so pure?
Clear but a moment hence and now obscure,
Ye fright the gentle day!
The thunder-balls, the lightning's forkéd ray,
Leap from its riven breast—
Terrific shapes it cannot keep at rest;
All the whole heaven a crown of clouds doth wear,
And with the curling mist, like streaming hair,

This mountain's brow is bound.
Outspread below, the whole horizon round
Is one volcanic pyre.
The sun is dead, the air is smoke, heaven fire.
Philosophy, how far from thee I stray,
When I cannot explain the marvels of this day!
And now the sea, upborne on clouds the while,
Seems like some ruined pile,
That crumbling down the wind as 'twere a wall,
In dust not foam doth fall.
And struggling through the gloom,
Facing the storm, a mighty ship seeks room
On the open sea, whose rage it seems to court,
Flying the dangerous pity of the port.
The noise, the terror, and that fearful cry,
Give fatal augury
Of the impending stroke.   Death hesitates,
For each already dies who death awaits.
With portents the whole atmosphere is rife,
Nor is it all the effect of elemental strife.
The ship is rigged with tempest as it flies.*
It rushes on the lee,
The war is now no longer of the sea ;
Upon a hidden rock
It strikes : it breaks as with a thunder shock.
Blood flakes the foam where helpless it is tost.
    [*The sound of the tempest increases, and voices are
        heard within.*
    Voices within. We sink ! we sink ! we're lost !
    DEMON (*within*). For what I have in hand,
I'll trust this plank to bear me to the land.
    CYPRIAN.   As scorning the wild wave

---

* Hartzenbusch remarks that there is no corresponding rhyme for
this line in the original, and that both the sense and the versification
are defective.—*Comedias de Calderon*, t. 2, p. 178.

One man alone his life attempts to save.
While lurching over, mid the billows' swell,
The great ship sinks to where the Tritons dwell ;
There, with its mighty ribs asunder rent,
It lies a corse of the sea, its grave and monument.

Enter The Demon, *dripping with wet, as if escaped from
the sea.*

DEMON (*aside*). For the end I wish to gain
It was of necessity
That upon this sapphire sea
I this fearful storm should feign,
And in form unlike that one
Which in this wild wood I wore,
When I found my deepest lore
By his keener wit outdone,
Come again to assail him here,
Trusting better now to prove
Both his intellect and his love.—
Earth, loved earth, O mother dear,   [*Aloud.*
From this monster, this wild sea,
Give me shelter in thy arms.
CYPRIAN.   Lose, my friend, the dread alarms,
And the cruel memory
Of thy peril happily past ;
Since we learn or late or soon,
That beneath the inconstant moon
Human bliss doth never last.
DEMON.   Who art thou, at whose kind feet
Has my fortune cast me here ?
CYPRIAN.   One who with a pitying tear,
For a ruin so complete,
Would alleviate your woe.
DEMON.   Ah, impossible !—for me
Never, never, can there be
Any solace.

CYPRIAN.   How, why so ?
DEMON.   All my priceless wealth I've lost . . .
But I'm wrong to thus complain,
I'll forget, nay, think it gain,
Since my life it hath not cost.
CYPRIAN.   Now that the wild whirl malign
Of this earthquake storm doth cease,
And the sky returns to peace,
Quiet, calm, and crystalline,
And the bright succeeds the dark
With such strange rapidity,
That the storm would seem to be
Only raised to sink thy bark,
Tell me who thou art, repay
Thus a sympathy so sincere.
DEMON.   It has cost me to come here
More than you have seen to-day,
More than I can well express ;
Of the miseries I recall
This ship's loss is least of all.
Would you see that clearly ?
CYPRIAN.   Yes.
DEMON.   I am, since you wish to know it,
An epitome, a wonder *
Of all happiness and misfortune,
One I have lost, I weep the other.
By my gifts was I so glorious,
So conspicuous in my order,
Of a lineage so illustrious,
With a mind so well informéd,
That my rare endowments feeling,
A great king (in truth the noblest
King of Kings, for all would tremble
If he looked in anger on them,)

---

* *Asonante* in *o e*, to the end of the speech.

In his palace roofed with diamonds
And with gems as bright as morning,
(If I called them stars, 'tis certain
The comparison were too modest,)
His especial favourite called me.
Which high epithet of honour
So enflamed my pride, as rival
For his royal seat I plotted,
Hoping soon my victor footsteps
Would his golden thrones have trodden.
It was an unheard-of daring,
That, chastized I must acknowledge,
I was mad ; but then repentance
Were a still insaner folly.
Obstinate in my resistance,
With my spirit yet unconquered,
I preferred to fall with courage
Than surrender with dishonour.
If the attempt was rash, the rashness
Was not solely my misfortune,
For among his numerous vassals
Not a few my standard followed.
From his court, in fine, thus vanquished,
Though part victor in the contest,
I went forth, my eyes outflashing
Flames of anger and abhorrence,
And my lips proclaiming vengeance
For the public insult offered
To my pride, among his people
Scattering murder, rapine, horror.
Then a bloody pirate, I
The wide plains of the sea ran over,
Argus of its dangerous shallows,
Lynx-eyed where the reefs lay covered ;
In that vessel which the wind
Bit by bit so soon demolished,

Since you here have given me welcome.
And even this is almost nothing
When compared with what my wishes
Hope hereafter to accomplish.
    CYPRIAN. Well to the sea, my thanks are due, that
        bore
You struggling to the shore,
And led you to this grove,
Where you will quickly prove
The friendly feelings that inflame my breast,
If happily I merit such a guest.
Then let us homeward wend,
For I esteem you now as an old friend.
My guest you are, and so you must not leave me
While my house suits you.
    DEMON.   Do you then receive me
Wholly as yours?
    CYPRIAN (*embracing him*). This act doth prove it true,
That seals an eternal bond betwixt us two.—
Oh ! if I could win o'er   [*Aside.*
This man to instruct me in his magic lore !
Since by that art my love might gain
Some solaee for its pain ;
Or yielding to its mighty laws
My love at length might win my love's sweet cause—
The cause of all my torment, madness, rage.
    DEMON (*aside*). The working of his mind and love I
        gauge.

SCENE VIII.

CLARIN *and* MOSCON *enter running from opposite sides.*
CYPRIAN, *and* The Demon.

CLARIN.   Oh ! are you, sir, alive ?
MOSCON.   My friend, do you
Speak civilly for once as something new ?
That he's alive requires no demonstration.
CLARIN.   I struck this lofty note of admiration,
Thou noble lackey, to express my wonder,
How from this storm of lightning, rain, and thunder,
Without a miracle he could survive.
MOSCON.   Will you stop wondering, now you see him
    alive ?
CYPRIAN.   These are my servants, sir.—
What brings you here ?
MOSCON.   Your spleen once more to stir.
DEMON.   They have a pleasant humour.
CYPRIAN.   Foolish pair,
Their weary wit is oft too hard to bear.
MOSCON.   This man, sir, waiting here,
Who is he ?
CYPRIAN.   He's my guest, so do not fear.
CLARIN. Wherefore have guests at such a time as this?
CYPRIAN (*to* The Demon). Your worth is lost on igno-
    rance such as his.
MOSCON. My master's right. Are you, forsooth, his heir ?
CLARIN.   No ; but our new friend there,
Looks like a guest, unless I deceive me, who
Will honour our poor house a year or two.
MOSCON.   Why ?
CLARIN.   When a guest soon means to go away,
Well, he'll not make much smoke in the house, we say.
But this . . . .
MOSCON.   Speak out.

CLARIN.   Will make, I do not joke . .
MOSCON.   What?
CLARIN.   In the house a deucéd deal of smoke.
CYPRIAN.   In order to repair
The danger done by the rude sea and air,
Come thou with me.
DEMON.   I'm thine, while thou hast breath.
                                        [*Aside.*

CYPRIAN.   I go to prepare thy rest.
DEMON (*aside*).   And I thy death :—
An entrance having gained
Within his breast, and thus my end obtained;
My rage insatiate now without control
Seeks by another way to win Justina's soul.   [*Exit.*
CLARIN.   Guess, if you can, what I am thinking about.
MOSCON.   What is it?
CLARIN.   That a new volcano has burst out
In the late storm, there's such a sulphur smell.
MOSCON.   It came from the guest, as my good nose
        could tell.
CLARIN.   He uses bad pastilles, then; but I can
Infer the cause.
MOSCON.   What is it?
CLARIN.   The poor gentleman
Has a slight rash on his skin, a ticklish glow,
And uses sulphur ointment.
MOSCON.   Gad! 'tis so.   [*Exeunt.*

SCENE IX.

THE STREET.

LELIUS *and* FABIUS.

FABIUS.   You return, then, to this street.
LELIUS.   Yes; the life that I deplore

I return to seek once more
Where 'twas lost.   Ah ! guide my feet,
Love, to find it !—
    FABIUS.   That house there
Is Justina's ; come away.
    LELIUS.   Wherefore, when I will to-day
Once again my love declare.
And as she, I saw it plain,
Trusted some one else at night,
'Tis not strange, in open light,
That I try to soothe my pain.
Leave me, go ; for it is best
That I enter here alone.
My rank in Antioch is known,
My father Governor; thus drest
In his robe as 'twere, my strong
Passion listening to no mentor,
I Justina's house will enter
To protest against my wrong.   [*Exeunt.*

SCENE X.

A HALL IN THE HOUSE OF LYSANDER.

JUSTINA, *and afterwards* LELIUS.

JUSTINA.   Livia .... But a step ! who's there ?

LELIUS *enters.*

LELIUS.   It is I.
JUSTINA.   What novelty,
What extreme temerity,
Thus, my lord, compels you? ...
    LELIUS.   Spare
Your reproaches.   Jealous-grown,

I can bear that you reprove.
Pardon me, for with my love
My respect has also flown.
    JUSTINA.   Why, at such a perilous cost
Have you dared . . .
    LELIUS.   Because I'm mad.
    JUSTINA.   To intrude . . . .
    LELIUS.   Heart-broken, sad.
    JUSTINA.   Here . . . .
    LELIUS.   Because, in truth, I'm lost.
    JUSTINA.   Nor perceive how scandal views
Such an act as now you do
'Gainst . . . .
    LELIUS.   Be not so moved, for you
Little honour now can lose.
    JUSTINA.   Lelius, spare at least my fame.
    LELIUS.   Ah, Justina, it were best
That this language you addressed
Unto him who nightly came
Down here from this balcony ;—
'Tis enough for me to show
All your lightness that I know,
That less coy and cold to me
Your pretended honour prove.
If I am disdained, displaced,
'Tis another suits your taste,
Not that you your honour love.
    JUSTINA.   Silence, cease, your words withhold.
Who with insult e'er before
Dared to pass my threshold's door ?
Are you then so blind and bold,
So audacious, so insane,
As my pure light to eclipse,
Through the libel of your lips,
By chimeras false and vain ?—
In my house a man ?

LELIUS. 'Tis so.
JUSTINA. From my balcony?
LELIUS. With shame
I repeat it.
JUSTINA. O, my fame,
O'er us twain your Ægis throw.

SCENE XI.

THE SAME.

The Demon *appears at the door which is behind* JUSTINA.

DEMON (*aside*). For the deep design I handle,
For my double plot I come
Raging to this simple home,
Now to work the greatest scandal
Ever seen.   Here, brooding o'er him,
This wild lover mad with ire,
I will fan his jealous fire,
I will place myself before him,
Catch his eye, and then as fleeing,
In invisible gloom array me.
        [*He affects to come in, and being seen by* LELIUS
            *muffles himself in his cloak, and re-enters the
            inner apartment.*
JUSTINA. Man, do you come here to slay me?
LELIUS. No, to die.
JUSTINA. What object seeing
Paralyses thus your senses?
LELIUS. What I see is your untruth.
Tell me now, the wish, forsooth,
Has invented my offences.
From that very chamber there
Came a man, I turned my head,

When he saw my face he fled
Back into the room.
    Justina.   The air
Must this phantasy display—
This illusion.
    Lelius.   Oh, that sight !
    Justina.   Is it not enough by night,
Lelius, but in open day
Thus fictitious forms to see ?
    Lelius.   Phantom shape or real lover,
Now the truth I will discover.
        [*He goes into the room where* The Demon *had*
            disappeared.
    Justina.   I no hindrance offer thee,
For my innocence, a way,
At the cost of this permission,
Thus finds out the night's submission
To correct by the light of day.

Scene XII.

Lysander *and* Justina ; Lelius, *within.*

    Lysander.   My Justina.
    Justina (*aside*).   Woe is me !
Ah, if here before Lysander *
Lelius from that room comes forth !
    Lysander.   My misfortunes, my disasters
Fly to be consoled by thee.
    Justina.   What can be the grief, the sadness,
That your face betrays so plainly?
    Lysander.   And no wonder, when the pallor
Springs even from the heart.   This sobbing

---

* *Asonante* in *a—e* to the end of Scene XVII.

Stops my weak words in their passage.
       [LELIUS *appears at the door of the apartment.*
  LELIUS (*aside*). I begin now to believe,
Since he is not in this chamber,
Jealousy can cause these spectres.
He, the man I saw, has vanished,
How I know not.
  JUSTINA (*aside to* LELIUS). Come not forth,
Lelius, here before my father.
  LELIUS.   Convalescent in my sickness
I will wait till he is absent.   [*Retires.*
  JUSTINA.   Why this weeping? why this sighing?
What, sir, moves thee, what unmans thee?
  LYSANDER.   I am moved by a misfortune,
I'm unmanned by a disaster,
Greater far than tender pity
Ever wept,—the dread example
Cruelty has sworn to make
In the innocent blood of martyrs.
To the Governor of this city
Decius Cæsar a strict mandate
Has despatched . . . I can speak no more.
  JUSTINA (*aside*). What position e'er was harder?
Moved with pity for the Christians
Hither comes to me Lysander
The sad news to tell, not knowing
Lelius to his words may hearken,—
Lelius, the Governor's son.
  LYSANDER. So, Justina . . .
  JUSTINA.   Sir, no farther,
Since you feel it so acutely,
Speak upon this painful matter.
  LYSANDER.   Let me, for I'll feel some solace
When to thee it is imparted.
In it he commands . . .
  JUSTINA.   Proceed not

Further now, when you should rather
Cheat your years with more repose.
    LYSANDER.   How? when I, to make you partner
In those lively fears whose bodings
Are sufficient to despatch me,
Would inform you of the edict,
The most cruel that the margin
Of the Tiber ever saw
Writ in blood to stain its waters,
Do you stop me?   Ah, Justina,
You were wont in another manner
Once to listen to me.
    JUSTINA.   Sir,
Different were the circumstances.
    LELIUS (*at the door, aside*). I can hear but indistinctly
Half-formed words and broken accents.

* * *

Scene XIII.

FLORUS *enters.*—JUSTINA *and* LYSANDER ; LELIUS, *peeping
at the door of the inner room.*

    FLORUS (*aside*). Licence has a jealous lover,
Who but enters to unmask here
A pretended purity,
To forego politer manners.
I come here with that intention . . .
But as she is with her father
I will wait a new occasion.
    LYSANDER.   Who is there? Some footstep passes.
    FLORUS (*aside*). Ah! 'tis now impossible
Without speaking to get back here.
Some excuse I'll try to offer :—
I am . . .

LYSANDER.   You here, sir?
FLORUS.   Your pardon.
I ask leave, sir, to speak with you
On a most important matter.
    JUSTINA (*aside*). Oh! take pity on me, fortune,
For these trials are too many.
    LYSANDER.   Well, sir, speak.
    FLORUS (*aside*).   What shall I say?
Never was I so embarrassed.
    LELIUS (*aside, at the door*). Florus in Justina's house
Leaves and enters like a master!—
These are not unfounded jealousies,
These are real and substantial.
    LYSANDER.   You grow pale, you change your colour.
    FLORUS.   Do not wonder, be not startled,
For I came to give a warning,
To your life of utmost value,
Of an enemy that you have,
Who your swift destruction planneth.
What I've said is quite sufficient.
    LYSANDER (*aside*). Florus, doubtless, must have gathered
Somehow that I am a Christian,
And thus comes in kindliest manner
Of my danger to apprise me.—
Speak, hide nothing in this matter.   [*Aloud.*

SCENE XIV.

LIVIA *enters.*—JUSTINA, LYSANDER, *and* FLORUS; LELIUS
at the door of the room.

    LIVIA.   Sir, the Governor, who is waiting
    At the door of the house, commanded
    Me to call you to his presence.
        FLORUS.   Best I wait for his departure:—

(Meantime my excuse I'll think of.)   [*Aside.*
So 'tis well that you despatch him.
     LYSANDER.   I appreciate your politeness.
Here I will return instanter.
           [*Exeunt* LYSANDER *and* LIVIA.

SCENE XV.

JUSTINA *and* FLORUS; LELIUS *at the door*.

     FLORUS.   Are you then that virtuous maiden,
Who, the very breeze that flatters
With its soft and sweet caresses,
You would call rude, bold, unmannered?
How then is it you surrendered
Even the very keys of the casket
Of your honour?
     JUSTINA.   Hold, hold, Florus,
Do not dare to throw a shadow
On that honour which the sun
After the most strict examen
Has proved bright and pure.
     FLORUS.   Too late
Comes this idle boast.   It happens
That I know to whom you have given
Free access . . .
     JUSTINA.   You dare this scandal?—
     FLORUS.   By a balcony . . .
     JUSTINA.   Do not say it.
     FLORUS.   To your honour.
     JUSTINA.   Thus will you blast me?
     FLORUS.   Yes, for hypocritical virtue
Merits something even harsher.
     LELIUS (*at the door, aside*).   Florus was not then the hero
Of the balcony; some more happy
Lover than us twain she welcomes.

JUSTINA.   Oh ! defame not noble damsels,
Since you noble blood inherit.

   FLORUS.   Noble damsel, dar'st thou call thee,
When thy very arms received him,
And from thy balcony he departed ?
Power subdued thee ; from the fact
That the Governor is his father,
Vanity led thee on to show
That in Antioch he commanded . . .

   LELIUS (*aside*).   Here he speaks of me.

   FLORUS.   Not seeing
Any graver defect of manner,
Than what in his birth and breeding
Rank may cover with its mantle,
But not so . . . .

LELIUS enters.

   LELIUS.   Be silent, Florus,
Nor attack me in my absence ;
For of a rival to speak ill,
Is the act but of a dastard.
'Tis to stop this I come forward,
Angry after so many passes
Which my sword has had with thine,
That I have not yet dispatched thee.

   JUSTINA.   Who, not guilty, ever saw her
In such dangerous straits entangled ?

   FLORUS.   What behind your back was spoken,
I before you will establish,
Truth is truth where'er 'tis uttered.

                             [*They grasp their swords.*

   JUSTINA.   Florus ! Lelius ! what would you have then.

   LELIUS.   I would have full satisfaction
Where I heard th' insulting language.

   FLORUS.   I'll maintain what I have said
Where I said it.

JUSTINA. From so many
Strokes of fortune, free me, Heaven !—
  FLORUS.   And I'll learn to chastise your rashness.

SCENE XVI.

The Governor *enters with* LYSANDER *and attendants.*—
  JUSTINA, LELIUS, *and* FLORUS.

All who enter.   Hold ! stand back !
JUSTINA.   Unhappy me !
  GOVERNOR.   What is this?   But empty scabbards,
Naked swords, are quite sufficient
To inform me what has happened.
  JUSTINA.   What misfortune !
  LYSANDER.   What affliction !—
  LELIUS.   Ah, my lord . . .
  GOVERNOR.   Enough, no farther.
Lelius, thou a son of mine,
A disturber?   Thou a scandal
To all Antioch through my favour ?
  LELIUS.   Think, my lord . . .
  GOVERNOR.   Arrest, disarm them,
Take them hence.   Make no distinction
On account of blood or rank here.
Let them suffer both alike,
Since in guilt alike they acted.
    LELIUS (*aside*). I came jealous, and go outraged.
    FLORUS (*aside*). To my pains new pains are added.
  GOVERNOR.   In distinct and separate prisons,
And with watchful eyes to guard them,
Place the two.—And you, Lysander,
Is it possible you have tarnished
Such a noble reputation,
Suffering . . . .

LYSANDER.   No ; let not these dazzling
False appearances mislead you,
For Justina in what happened
Was quite blameless.
          GOVERNOR.   In her house here,
Would you have her live regardless
Of the fact that they were young,
And that she was fair ?   My anger
I restrain, lest people say,
I, an interested party,
Sentence passed as partial judge.—
But of you who caused this quarrel,
Now that maiden shame has left you,
Well I know that you will glad me
With the occasion I desire,
Of exposing, of unmasking,
In the light of actual vices,
The false virtuous part you've acted.

> [*Exeunt* The Governor *and his attendants ;*
> LELIUS *and* FLORUS *follow as prisoners.*

SCENE XVII.

JUSTINA *and* LYSANDER.

JUSTINA.   I reply but with my tears.
     LYSANDER.   Tears as vain as they are tardy.
What an act was mine, Justina,
When to thee my lips imparted
Who thou art !   Oh, would I never
Told thee, that upon the margin
Of a rivulet in this forest,
A dead mother's womb here cast thee !
     JUSTINA.   I . . . .
          LYSANDER.   Do not attempt excuses.

JUSTINA. Heaven will make them, then, hereafter
LYSANDER. When too late, perhaps.
JUSTINA.   No limit
Can be late here while life lasteth.
  LYSANDER. For the punishment of crimes.
  JUSTINA. Injured truth to re-establish.
  LYSANDER. I, from what I have seen, condemn thee.
  JUSTINA. I thee, from what thou knowest not, rather.
  LYSANDER. Leave me; I go forth to die
Where my grief will soon dispatch me.
  JUSTINA. At thy feet I would lose my life;
But do not reject me, father.   *[Exeunt.*

SCENE XVIII.

A HALL IN CYPRIAN'S HOUSE.

AT THE END IS AN OPEN GALLERY, THROUGH WHICH IS SEEN
THE COUNTRY.

CYPRIAN, The Demon, MOSCON, *and* CLARIN.

  DEMON. Since the hour that I have been
In your house a guest, you ne'er
Show a gay and cheerful air.
Sadness in your face is seen.
It is wrong your cure to shun,
Seeking to mislead mine eyes,
Since I would unsphere the skies,
Shake the stars, and shroud the sun,
For the least desire you feel
That more pleasantly you might live.
  CYPRIAN. Magic has no power to give
The impossible I conceal,
Though the misery I betray.
  DEMON. Come, confess the longed-for bliss.

CYPRIAN.   I love a woman.
DEMON.   And is this
The impossible that you say?
    CYPRIAN.   If you knew her, you'd agree.
    DEMON.   Well, describe her, I'm resigned;
Though I can't but smile to find
What a coward you must be.
    CYPRIAN.   The fair cradle of the skies,
Where the infant sun reposes,
Ere he rises, decked with roses,
Robed in snow, to dry heaven's eyes.
The green prison-bud that tries
To restrain the conscious rose,
When the crimson captive knows
April treads its gardens near,
Turning dawn's half frozen tear
To a smile where sunshine glows.
The sweet streamlet gliding by,
Though it scarcely dares to breathe
Softest murmurs through its teeth,
From the frosts that on it lie.
The bright pink, in its small sky
Shining like a coral star.
The blithe bird that flies afar,
Drest in shifting shades and blooms—
Soaring cithern of plumes
Harping high o'er heaven's blue bar.
The white rock that cheats the sun
When it tries to melt it down, ·
What it melts is but the crown
Which from winter's snow it won.
The green bay that will not shun,
Though the heavens are all aglow,
For its feet a bath of snow,—
Green Narcissus of the brook,
Fearless leaning o'er to look,

Though the stream runs chill below.
In a word, the crimson dawn,
Sun, mead, streamlet, rosebud, May,
Bird that sings his amorous lay,
April's laugh that gems the lawn,
Pink that sips the dews up-drawn,
Rock that stands in storm and shine,
Bay-tree that delights to twine
Round its fadeless leaves the sun,
All are parts which met in one
Form this woman most divine.
For myself, in blind unrest,
(Guess my madness if you can)
I, to seem another man,
In these courtly robes am drest.
Studious calm I now detest,
Fame no longer fires my mind,
Passion reigns where thought refined,
I my firmness fling to tears,
Courage I resign to fears,
And my hopes I give the wind.
I have said, and so will do,
That to some infernal sprite
I would offer with delight
(And the pledge I now renew)
Even my soul for her I woo.
But my offer is in vain,
Hell rejects it with disdain,
For my soul, it may allege,
Is a disproportionate pledge
For the interest I would gain.
    DEMON.	Is this, then, your boasted courage,
In the footsteps of dejected *
Swains to follow, who grow timid

-----

* *Asonante* in *e – e* to the end of the Act.

When their first assault's rejected ?
Are examples then so distant
Of fair ladies who surrender
All their vanities to entreaties,
All their pride to fond addresses ?
Would you make your breast the prison
Of your love, your arms her fetters ?
   CYPRIAN.   Can you doubt it ?
   DEMON.   Then command them
To retire, those two, your servants,
So that we remain here only.
   CYPRIAN.   Go : both leave me for the present.
   MOSCON.   I obey.   [*Exit.*
   CLARIN.   And I as well.—
Such a guest must be the devil.   [*Aside, concealing himself.*
   CYPRIAN.   They are gone.
   DEMON (*aside*).   That Clarin's hiding,
Is to me of small concernment.
   CYPRIAN.   What more wish you now ?
   DEMON.   First fasten
Well this door.
   CYPRIAN.   Yes ; none can enter.
   DEMON.   For the possession of this woman,
With your lips you have asserted
You would give your soul.
   CYPRIAN.   'Tis so.
   DEMON.   Then the contract is accepted.
   CYPRIAN.   What do you say ?
   DEMON.   That I accept it.
   CYPRIAN.   How ?
   DEMON.   So much have I effected
By my science, that I will teach you
How by it to get possession
Of the woman that you worship ;
For I (though so wise and learnéd)
Have no other means to win her.

Let us now in writing settle
What we have resolved between us.
   CYPRIAN.   Do you wish by new pretences
To prolong the pains I suffer?
In my hand is what I tender,
But in yours is not the offer
That you make me ; no, for never
Conjurations or enchantments
Can free will control or fetter.
   DEMON.   Give me, on the terms you spoke of,
Your signed bond.
   CLARIN (*peeping*). The deuce !   This fellow
Is no fool, I see.   No greenhorn
In his business is this devil.
I give him my bond !   No, truly,
Though my lodgings wanted a tenant
For the space of twenty ages,
I wouldn't do it.
   CYPRIAN.   Sir, such jesting
May with merry friends be pastime,
Not with those who are dejected.
   DEMON.   I, in proof of what I am able
To effect, will now present you
With an example, though it faintly
Shows the power my art possesses.
From this gallery what is seen ?
   CYPRIAN.   Much of sky, and much of meadow,
Wood, a rivulet, and a mountain.
   DEMON. Which to you doth seem most pleasant ?
   CYPRIAN.   The proud mountain, for in it
Is my adored one represented.
   DEMON.   Proud competitor of time,
Rival of the years for ever,
Who as king of fields and plains
Crown'st thee with the cloud and tempest,
Move thyself, change earth and air ;

Look, see who I am that tell thee.—
And, look thou, too, since a mountain
I can move, thou mayest a maiden.
  [*The mountain moves from one side to the other in
   the perspective of the theatre.*

CYPRIAN. Never saw I such a wonder !
Ne'er a sight of so much terror !
  CLARIN (*peeping*). With the fright and with the fear,
I enjoy a twofold tremble.
  CYPRIAN. Mighty mountain bird that fliest,
Trees for wings replacing feathers,
Boat, whose rocks supply the tackle,
As thou furrowest through the zephyr,
To thy centre back return thee,
And so end this fear, this terror.
  [*The mountain returns to its original position.*
  DEMON. If one proof is not sufficient,
I will give you then a second.
Do you wish to see the woman
You adore?
  CYPRIAN. Yes.
  DEMON.   Then, thy entrails
Ope, thou monster, to whose being
The four elements are servants.
Show to us the perfect beauty
That thou hidest in thy centre.
  [*A rock opens and* JUSTINA *is seen sleeping.*
Is this she whom you adore?
  CYPRIAN. Whom I idolize beyond measure.
  DEMON. But since I have power to give her,
I can take her too, remember.
  CYPRIAN. Now impossible dream of mine,
Now thy arms will be the centre
Of my love, thy lips the sun,
Burning, brimming as with nectar.
  DEMON. Stay; for till the word you gave me

Is affirmed, and well attested,
You can touch her not.
        [Cyprian *rushes towards the rock, which closes.*
    Cyprian.   Oh, stay
Cloud that hides the most resplendent
Sun, that on my bliss e'er dawned !—
But 'tis air my void arm presses.—
I believe your art, acknowledge
Now I am your slave for ever.
What do you wish I do for thee ?
What do you ask ?
    Demon.   To be protected
By your signature here written
In your blood, at the foot of a letter.
    Clarin (*peeping*). Oh ! I'd give my soul that I
To stay here had not been tempted.
    Cyprian.   For my pen I use this dagger,
Paper let this white cloth serve for,
And the ink wherewith I write it,
Be the blood my arm presents me.
        [*He writes with the point of a dagger upon a piece of
            linen, having drawn blood from one of his arms.*
Oh ! I freeze with fear, with horror !   [*Aside.*
I, great Cyprian, say expressly
I will give my immortal soul,
(Oh ! what lethargy, what frenzy !)
Unto him whose art will teach me
(What confusion ! what strange terror !)
How I may of fair Justina,
Haughty mistress mine, possess me.
I have signed it with my name.
    Demon (*aside*). Now to my deceits is rendered
Valid homage, when such reason,
When discourse like his must tremble
Even when my help is sought for.—
Have you written ?

CYPRIAN.   And signed the letter.

DEMON.   Then the sun you adore is thine.

CYPRIAN.   Thine too, for the years eternal,
Is the soul I offer thee.

DEMON.   Soul for soul I pay my debtors,
Then for thine I give to thee
Thy Justina's.

CYPRIAN.   In what term then,
Think you you can teach to me
All your magic art ?

DEMON.   A twelvemonth ;
But on this condition . . . .

CYPRIAN.   Speak.

DEMON.   That within a cavern buried,
Without any other study,
We may live there both together,
In our service having no one
For us two but this attendant,

       [*Drags out* CLARIN.

Who being curious hid him here ;—
By securing thus his person
That our secret is well kept,
We, I think, may be quite certain.

CLARIN (*aside*). Oh, that I had never waited !
How does it happen though, so many
Neighbours prone to pry, as I am,
Are not caught thus by the devil ?

CYPRIAN.   So far well.   My love, my genius
Have this happy end effected :
First Justina will be mine,
Then by my new lights, new learning,
I will wake the world's surprise.

DEMON.   I have gained what I intended.

CLARIN.   I not so.

DEMON.   You come with us.—
O'er my great foe I've got the better.   [*Aside.*

CYPRIAN.   Ah, how happy my desires,
If I reach to such possession !—-
    DEMON (*aside*). Never will my envy rest
Till I gain both souls to serve me.—
Let us go, and in the deepest
Cavern this wild world presenteth
You to-day will learn in magic
Your first lesson.
    CYPRIAN.   Let us enter,
For my mind with such a master,
For my love with such incentive,
Will the sorcerer Cyprian's name
Live before the world for ever.

ACT THE THIRD.

SCENE I.

A WOOD; AT THE EXTREMITY A GROTTO.

CYPRIAN.

CYPRIAN.   Ungrateful beauty mine,
At length the day, the happy day doth shine—
My hope's remotest range,
The limits of my love and of thy change,
Since I to-day will gain
At last my triumph over thy disdain.
This lofty mountain nigh,
Raised to the star-lit palace of the sky,
And this dark cavern's gloom,
Of two that live, so long the dismal tomb,
Are the rough school wherein
From magic art its mystic lore I win,
And such perfection reach
That I can now my mighty master teach.
Seeing, that on this day, since I came here
The sun completes its course from sphere to sphere,
I from my prison cell come forth to view
What in the light I now have power to do.
Ye skies of cloudless day
List to my magic spell-words and obey;
Swift zephyrs that rejoice
In heaven's warm light, stand still and hear my voice;
Stupendous mountain rock
Shake at my words as at an earthquake shock;

Ye trees in rough bark drest
Be frightened at the groanings of my breast ;
Ye flowers so fair and frail
Faint at the echoing terror of my wail ;
Ye sweet melodious birds
Hush all your songs before my awful words ;
Ye cruel beasts of prey
See the first fruits of my long toil to-day ;
For blinded, dazzled, dazed,
Confused, disturbed, astonished and amazed,
Ye skies and zephyrs, rocks, and trees, and flowers,
And birds, and beasts, behold my magic powers,
And thus to all make plain
Cyprian's infernal study is not vain.

Scene II.

The Demon *and* Cyprian.

Demon.   Cyprian !
Cyprian.   Wise friend and master still !
Demon.   Why, how is this, that using your free-will
More than my precept meant,
Say for what end, what object, what intent,
Through ignorance or boldness can it be,
You thus come forth the sun's bright face to see ?
    Cyprian.   Seeing that now my spell
Can fill with fear, with horror even hell,
Since I, with so much care
Have studied magic and its depths laid bare,
So that yourself can scarcely tell
Whether 'tis I or you that most excel,
Seeing that now there is no place or part
That I with study, diligence and art,

Have not attained,
Since necromancy's secret I have gained,
That art whose lines of gloom
Can ope to me the dark funereal tomb,
And bring before mine eyes
Each corpse that in it lies,
Regaining them, as 'twere by a new birth
From the hard avarice of the grasping earth.
The pale ghosts, one and all,
Rise and respond my call ;—
And seeing that at length the sun
My goal of life had won,
Since from its innate force
Swift-speeding on its course,
Climbing the heavens each day,
It turns as 'twere reluctantly away,
And with a natural fear
Completes to-day the lifetime of a year,
I wish to attain the scope
At last of all my dreams, of all my hope.
To-day the rare, the beautiful, the divine
Justina will be mine,
Here summoned by my charms,
Here lured by love she'll come unto my arms,
For you from me no longer can require
Postponement of my hope's, my heart's desire.
    DEMON.   Nor do I wish to do it, no,
Since thus so earnestly you wish it so.
Now trace upon the ground
Mute mystic symbols, and the deep profound
Of air, with powerful incantations move
Obedient to your hope and to your love.
    CYPRIAN.   For that I will retire ;
You soon shall see the heaven and earth admire. [*Exit.*
    DEMON.   I give you leave to go,
Because our science being the same, I know

That the abyss of hell
Obedient to your spell
Will yield through me, this way,
The fair Justina to your arms to-day :
For, though my mighty power
Cannot enslave free-will even for an hour,
It may present
The outward show of rapture and content,
Suggesting thoughts impure :—
If force I cannot use, at least I lure.

SCENE III.

CLARIN *and* The Demon.

CLARIN. Ungrateful fair, who still my heart doth hold,
Not burning Libya sure, but Livia cold,
The time is come to show
Whether in love you have been true or no,
Whether, since I within this cave was placed,
Not chased by me you have yourself been chaste ;
For I have studied here
At second hand some magic for a year,
Just to find out (alack ! I can't but wince)
Whether with Moscon you have wronged me since :—
Ye watery skies (some people call them pure)
List to my conjurations I conjure,
Mountains . . . .
DEMON.   How, Clarin ?
CLARIN.   Oh ! my master wise !
By the concomitance of my hands and eyes,
I've learned some magic, and would know by it
If Livia, that ungrateful little chit,
Has played me false since I have been away,
Embracing that rogue Moscon on my day.

DEMON.   Have done with these buffooneries : leave
    me, go.
And 'mid these intricate rocks whose paths you know,
Assist your master, who will let you see
(If you would witness such a prodigy)
The end of all his woe.
I wish to be alone.
    CLARIN.   And I not so.
I now perceive
Why to use magic I have not your leave,
The fault was mine, neglecting to attest
My bond, and sign it with the blood of my breast.—
Upon this linen handkerchief
          [He takes out a soiled pocket-handkerchief.
(None cleaner he can have who cries for grief)
I'll sign it now, the method I propose
Is but to give myself a box on the nose,
For there is little harm
Whether the blood is drawn from nose or arm.
        [He writes with his finger on the handkerchief,
            after having drawn some blood.
I, the great Clarin, say, if I can level
Pert Livia's cruel pride, whom I give to the devil . . . .
    DEMON.   Leave me, I say again,
Go seek your master and with him remain.
    CLARIN.   Yes, I will do so, don't get angry though.
The reason you reject my bond I know :
'Tis this, because you see,
Do what I will that you are sure of me.

SCENE IV.

The Demon.

DEMON.   Abyss of hell prepare !
Thyself the region of thine own despair.—
From out each dungeon's dark recess
Let loose the spirits of voluptuousness,
To ruin and o'erthrow
Justina's virgin fabric pure as snow.
A thousand filthy phantoms with thee brought
So people her chaste thought
That all her maiden fancies may be filled
With their deceits ; let sweetest notes be trilled
From every tuneful grove,
And all, birds, plants, and flowers, provoke to love.
Let nothing meet her eyes
But spoils of love's delicious victories,
Let nothing meet her ears
But languid sighs that listening passion hears :
That thus unguarded by the faith, and weak,
She here may Cyprian seek
Invoked by his strong spell,
And by my blinding spirit lured as well.
Begin, in silence I will here remain
Unseen, that you may now begin the strain.   [*Exit.*

SCENE V.

JUSTINA ; *music within.   (They sing within.)*

A VOICE.   *What is the glory far above,
All else that life can give ?*

CHORUS OF VARIOUS VOICES.   *Love, love.*
A VOICE.   *No creature lives on which love's flame*
Has not impressed its burning seal,
The man feels more who love doth feel
Than when Love's breath first warmed his frame.
Love owns one universal claim,—
To Love, it only needs To Be,—
Whether a bird, a flower, a tree:
Then the chief glory, far above
All else in life must be . . . .
CHORUS (*within*).   *Love, love.*
JUSTINA (*alarmed and restless*). Fancy, flatterer that
        thou art,
Though thou should'st be sad to-day,
When did I to thee impart,
In this strange and sudden way,
Licence to afflict my heart?
What thus makes my pulses move?
What strange fire is this I prove
Which each moment doth increase?
Ah! this pain that ends my peace,
This sweet unrest, ah, what?
CHORUS.   *Love, love.*
JUSTINA (*more composed*). 'Tis that enamoured night-
        ingale
Who thus gives me the reply :—
To his partner in the vale
Listening on a bough hard by
Warbling thus his tuneful wail.
Cease, sweet nightingale, nor show
By thy softly witching strain
Trilling forth thy bliss and woe,
How a man might feel love's pain,
When a bird can feel his so.
No : it was that wanton vine
That in fond pursuit has sought

The tall tree it doth entwine,
Till the green weight it hath brought
Makes the noble trunk decline.
Green entwining boughs that hold
What you love in your embrace,
Make my fancy not too bold :—
Ah, if boughs thus interlace,
How would clasping arms infold !—
And if not the vine, 'twill be
That bright sunflower which we see
Turning with its tearful eyes
To its sun-god in the skies,
Whatsoe'er his movements be.
Flower, thy watch no longer keep,
Drooping leaflets fold in sleep,
For the fond thought reappears,
Ah, if leaves can shed such tears,
What are those that eyes can weep !
Cease then, lyrist of the grove,
Leafy vine, unclasp thy arms,
Fickle flower, no longer move,
And declare, these poisoned charms
That you use, what yields ?

    CHORUS (*within*).   *Love, love.*

    JUSTINA.   Love ! it cannot be.   Its chain
Have I ever worn for man ?
No, the fond deceit is vain.
All received a like disdain,
Lelius, Florus, Cyprian.
Lelius did I not despise ?
Florus did I not detest ?
Cyprian, the good and wise,
    [*She pauses at* CYPRIAN'S *name and resumes for
        a time her unquiet manner.*
Spurn with such a haughty breast,
That he vanished from my eyes,

As if frightened by their ire ?—
Where he went I do not know.
But save this, the faintest fire
Love e'er lit, ne'er dared to glow
In the depths of my desire.
Yes, for since I said that he
Should submit without appeal
Never more my face to see,
Ah, I know not what I feel !— [*She grows calmer.*
Pity it must surely be,
That a man so widely known
Should through love of me be lost,
When he pays at such a cost
For the preference he has shown.

[*She becomes troubled again.*

Were it pity though, 'tis true,
The same pity I should give
Lelius and to Florus too,
Who in separate dungeons live,
Ah ! for daring me to woo.   [*She grows calmer.*
But my thoughts, ye mutinous crew,
If my pity is enough
It should not be clogged by you.
Still your promptings press me so,
That I feel in my despair,
Where he is, if **I** could know,
I to seek him now would go.

SCENE VI.

The Demon *and* JUSTINA.

DEMON.   Come, and I will tell thee where.
JUSTINA.   Who art thou who hast procured
Entrance to this lone retreat,

Though the entrance is secured ?
Or, my senses being obscured,
Art thou but delusion's cheat ?
   Demon.   No, not so ; but having known
How this passion pressed thee so,
I have sought thee here alone,
Having promised thee to show
Whither Cyprian has flown.
   Justina.   Then thou'lt reach not thy intent ;
For this passion, this strange pain,
Which my thought doth so torment,
Though my fancy it may gain,
It will never my consent.
   Demon.   But in thought to enter in
Shows that half the deed is done ;
Since accomplished is the sin :—
Stop not half way, ere is won
What the wish desired to win.
   Justina.   Even in this desponding hour,
Though to think may taint the flower,
Thy suggestion comes to nought,—
In my power is not my thought,
But my act is in my power.
I can follow to the brink,
Free to pause or to pursue,
Move my foot, or backward shrink,
For it is one thing to do,
And another thing to think.
   Demon.   If a stronger power than thine,
Drawn from a profounder source,
With thine own desires combine,
How resist the double force
Which with force thy steps incline ?
   Justina.   I will trust a safer spell :—
My free will suffices me.
   Demon.   But my power will it excel.

JUSTINA.   Then the will no more were free
If a force could it compel.
      DEMON.   Come where every bliss thou'lt meet.
      [*Attempts to draw her with him, but cannot
            move her.*
JUSTINA.   Ah ! the bliss were bought too dear.
DEMON.   It is peace, serene and sweet.
JUSTINA.   'Tis a slavery most severe.
DEMON.   Life, 'tis joy.
JUSTINA.   'Tis death, deceit.
DEMON.   Thy defence, what can it be,
If my power thus forces thee ?
                              [*Drags her with more force.*
JUSTINA.   In my God it doth consist.
DEMON.   By persisting to resist,
Woman, thou hast conquered me.   [*Releases her.*
Thy defence to God is due,
And my counsel is disdained ;
Yes, but raging I'll renew
My attempt and have thee feigned,
If I cannot have thee true.
To a spirit I will give
Shape like thine though fugitive,
It will counterfeit thy form,
As with seeming life be warm,
And in it disgraced thou'lt live.
Thus two triumphs at one time
I am sure to win by this,
Be thy virtue so sublime,
Since through an ideal bliss
I will consummate a crime.   [*Exit.*

Scene VII.

Justina.

Justina.   'Gainst the clouds that round me lower
I appeal to heaven's high power ;
Let this spectre of my fame—
As before the wind the flame—
As before the frost the flower,
Vanish, die . . . . But, woe is me !
Who is here to heed my moan ?
Was there not a man with me ?
Yes.   But no : I am alone :
No.   But yes : for I could see.
Where so quickly could he fly ?
Was he born of my unrest ?
Oh ! my danger's manifest . . .
Father ! friend ! Lysander ! I
Call . . . .

Scene VIII.

Lysander *and* Livia *enter from opposite doors.*—Justina.

Lysander.   My child ?
Livia.   What means this cry ?
Justina.   Saw you not a man (ah, me !)
Who but left me instantly ?
I can scarce express my thought.
Lysander.   A man here ?
Justina.   You saw him not ?
Livia.   No, señora.
Justina.   I could see.

LYSANDER.   Saw a man here?   That is hard,
When the place was locked and barred.
    LIVIA (*aside*). Moscon sure she must have seen,
Whom I have contrived to screen
In my chamber.
    LYSANDER.   I regard
What you saw but as the play
Of your fancy and your fear.
Melancholy surely may
Have, the man that you saw here,
Formed from atoms of the day.
    LIVIA.   Yes, I think my master's right.
    JUSTINA.   No, 'twas no defect of sight,
No illusion : since my heart,—
Ah ! too well I feel the smart—
Has been broken by the fright.
Some strange witchery of my will
Must have been effected here.
And with such consummate skill,
That if God had not been near
I might have pursued my ill.
He who at such timely hour
Helped me to resist the power
Of this fearful violence,
Will my humble innocence
Guard, whatever dangers lower.—
Livia, my cloak : whene'er   [*Exit* LIVIA.
Overwhelming griefs oppress,
I to holy church repair,
Where we secretly confess
The true faith.
        [LIVIA *returns with the cloak, which she*
           places on JUSTINA.
    LIVIA.   'Tis this you wear.
    JUSTINA.   There perchance I may appease
This strange fire that burns me so.

LYSANDER.   I desire with thee to go.
LIVIA (*aside*). I will breathe much more at ease
When they're out of the house, I know.
JUSTINA.   Since I wholly trust to thee
Heaven, thy hold to me afford.
Save me . . . .
LYSANDER.   Come : so it may be.
JUSTINA.   Since the cause is thine, O Lord !
Oh, defend Thyself and me !

[Exeunt JUSTINA and LYSANDER.

SCENE IX.

MOSCON *and* LIVIA.

MOSCON.   Have they gone?
LIVIA.   They're gone : all right.
MOSCON.   Why, I'm almost dead with fright.
LIVIA.   Were you of your sense bereft
When but now my room you left
And appeared before her sight?
MOSCON.   Left your room?   Be seen by her?
Why, I swear it, Livia dear,
Not one moment did I stir.
LIVIA.   Who then was it she saw here?
MOSCON.   Well, the devil, as I infer.
How know I?   But then do not
Take it so to heart, my soul.
LIVIA.   Oh ! that's not the cause.   [*She weeps.*
MOSCON.   Then what ?
LIVIA.   Such a question, when the whole
Of a day it was his lot
With me here locked up to stay?
For his comrade far away

Must I not a tear then shed,
Though I take this day instead,
Having wept not yesterday?
Would I have him think of me
As a woman who could be
So forgetful and so frail,
As for half a year to fail
In what we did both agree?

MOSCON.   Half a year?   It is above
One whole year since he went away.

LIVIA.   Quite an error, as I'll prove.
Mind, I cannot count a day
When I Clarin could not love.
This being so, if I to thee
Gave up half the year (ah, me!),
It would give a false amount
To place all to his account.

MOSCON.   Ah, ungrateful! can it be
When my heart on thee depends
For its peace, that thine attends
To such trifles?

LIVIA.   Moscon, yes,
For I find, I must confess,
Short accounts make longest friends.

MOSCON.   Such being then thy constancy,
Livia, I must say good-bye,
Till to-morrow.   Ah! if he
Is thy two-day fever, I
Hope he's not thy syncope.

LIVIA.   Well, my friend, from this you know
I no malice bear.

MOSCON.   Just so.

LIVIA.   See me then no more to-day,
But to-morrow, sir, you may:
I'll not need to send.   Heigho!   [*Exeunt.*

SCENE X.

A WOOD.

CYPRIAN, *as frightened;* CLARIN, *stealthily after him.*

CYPRIAN.   Doubtless something must have happened
'Mong the stars' imperial clusters,*
Since I find their influences
To my wishes so repugnant.
Up from the profound abysses
Some dark caveat must be uttered,
Which prohibits the obedience
Which they owe me as my subjects.
I, a thousand times, with spell-words
Made the winds of heaven to shudder,
I, a thousand times, the bosom
Of the earth with symbols furrowed,
Yet mine eyes have not been gladdened
By the human sun refulgent
That I seek, nor in mine arms
Hold that human heaven.
CLARIN.   What wonder?
When a thousand times have I
Scraped the earth as if for nuggets,
When a thousand times the wind
By my screeching was perturbéd,
And yet Livia was oblivious.
CYPRIAN.   Once again then I am humbled
To invoke her thus.   Oh, listen,
Beautiful Justina . . . . .

---

* *Asonante* in *u—e* to the end of Scene XV.

SCENE XI.

A phantom Figure *of* JUSTINA *appears.*

The Figure, CYPRIAN, *and* CLARIN.

FIGURE.   Summoned,
As I wander through these mountains,
I obey a call so urgent.
What, then, wouldst thou ? what, then, wouldst thou,
Cyprian, with me ?
    CYPRIAN.   Oh, I shudder !
    FIGURE.   And since now . . . .
    CYPRIAN.   I am astonished !
    FIGURE.   I have come . . . .
    CYPRIAN.   What thus disturbs me ?
    FIGURE.   To this place . . . .
    CYPRIAN.   What makes me tremble ?
    FIGURE.   Where . . . .
    CYPRIAN.   Oh ! whence this doubt that
        numbs me ?
    FIGURE.   Love doth call me . . . .
    CYPRIAN.   Why, this terror ?
    FIGURE.   And the powerful spell thou workest
Thus complied with, to this forest's
Deepest depths I fly to shun thee.
               [*Exit, covering her face with the cloak.*
    CYPRIAN.   Listen, hear me, stay, Justina !
But why linger spell-bound, stunned here ?
I'll pursue her, and this forest,
Whither by my spells conducted
She has flown, will be the leafy
Theatre, the rude-constructed
Bride-bed of the strangest bridal
Heaven e'er witnessed.   [*Exit.*

Scene XII.

CLARIN.   Stop : Renuncio
Bride like this who smells of smoke
Stronger than a blacksmith's furnace.
But perhaps the incantation,
Being so extremely sudden,
Caught her leaning o'er the lye-tub,
If not cooking tripe for supper.
No.   Thus cloaked and in a kitchen !
That excuse won't do : another
Let me try.   (I have it now,
For an honourable woman
Never smells then any sweeter,)
She with fright must have been flustered.—
He has overtaken her now,
And from that rude vale uncultured,
Struggling in closed clasping arms,
(For I think when lovers struggle,
Open arms are not the weapon
Even for the lustiest lover,)
To this very spot they come :
I will watch them under cover,
For I wish for once to witness
How young women are abducted. [*Conceals himself.*

Scene XIII.

CYPRIAN *embracing the* Figure *of* JUSTINA, *which he
carries in his arms.*

CYPRIAN.   Now, O beautiful Justina,
In this sweet and secret covert,
Where no beam of sun can enter,

Nor the breeze of heaven blow roughly,
Now the trophy of thy beauty
Makes my magic toils triumphant,
For here folding thee, no longer
Have I need to fear disturbance.
Fair Justina, thou hast cost me
Even my soul.   But in my judgment,
Since the gain has been so glorious,
Not so dear has been the purchase.
Oh ! unveil thyself, fair goddess,
Not in clouds obscure and murky,
Not in vapours hide the sun,
Show its golden rays refulgent.
          [*He draws aside the cloak and discovers a skeleton.*
But, O woe ! what's this I see ?
Is it a cold corse, mute, pulseless,
That within its arms expects me ?
Who, in one brief moment's compass,
Could upon these faded features,
Pallid, motionless, and shrunken,
Have extinguished the bright beauties
Of the blush-rose and the purple ?
   THE SKELETON.   Cyprian, such are all the glories
Of the world that you so covet.
          [The Skeleton *disappears.*   CLARIN *rushes in*
               frightened, and embraces CYPRIAN.

SCENE XIV.

CLARIN *and* CYPRIAN.

   CLARIN.   Fear, for any one who wants it,
Wholesale or retail I'll furnish.
   CYPRIAN.   Stay ! funereal shadow, stay !
Now for other ends I urge thee.

CLARIN.   I am a funereal body :—
Don't you see it by my bulk here ?
   CYPRIAN.   Ah ! who are you?
   CLARIN.   Who I am, sir,
Or am not, myself doth puzzle.
   CYPRIAN.   Did you in the air's void spaces,
Or earth's caverns yawning under,
See an icy corse here vanish,
See to dust and ashes turning
All the freshness and the beauty
That it promised in its coming ?
   CLARIN.   Do you take me, sir, for one
Of those pitiful poor lurkers
Men call spies ?
   CYPRIAN.   What could it be ?
   CLARIN.   And not be, in such a hurry.
   CYPRIAN.   Let us seek it.
   CLARIN.   Let's not seek it.
   CYPRIAN.   I must sift this matter further.
   CLARIN.   I would rather not.

SCENE XV.

The Demon, CYPRIAN, *and* CLARIN.

DEMON (*aside*).   Just heavens,
If my nature, in conjunction,
Once possessed both grace and science,
When 'mongst angels I was numbered,
Grace alone is what I've lost,
Science no.   Then why unjustly,
If 'tis so, deprive my science
Of its proper power and function ?
   CYPRIAN.   Lucifer, wise master mine.

CLARIN.   Pray don't call him: for he'll come here
In another corse, I warrant.
    DEMON.   Speak, what would you?
    CYPRIAN.   The annulling,
The redemption of those pledges,
At whose very thought I shudder.
    CLARIN.   As I don't redeem my pledges,
I'll slip off here through the bushes.   [*Exit.*

SCENE XVI.

CYPRIAN *and* The Demon.

CYPRIAN.   Scarcely o'er earth's wounded bosom
Had I the true spell-word uttered,
When in the ensuing action,
She, of all my dreams the subject,
My adored, divine Justina . . . .
But why take the useless trouble,
That to tell you know already?
I embraced her, would unmuffle
Her fair face, when (woe is me!)
In her beauty I discovered
A gaunt skeleton, a statue,
A pale image, a sepulchral
Show of death, which in these measured
Words thus spoke (even yet I shudder),
" Cyprian, such are all the glories
Of the world that you so covet."—
To assert, that on thy magic
As expressed by me, the burden
Of the fault should lie, is vain,
For I, point by point, so worked it,
That of all its silent symbols
There was not a line but somewhere

Had its place, of all its spell-words
Not one word that was not uttered.
Then, 'tis plain thou hast deceived me,
For though acting as instructed,
I but found an empty phantom
Where I sought a blissful substance.
    DEMON.   Cyprian, this defect from thee,
Nor from me, in truth, resulted :
Not from thee, because the magic
Thou didst exercise with subtle
Thought and skill ; and not from me,
For I could not teach thee further.
From a higher cause, believe me,
Came this injury thou hast suffered.
But be not cast down : for I,
Who in tranquil rest would lull thee,
Will to thee unite Justina,
By a different way and juster.
    CYPRIAN.   That is not my intention now.
For this strange event has struck me
With such terror and confusion,
That thy ways I do not covet.
And since thou hast not complied with
The conditions, the assumptions
Of my love, I only ask thee,
Now that from thy face I'm rushing,
As the contract is annulled,
That my bond thou shouldst return me.
    DEMON.   What I promised was to teach thee,
By a course of secret study,
How to draw to thee Justina
By the potent power impulsive
Of thy words : and since the wind
Here Justina hath conducted,
I have then fulfilled my contract,
I have kept my plighted word then.

CYPRIAN.   What was offered to my love
Was that I should surely pluck here
The sweet fruit whose seeds my hope
Had to these wild wastes entrusted.
    DEMON.   Cyprian, I was only bound
Her to bring here.
    CYPRIAN.   A mere shuffle:
To my arms you swore to give her.
    DEMON.   In thy arms I saw her struggle.
    CYPRIAN.   'Twas a phantom.
    DEMON.   "Twas a portent.
    CYPRIAN.   Worked by whom?
    DEMON.   By one who worked it
To protect her.
    CYPRIAN.   Who was he?
    DEMON (*trembling*). I don't wish the name to utter.
    CYPRIAN.   I will turn my magic science
'Gainst thyself.   By its compulsion
Speak, inform me who he is.
    DEMON.   Well, a god who takes this trouble
For Justina.
    CYPRIAN.   What's one God,
When of gods there's such a number?
    DEMON.   'All their power in Him is centred.
    CYPRIAN.   Then One only, sole and Sovereign,
Must He be, whose single will
Their united wills outworketh.
    DEMON.   I know nothing, I know nothing.
    CYPRIAN.   I renounce then with my utmost
Power the pact that I made with thee;
What compelled Him (this I urge thee
In that God's great name) to guard her?
    DEMON (*after having struggled ineffectually not to say it*).
        To preserve her pure, unsullied.
    CYPRIAN.   Then He is the sovereign goodness
Since a wrong He will not suffer.

But if she remained here hidden
Say what loss would have resulted?
   DEMON.   Loss of honour, if the secret
Leaked out to the gossiping vulgar.
   CYPRIAN.   Then that God must be all sight,
Since he could foresee these troubles.
But, why could not thy enchantment
Be as potent and consummate?
   DEMON.   Ah! His power is ampler, fuller.
   CYPRIAN.   Then that God must be all hands,
Since whate'er He wills He worketh.
Tell me then who is that God,
Whom to-day I have discovered
The supreme of good to be,
The Creator, the Annuller,
The Omniscient, the All-seeing,
Whom I've sought for years unnumbered?
   DEMON.   Him I know not.
   CYPRIAN.   Speak, who is He?
   DEMON.   As I speak it, how I shudder!
He—He is the God of the Christians.
   CYPRIAN.   Say what moved Him to obstruct me
In my wish?
   DEMON.   Her Christian faith.
   CYPRIAN.   Does He guard so those who love Him?
   DEMON.   Yes; but now too late, too late,
Dost thou hope to gain His succour,
Since, in being my slave, thou canst not
Claim the privilege of His subject.
   CYPRIAN.   I thy slave?
   DEMON.   In my possession
Is thy signature.
   CYPRIAN.   I'll struggle
To regain it from thee, since
'Twas conditional at the utmost.
I don't doubt I will get it.

DEMON.   How?

CYPRIAN.   In this way.

> [*He draws his sword, strikes at* The Demon, *but cannot touch him.*

DEMON.   Although the lunges
Of thy naked sword against me
Are well aimed, thou hast not struck me,
Fierce as were thy blows.   And now,
Even in more despair to plunge thee,
I would have thee learn at last
That the Devil is thy instructor.

CYPRIAN.   What do you say?

DEMON.   That I am he.

CYPRIAN.   Oh! to hear thee how I shudder!—

DEMON.   Not alone a slave art thou,
But *my* slave; be that thy comfort.

CYPRIAN.   I the slave of the Devil!   I
Own a master so unworthy?

DEMON.   Yes; for since thy soul thou gav'st me,
Thenceforth it to me was subject.

CYPRIAN.   Is there then no gleam of hope,
No appeal, no aid, no succour,
By which I so great a crime
Can blot out?

DEMON.   No.

CYPRIAN.   Why doubt further?
Let not this sharp sword rest idly
In my hand, but swiftly cutting
Through my breast, become the willing
Instrument of mine own murder.
But what say I?   He who could
Snatch Justina from thy clutches,
Can He not, too, rescue me?

DEMON.   No.   By choice thou wert a culprit,
And He does not favour crimes,
Virtues only.

CYPRIAN.   If the summit
Of all power He be, to pardon
Is as easy as to punish.

DEMON.   He rewardeth by His power,
He chastiseth from His justice.

CYPRIAN.   One who yields He'll not chastise.
I am one, since I am humbled.

DEMON.   Thou art mine, my slave : no master
Canst thou have but me.

CYPRIAN.   I trust not.

DEMON.   How, when still in my possession
Is that bond of thine, that bloody
Scroll inscribed by thine own hand?

CYPRIAN.   He who is supreme and sovereign,
And depends not on another,
Will yet bear me through triumphant.

DEMON.   In what way?

CYPRIAN.   He is all sight,
And will see the fitting juncture.

DEMON.   It I hold.

CYPRIAN.   He is all hands,
And will burst my bonds asunder.

DEMON.   Ere that comes I'll see thee dead :
Thus my clasping arms shall crush thee.

                    [*They struggle together.*

CYPRIAN.   Thou great God, the Christians' God,
Oh, assist me in this struggle !

DEMON (*flinging* CYPRIAN *from his arms*). It is He
      who has saved thy life.

CYPRIAN.   More He'll do since I seek Him humbly.

                              [*Exeunt.*

Scene XVII.

HALL IN THE PALACE OF THE GOVERNOR.

The Governor, Fabius, *and* Soldiers.

GOVERNOR.   How then was the capture made?
FABIUS.   In their church, as we suspected,
We discovered them collected,
Where before their God they prayed.
With an armed guard I traced them
To this secret sacred hall,
Made them prisoners one and all,
And in different prisons placed them.
But, your patience not to tire,
The chief point I may declare,—
Captured is Justina fair,
And Lysander her old sire.
GOVERNOR.   If for gold, a fair pretence,
If for rank, you would not miss,
Wherefore bring me news like this
And not claim your recompense?
FABIUS.   If you deign to value thus
My poor service, you may pay it.
GOVERNOR.   How?
FABIUS.   With great respect I say it,
Florus free, and Lelius.
GOVERNOR.   Though I seemed austere and cold,
Them chastising without pity
To strike terror through the city,
Yet if the whole truth were told,
Then the cause were plain why they
Have been prisoned a whole year.
It is this, a father's fear
Lelius would preserve this way.

Florus was his rival, he
Had a host of powerful friends,
Each was jealous, and his ends
Would attain whate'er might be.
I was fearful a collision
Would ensue if they should meet,
So I thought it more discreet
Not to come to a decision.
So with this intent I sought
Some pretext, Justina's face
To expel from out this place,
But I could discover nought.
But since this event to-day,
With her damaged character,
Gives a right to banish her,
Nay, to take her life away,
Let them be released.   No fear
Need you have about their fate ;
Go, and Lelius liberate,
Go, and Florus bring me here.
    FABIUS.   Myriad times I kiss thy feet
For a favour so immense.   [*Exit.*

SCENE XVIII.

The Governor *and* Soldiers.

    GOVERNOR.   And since now this fair pretence,
This hypocritical deceit,
In my power at last doth lie,
Wherefore my revenge postpone
For the sorrows I have known
Through her fault?   Yes, she shall die
By the bloody headsman's hand.

Bring her hither in my name,   [*To a* Soldier.
Let her punishment and shame
Be a terror to the land.
Let the palace she thought sweet
But her scaffold scene present.

> [*Exit the* Soldier *with others.*

SCENE XIX.

FABIUS, LELIUS, *and* FLORUS.—THE SAME.

FABIUS.   Sir, the two for whom you sent
Here are kneeling at your feet.
    LELIUS.   I, whose wish it is to be
Welcomed as thy son this time,
With no consciousness of crime
Do not see a judge in thee,
I an angry sire may see
With a son's respectful fear
And obedience.
    FLORUS.   Being here,
I infer that it must be
(Though no guilt can I discern)
Thy chastising hand to feel.
See.   Submissive here I kneel.
    GOVERNOR.   Lelius, Florus, I was stern,
Justly stern against ye two,
For as judge or father I
Could not unchastised pass by
Your offence.   But then I knew
That in noble hearts the feeling
Of resentment does not last,
And as now the cause is past,
I resolved, to both appealing,
Friends to make of you once more.

So to consecrate the tie
Now embrace in amity.
    LELIUS.   I am glad that, as of yore,
Florus is my friend to-day.
    FLORUS.   That thou'rt mine this act may show.
Here's my hand.
    GOVERNOR.   This being so,
You are free to go or stay:—
When I tell you of the sad
Fall of her you once admired,
Nothing further is required.

SCENE XX.

The Demon, *a crowd of* People.—THE SAME.

DEMON (*within*). Ware! beware! He's mad! he's mad!
GOVERNOR.   What is this?
LELIUS.   I'll go and see.
       [*He goes to the door, and after a pause returns.*
GOVERNOR.   In this palace hall these cries,
From what cause can they arise?
    FLORUS.   Something serious it must be.
    LELIUS.   This confusion is occasioned
(Hear a singular adventure),
Sir, by Cyprian, who being absent
Many days again has entered *
Antioch completely mad.
    FLORUS.   It was doubtless the fine essence
Of his mind that thus has brought him
To this lamentable ending.
    PEOPLE (*within*). Ware the madman! ware the mad-
    man!

---

   * *Asonante* in *e—e*, which continues to the end.

SCENE XXI.

CYPRIAN, *half naked;* People.—THE SAME.

CYPRIAN.   Never was I more collected;
It is you yourselves are mad.
    GOVERNOR.   Cyprian, what is all this ferment?
    CYPRIAN.   Governor of Antioch,
Viceroy of great Cæsar Decius,
Florus, Lelius, my young friends,
Whom I valued and respected,
Proud nobility, great people,
To my words be all attentive :
I am Cyprian, I am he
Once so studious, and so learnëd,
I the wonder of the schools,
Of the sciences the centre.
What I gained from all my studies
Was one doubt, a doubt that never
Left my wildered mind a moment,
Ever troubling and perplexing.
I Justina saw, and seeing,
To her charms my soul surrendered,
And for soft voluptuous Venus
Left the wise and learn'd Minerva.
Baffled by Justina's virtue,
I, pursuing though rejected,
And from one extreme to another
Passing on as passion led me,
To my guest, who from the sea
Found my feet a port of shelter,
For Justina pledged my soul,
Since at once he charmed my senses
And my intellect, by giving

Love its hopes, and thought its treasures.
From that hour, as his disciple
Lived I in these lonely deserts,
And to his laborious teaching
I am for a power indebted,
By which I can move even mountains
And in different places set them :
Yet although these mighty wonders
I can do to-day, I'm helpless
By the voice of my desire
To draw towards me one fair vestal.
And the cause why I am powerless
To subdue that beauteous virgin
Is that by a God she's guarded,
Whom, now knowing by His blessèd
Grace bestowed, I come to acknowledge
As the Infinite, the Eternal.
Yes, the great God of the Christians
I now openly confess here.
And though true it is I am
Still of hell the slave and servant,
Having with my very blood
Signed a certain secret cedule,
Yet my blood that blood may blot out
In the martyrdom I'm expecting.
If you are a judge, if Christians
You pursue with bloody vengeance,
I am one : for in these mountains
A grave venerable elder
The first sacrament conferring
With its sacred sign impressed me.
This being so, why wait ?   Your orders
Give unto the bloody headsman,
Tell him here to strike this neck
And from it my head dissever.
Try my firmness as you will,

For I, resolute and determined,
Will endure a thousand deaths
Since this truth at last I've learnéd,
That without the great God, whom
Now I seek, adore, and reverence,
Human glories are but ashes,
Dust, smoke, wind, delusive, empty.
　　　　　[*He falls as if in a swoon, with his face to the
　　　　　　　　ground.*
　　GOVERNOR.　So absorbed, so lost in wonder,
Cyprian, has thy daring left me,
That considering modes of torture
I have yet not one selected.
Rise.　Bestir thee.　　　　　[*Spurns him with his foot.*
　　FLORUS.　　　　　As a statue
Formed of ice he lies extended.

SCENE XXII.

Soldiers, JUSTINA.—THE SAME.

　　A SOLDIER.　Here, your Highness, is Justina.
　　GOVERNOR (*aside*). I must go, her face unnerves me.—
With this living corse here lying
Let us leave her for the present.
　　　　　　　　　[*Aside to his retinue.*

For the two being here confined,
It may alter their intentions,
Seeing that they are condemned
Both to die : if not, 'tis certain,
That unless they adore our gods
Frightful torments soon shall end them.
　　LELIUS (*aside*). I remain, 'twixt love and fear
Quite bewildered and suspended.

FLORUS (*aside*). So affected have I been,
I scarce know what most affects me.
> [*Exeunt all, except* JUSTINA.

SCENE XXIII.

JUSTINA ; CYPRIAN, *insensible on the ground.*

JUSTINA.   What ! without a word you leave me ?
When I come here, calm, contented,
Even to die.   Ah ! wishing death,
Am I then of death prevented ?—
> [*She perceives* CYPRIAN.

But my punishment is, doubtless,
Thus locked up to face the terrors
Of a slow and lingering death,
With the body of this wretch here
Left alone, my sole companion
Being a corse.   O thou, re-entered
Into thy original earth,
Happy wert thou, if thy sentence
Was passed on thee for the faith
I adore !
CYPRIAN (*recovering consciousness*). O proud avenger
Of your gods, why wait, the thread
Of my life to cut ? . . . [*He perceives* JUSTINA, *and rises.*
> Heaven bless me !—
Can I trust my eyes ?   Justina !   [*Aside.*
JUSTINA (*aside*). Cyprian, do I see ?   O Heaven !
CYPRIAN (*aside*). No, it is not she, my thought
Fills the void air with her presence.
JUSTINA (*aside*). No, it is not he, the wind
Forms this phantom to divert me.
CYPRIAN.   Shadow of my fantasy . . .

JUSTINA.　Of my wish, delusive spectre . . .
CYPRIAN.　Terror of my startled senses . . .
JUSTINA.　Horror of my heart's dejection . . .
CYPRIAN.　What, then, wouldst thou?
JUSTINA.　　　　　　　　What, then, wouldst thou?
CYPRIAN.　I invoked thee not.　What errand
Hast thou come on?
JUSTINA.　　　　　Why thus seek me?
I to thee no thought directed.
CYPRIAN.　Ah! I sought thee not, Justina.
JUSTINA.　Nor here at thy call I entered.
CYPRIAN.　Then, why here?
JUSTINA.　　　　　　　I am a prisoner.—
Thou?
CYPRIAN.　I, too, have been arrested.
But, Justina, say what crime
Could thy virtue have effected?
JUSTINA.　It is not for any crime,
It is from their deep resentment,
Their abhorrence of Christ's faith,
Whom I as my God confess here.
CYPRIAN.　Thou dost owe Him that, Justina,
For thy God was thy defender,
He watched o'er thee in His goodness.
Get my prayers to Him accepted.
JUSTINA.　Pray with faith, and He will listen.
CYPRIAN.　Then with that I will address Him.
Though a fear, that's not despair,
Makes me for my great sins tremble.
JUSTINA.　Oh! have confidence.
CYPRIAN.　　　　　　　　My crimes are
So immense.
JUSTINA.　　　But more immense are
His great mercies.
CYPRIAN.　　　　Then, will He
Pardon have on me?

JUSTINA.   'Tis certain.
CYPRIAN.   How, if I my soul surrendered
To the Demon's self, as purchase
Of thy beauty?
JUSTINA.   Oh, there are not
Stars as many in the heavens,
Sands as many on the shore,
Sparks within the fire as many,
Motes as many in the beam,
On the winds so many feathers,
As the sins He can forgive.
CYPRIAN.   I believe it, and am ready
Now a thousand lives to give Him.—
But I hear some people enter.

SCENE XXIV.

FABIUS, *leading in* MOSCON, CLARIN, *and* LIVIA, *as
prisoners;* CYPRIAN *and* JUSTINA.

FABIUS.   With your master and your mistress
Here remain confined together.   [*Exit.*
LIVIA.   If *they* fancy to be Christians,
What have *we* done to offend them?
MOSCON.   Much: 'tis crime enough for us
That we happen to be servants.
CLARIN.   Flying peril in the mountain,
I find here a greater peril.

Scene XXV.

A Servant.—The Same.

Servant.   The Lord Governor Aurelius
Summons Cyprian to his presence,
And Justina.
    Justina.   Ah ! how happy,
If 'tis for the wished-for ending.
Do not, Cyprian, be disheartened.
    Cyprian.   Faith, zeal, courage, all possess me :
For if life must be the ransom
Of my slavery to the devil,
He who gave his soul for thee,
Will he not give God his person ?
    Justina.   I once said that I could love thee
But in death, and since together,
Cyprian, we now must die,
What I promised I present thee.
                    [*They are led out by the* Servant.

———————————— —— —— -

Scene XXVI.

Moscon, Livia, *and* Clarin.

Moscon.   How contentedly to die
They go forth.
    Livia.   Much more contented
Are we three to remain alive.
    Clarin.   Not much more; for we must settle
Our account now, though I own
The occasion might be better,

And the place too, still 'twere wrong
To neglect the time that's present.
   MOSCON.   What account pray ?
   CLARIN.   I have been
Absent . . .
   LIVIA.   Speak.
   CLARIN.   The whole of a twelvemonth,
When without my intermission
Moscon in possession held thee.
Now my quota in the business,
If we both have equal measure,
Is that I must have my year.
   LIVIA.   Can it be that I'm suspected
Of thus wronging thee so basely ?
Why, I wept whole days together
When it was the day for weeping.
   MOSCON.   Yes, for I myself was present :
Every day that was not mine
She thy friendship quite respected.
   CLARIN.   That's a bounce ; for not a tear,
When this day her house I entered,
Did she shed, and there I found thee
Sitting with her quite contented.
   LIVIA.   But this day is not a fast.
   CLARIN.   Yes, it is ; for I remember
That the day I went away
Was my day.
   LIVIA.   Oh ! that's an error.
   MOSCON.   Yes, I see how that arises,
This year is a year bissextile,
And our days are now the same.
   CLARIN.   Well, I'm satisfied, 'tis better
That a man should not too deeply
Pry into such things.—Good heavens ! —
               [*The sound of a great tempest is heard.*

SCENE XXVII.

The Governor, *a crowd of* People ; *then* FABIUS, LELIUS, *and* FLORUS, *all astonished ; afterwards* The Demon.

LIVIA.   Sure the house is tumbling down.
MOSCON.   How terrific ! what a tempest !
GOVERNOR.   Doubtless in disastrous ruin
Topple down the walls of heaven.
    [*The tempest is renewed, and enter* FABIUS, LELIUS,
        and FLORUS.
FABIUS.   Scarcely on the public scaffold
Had the headsman's hand dissevered
Cyprian and Justina's necks,
When the earth, even to its centre,
Seemed to tremble.
LELIUS.   And a cloud,
From whose burning womb extended
The wild lightnings, the loud thunders,
Awful embryos were projected,
Fell upon us.
FLORUS.   From which issued
A most horrid, most repelling
Shape, who on the scaly shells
Of a mailed and mighty serpent,
O'er the scaffold made a sign
Motioning silence and attention.
      [*The Scene opens, and a scaffold with the heads
        and bodies of* JUSTINA *and* CYPRIAN *is seen.
        Over it in the air, upon a winged serpent, is*
        The Demon.
DEMON.   Hear, O mortals, hear what I,
By the orders of high Heaven,
For Justina's exculpation,
Must declare to all here present.

I it was, who to dishonour
Her pure fame, in form dissembled
For the purpose, scaled her house,
And her very chamber entered.
And in order that her fame
Should not by that fraud be lessened,
I come here her injured honour
To exhibit pure and perfect.
Cyprian, who with her lieth
On a happy bier at rest there,
Was my slave.   But he effacing,
With the blood his neck outsheddeth,
The red signature, the linen
Is now spotless and unblemished.
And the two, in spite of me,
Having to the spheres ascended
Of the sacred throne of God,
Live there in a world far better.—
This, then, is the truth, which I
Tell, because God makes me tell it,
Much against my will, my practice
Not being great as a truth-teller.

     [*He falls swiftly, and sinks into the earth.*

 Livia. Oh ! what horror !
 Florus.   What confusion !
 Livia. What a prodigy !
 Moscon.   What terror !
 Governor. These are all but the enchantments
Which this sorcerer effected
At his death.
 Florus. I am in doubt
To believe them or reject them.
  Lelius. The mere thought of them confounds me.
  Clarin. If magician, it is certain,
  As I hold, he must have been
  The magician then of heaven.

MOSCON.   Leaving our partitioned love
In a rather odd dilemma,
For *The Wonderful Magician*
Ask the pardon of its errors.

THE

PURGATORY OF ST. PATRICK.

TO

AUBREY DE VERE,

WHOSE

"LEGENDS OF ST. PATRICK"

ARE AMONG THE MOST BEAUTIFUL OF ENGLISH POEMS,

This Version

OF THE CELEBRATED LEGEND OF ST. PATRICK'S PURGATORY,
AS TOLD BY CALDERON,

IS AFFECTIONATELY INSCRIBED BY

THE AUTHOR.

PERSONS.

—•—

EGERIUS, *King of Ireland.*

PATRICK.

LUIS ENIUS.

A GOOD ANGEL.

A BAD ANGEL.

PHILIP.

LEOGAIRE.

A CAPTAIN.

POLONIA, *Daughter of the King.*

LESBIA, *her Sister.*

PAUL, *a Peasant.*

LUCY, *his Wife.*

Two Canons Regular.

Two Peasants.

An Old Countryman.

A Muffled Figure.

Attendants, Friars, and others.

———

*The Scene passes in Ireland, in the Court of King Egerius,
and other parts.*

THE PURGATORY OF SAINT PATRICK.

ACT THE FIRST.

THE SEA-SHORE, WITH PRECIPITOUS CLIFFS.

SCENE I.

The King EGERIUS, *clad in skins*, LEOGAIRE, POLONIA, LESBIA, *and a* Captain.

KING (*furious*). Here let me die. Away!
LEOGAIRE.   Oh, stop, my lord!
CAPTAIN.   Consider . . .
LESBIA.   Listen . . .
POLONIA.   Stay . . .
KING.   Yes, from this rocky height,
Nigh to the sun, that with one starry light
Its rugged brow doth crown,
Headlong among the salt waves leaping down
Let him descend who so much pain perceives;
There let him raging die who raging lives.
LESBIA.   Why wildly seekest thou the sea?
POLONIA.   Thou wert asleep, my lord; what could it
    be?
KING.   Every torment that doth dwell
For ever with the thirsty fiends of hell—
Dark brood of that dread mother,

R

The seven-necked snake, whose poisoned breath doth
    smother
The fourth celestial sphere ;
In fine, its horror and its misery drear
Within me reach so far,
That I myself upon myself make war,
When in the arms of sleep
A living corse am I, for it doth keep
Such mastery o'er my life, that, as I dream,
A pale foreshadowing threat of coming death I seem.
    POLONIA.   How could a dream, my lord, provoke you
    so ?
    KING.   Alas ! my daughters, listen, you shall know.
From out the lips of a most lovely youth
(And though a miserable slave, in sooth
I dare not hurt him, and I speak his praise),
Well, from the mouth of a poor slave, a blaze
Of lambent lustre came,
Which mildly burned in rays of gentlest flame ;
Till reaching you,
The living fire at once consumed ye two.
I stood betwixt ye both, and though I sought
To stay its fury, the strange fire would not
Molest or wound me, passing like the wind,
So that despairing, blind,
I woke from out a deep abysm
Of dream, a lethargy, a paroxysm ;
But find my pains the same,
For still it seems to me I see that flame,
And flying, at every turn
See you consumed ; but now I also burn.*

---

* The Dream of Egerius, as given by Calderon, agrees substantially with Jocelin's description, and differs only in one slight par-
ticular (the number of the flames) from that in Montalvan's *Vida y
Purgatorio de San Patricio.* In the latter, the name of the Irish
prince to whom Patrick was sold is not given ; in Jocelin he is

LESBIA.   Light phantoms these,
Chimeras which an entrance find with ease
Into the dreamer's brain.   [*A trumpet sounds.*
But wherefore sounds this trumpet?
    CAPTAIN.   It is plain
Ships are approaching to our port below.
    POLONIA.   Grant me thy leave, great lord, since thou
        dost know
A trumpet in my ear
Sounds like a siren's voice, serene and clear;
Ever to war inclined,
In martial music my chief joy I find ;
Its clangour and its din
Lead my rapt senses on : for I may win
Through it my highest fame,
When soaring to the sun on waves of flame,
Or wings as swift, my proud name shall ascend,
There it may be with Pallas to contend.
A stronger motive urges me to go :   [*Aside.*
If it is Philip's ship I wish to know.   [*Exit.*
    LEOGAIRE.   Descend, my lord, with me
Down where the foam-curled head of the blue sea
Bows at the base of this majestic hill,
Whose sands, like chains of gold, restrain its wilder will.

---

called " Milcho."   Calderon was either ignorant of this, and gave
the king a name that was purely imaginary, or, considering it less
musical than he would wish, gave him the more harmonious one of
Egerio.   The following is Jocelin's version : " And Milcho beheld
a vision in the night : and behold Patrick entered his palace as all
on fire, and the flames, issuing from his mouth, and from his nose,
and from his eyes, and from his ears, seemed to burn him ; but Milcho
repelled from himself the flaming hair of the boy, nor did it prevail
to touch him any nearer ; but the flame, being spread, turned aside
to the right, and catching on his two little daughters, who were lying
in one bed, burned them even to ashes : then the south wind blowing
strongly dispersed their ashes over many parts of Ireland." —*Jocelin's
Life of St. Patrick, translated by Swift* (Dublin, 1804), pp. 17, 18.

CAPTAIN.   Let it divert thy care,
This snow-white monster fair,
Whose waves of dazzling hue
Shape silver frames round mirrors sapphire blue.
   KING.   Nothing can give relief;
Nothing can now divert me from my grief;
That mystic fire will give my life no rest,—
My heart an Etna seems within my breast.
   LESBIA.   Is any sight more fair? can aught surpass
That of a vessel breaking through the glass
Of crystal seas, and seeming there to be,
As with light share it cuts the azure mass,
A fish of the wind, a swift bird of the sea,
And being for two elements designed,
Flies in the wave and swims upon the wind?
But now no witchery
Were it to any eyes that sight to see;
For, lo! the roused-up ocean,
Heaving with all its mountain waves in motion,
Wrinkles its haughty brow,
And suddenly awaking,
Neptune, his trident shaking,
Ruffles the beauteous face so sweet and calm but now.
Well may the sailor in his floating home
Expect a storm, for, lo! in heaven's high vault
Rise pyramids of ice, mountains of salt,
Turrets of snow, and palaces of foam.

POLONIA returns.

POLONIA.   O dire misfortune!
   KING.   What so suddenly
Has chanced, Polonia?
   POLONIA.   This inconstant sea,
This Babel of wild waves that seeks heaven's gate,
So great its fury, and its rage so great,
Driven by a drought accursed,

(Who would have thought that waves themselves could
        thirst?)
Has swallowed in the depths of its dread womb,
But now, a numerous company, to whom
It consecrates below
Red sepulchres of coral, tombs of snow,
In silver-shining caves;
For from their prison out o'er all the waves
Has Æolus the winds let loose, and they,
Without a law to guide them on their way,
Fell on that bark from which the trumpet rang,
A swan whose own sad obsequies it sang.
I from that cliff's stupendous height,
Which dares to intercept the great sun's light,
Looked full of hope along that vessel's track,
To see if it was Philip who came back;
Philip whose flag had borne upon the breeze
Thy royal arms triumphant through the seas;
When his sad wreck swept by,
And every sound was buried in a sigh,
His ruin seemed not wrought by seas or skies,
But by my lips and eyes,
Because my cries, the tears that made me blind,
Increased still more the water and the wind.
    KING.   How ! ye immortal deities,
Would you still try by threatenings such as these
What I can bear?
Is it your wish that I should mount and tear
This azure palace down, as if the shape
Of a new Nimrod * I assumed, to show
How on my shoulders might the world escape,
Nor as I gazed below

-----

* Nimrod is here used for Atlas. "Nimrod aber ist hier, was
den Profandichtern und auch dem Calderon oft Atlas ist."—Schmidt,
Die Schauspiele Calderon's, &c., p. 426.

Feel any fear, though all the abysses under
Were rent with fire and flame, with lightning and with
    thunder.

SCENE II.

PATRICK, *and then* LUIS ENIUS.

PATRICK (*within*). Ah me !
LEOGAIRE.   Some mournful voice.
KING.   What's this ?
CAPTAIN.   The form,
As of a man who has escaped the storm,
Swims yonder to the land.
    LESBIA.   And strives to give a life-sustaining hand
Unto another wretch, when he
Appeared about to sink in death's last agony.
    POLONIA.   Poor traveller from afar,
Whom evil fate and thy malignant star
On this far shore have cast,
Let my voice guide thee, if amid the blast
My accents thou canst hear ; since it is only
To rouse thy courage that I speak to thee.
Come !

    Enter PATRICK *and* LUIS ENIUS, *clasping each other.*

PATRICK.   Oh, God save me !
LUIS.   Oh, the devil save *me !*
LESBIA.   They move my pity, these unhappy two.
KING.   Not mine, for what it is I never knew.
PATRICK.   Oh, sirs, if wretchedness
Can move most hearts to pity man's distress,
I will not think that here
A heart can be so cruel and severe

As to repel a wretch from out the wave.
Pity, for God's sake, at your feet I crave.
　　LUIS.   I don't, for I disdain it.
From God or man I never hope to gain it.
　　KING.   Say who you are ; we then shall know
What hospitable care your needs we owe.
But first I will inform you of my name,
Lest ignorance of that perchance might claim
Exemption from respect, and words be said
Unworthy of the deference and the dread
That here my subjects show me,
Or wanting the due homage that you owe me.
I am the King Egerius,
The worthy lord of this small realm, for thus
I call it being mine ;
Till 'tis the world, my sword shall not resign
Its valorous hope.　　The dress,
Not of a king, but of wild savageness
I wear : to testify,
Thus seeming a wild beast, how wild am I.
No god my worship claims ;
I do not even know the deities' names :
Here they no service nor respect receive ;
To die and to be born is all that we believe.
Now that you know how much you should revere
My royal state, say who you are.
　　PATRICK.　　　　　　　　　　　　Then hear :
Patrick is my name, my country
Ireland, and an humble hamlet,*
Scarcely known to men, called Empthor,†
Is my place of birth : it standeth

---

* The *asonante* in *a—e*, or their vocal equivalents, commences
here, and is continued to the commencement of the speech of Enius,
when it changes to the asonante in *e—e*, which is kept up through
the remainder of the Scene, and to the end of Scene III.

† " Empthor "—see note on this name.

Midway 'twixt the north and west,
On a mountain which is guarded
As a prison by the sea,—
In the island which hereafter
Will be called the Isle of Saints,
To its glory everlasting;
Such a crowd, great lord, therein
Will give up their lives as martyrs
In religious attestation
Of the faith, faith's highest marvel.
Of an Irish cavalier,
And of his chaste spouse and partner,
A French lady, I was born,
Unto whom I owe (oh, happy
That 'twas so !), beyond my birthright
Of nobility, the vantage
Of the Christian faith, the light
Of Christ's true religion granted
In the sacred rite of baptism,
Which a mark indelibly stampeth
On the soul, heaven's gate, as it
Is the sacrament first granted
By the Church.   My pious parents,
Having thus the debt exacted
From all married people paid
By my birth, retired thereafter
To two separate convents, where
In the purity and calmness
Of their chaste abodes they lived,
Till the fatal line of darkness,
Ending life, was reached, and they,
Fortified by every practice
Of the Catholic faith, in peace
Yielded up their souls in gladness,
Unto heaven their spirits giving,
Giving unto earth their ashes.

I, an orphan, then remained
Carefully and kindly guarded
By a very holy matron,
Underneath whose rule I hardly
Had completed one brief lustrum—
Five short years had scarce departed—
Five bright circles of the sun
Wheeling round on golden axles,
Twelve high zodiac signs illuming
And one earthly sphere, when happened
Through me an event that showed
God's omnipotence and marvels;
Since of weakest instruments
God makes use of, to enchance his
Majesty the more, to show
That for what men think the grandest
And most strange effects, to HIM
Should alone the praise be granted.—
It so happened, and Heaven knoweth
That it is not pride, but rather
Pure religious zeal, that men
Should know how the Lord hath acted,
Makes me tell it, that one day
To my doors a blind man rambled,
Gormas was his name, who said,
" God who sends me here commands thee
In His name to give me sight ; "
I, obedient to the mandate,
Made at once the sign of the cross
On his sightless eyes, that started
Into life and light once more
From their state of utter darkness.
At another time when heaven,
Muffled in the thickest, blackest
Clouds, made war upon the world,
Hurling at it lightning lances

Of white snow, which fell so thickly
On a mountain, that soon after
They being melted by the sun,
So filled up our streets and alleys,
So inundated our houses,
That amid the wild waves stranded
They were ships of bricks and stones,
Barks of cement and of plaster.
Who before saw waves on mountains?
Who 'mid woods saw ships at anchor?
I the sign of the cross then made
On the waters, and in accents,
In a tone of grave emotion,
In God's name the waves commanded
To retire : they turned that moment
And left dry the lands they ravaged.
Oh, great God ! who will not praise Thee?
Who will not confess Thee Master?—
Other wonders I could tell you,
But my modesty throws shackles
On my tongue, makes mute my voice,
And my lips seals up and fastens.
I grew up, in fine, inclined
Less to arms than to the marvels
Knowledge can reveal : I gave me
Almost wholly up to master
Sacred Science, to the reading
Of the Lives of Saints, a practice
Which doth teach us faith, hope, zeal,
Charity and Christian manners.
In these studies thus immersed,
I one day approached the margin
Of the sea with some young friends,
Fellow-students and companions,
When a bark drew nigh, from which
Suddenly out-leaping landed

Armed men, fierce pirates they,
Who these seas, these islands, ravaged ;
We at once were captives made,
And in order not to hazard
Losing us their prey, they sailed
Out to sea with swelling canvas.
Of this daring pirate boat
Philip de Roqui was the captain,
In whose breast, for his destruction,
Pride, the poisonous weed, was planted.
He the Irish seas and coast
Having thus for some days ravaged,
Taking property and life,
Pillaging our homes and hamlets ;
But myself alone reserved
To be offered as a vassal,
As a slave to thee, O king !
In thy presence as he fancied.
Oh ! how ignorant is man,
When of God's wise laws regardless,
When, without consulting Him,
He his future projects planneth !
Philip well, at sea, might say so ;
Since to-day, in sight of land here,
Heaven the while being all serene,
Mild the air, the water tranquil,
In an instant, in a moment,
He beheld his proud hopes blasted.
In the hollow-breasted waves
Roared the wind, the sea grew maddened,
Billows upon billows rolled
Mountain high, and wildly dashed them
Wet against the sun, as if
They its light would quench and darken.
The poop-lantern of our ship
Seemed a comet most erratic·· ·

Seemed a moving exhalation,
Or a star from space outstarted ;
At another time it touched
The profoundest deep sea-caverns,
Or the treacherous sands whereon
Ran the stately ship and parted.
Then the fatal waves became
Monuments of alabaster,
Tombs of coral and of pearl.
I (and why this boon was granted
Unto me by Heaven I know not,
Being so useless), with expanded
Arms, struck out, but not alone
My own life to save, nay rather
In the attempt to save this brave
Young man here, that life to barter ;
For I know not by what secret
Instinct towards him I'm attracted ;
And I think he yet will pay me
Back this debt with interest added.
Finally, through Heaven's great pity
We at length have happily landed,
Where my misery may expect it,
Or my better fate may grant it ;
Since we are your slaves and servants,
That being moved by our disasters,
That being softened by our weeping,
Our sore plight may melt your hardness,
Our affliction force your kindness,
And our very pains command you.*

    KING. Silence, miserable Christian,
For my very soul seems fastened
On thy words, compelling me,

---

* See note for some extracts from Montalvan's *Vida y Purgatorio
de San Patricio.*

How I know not, to regard thee
With strange reverence and fear,
Thinking thou must be that vassal—
That poor slave whom in my dream
I beheld outbreathing flashes,
Saw outflashing living fire,
In whose flame, so lithe and lambent,
My Polonia and my Lesbia
Like poor moths were burned to ashes.
    PATRICK. Know, the flame that from my mouth
Issued, is the true Evangel,
Is the doctrine of the Gospel :—
'Tis the word which I'm commanded
Unto thee to preach, O King !
To thy subjects and thy vassals,
To thy daughters, who shall be
Christians through its means.
    KING.   Cease, fasten
Thy presumptuous lips, vile Christian,
For thy words insult and stab me.
    LESBIA.   Stay !
    POLONIA.   And wilt thou in thy pity
Try to save him from his anger?
    LESBIA.   Yes.
    POLONIA.   Forbear, and let him die.
    LESBIA.   Thus to die by a king's hands here
Were unjust.   (It is my pity   [Aside.
For these Christians prompts my answer.)
    POLONIA.   If this second Joseph then,
Like the first one, would unravel,
Would interpret the king's dreams,
Do not dread the result, my father;
For if my being seen to burn
Indicates in any manner
I should ever be a Christian,
As impossible a marvel

Such would be, as if, being dead,
I could rise and live thereafter.
But in order that your mind
May be turned from such just anger,
Let us hear now who this other
Stranger is.

    LUIS.   Then be attentive,
Beautiful divinity,
For my history thus commences :—
Great Egerius, King of Ireland,
I by name am Luis Enius,
And a Christian also, this
Being the sole point of resemblance
Betwixt Patrick and myself,
Yet a difference presenting :
For although we two are Christians,
So distinct and so dissevered
Are we, that not good from evil
Is more opposite in its essence.
Yet for all that, in defence
Of the faith I believe and reverence,
I would lose a thousand lives
(Such the esteem for it I cherish).
Yes, by God !   The oath alone
Shows how firmly I confess Him.
I no pious tales or wonders,
Worked in my behalf by Heaven,
Have to speak of: no ; dark crimes,
Robberies, murders, sacrileges,
Treasons, treacheries, betrayals,
Must I tell instead, however
Vain it be in me to glory
In my having such effected.
I in one of Ireland's many
Isles was born ; the planets seven,
I suspect, in wild abnormal

Interchange of influences,
Must have at my hapless birth-time
All their various gifts presented.
Fickleness the Moon implanted
In my nature ; subtle Hermes
Wit and genius ill-employed ;
(Better ne'er to have possessed them) ;
Wanton Venus gave me passions—
All the flatteries of the senses,
And stern Mars a cruel mind
(Mars and Venus both together
What will they not give ?) ; the Sun
Gave to me an easy temper,
Prone to spend, and when means failed me
Theft and robbery were my helpers ;
Jupiter presumptuous pride,
Thoughts fantastic and unfettered,
Gave me ; Saturn, rage and anger,
Valour and a will determined
On its ends ; and from such causes
Followed the due consequences.
Here from Ireland being banished,
By a cause I do not mention
Through respect to him, my father
Came to Perpignan, and settled
In that Spanish town, when I
Scarce my first ten years had ended,
And when·sixteen came, he died.
May God rest his soul in heaven !—
Orphaned, I remained the prey
Of my passions and my pleasures,
O'er whose tempting plain I ran
Without rein or curb to check me.
The two poles of my existence,
On which all the rest depended
For support, were play and women.

What a base on which to rest me!
Here my tongue would not be able
To acquaint you *in extenso*
With my actions : a brief abstract
May, however, be attempted.
I, to outrage a young maiden,
Stabbed to death a noble elder,
Her own father : for the sake
Of his wife, a most respected
Cavalier I slew, as he
Lay beside her in the helpless
State of sleep, his honour bathing
In his blood, the bed presenting
A sad theatre of crimes,
Murder and adultery blended.
Thus the father and the husband
Life for honour's sake surrendered ;
For even honour has its martyrs.
May God rest their souls in heaven !—
Dreading punishment for this,
I fled hastily, and entered
France, where my exploits, methinks,
Time will cease not to remember ;
For, assisting in the wars
Which at that time were contended
Bravely betwixt France and England,
I took military service
Under Stephen, the French king,
And a fight which chance presented
Showed my courage to be such,
That the king himself, as guerdon
Of my valour, gave to me
The commission of an ensign.
How that debt I soon repaid,
I prefer not now to tell thee.
Back to Perpignan, thus honoured,

I returned, and having entered
Once a guard-house there to play,
For some trifle I lost temper,
Struck a serjeant, killed a captain,
And maimed others there assembled.
At the cries from every quarter
Speedily the watch collected,
And in flying to a church,
As they hurried to prevent me,
I a catch-pole killed.   ('Twas something
One good work to have effected
'Mid so many that were bad.)
May God rest his soul in heaven !—
Far I fled into the country,
And asylum found and shelter
In a convent of religious,
Which was founded in that desert,
Where I lived retired and hidden,
Well taken care of and attended.
For a lady there, a nun,
Was my cousin, which connection
Gave to her the special burden
Of this care.   My heart already
Being a basilisk which turned
All the honey into venom,
Passing swiftly from mere liking
To desire—that monster ever
Feeding on the impossible—
Living fire that with intensest
Fury burns when most opposed —
Flame the wind revives and strengthens,
False, deceitful, treacherous foe
Which doth murder its possessor—
In a word, desire in him,
Who nor God nor law respecteth,
Of the horrible, of the shocking,

s

Thinks but only to attempt it.—
Yes, I dared . . . . But here disturbed,
When, my lord, I this remember,
Mute the voice in horror fails,
Sad the accent faints and trembles,
And as 'mid the night's dark shadows,
The hair stands on end through terror ;
Thus confused, so full of doubt,
Sad remembrance so o'erwhelms me,
That the thing I dared to do
I scarce dare in words to tell thee.
For, in fine, my crime is such,
So to be abhorred, detested,
So profane, so sacrilegious
(Strange upon thee so to press it),
That for having such committed
I at times feel some repentance.
Well, in fine, I dared one night,
When deep silence had erected
Sepulchres of fleeting sleep
For men's overwearied senses,
When a dark and cloudy veil
Heaven had o'er its face extended—
Mourning which the wind assumed
For the sun whose life had ended—
In whose obsequies the night-birds
Swan-notes sang instead of verses,
And when back from waves of sapphire,
Where their beauty was reflected,
The clear stars a second time
Trembling lights to heaven presented :—
Well, on such a night, by climbing
O'er the garden wall, I entered
With the assistance of two friends
(For when such things are attempted
An associate never fails),

And in horror and in terror,
Seeking in the dark my death,
Reached at length the cell (I tremble
To remember it) in which
Was my cousin, whom respectful
Silence bids me not to name,
Though all self-respect has left me.
Frightened at such nameless horror,
On the hard floor she fell senseless,
Whence she passed into my arms,
And ere she regained her senses,
She already was outside
Her asylum, in a desert,
When if heaven possessed the power,
It had not the will to help her.
Women, when they are persuaded
That the wildest of excesses
Are the effects of love, forgive them
Easily; and, therefore, pleasure
Following tears, some consolation
In her miseries was effected;
Though, in fact, they were so great,
That united in one person
She saw violence, violation,
Incest, nay, adultery even,
Against God who was her spouse,
And a sacrilege most dreadful.
Finally we left that place,
Being carried to Valencia
By two steeds that well might claim
From the winds to be descended:
Feigning that she was my wife,
But with little peace we dwelt there;
For I quickly having squandered
Whatsoever little treasure
I brought with me, without friends,

Without any hope of help there,
In my dire distress appealed
To the beauty still so perfect
Of my poor pretended wife :
If for aught I did I ever
Could feel shame, this act alone
Would most surely overwhelm me ;
Since it is the lowest baseness
That the vilest breast descends to,
To put up to sale one's honour,
And to trade in love's caresses.
Scarce with shameless front had I
This base plan to her suggested,
When concealing her design
She gave seeming acquiescence ;
But I scarce had turned my back,
Hardly had I left her presence,
When she, flying from me, found
Grace a convent's walls to enter.
There, a holy monk advising,
She a saving port and shelter
Found against the world's wild storms,
And there died, her sin, her penance,
Giving all a great example ;
May God rest her soul in heaven !—
Seeing that the narrow world
Now took note of my offences,
And that soon the very land
Might reject me, I determined
To re-seek my native country ;
For at least I there expected
To be safer from my foes,
In a place so long my centre
And my home.   The way I took
And to Ireland came, which welcomed
Me at first as would a mother,

But a step-mother resembled
Before long, for seeking a passage
Where a harbour lay protected
By a mole, I found that corsairs
Lay concealed within the shelter
Of a little creek which hid
Out of view their well-armed vessel.
And of these, their captain, Philip,
Took me prisoner, after efforts
Made in my defence so brave,
That in deference to the mettle
I displayed, my life he spared.
What ensued you know already,
How the wind in sudden anger
Rising into raging tempest,
Now chastised us in its pride,
Now our lives more cruelly threatened,
Making in the seas and mountains
Such wild ruin and resemblance,
That to mock the mountain's pride
Waves still mightier forms presented,
Which with catapults of crystal
Made the cliffs' foundations tremble,
So that neighbouring cities fell,
And the sea, in scornful temper,
Gathering up from its abysses
The munition it collecteth,
Fired upon the land its pearls
In their shells, wherein engendered
By the swift breath of the morning
In its dew, they shine resplendent
Tears of ice and fire ; in fine,
Not in pictures so imperfect
All our time to waste, the crew
Went to sup in the infernal
Halls themselves ; I, too, a guest

Would have equally attended
With them, if this Patrick, here,
Whom I know not why I reverence,
Looking with respect and fear
On his beauteous countenance ever,
Had not drawn me from the sea,
Where, exhausted, sinking, helpless,
I drank death in every draught,
Agony in each salt wave's venom.
This my history is, and now
I wish neither life nor mercy,
Neither that my pains should move thee,
Nor my asking should compel thee,
Save in this, to give me death,
That thus may the life be ended
Of a man who is so bad,
That he scarcely can be better.*

    KING.   Luis, though thou art a Christian,
Which by me is most detested,
Yet I so admire thy courage
That I wish, before all present,
Between thee and him to show
How my power can be exerted,
How it punishes as rewards,
How it elevates and depresses.
And so thus my arms I give thee,
That within them thus extended
Thou may'st reach my heart; to thee
Thus beneath my feet to tread thee;
      [*He throws* PATRICK *on the ground and places
        his foot upon him.*
The two actions signifying
How the heavier scale descendeth.
And that, Patrick, thou may'st see

---

* See note as to Montalvan's invention of this story.

How I value or give credit
To thy threats, thy life I spare.
Vomit forth the flame incessant
Of the so-called word of God,
That by this thou may'st be certain
I do not adore his Godship,
Nor his miracles have dread of.
Live then; but in such a state
Of poor, mean, and abject service,
As befits a useless hind
In the fields; and so as shepherd
I would have thee guard my flocks,
Which are in these vales collected.
Let us see, if for the purpose
Of this mystic fire outspreading,
Being my slave, thy God will free thee
From captivity and thy fetters.   [*Exit.*

    LESBIA.   Patrick moves my heart to pity.   [*Exit.*

    POLONIA.   Not so mine, for none I cherish.
Had I any, none would move me
Sooner than this Luis Enius.*   [*Exit.*

---

* It is difficult to account for Calderon giving the name of
" Egerio " to the King of Ireland, when he bestows the proper one
—" Leogaire "—on an inferior character.   The name of the King of
Ireland at the time of St. Patrick's mission is given correctly by
Montalvan.   " Era Rey de aquella, y de otras islas comarcanas
Leogario, hijo de Neil."—Cap. I., p. 19, ed. 1628.   Calderon had to
invent names for the king's daughters, as he did not find them in
Montalvan.   In the Book of Armagh they are called " Ethne the
fair " and " Fedelm the ruddy."—*Todd*, p. 451.   Miss Cusack gives
the names " Ethna " and " Fethlema."—*Life of St. Patrick*, p. 291.
Of their baptism, the distinguished poet to whom this drama is dedi-
cated, has thus sung : —

> " They knelt : on their heads the wave he poured
> Thrice, in the name of the Triune Lord :
> And their foreheads he signed with the Sign adored.
> On Fedelm the ' Red Rose,' on Ethna ' The Fair,'
> God's dew shone bright in that morning air."
>
>   AUBREY DE VERE'S *Legends of St. Patrick.*

SCENE III.

PATRICK *and* LUIS.

PATRICK.   Luis, though a low position
Mine is here, and I observe thee
Raised to fortune's highest summit,
Yet I feel more grief than envy
At thy rise.   Thou art a Christian ;
Show thyself one now in earnest.
   LUIS.   Patrick, let me now enjoy
The first favours fate has sent me
After so much sad misfortune.
   PATRICK.   One word, then (if thou wilt let me
So presume), I ask of thee.
   LUIS.   What is that?
   PATRICK.   Upon this earth here,
Once again, alive or dead,
That we two shall meet together.
   LUIS.   Such a word dost ask me?
   PATRICK.   Yes.
   LUIS.   Then I give it.
   PATRICK.   I accept it.   [*Exeunt.*

SCENE IV.

A HAMLET NEAR THE COURT OF EGERIUS.

PHILIP *and* LUCY.

LUCY.   Pardon, if I have not known
How to serve you as I ought.
   PHILIP.   For much more than you have thought
Must you my forgiveness own.

For when I your kind face view,
Pain and pleasure being at war,
I have much to thank you for,
And have much to pardon too.
Thanks, with which my heart is rife,
Are for life restored and breath;
Pardon, for you give me death,
As before you gave me life.
    Lucy.   For such flattering declarations
Rude and ignorant am I,
So my arms will give reply;
Which gets rid of explanations.
Let their silent interlacing
Figure what my words should be.

Scene V.

Paul.—The Same.

    Paul (*aside*). Eh, sirs ! what is this I see ?
Some one here my wife's embracing.
What's to do ?   I burn, I burst.
Kill her ?   Yes.   'Twas fortune sent me.
One thing only doth prevent me,
Which is, she might kill me first.
    Philip.   For your hospitable care,
Beauteous mountaineer, I would
That this ring's bright diamond could
Far outshine a star of air.
    Lucy.   Think me not a woman who
Lives intent her gain to make;
But I take it for your sake.
    Paul (*aside*). What I wonder should I do ?

But if I'm her husband, then,
As I saw him give the ring,
Silence is the proper thing.
   Lucy.   In these arms I once again
Give to you my soul, for I
Have no other ring or chain.
   Philip.   Where I ever could remain :—
For such sweet captivity
Lures me from the miseries
Of remembering my sad fate,
Caused, as you have seen, so late,
By these crystalline blue seas.
   Paul (*aside*). What ! a new embrace !   Halloo !
Don't you see, sir, Od's my life,
That this woman is my wife ?
   Philip.   Here's your husband full in view ;
He has seen us.   I must straight
Leave you and return-—Ah, me !   [*Aside.*
Couldst thou this, Polonia, see,
Thou mightst mourn, perhaps, the state
Unto which I see me doomed.
And, O heaven-aspiring sea,
Say in what vast depths can be
All the lives thou hast entombed ?   [*Exit.*

Scene VI.

Paul *and* Lucy ; *afterwards* Philip.

   Paul (*aside*). As he's gone, I'll louder speak.—
This time, Lucy mine, I've caught you,
So a present I have brought you :
See this window-bar, 'twill wreak
My revenge.

LUCY.   Oh, how malicious !
Bless me, grumbler, what grimaces !
    PAUL.   Then, to witness two embraces
Does not look at all suspicious ?—
Was it malice, then, in me,
Not plain seeing ?
    LUCY.   Malice merely :
For a husband, how so nearly
He may pry, should never see
More than half his wife doth do.
    PAUL.,   Well, with that I'm quite content,
To that condition I assent,
And since twice embraced by you
Has that rascal soldier been,
Whom the sea spewed out in spite,
I will juggle with my sight,
And pretend but once to have seen ;
And as I for two embraces
Meant to give a hundred blows,
I but fifty now propose
For one half of my disgraces.
I have totted up the score ;
You yourself the sentence gave ;
Yes, by God I swear, you'll have
Fifty strokes and not one more.
    LUCY.   I've admitted far too much.
For a husband it would be
Quite preposterous ; he should see
But the quarter.
    PAUL.   Even as such
I acknowledge the appeal.
Patience, and your back prepare,
For the now admitted share,
Five-and-twenty blows you'll feel.
    LUCY.   No, not so ; you're still astray.
    PAUL.   Then say what ?

LUCY.　　　　　　　　Between us two,
You're to trust not what you view,
But what I am pleased to say.
　　PAUL.　Better far, I think, 'twould be,
Daughter of the devil, that you
Held the stick and used it too,
With it well belabouring me ;
Is't agreed what I propose ?
Yes ; then let us both change places.
Give to him the two embraces,
And to me the hundred blows.

　　　　　PHILIP *returns*.

　　PHILIP (*aside*). Has the peasant gone, I wonder ?
　　PAUL.　At the nick of time you're here,
So, Sir Soldier, lend an ear.
Obligation I am under
For the favours you have meant
To bestow so liberally
On my cot, my wife, and me ;
And although I'm well content
With you, yet as you're progressing
Day by day and getting stronger,
It is best you stay no longer.
Take the road, then, with God's blessing,
Leave my house, for it would be
Sad in it to raise my hand,
Leaving you dead flesh on land
Who wert living fish at sea.
　　PHILIP.　The suspicion that you show
Is quite groundless, do not doubt it.
　　PAUL.　Zounds ! with reason or without it,
Am I married, sir, or no ?

SCENE VII.

LEOGAIRE, *an* Old Peasant, *and* PATRICK.

LEOGAIRE.   So 'tis ordered, and that he
Serving here from day to day,
In the open field should stay.
    OLD MAN.   Yes ; I say it so shall be.
    LEOGAIRE.   But who's this?   O happiness !
Since 'tis Philip's form I greet.
Mighty lord, I kiss thy feet.
    PAUL.   Mighty lord does he call him ?
    LUCY.   Yes.
Now lay on the blows you owe.
Now, friend Paul, the moment charms.
    PHILIP.   Give me, good Leogaire, your arms.
    LEOGAIRE.   Honour in them you bestow.
Is it possible, once more
That alive I see thee ?
    PHILIP.   Here,
Trophy of a fate severe,
The sea flung me on this shore,
Where, their willing aid secured,
I have lived these peasants' guest,
Till I could repair with rest
All the sufferings I endured.
And, besides, I thought with dread
On the angry disposition
Of the king : for his ambition
When has it or bowed the head,
Or with patience heard related
The sad tragedies of fate ?
Hopeless and disconsolate
In this solitude I've waited,
Till some happy chance might rise

When no longer I should grieve,
And the king would give me leave
To appear before his eyes.
    LEOGAIRE.   That already has been given thee;
For so sad was he, believing
Thou wert dead, so deep his grieving,
All the past will be forgiven thee
Since thou livest.   Come with me,
Fortune will once more embrace thee,—
In his favour to replace thee
Let my happy privilege be.
    PAUL.   For that late unseemly brawl
See me humbly bending low ;
You, my lord Prince Philip, know
That I am one Juan Paul.
My suspicion and abuse
Pray forgive, your majesty,
Think that what I said to thee
Was but cackled by a goose.
At your service, night and day,
Are whatever goods I've got—
Lucy here, myself and cot ;
And God bless us all, I pray.
    PHILIP.   For your hospitality
I am grateful, and I trust
To repay it.
    PAUL.   If you must,
Let the first instalment be
Just to take my wife away.
Thus you will reward us two :
She'll be glad to go with you,
I, without her, glad to stay.
                [*Exeunt* PHILIP *and* LEOGAIRE.
    LUCY (*aside*). Was there ever love so vain
As is mine, a brief caress
Cradled in forgetfulness ?

OLD MAN.   Juan Paul, as we remain
Here alone, 'twere well to greet
As a friend this labourer,
Newly sent us.
PATRICK.   Nay, good sir,
I'm a slave, and I entreat
That as such you understand me ;
I, the lowest of the low,
Hither come to serve, and so
I implore that you command me
As a slave, since I am one.
OLD MAN.   Oh, what modesty !
PAUL.   What humility !
LUCY.   What good looks, too, and gentility !
I, in truth, can't help being drawn
By his face.
PAUL.   Came ever here
(This is quite between us two)
Any wandering stranger who
Did not draw you so, my dear ?
Eh, my Lucy ?
LUCY.   Boorish, base,
Is your vile insinuation
'Gainst my innocent inclination
For the whole of the human race !   [*Exit.*
OLD MAN.   To your sharpness and good will,
Paul, I trust a thing that may
Cost my life.
PAUL.   Then don't delay.
Tell it, since you know my skill.
OLD MAN.   This new slave that here you see,
I suspect is not secure,
And I hasten to procure
Means by which he more may be.
For the present I confide him
To your care, by day or night

Let him not escape your sight,
Ever watchful keep beside him.   [*Exit.*

Scene VIII.

Patrick *and* Paul.

Paul (*aside*). I'm to keep what you discarded !
Good in faith !—Behold in me   [*To* Patrick.
Your strict guard ; in you I see
The sole thing I ever guarded
In my life ; with such a care
I can neither sleep nor eat.
If you wish to use your feet
You can go, your road lies there.
Nay, in flying quickly hence
You to me a good will do,
Since my care will fly with you.
Go in peace.
        Patrick.   With confidence
You may trust me, for I'm not,
Though a slave, a fugitive.
Lord ! how gladly do I live
In this solitary spot,
Where my soul in raptured prayer
May adore Thee, or in trance
See the living countenance
Of Thy prodigies so rare !
Human wisdom, earthly lore,
Solitude reveals and reaches ;
What diviner wisdom teaches
In it, too, I would explore.
        Paul.   Tell me, talking thus apart,
Who it is on whom you call ?

PATRICK.   Great primeval cause of all,
Thou, O Lord, in all things art !
These blue heavens, these crystal skies
Formed of dazzling depths of light,
In which sun, moon, stars unite,
Are they not but draperies
Hung before Thy heavenly land ?—
The discordant elements,
Water, fire, earth, air immense,
Prove they not Thy master hand ?
Or in dark or brightsome hours,
Praise they not Thy power and might ?
O'er the earth dost Thou not write
In the characters of flowers
Thy great goodness ?   And the air,
In reverberating thunder,
Does it not in fear and wonder
Say, O Lord, that Thou art there ?
Are not, too, Thy praises sung
By the fire and water—each
Dowered for this divinest speech,
With tongue the wave, the flame with tŏngue ?
Here, then, in this lonely place
I, O Lord, may better be,
Since in all things I find Thee.
Thou hast given to me the grace
Of Obedience, Faith, and Fear ;
As a slave, then, let me stay,
Or remove me where I may
Serve Thee truly, if not here.*

    [An Angel *descends, holding in one hand a shield
       in which is a mirror, and in the other hand
       a letter.*

---

* For the earlier version of this prayer, see Note.

SCENE IX.

An Angel.—THE SAME.

ANGEL.   Patrick !
PATRICK.   Ah ! who calls me ?
PAUL.   Why,
No one calls.   (*Aside.*) The man is daft,
Poetry should be his craft.
ANGEL.   Patrick !
PATRICK.   Ah ! who calls me ?
ANGEL.   I.
PAUL (*aside*). Who he speaks to, I can't see.
Well, to stop his speech were hard,
I'm not here his mouth to guard.   [*Exit.*

SCENE X.

The Angel *and* PATRICK.

PATRICK.   Ah ! it cannot be to me
Comes such glory !   For, behold !
Pearl and rosy dawn in one,
Shines a cloud, from which its sun
Breaks in crimson and in gold !
Living stars its robe adorning,
Rose and jasmine sweetly blended,
Dazzling comes that vision splendid,
Scattering purple pomps of morning.
ANGEL.   Patrick !
PATRICK.   Sunlight strikes me blind !
Heavenly Lord, who canst thou be ?

ANGEL.   I am Victor, whom to thee
God thy angel-guard assigned :
With this scroll, to give it thee
I am sent.   [*Gives him the letter.*
    PATRICK.   Sweet messenger,
Paranymph of all things fair,
Who amidst the hierarchy
Of the highest hosts of heaven
Singest in melodious tone—
" Glory unto Thee alone,
Holy, Holy Lord, be given ! "
    ANGEL.   Read the letter.
    PATRICK.   With amaze,
I see here " To Patrick " Oh,
Can a slave be honoured so ?
    ANGEL.   Open it.
    PATRICK.   It also says—
" Patrick ! Patrick ! hither come,   [*Reads.*
Free us from our slavery !"—
More it means than I can see,
Since I do not know by whom
I am called.   Oh, faithful guide,
Speedily dispel my error !
    ANGEL.   Look into this shining mirror.
    PATRICK.   Heavens !
    ANGEL.   What seest thou inside ?
    PATRICK.   Numerous people there seem thronging,
Old men, children, women, who
Seem to call me.
    ANGEL.   Nor do you
Stay, but satisfy their longing.
You behold the Irish nation,
Who expect to hear God's truth
From your lips.   Oh, chosen youth,
Leave your slavery.   The vocation
God has given thee is to sow

Faith o'er all the Irish soil.
There as Legate thou shalt toil,
Ireland's great Apostle.   Go
First to France, to German's home,
The good bishop : there thou'lt make
Thy profession : there thou'lt take
The monk's habit, and to Rome
Pass, where letters thou'lt procure
For that mighty work of thine,
In the bulls of Celestine :
Thou wilt visit, then, in Tours
Martin, the great bishop there.
Now upborne upon the wind
Come with me, for thou wilt find
God has given with prescient care
His commands to all, that so
Fitly thy great work be done ;
But 'tis time we should be gone :
Let us on our journey go.   [*They disappear.*

ACT THE SECOND.

HALL OF A TOWER IN THE PALACE OF EGERIUS.

SCENE I.

LUIS *and* POLONIA

LUIS.   Yes, Polonia, yes, for he
Who betrays inconstancy
Has no reason for complaining
That another love is gaining
On his own ; that fault will be
Ever punished so.   For who
Proudly soars that doth not fall?
Therefore 'tis that I forestall
Philip's love howe'er so true.
He is nobler to the view,
As one nobly born may be ;
But in that nobility,
Which one's self can win and wear,
I with justice may declare
I am nobler far than he ;
I more honour have obtained
Than on Philip's cradle rained :
Let the fact excuse the boast,
For this land from coast to coast
Rings with victories I have gained.
Three years is it since I came
To these isles (it seems a day);
Three swift years have rolled away
Since I made it my chief aim
Thee to serve—my highest fame.
Trophies numerous as the sand,
Mars might envy, has my hand

Won for thy great sire and thee—
Being the wonder of the sea,
And th' amazement of the land.
    POLONIA.   Luis, yes, thy gallant bearing,
Or inherited or acquired,
Has within my breast inspired
A strange fear, a certain daring,—
Ah, I know not if, declaring
This, 'tis love, for blushes rise
At perceiving with surprise
That at last hath come the hour,
When my heart must own the power
Of a deity I despise.
This alone I'll say, that here
Long thy hope had been fruition,
But that I the disposition
Of the king, my father, fear,
But still hope and persevere.

SCENE II.

PHILIP.—THE SAME.

    PHILIP (*aside*). If to find my death I come,
Why precipitate my doom?
But so patient who could be
As to not desire to see
What impends, how dark its gloom?
    LUIS.   Then, what pledge may I demand
Of your faith?
    POLONIA.   This hand.
    PHILIP.   Not so,
How to hinder it I shall know;
More of this I must withstand.

POLONIA.   Woe is me !

PHILIP.   Wilt give thy hand
To this outcast of the wave ?
And, oh thou, to whom pride gave
The presumption to aspire
To a sun's celestial fire,
Knowing that thou wert my slave,
Why thus dare to come between
Me and mine ?

LUIS.   Because I dare
Be what now I am, nor care
More to be what I have been.
It is true that I was seen
Once your slave : for who, indeed,
Can the fickle wheel control ?
But in nobleness of soul
The best blood of all your breed
I can equal, nay, exceed.

PHILIP.   Exceed *me ?*   Vile homicide !
Wretch . . . .

LUIS.   In having thus replied
You have made a slight mistake.

PHILIP.   No.

LUIS.   If such you did not make,
You've done worse.

PHILIP.   Say, what ?

LUIS.   You've lied !

PHILIP.   Villain ! traitor !

                              [*Strikes him in the face.*

POLONIA.   Oh, ye skies !

LUIS.   For so many injuries
Why not instant vengeance take,
When volcanic fires awake
In my breast, and hell-flames rise ?

                              [*They draw their swords.*

SCENE III.

 EGERIUS *and* SOLDIERS.—THE SAME.

KING.　　What is this?
LUIS.　　　　　　　　A lasting woe,
A misfortune, an abuse,
A sharp pain, a fiend let loose
From the infernal pit below.
Let no one presume to go
'Twixt me and revenge.　Reflect,
Fury breathes immortal breath,
Vengeance has no fear of death,
Nor for any man respect.
I my honour must protect.
　KING.　Seize him.
　LUIS.　　　　　　Let the man who sighs
For his death obey!　You'll see
How the boldest fares, for he,
Even before your very eyes,
Shall be slain.
　KING.　　　　That this should rise!—
Follow him.
　LUIS.　　　In desperate mood,
Plunging headlong in red blood,
Like a sea both wide and deep,
Thus courageously I leap,
Seeking Philip through the flood.

[All enter fighting.

Scene IV.

KING.   I but wanted this alone
After what I've heard, that he
Who escaped from slavery,
And to distant Rome had flown,
Now with purpose too well known,
Has to Ireland come again,
Where proclaiming the new reign
Of the faith, he has enticed
Many to believe in Christ,
Rending all the world in twain.
A magician he must be,
Since condemned, so rumour saith,
By some other kings to death,
He though tied upon the tree
In an instant set him free,
With such prodigies of wonder
That the earth (within whose womb
The dead lie as in a tomb)
Trembled, the air groaned in thunder,
Dark eclipse the sun lay under,
Deigning not a single glance
Of his radiant countenance
To the moon : from which I see
That this Patrick, for 'tis he,
Lords it over fate and chance ;
Awe-struck by the prodigy,
Fearing they may punished be,
Crowds attend him on his way.
And 'tis said that he to-day
Comes to try his spells on me.
Let him come, and once for all
Wave in vain his conjuring rod !

We shall see who is this God,
Whom their God the Christians call.
By my hand must Patrick fall,
Were it but to see if he
Can escape his destiny,
Or my will subvert and master,
He this Bishop, he this Pastor,
He Pope's Legate, though he be.

SCENE V.

The Captain, Soldiers, LUIS *a prisoner*, The King.

CAPTAIN.   Luis, sire, without delay
We secured; but not before
He killed three, and wounded more,
Of our company.
KING.   Christian, say,
Why do you no fear display,
Seeing now in angry mood
My hand raised to shed your blood?
But in vain do I deplore,
Since he this deserves and more
Who has done a Christian good.
Gifts, not chastisement, should be
Thine to-day, for it is plain
It is I should feel the pain
For conferring good on thee.
Take him hence, and presently
Let him die; and be it known
Why from him has mercy flown.
'Tis not for his crimes or guilt
That this Christian's blood is spilt,
'Tis for Christ's belief alone.   [*Exeunt.*

SCENE VI.

LUIS.

LUIS.   If for this I die, to me
Thou the happiest death allottest,
Since he for his God will die,
He who dies to do Him honour.
And a man whose life is here
But a round of cares and crosses,
Should be grateful unto death
As the end of all his sorrows;
Since it comes the tangled thread
Of a wretched life to shorten,
Which to-day the evil Phœnix
Of its works that now prove mortal
Would revive amid the ashes
Of my wrong and my dishonour.
Then my life, my breath were poison,
Venom would my breast but foster,
Until I had shed in Ireland
Blood in such a copious torrent,
That though base it might wash out
The remembrance of my wronger.
Ah, my honour, low thou liest,
By a ruthless foot down trodden!—
I will die with thee, united
We two will together conquer
These barbarians.   Then since little,
But a span at best, belongeth
To my life, a noble vengeance
Let this dagger take upon me!—
But, good God! what evil impulse
With demoniac instinct prompteth
Thus my hand?   I am a Christian,

I've a soul, and share the godly
Light of faith : then were it right,
'Mid a crowd of Gentile mockers,
Thus the Christian faith to tarnish
By an action so improper ?
What example would I give them
By a death so sad and shocking,
Save that I thus gave the lie
To the works that Patrick worketh.
Since they'd say, who worship only
Their own vices most immodest,
Who deny unto the soul
Its eternal joy or torment,
" Of what use is Patrick's preaching
That man's soul must be immortal,
If the Christian, Luis Enius,
Kills himself?   He can't acknowledge
Its eternal life who'd lose it."—
Thus with actions so discordant,
He the light and I the shadow,
We would neutralize each other.
'Tis enough to be so wicked
As even now to feel no sorrow,
No repentance for past sins,
Rather a desire for others.
Yes, by God ! for if escape
Fortune now my life would offer,
Europe, Africa, and Asia
I would fill with fear and horror ;
First exacting here the debt
Of a vengeance so enormous,
That these islands of Egerius
Would not hold a single mortal
Who should not appease the thirst,
The insatiable longing
That I have for blood.   The lightning,

When it bursts its prison portals,
Warns us in a voice of thunder,
And then 'twixt dark smoke and forkéd
Fires that take the shape of serpents,
Fills the trembling air with horror.
I, too, gave that thunder voice,
So that all men heard the promise,
But the lightning bolt was wanting.
Yes, ah me! it proved abortive,
And before it touched the earth
Was by dallying winds made sport of.
No, it is not death that grieves me,
Even a death of such dishonour,
'Tis because at last are ended,
In my youth's fresh opening blossom,
My offences.   Life I wish for
To begin from this day forward
Greater and more dread excesses.
Heavens ! 'tis for no other object.

SCENE VII.

POLONIA.—LUIS.

POLONIA (*aside*). (Now with mind made up I come.)
Luis, an occasion offers
Ever as the test and touchstone
Of true love.   By certain knowledge
Have I learned the imminent danger
Of thy life.   The wrath grows hotter
Of my father, and his fury
To evade is most important.
All the guards that here are with thee
Has my liberal hand subornéd,
So that at the clink of gold
Have their ears grown deaf and torpid.

Fly ! and that thou mayest see
How a woman's heart can prompt her,
How her honour she can trample,
How her self-respect leave prostrate,
With thee I will go, since now
It is needful that henceforward
I in life and death am thine,
For without thee life were worthless,
Thou who in my heart dost live.
I bring with me gems and money
Quite enough to the most distant
Parts of India to transport us,
Where the sun with beams and shadows
Scatters frost, or burning scorches.
At the door two steeds are standing,
I should rather call these horses
Two swift lynxes, air-born creatures,
Thoughts by liveliest minds begotten ;
They so rapid are, that though
We as fugitives fly on them,
An assurance of our safety
We shall feel.   At once resolve then.
Why thus ponder ? what delays thee ?
Time is pressing, therefore shorten
All discourse ; and that mischance,
Which disturbs love's plans so often,
May not offer an obstruction
To so well-prepared a project,
First before thee I will go.
Issue, while in specious converse
I divert thy guards, and give
To thy coming forth a cover.
Even the sun our project favours,
Which amid the west waves yonder,
Sinking, dips his golden curls
To refresh his glowing forehead.   [*Exit.*

Scene VIII.

Luis.

Luis.   A most opportune occasion
To my hands has fortune offered ;
Since Heaven knows that all the show
Of apparent love and fondness
Which I proffered to Polonia
Was assumed, it being my object
She should go with me, where I,
Seizing on the gold and costly
Gems she carries, so might issue
From this Babylonian bondage.
For although in it my person
Was esteemed and duly honoured,
Still 'twas slavery after all,
And my free wild life was longing
For that liberty, heaven's best gift,
Which I had enjoyed so often.
But a great embarrassment
And a hindrance were a woman
For the end I have in view,
Since in me is love a folly
That ne'er passes appetite,
Which being satisfied, no longer
Care I for a woman's presence,
How so fair or so accomplished.
And since thus my disposition
Is so free, of what importance
Is a murder more or less ?
At my hands must die Polonia
For her loving at a time
When there's no one loved or honoured.

Had she loved as others love,
Then she would have lived as others.   [*Exit.*

SCENE IX.

The Captain ; *then* The King, PHILIP, *and* LEOGAIRE.

CAPTAIN.   The sad sentence of his death
Have I come, by the king's orders,
Here to read to Luis Enius.—
But what's this ?   The door lies open,
And the tower deserted.   Ha !
Soldiers !   No one answers.   Ho, there !
Guards, come hither, treason! treason !
            [*Enter* The King, PHILIP, *and* LEOGAIRE.
KING.   Why these outcries? this commotion ?
What is this ?
CAPTAIN.   That Luis Enius
Has escaped, and from the fortress
All the guards have fled.
LEOGAIRE.   My lord,
I saw entering here Polonia.
PHILIP.   Heavens ! beyond all doubt 'twas she
Who released him.   That her lover
He dared call him, you well know.
Jealousy and rage provoke me
To pursue them.   A new Troy
Will to-day be Ireland's story.   [*Exit.*
KING.   Give me, too, a horse ; in person
I these fugitives will follow.
Ah, what Christians are these two
Who with actions so discordant,
One deprives me of my rest,
And the other robs my honour ?

But the twain shall feel the weight
Of my vengeful hands fall on them ;
For not safe from me would be
Even their sovereign Roman Pontiff.   [*Exeunt.*

Scene X.

A WOOD, AT WHOSE EXTREMITY IS PAUL'S CABIN.

Polonia *flying wounded, and* Luis *with a naked dagger in
his hand.*

Polonia.   Oh, hold thy bloody hand !
Though love be dead, let Christian faith command.
My honour take ; but, oh, my poor life spare,
That suppliant at thy feet pours out its humble prayer.
     Luis.   Hapless Polonia, since creation's hour
Beauty has ever one unvarying dower,
It brings misfortune with it, it is this
Makes beauty rarely live long time with bliss.
I, who less pity feel
Than any headsman who e'er held death's steel,
May by thy death procure
My life, since with it I will go secure.
If thee I bring where fortune's hand may guide me
I bring the witness of my woes beside me,
By whom they may pursue me,
Track me, discover me, in fact, undo me.
If here I leave thee living,
I leave thee angry, vengeful, unforgiving ;
Leave thee, in fact, to be
One enemy more (and what an enemy !) ;
Thus equally I grieve thee,
Thus evil do whether I take or leave thee ;
And so 'tis better thus,

That I a wretch, cruel and infamous,
False, impious, fierce, abandoned, wicked, banned
By God and man, should slay thee by my hand,
Since buried here,
Within the rustic entrails dark and drear
Of this rude realm of stone,
My worst misfortune shall remain unknown.
My fury, too, shall gain
A novel kind of vengeance when thou'rt slain,
Remaining satisfied
That Philip, too, by the same stroke has died,
If in thy heart he lived ; and then mine ire
Will need no victim more except thy sire.
Through thee first came
My first disgrace, the cause of all my shame,
And so the first of all
On thee my vengeful strokes shall furious fall.

    POLONIA.   Ah me ! my fate pursuing,
I have but only worked my own undoing,
Like to the worm that by its subtle art
Spins its own grave.   Hast thou a human heart?

    LUIS.   I am a demon.   So to prove it, die.
Thus——

    POLONIA.   God of Patrick, listen to my cry !
        [*He stabs her several times, and she falls within.*

    LUIS.   She fell on flowers, there sowing
Both lives and horrors in her blood outflowing.
Thus now with greater ease
I can escape, and carry o'er the seas,
In many a gem and chain,
Treasure enough to make me rich in Spain,
Until so changed by time,
Disguised by wandering in a foreign clime,
I may return to reap
My vengeance ; for a wrong doth never sleep.
But whither do I stray,

Treading the shades of death in this dark way?
My path is lost : I go
Whither I do not know ;
Perchance escaping from my prison bands
To fall again into my tyrant's hands.
If the dark night doth not my sight deceive,
Yonder a rustic cabin I perceive.
Yes, I am right.   I'll knock ; I can't much err,
They'll know the way.   [*He knocks.*

SCENE XI.

PAUL *and* LUCY.—LUIS.

LUCY (*within*).   Who's there ?
LUIS.   A traveller,
Benighted, his way lost, confused, distressed,
Good worthy husbandman, disturbs thy rest.
   LUCY (*within*). Ho, Juan ! how you snore !
Awake ! there's some one knocking at the door.
   PAUL (*within*). Why, I am well enough here in my bed.
He knocks for you, so answer him instead.
   LUCY (*within*). Who's there ?
LUIS.   A traveller, I say.
PAUL (*within*). A traveller?
LUIS.   Yes.
PAUL (*within*).   Then travel on, I pray.
This cabin is no inn, sir, not a bit.
   LUIS.   I'm getting weary of this fellow's wit.
I'll try what kicking in the door will do.
Ay, there it goes.   [*Drives in the door.*
   LUCY (*within*).   Why, Juan Paul, halloo !
Awake, I say, for if I don't mistake,
The door's knocked in.

PAUL (*within*).   Well, one eye is awake,
But underneath its lid the other's laid.—
Come with me, Lucy, for I'm sore afraid.

Enter PAUL *and* LUCY.

Who's there?
    LUIS.   Be silent, peasants, and attend
If you would not that now your lives should end.
Lost in this woodland waste
I sought your door; and so, my friend, make haste
To tell me the best way
From this to the port, where I by break of day
May from the coast get clear.
    PAUL.   Go right ahead : first take the pathway here,
Then left, then right again, .
Rise where there's hill, descend where there's a plain,
And going thus, in short,
The port you'll reach when you have reached the port.
    LUIS.   'Tis better that you come
Along with me, or by the heavens o'erhead,
Your blood shall stain the ground on which you tread.
    LUCY.   Were it not better, cavalier,
To pass the night here till the dawn appear ?
    PAUL.   How very kind you are when least expected !
Are you already to this knight infected?
    LUIS.   Choose now, at once, I say,
To die or guide me.
    PAUL.   Don't be vexed, I pray ;
If I without more haggling or vain clack
Select to go, and carry you on my back,
If so you chose, 'tis not that death I fear,
But just to disappoint my Lucy here.
    LUIS (*aside*).   That he may not betray
Whither I go, to those who track my way,
Him from some cliff I'll throw
Headlong amid the icy waves below.—

You with this consolation here remain, [*To* Lucy.
Your husband will be with you soon again.
    [*Exeunt the two at one side, and she at the other.*

Scene XII.

The King Egerius, Lesbia, Leogaire, The Captain ;
afterwards Philip.

Lesbia.   Not a trace of them is found ;
All the mountain, hill and valley,
Leaf by leaf has been explored,
Bough by bough has been examined,
Rock by rock has been searched through,
Still no clue wherewith to track them
Can we light on.
   King.   Without doubt,
To preserve them from my anger,
Has the earth engulphed the two ;
For not heaven itself could guard them
From my wrath if still they lived.
   Lesbia.   See the sun his disentangled
Golden tresses far extends
Over mountains, groves and gardens,
Showing that the day hath come.

Enter Philip.

Philip.   Deign, your majesty, to hearken
To a tragedy more dreadful,
To a crime more unexampled
Than has time or fortune ever
Yet recorded in earth's annals.
Seeking traces of Polonia
Through these savage woods distracted

Roamed I restless all the night-time,
Till at length amid the darkness
Half awakened rose the dawn ;
Not in veils of gold and amber
Was she dressed, a robe of mourning
Formed of clouds composed her mantle,
And with discontented light
Hidden were the stars and planets,
Though for this one time alone
They were happy in their absence.
Searching there in every part,
We approached where blood was spattered
On the tender dewy flowers,
And upon the ground some fragments
Of a woman's dress were strewn.
By these signs at once attracted,
We went on, 'till at the foot
Of a great rock overhanging,
In a fragrant tomb of roses
Lay Polonia, dead and stabbed there.

Scene XIII.

Polonia *dead; and afterwards* Patrick.—The Same.

PHILIP.   Turn your eyes, and here you see
The young tree of beauty blasted,
Pale and sad the opening flower,
The bright flame abruptly darkened ;
See here loveliness laid prostrate,
See warm life here turned to marble,
See, alas ! Polonia dead.
KING.   Philip, cease ! proceed no farther !
For I have not resignation

To bear up with any calmness
'Gainst so many forms of wrong,
'Gainst so many shapes of sadness,
'Gainst such manifold misfortunes.
Ah, my daughter !   Ah, thou hapless
Treasure fatally found for me !
     LESBIA.   Grief my feeling so o'ermasters
That I have not breath to mourn.
Ah ! of all thy woes the partner
Let thy wretched sister be !
     KING.   What rude hand in ruffian anger
Raised its bloody steel against
Beauty so divinely fashioned ?
Sorrow, sorrow ends my life.
     PATRICK (*within*). Woe to thee, sin-stained Irlanda !
Woe to thee, unhappy people !
If with tears thou dost not water
The hard earth, and night and day
Weeping in thy bitter anguish,
Ope the golden gates of heaven
Which thy disobedience fastened.
Woe to thee, unhappy people !
Woe to thee, sin-stained Irlanda !
     KING.   Heavens ! what mournful tones are these ?
What are these sad solemn accents
That transpierce my very heart,
That cut through me like a dagger ?
Learn who thus disturbs the flowing
Of my grief's most tender channels.
Who but I should so lament ?
Who but I should wail thus sadly ?
     LEOGAIRE.   This, my lord, is Patrick, who
Having, as you know, departed
From this country went to Rome,
Where the Pontiff, the great father,
Made him bishop, and a post

Of pre-eminence imparted
To him here ; through all the islands
He proceedeth in this manner.

PATRICK *enters.*

   PATRICK.   Woe to thee, unhappy people !
Woe to thee, sin-stained Irlanda !
   KING.   Patrick, thou who thus my grief
Interrupted, and my sadness
Doubled with thy golden words,
Hiding false and poisonous matter,
Why thus persecute me ?   Wherefore
Thus disturb the hills and valleys
Of my kingdom with deceptions
And new-fangled laws and maxims ?
Here we know but this alone,
We are born and die.   Our fathers
Left us this, the simple doctrine
Taught by nature, and no farther
Have we sought to learn.   What God
Can be this, of whom such marvels
You relate, who life eternal
Gives when temporal life departeth ?
Can the soul, when it is severed
From the body, be so active
As to have another life,
Or of bale or bliss, hereafter ?
   PATRICK.   Being loosened from the body,
And the human portion having
Given to nature, it being only
But a little dust and ashes,
Then the spirit upward rises,
To the higher sphere attracted,
Where its labours find their centre,
If it dies in grace, which baptism

First confers upon the soul,
And then penance ever after.
    KING.   Then this beauteous one, that here
Lies in her own blood bedabbled,
There, is living at this moment?
    PATRICK.   Yes.
    KING.   A sign, a proof, then, grant me
Of this truth.
    PATRICK (*aside*).   Almighty Lord!
For Thy glory deign to hearken!
It behoveth Thee to show
Here Thy power by an example.
    KING.   What! you do not answer?
    PATRICK.   Heaven
Wishes for itself to answer.—
In the name of God, O corse,
        [*He extends his hands over the dead body of*
         POLONIA.
Lying stiff here, I command thee
To arise and live, resuming
Thine own soul, and thus make patent
This great truth, before us preaching
The true doctrine and evangel.
    POLONIA (*arising*). Woe is me! Oh, save me, heaven!
Ah, what secrets are imparted
To the soul! O Lord! O Lord!
Stay the red hand of Thy anger,
Of Thy justice. Do not threaten,
'Gainst a woman weak and abject,
The dread thunders of Thy rigour,
Of Thy power the lightning's flashes.
Where, oh, where shall I conceal me
From Thy countenance, if haply
Thou art wroth? Ye rocks, ye mountains,
Fall upon and overcast me.
Hating mine own self, to-day

Would that to my prayer 'twas granted
In the centre of the earth
From Thy sight to hide and mask me !
Ah, but why ? if wheresoever
My unhappy fate might cast me
There I brought with me my sin ?
See ye, see ye not this Atlas
Back recede, and this huge mountain
Tremble to its base ?   The axes
Of the firmament are loosened,
And its perfect fabric hangeth
Threatening ruin o'er my head,
With terrific pride and grandeur.
Darker grows the air around me,
Chained, my feet proceed no farther,
Even the seas retire before me.
What, here fly me not nor startle,
Are the wild beasts, which to rend me
Bit by bit come on to attack me.
Mercy, mighty Lord, oh, mercy !
Pardon, gracious Lord, oh, pardon !
Holy baptism I implore,
That in grace I may depart hence.
Mortals, hear, oh, mortals hear,
Christ is living, Christ is master,
Christ is god, the one true God !
Penance, penance, penance practice !   [*Exit.*

Scene XIV.

The Same, *with the exception of* Polonia.

Philip.   How prodigious !
Captain.   How stupendous !

LESBIA.   What a miracle !
LEOGAIRE.   What a marvel!
KING.   What enchantment! what bewitchment!
Who can bear this? who can grant this?
    ALL.   Christ is God, the one true God.
    KING.   What a bold deceit is practised
Here, blind people, to deceive you,
In the making of these marvels,
Which you have not sense to see
Are in outward show but acted
And within are fraud!   However,
That the truth be now established,
I will own myself convinced,
If in argument shall Patrick
Prove his case : and so attend
As the grave dispute advances.
If the soul was made immortal
It could never be inactive
Even for a single moment.
    PATRICK.   Yes ; and every dream that passes
Proves this truth ; because the dreams
That engender numerous phantoms
Are discourses of the soul
That ne'er sleeps, and as these shadows
Simulate the imperfect actions
Of the senses, a strange language
And imperfect is produced ;
And 'tis thus that in their trances
Men dream things that are at once
Inconsistent and fantastic.
    KING.   Well, then, this being so, I ask
Was Polonia when this happened
Dead or not?   For if but only
In a swoon, what mighty marvel,
Then, was done?   But this I pass.
If she really had departed,

Then to one of the two places,
Heaven or hell, so named, O Patrick,
By yourself, it must have gone.
If it was in heaven, 'twas hardly
Merciful in God to send it
Back into this world, to hazard
A new chance of condemnation,
When 'twas once in grace and happy.
This is surely true.   If, likewise,
It had been in hell, 'tis adverse
To strict justice, since it were not
Just that that which by its badness
Once had earned such punishment,
Should again be given the chances
Of regaining grace.   It must,
I presume, be taken as granted
That God's justice and His mercy
Cannot possibly be parted.
Where, I ask then, was her soul?
    PATRICK.   Hear, Egerius, the answer.
I concede that for the soul,
Sanctified by holy baptism,
Heaven or hell must be its goal,
Out of which, by God's commandment,
Speaking of His usual power,
It can never more be absent.
But if of His absolute power
There is question, God could drag it
Even from hell itself; but this
Is not what we have to argue.
That the soul doth go to either
Of those places, must be granted
When 'tis severed from the body
Once for all by mortal absence
To return to it no more ;
But when otherwise commanded

To it to return, it waiteth
In a certain state of passage,
And remains as 'twere suspended
In the universe, not having
Any special place allotted.
For the Almighty mind forecasting
All things, when from out His essence,
As th' exemplar, the fair pattern
Of His thought, this glorious fabric
He brought forth to light and gladness,
Saw this very incident,
And well knowing what would happen,
That this soul would here return,
Kept it for awhile inactive,
Seemingly unfixed, yet fixed.
This is the authentic answer
That theology, that sacred
Science, gives to what you have asked me.
But another point remaineth :
There are other places, mark me,
Both of glory and of pain,
Than you think ; and of these latter
One is called the Purgatory,
Where the soul of him who haply
Dies in grace, is purged from stains,
Sinful stains which it contracted
In the world : for into heaven
None can pass till these are cancelled.
And thus, there 'tis purified,
Cleansed by fire from all that tarnished,
Till to God's divinest presence
Pure and clean at length it passes.
    KING.   So you say, and I have nothing
To confirm what you advance here
But your word.   Some proof now give me,
Give me something I can handle,

Something tangible to convince me
Of this truth, that I may grasp it,
And know what it is.   And since
So much power and influence have you
With your God, implore His grace,
That I may believe the faster,
Some material fact to give me,
Something that we all can grapple,
Not mere creatures of the mind.
And remember that at farthest
But an hour remains in which
You must give me sure and ample
Signs of punishment and glory,
Or you die.   These mighty marvels
Of your God here let them come,
Where the truth we can examine
For ourselves.   And if we neither
Heaven or hell deserve to have here,
Show us, then, this Purgatory,
Which is different from the latter,
So that here we all may know
His omnipotence and grandeur.
Mind, God's honour rests upon you,
Tell Him to defend and guard it.
[Exeunt all but PATRICK.

Scene XV.

Patrick.

PATRICK.   Here, mighty Lord, dart down thy
    searching glance,
Arm'd with the dreadful lightnings of Thine ire,
Wing'd with Thy vengeance, as the bolt with fire,

And rout the squadrons of fell ignorance :
Come not in pity to the hostile band,
   Treat not as friends Thy enemies abhorr'd,
   But since they ask for portents, mighty Lord,
Come with the blood-red lightnings in Thy hand.
Of old Elias asked with burning sighs
   For chastisement, and Moses did display
   Wonders and portents ; in the self-same way
Listen, O Lord, to my beseeching cries,
   And though I be not great or good as they,
Still let my accents pierce the listening skies !
   Portents and chastisement, both day and night
I ask, O Lord, may from Thy hand be given,
That Purgatory, Hell and Heaven,
   May be revealed unto these mortals' sight.

Scene XVI.

A Good Angel *at one side, and on the other a* Bad Angel.—
Patrick.

Bad Angel (*to himself*). Fearful that the favouring
    skies
May accede to Patrick's prayer,
And discover to him where
Earth's most wondrous treasure lies,
Like a minister of light,
Full of scorn, I hither fly
It to chill and nullify.
Covering with my poison blight
His petition.
   Good Angel. Then give o'er,
Cruel monster ; for in me
His protecting angel see.

But be silent, speak no more.—
Patrick, God has heard Thy prayer,   [*To him.*
He has listen'd to thy vows,
And, as thou hast asked, allows
Earth's great secrets to lie bare.
Seek along this island ground
For a vast and darksome cave,
Which restrains the lake's dark wave,
And supports the mountains round ;
He who dares to go therein,
Having first contritely told
All his faults, shall there behold
Where the soul is purged from sin.
He shall see, with mortal eyes,
Hell itself, where those who die
In their sins for ever lie
In the fire that never dies.
He shall see, in blest fruition,
Where the happy spirits dwell.
But of this be sure as well—
He who without due contrition
Enters there to idly try
What the cave may be, doth go
To his death ; he'll suffer woe,
While the Lord doth reign on high,
Who thy soul this day shall free
From this poor world's weariness.
It is thus that God doth bless
Those who love His name like thee.
He shall grant to thee in pity,
Bliss undreamed by mortal men,
Making thee a denizen
Of His own celestial city.
He shall to the world proclaim
His omnipotence and glory,
By the wondrous Purgatory

Which shall bear thy sainted name.
Lest thou think the promise vain
Of this miracle divine,
I will take this shape malign,
Which came hither to profane
Thy devotion, and within
This dark cavern's dark abyss
Fling it,—there to howl and hiss
In the everlasting din.   [*They disappear.*
   Patrick.   Glory, glory unto Thee,
Mighty Lord ; the heavens proclaim,
Miracles attest Thy name,
Wonders show that Thou must be.—
King !   [*Calling.*

Scene XVII.

The King, Philip, Lesbia, Leogaire, The Captain,
People.—Patrick.

   King.   What would'st thou ?
   Patrick.   Come with me
Through this mountain woodland drear,
Thou and all thy followers here,
Thou and they shall see therein
The dark place reserved for sin,
And rewards delightful sphere.
They shall have a passing view
Of a sight no tongue can tell,
An unending miracle,
To whose greatness shall be due
Their amazement ever new
Who its secrets shall unveil.
Yes, a perfect image pale

x

In the wonders guarded here,
Shall they see with awe and fear,
Of the realms of bliss and bale.

                    [*Exit, followed by all.*

Scene XVIII.

A REMOTE PART OF THE MOUNTAIN WITH THE MOUTH OF A HORRIBLE CAVE.

The Same.

    King.   Look, O Patrick, for you go
Turning towards a part forbidden,
Where the light of the sun is hidden
Even in the noon-tide's glow.
Through this wilderness of woe
Even the hunter in pursuit
Of his prey ne'er placed a foot
On its trackless wild walks green,
Since for ages it has been
Shunned alike by man and brute.
    Philip.   We for many and many a year,
Who have lived here from our youth,
Never dared to learn the truth
Of the secrets hidden here ;
For the entrance did appear
In itself enough to make
Even the bravest heart to quake.
No one yet has dared to brave
The wild rocks that guard this cave,
Or the waters of this lake.
    King.   And for auguries we heard,
Borne the troubled wind along,

Oft the sad funereal song
Of some lone nocturnal bird.
    PHILIP.   Be the rash attempt deferred.
    PATRICK.   Let not causeless fear arise ;
For a treasure of the skies
Here is hidden.
    KING.   What is fear ?
Could it ever me come near
In an earthquake's agonies ?
No ; for though the flames should break
As from some sulphureous lake,
And the mountains' sides run red
From the molten fires outshed,
They could ne'er my courage shake,
Never make me fear.

SCENE XIX.

POLONIA.—THE SAME.

POLONIA.   Oh, stay,
Wandering from the path astray,
Hapless crowd, rash, indiscreet,
Turn away your erring feet,
For misfortune lies that way.

Here from myself with hurried footsteps flying,
  I dared to tread this wilderness profound,
  Beneath the mountain whose proud top defying
  The pure bright sunbeam is with huge rocks crowned,
  Hoping that here, as in its dark grave lying,
  Never my sin could on the earth be found,
  And I myself might find a port of peace
  Where all the tempests of the world might cease.

No polar star had hostile fate decreed me,
　　As on my perilous path I dared to stray,
　　So great its pride, no hand presumed to lead me,
　　And guide my silent footstep on its way.
　　Not yet the aspect of the place has freed me
　　From the dread terror, anguish and dismay,
　　Which were awakened by this mountain's gloom,
　　And all the hidden wonders of its womb.

See ye not here this rock some power secureth,
　　That grasps with awful toil the hill-side brown,
　　And with the very anguish it endureth
　　Age after age seems slowly coming down?
　　Suspended there with effort, it obscureth
　　A mighty cave beneath, which it doth crown;—
　　An open mouth the horrid cavern shapes,
　　Wherewith the melancholy mountain gapes.*

---

*　　　　　　　　　　　　　　"But I remember,
　　Two miles on this side of the fort, the road
　　Crosses a deep ravine; 'tis rough and narrow,
　　And winds with short turns down the precipice;
　　*And in its depth there is a mighty rock
　　Which has from unimaginable years,
　　Sustained itself with terror and with toil
　　Over the gulf, and with the agony
　　With which it clings seems slowly coming down:*
　　Even as a wretched soul hour after hour
　　Clings to the mass of life: yet, clinging, leans;
　　And leaning, makes more dark the dread abyss
　　In which it fears to fall.　Beneath this crag,
　　Huge as despair, as if in weariness
　　The melancholy mountain yawns."—THE CENCI.

Shelley says, "An idea in this speech was suggested by a most sublime passage in 'El Purgatorio de San Patricio' of Calderon." The same idea is to be found in "Amor despues de la Muerte," "Los dos amantes del Cielo," and other dramas of Calderon.

This, then, by mournful cypress trees surrounded,
  Between the lips of rocks at either side,
  Reveals a monstrous neck of length unbounded,
  Whose tangled hair is scantily supplied
  By the wild herbs that there the wind hath grounded,
  A gloom whose depths no sun has ever tried,
  A space, a void, the gladsome day's affright,
  The fatal refuge of the frozen night.

I wished to enter there, to make my dwelling
  Within the cave ; but here my accents fail,
  My troubled voice, against my will rebelling,
  Doth interrupt so terrible a tale.—
  What novel horror, all the past excelling,
  Must I relate to you, with cheeks all pale,
  Without cold terror on my bosom seizing,
  And even my voice, my breath, my pulses freezing ?

I scarcely had o'ercome my hesitation,
  And gone within the cavern's vault profound,
  When I heard wails of hopeless lamentation,
  Despairing shrieks that shook the walls around,
  Curses, and blasphemy, and desperation,
  Dark crimes avowed that would even hell astound,
  Which heaven, I think, in order not to hear,
  Had hid within this prison dark and drear.

Let him come here who doubts what I am telling,
  Let him here bravely enter who denies,
  Soon shall he hear the sounds of dreadful yelling,
  Soon shall the horrors gleam before his eyes.
  For me, my voice is hushed, my bosom swelling,
  Pants now with terror, now with strange surprise.
  Nor is it right that human tongue should dare
  High heaven's mysterious secrets to lay bare.

PATRICK.   This cave, O king, which here you see, concealeth
The mysteries of life as well as death :
Not, I should say, for him whose bosom feeleth
No true repentance, or no real faith ;
But he who boldly enters, who revealeth
His sins, confessing them with penitent breath,
Shall see them all forgiven, his conscience clear,
And have alive his Purgatory here.

KING.   And dost thou think, O Patrick, that I owe
My blood so little, as to yield to dread,
And trembling fear like a weak woman show ?
Say, who shall be the first this cave to tread ?
What silent ! Philip?
    PHILIP.   Sire, I dare not go.
    KING.   Then, Captain, thou ?
    CAPTAIN.   Enough to strike me dead
Is even the thought.
    KING.   Leogaire, thou'lt surely dare ?
    LEOGAIRE.   The heavens, my lord, themselves exclaim
        forbear !

KING.   O cowards, lost to every sense of shame,
Unfit to gird the warrior's sword around
Your shrinking loins !   Men are ye but in name.
Well, I myself shall be the first to sound
The depths of this enchantment, and proclaim
Unto this Christian that my heart unawed
Nor dreads his incantations nor his God !
            [EGERIUS *advances to the cave, and on entering*
                sinks into it with much noise, flames rise
                from below, and many voices are heard.

POLONIA.   How terrible !
LEOGAIRE.   How awful !

Philip.   What a wonder!
Captain.   The earth is breathing out its central fire.
                                                   [*Exit.*
Leogaire.   The axes of the sky are burst asunder.
                                                   [*Exit.*
Polonia.   The heavens are loosening their collected
    ire.   [*Exit.*
Lesbia.   The earth doth quake, and peals the sullen
    thunder.   [*Exit.*
Patrick.   O, mighty Lord, who will not now admire
Thy wondrous works?   [*Exit.*
Philip.   Oh! who that's not insane
Will enter Patrick's Purgatory again?   [*Exit.*

ACT THE THIRD.

A STREET. IT IS NIGHT.

SCENE I.

JUAN PAUL, *dressed ridiculously as a soldier, and* LUIS
ENIUS, *very pensive.*

PAUL. Yes, the day would come I knew,
After long procrastination,
When a word of explanation
I should ask to have with you.
" Come with me," you said.   Though dark,
Off I trudged with heavy heart
To point out to you the part
Where at morn you could embark ;
Then again, with thundering voice,
Thus you spoke, " Where I must fly
Choose to come with me, or die."
And, since you allowed a choice,
Of two ills I chose the worst,
Which, sir, was to go with you.
As your shadow then I flew
'Cross the sea to England first,
Then to Scotland, then to France,
Then to Italy and Spain,
Round the world and back again,
As in some fantastic dance.
Not a country great or small
Could escape you, 'till, good lack !
Here we are in Ireland back :—
Now, sir, I, plain Juan Paul,

Being perplexed to know what draws
You here now, with beard and hair
Grown so long, your speech, your air,
Changed so much, would ask the cause
Why you these disguises wear?
You by day ne'er leave the inn,
But when cold night doth begin
You a thousand follies dare,
Without bearing this in mind,
That we now are in a land
Wholly changed from strand to strand,
Where, in fact, we nothing find
As we left it.   The old king
Died despairing, and his heir,
Lesbia, now the crown doth wear,
For her sister, hapless thing!
Poor Polonia . . . .

    LUIS.   Oh, that name
Do not mention!   Do not kill me
By repeating what doth thrill me
To the centre of my frame
As with lightning.   Yes, I know
That at length Polonia died.

    PAUL.   Yes; our host was at her side
(He himself has told me so),
When they found her dead, and . . . .

    LUIS.   Cease!
Of her death, oh! speak no more,
'Tis sufficient to deplore,
And to pray that she's at peace.

    PAUL.   Leaving heathen sin and crime,
All the people far and near
Are become good Christians here.
For one Patrick, who some time
Now is dead . . . .

    LUIS.   Is Patrick dead?

PAUL. So I from our host have heard.

LUIS (*aside*). Badly have I kept my word!—
But proceed.

PAUL.   The teaching spread
Of the faith of Christ, and gave,
As a proof complete and whole
Of the eternity of the soul,
The discovery of a cave.—
Oh ! it's very name doth send
Terror through me.

LUIS.   Yes, I have heard
Of that cave, and every word
Made my hair to stand on end.
Those who in the neighbourhood
Dwell, see wonders every day.

PAUL. Since, 'mid terror and dismay,
In your melancholy mood
You will no one hear or see,
Ever locked within your room,
It is plain you have not come
Aught to learn, how strange they be,
Of these things. It doth appear
Other work you are about.
Satisfy my foolish doubt,
And say why we have come here.

LUIS. To your questions thus I yield :
Yes, I forced you, as you mention,
From your house, and my intention
Was to kill you in the field ;
But I thought it best instead
You to make my steps attend
As my comrade and my friend,
Shaking off the mortal dread
Which forbad me to endure
Any stranger, and in fine,
That your arms being joined with mine,

I might feel the more secure.
Many a land, both far and near,
Passing through you fared right well;
And now answering I will tell
Why it is that we come here.
And 'tis this : I come to slay
Here a man who did me wrong,
'Tis for this I pass along,
Muffled in this curious way,
Hiding country, dress, and name ;
And the night suits best for me,
For my powerful enemy
Can the first position claim
In the land.   Since I avow
Why I hither have been led,
Listen now how I have sped
In my project until now.
I three days ago was brought
To this city in disguise,
For two nights, beneath the skies,
I my enemy have sought
In his street and at his door ;
Twice a muffled figure came
And disturbed me in my aim,
Twice he called and stalked before
Him I followed in the street ;
But when I the figure neared,
Suddenly he disappeared
As if wings were on his feet.
I this third night have brought *you*,
That should this mysterious shape
Come again, he sha'nt escape,
Being caught between us two ;
Who he is we then can see.

   PAUL.   Two? who are they ?
   LUIS.   You and I.

Paul.   I'm not one.

Luis.   Not one? How? Why?

Paul.   No, sir, no, I cannot be
One, nor half a one.   These stories,
Faith! would frighten fifty Hectors;
What know I of Lady Spectres,
Or of Lord Don Purgatories?
All through life I've kept aloof
From the other world's affairs,
Shunning such superfluous cares;
But, my courage put to proof,
Bid me face a thousand men,
And if I don't cut and run
From the thousand, nay, from one,
Never trust to me again.
For I think it quite a case
Fit for Bedlam, if so high,
That a man would rather die,
Than just take a little race.
Such a trifle!   Sir, to me
Life is precious; leave me here,
Where you'd find me, never fear.

Luis.   Here's the house; to-night I'll be,
Philip, your predestined fate.
Now we'll see if heaven pretends
To defend him, and defends.—
Watch here, you, beside the gate.

Scene II.

A Muffled Figure.—Luis *and* Paul.

Paul.   There's no need to watch, for hither
Some one comes.

LUIS.   A lucky mortal
Am I, if the hour draws nigh
That will two revenges offer.*
Since this night there then will be
Naught to interrupt my project,
Slaying first this muffled figure
And then Philip.   Slow and solemn
Comes this man again.   I know him
By his gait.   But whence this horror
That comes o'er me as I see him,
This strange awe that chills, that shocks me?
   THE FIGURE.   Luis Enius!
   LUIS.   Sir, I've seen you
Here the last two nights ; your object?
If you call me, wherefore fly thus?
If 'tis me you seek, why mock me
By retiring?
   THE FIGURE.   Follow me,
Then you'll know my name.
   LUIS.   I'm stopped here
In this street by a little business.—
To be quite alone imports me.—
Wherefore first by killing you
I'll be free to kill another.
       [*He draws his sword, but merely cuts the air.*
Draw, then, draw your sword or not,
Thus the needful path I shorten
To two acts of vengeance.   Heavens !
I but strike the air, cut nothing,
Sever nothing else.   Quick ! Paul,
Stop him as he stalks off yonder,
Near to you.
   PAUL.   I'm bad at stopping.
   LUIS.   Then your footsteps I will follow

---

* *Asonante* in *o—e* to the end of Scene VIII.

Everywhere, until I learn
Who you are.   (*Aside.* In vain his body
Do I strive to pierce.   Oh, heavens !
Lightnings flash from off my sword here ;
But in no way can I touch him,
As if sword and arm were shortened.)
> [*Exit following the figure, striking at it without touching it.*

SCENE III.

PHILIP.—PAUL.

PAUL (*aside*). God be with you both !   But scarce
Has one vanished, when another
Comes to haunt me.   Why, I'm tempted
By strange phantoms and hobgoblins
Like another San Antonio :—
In this doorway I'll ensconce me,
Till my friend here kindly passes.
PHILIP.   Love, ambitious, bold, deep-plotted,
With the favours of a kingdom
Me thou mak'st a prosperous lover.
To the desert fled Polonia,
Where, mid savage rocks and forests,
Citizen of mighty mountains,
Islander of lonely grottoes,
She doth dwell, to Lesbia leaving
Crown and kingdom ; through a stronger
Greed than love I Lesbia court,—
For a queen is worth my homage.
From her trellis I have come,
From a sweet and pleasant converse.
But, what's this ?   Each night I stumble

On a man here at my doorstep.
Who is there ?
    Paul (*aside*).   To me he's coming.
Why on earth should every goblin
Pounce on me ?
    Philip.   Sir, Caballero.
    Paul.   These are names I don't acknowledge ;
He can't speak to *me*.
    Philip.   This house
Is my home.
    Paul,   Which I don't covet ;
May you for an age enjoy it,
Without billets.
    Philip.   If important
Business in this street detains you
(Not a word whereon I offer),
Give me room that I may pass.
    Paul (*aside*). Somewhat timid, though quite proper,
Goblins can be cowards too.—
Yes, sir, for a certain office
I am here ; go in, and welcome ;
I no gentleman would stop here
Bound for bed, nor is it right.
    Philip.   The condition I acknowledge.—
Well, fine spectres, to be sure,   [*Aside.*
Haunt this street : each night I notice
That a man here comes before me,
But when I approach him softly,
Hereabouts on my own threshold,
I, as now, have always lost him.
But what matters this to me ?   [*Exit.*
    [Paul *draws his sword and makes several flourishes.*
    Paul.   As he's gone, the right and proper
Thing is this :—Stay, stay, cold shadow,
Whether you're a ghost or ghostess,
I can't reach it.   Why, by heaven !

Air alone I cut and chop here.
But if this is he we wait for
In the night-time like two blockheads,
Faith ! he is a lucky fellow
To have got to bed so promptly.
But another noise I hear
Sounding from that dark street yonder,
'Tis of swords and angry voices :—
There I run to reconnoitre.   [*Exit.*

SCENE IV.

ANOTHER STREET.

The Muffled Figure *and* LUIS.

LUIS.   Sir, already we have issued
From that street ; if aught there stopped us,
We are here alone, and may
Hand to hand resume the combat.
And since powerless is my sword
Thee to wound, I throw me on thee
To know who thou art.   Declare,
Art thou demon, man, or monster ?
What ! no answer ?   Then I thus
Dare myself to solve the problem,
    [*He tears the cloak from the Figure, and finds
        beneath it a skeleton.*
And find out . . . . Oh, save me, heaven !
God ! what's this I see ?   What horrid
Spectacle !   What frightful vision !
What death-threatening fearful portent !
Stiff and stony corse, who art thou ?
That of dust and ashes forméd
Now dost live ?

THE FIGURE.   Not know thyself?
This is thy most faithful portrait ;
I, alas! am Luis Enius.   [*Disappears.**
    LUIS.   Save me, heaven! what words of horror!
Save me, heaven ! what sight of woe !
Prey of shadows and misfortunes,
Ah, I die.   [*He falls on the ground.*

SCENE V.

PAUL.—LUIS.

    PAUL.   It is the voice
Of my master.   Succour cometh
Opportunely now in me.
Sir !
    LUIS.   Ah ! why return, dread monster?
I am overwhelmed, I faint here
At your voice.
    PAUL (*aside*).   God help his noddle !
He's gone mad !—Dread monster ?   No,   [*Aloud.*
I am Juan Paul, that donkey
Who, not knowing why or wherefore,
Is your servant.
    LUIS.   Ah ! good, honest
Paul, I knew you not, so frightened

---

* The interview between *Luis Enius* and the *Skeleton*, says
a recent writer, "is a scene truly Calderonic—the hour, the place,
the intended assassin, and the sudden reflection of himself, with his
guilty conscience impersonate before him ; it reminds us of that wild
fable of Jeremy Taylor or Fuller, about the bird with a human face,
that feeds on human flesh until it chances to see its reflection in a
stream, and then it pines away for grief that it has killed its fellow."
—WESTMINSTER REVIEW, vol. liv. p. 306.

Am I.   But at that why wonder,
If myself I do not know ?
Did you see a fearful corse here,
A dead body with a soul,
An apparent man supported
By his skeleton alone,
Bones from which the flesh had rotted,
Fingers rigid, gaunt, and cold,
Naked trunk, uncouth, abhorrent,
Vacant spaces whence the eyes,
Having fallen, left bare the sockets ?—
Whither has he gone?
    PAUL.   If I
Saw that ghost, upon my honour,
I could never say I saw it;
For more dead than that dead body
I had fallen on the other side
At the moment.
    LUIS.   And no wonder;
For my voice was mute, my breath
Choked, my heart's warm beat forgotten,
Clothed with ice were all my senses,
Shod with lead my feet, my forehead
Cold with sweat, I saw suspended
Heaven's two mighty poles upon me,
The brief Atlases sustaining
Such a burden being my shoulders.
It appeared as if there started
Rocks from every tender blossom,
Giants from each opening rose;
For the earth's disrupted hollows
Wished from out their graves to cast
Forth the dead who lay there rotten ;
Ah, among them I beheld
Luis Enius !   Heaven be softened !
Hide me, hide me, from myself !

Bury me in some deep corner
Of earth's centre !   Let me never
See myself, since no self-knowledge
Have I had !   But now I have it ;
Now I know I am that monster
Of rebellion, who defied,
In my madness, pride, and folly,
God Himself ; the same, whose crimes
Are so numerous and so horrid,
That it were slight punishment,
If the whole wrath of the Godhead
Was outpoured on me, and whilst
God was God, eternal torments
I should have to bear in hell.
But I have this further knowledge,
They were done against a God
So divine, that He has promised
To grant pardon, if my sins
I with penitent tears acknowledge.
Such I shed ; and, Lord, to prove
That to-day to be another
I begin, being born anew,
To Thy hands my soul I offer.
Not as a strict judge then judge me,
For the attributes of the Godhead
Are His justice and His mercy ;
With the latter, not the former,
Judge me, then, and fix what penance
I shall do to gain that object.
What will be the satisfaction
Of my life ?

             [*Music (within).   The Purgatory.*

  Luis.   Bless me, heaven ! what's this I hear ?
A sweet strain divine and solemn ;
It appears a revelation
From on high, since heaven doth often

Y 2

Help mysteriously the sinner.
And since I herein acknowledge
A divine interposition,
I will go into the Purgatory,
Called, of Patrick, and fulfil,
Humbly, faithfully, the promise
Which I gave him long ago,
If it is my happy fortune
To see Patrick.   If the attempt
Is, as rumour hath informed me,
Most terrific, since no human
Strength avails against the horrors
Of the place, or resolution
To endure the demons' torments,
Still my sins I must remember
Were as dreadful.   Skilful doctors
Give for dangerous diseases
Dangerous remedies to stop them.—
Come, then, with me, Paul, and see
How here penitent and prostrate
At the bishop's feet I'll kneel,
And confess, for greater wonder,
All my awful sins aloud.

 PAUL.   Go alone, then, for that project,
Since so brave a man as you are
Has no need of an accomplice ;
And there's no one I have heard of
Who e'er went to hell escorted
By his servant.   I'll go home,
And live pleasantly in my cottage
Without care.   If ghosts there be,
I'm content with matrimony.   [*Exit.*

 LUIS.   Public were my sins, and so
Public penance I will offer
In atonement.   Like one crazed,
Crying in the crowded cross-ways,

I'll confess aloud my crimes.
Men, wild beasts, rude mountains, forests,
Globes celestial, flinty rocks,
Tender plants, dry elms, thick coppice,
Know that I am Luis Enius,
Tremble at my name, that monster
Once of pride, as now I am
Of humility the wonder.
I have faith and certain hope
Of great happiness before me,
If in God's great name shall Patrick
Aid me in the Purgatory.   [*Exit.*

SCENE VI.

A WOOD, IN THE CENTRE OF WHICH IS SEEN A
MOUNTAIN, FROM WHICH POLONIA DESCENDS.

POLONIA.

POLONIA.   To Thee, O Lord, my spirit climbs,
To Thee from every lonely hill
I burn to sacrifice my will
A thousand and a thousand times.
And such my boundless love to Thee
I wish each will of mine a living soul could be.

Would that my love I could have shown,
By leaving for Thy sake, instead
Of that poor crown that press'd my head,
Some proud, imperial crown and throne—
Some empire which the sun surveys
Through all its daily course and gilds with constant rays.

This lowly grot, 'neath rocks uphurled,
In which I dwell, though poor and small,

A spur of that stupendous wall,
The eighth great wonder of the world,
Doth in its little space excel
The grandest palace where a king doth dwell.

Far better on some natural lawn
To see the morn its gems bestrew,
Or watch it weeping pearls of dew
Within the white arms of the dawn ;
Or view, before the sun, the stars
Drive o'er the brightening plain their swiftly-fading cars.

Far better in the mighty main,
As night comes on, and clouds grow grey,
To see the golden coach of day
Drive down amid the waves of Spain.
But be it dark, or be it bright,
O Lord ! I praise Thy name by day and night.

Than to endure the inner strife,
The specious glare, but real weight
Of pomp, and power, and pride, and state,
And all the vanities of life ;
How would we shudder could we deem
That life itself, in truth, is but a fleeting dream.

Scene VII.

Luis.—Polonia.

Luis (*aside*). True to my purpose on I go,
With footsteps firm and bosom brave,
Seeking for that mysterious cave
Wherein the pitying heavens will show
How I salvation there may gain,
By bearing in this life the Purgatorial pain.

Tell me, O holy woman ! thou   [*To* POLONIA.
Who in these wilds a home hast found,
A dweller in this mountain ground
Obedient to some sacred vow,
Which is the road to Patrick's cave,
Where penitential man his soul in life may save ?

POLONIA.   O, happy traveller ! who here
Hast come so far in storm and shine,
Within this treasury divine
To feel and find salvation near,
Well can I guide thee on thy way,
Since 'tis for this alone amid these wilds I stray.

Seest thou this mountain ?
    LUIS.   Ah ! I see
My death in it.
    POLONIA (*aside*).   My heart grows cold.
Ah ! who is this that I behold ?
    LUIS (*aside*). I cannot think it.   Is it she ?
    POLONIA (*aside*). Can it be he ? Oh, pain ! oh, woe !
    LUIS (*aside*). Polonia sure it is.
    POLONIA (*aside*).   'Tis Luis, now I know.
    LUIS (*aside*). Perhaps illusion it may be
To baffle my intent, and lead
My erring feet astray.—Proceed.   [*To* POLONIA.
    POLONIA (*aside*). Say, can it be to conquer me
The common enemy doth send
This spectre here ?
    LUIS.   You do not speak.
    POLONIA.   Attend.
This mighty mountain, rock bestrown,
Full well the dreaded secret knows ;
But no one to its centre goes
By any path o'er land alone :

He who would see this wondrous cave
Must in a bark put forth and tempt the lake's dark wave.

I struggle with a wish to wreak   [*Aside.*
Revenge, which pity doth subdue.
   Luis (*aside*). It doth my happiness renew
Once more to see and hear her speak.
   Polonia (*aside*). Within me opposite thoughts
     contend.
   Luis (*aside*). Ah, me ! I die.—You do not speak.

   Polonia.   Attend.
This darksome lake doth all surround
The lofty mountain's rugged base,
And so to reach the awful place
An easy passage may be found :
A sacred convent in the island stands,
Midway between the mountain and the sands.

Some pious priests inhabit there,
And for this task alone they live,
With loving zeal to freely give
The helping hand, the strengthening prayer—
Confession, and the Holy Mass,
And every needful help to all who thither pass.

Telling them what they first must do,
Before they dare presume to go,
Alive, within the realm of woe.—
Let not this enemy subdue   [*Aside.*
My soul, O Lord !
  Luis (*aside*).   My hopes are fair.
Let me not feel, O Lord ! the anguish of despair,

Seeing before my startled sight
My greatest, deepest crime arise ;

Let not the fiend, my soul that tries,
Subdue me in this dreadful fight.
  POLONIA (*aside*). 'Gainst what a powerful foe must I
   defend
Myself to-day !

  LUIS.   You do not speak.
  POLONIA.   Attend.
  LUIS. With quicker speed your story tell,
For well I know my soul hath need
That I should go with swifter speed !
  POLONIA. And me it doth import as well
That you should go away.
  LUIS.   Agreed.
Now, woman, point the way to where my path doth lead.

  POLONIA. No one accompanied can brave
The terrors of this gloomy lake ;
And so a skiff you needs must take,
And try alone the icy wave ;
Being in that most trying strait
The absolute master of your acts and fate.

Come where within a secret cave
Beside the shore the boat doth lie,
And trusting in the Lord on high,
Embark upon the crystal wave
Of this remote lone inland sea.

LUIS. My life and all I have I place, O Lord ! in Thee.
  And so I trust me to the bark ;
  But, O my soul ! what sight is here,
  A coffin doth the bark appear ;
  And I upon the waters dark
  Alone must cross the icy tide.   [*He enters.*
POLONIA. Oh ! turn not back, but follow and confide.

Luis (*within*).   I've conquered! sweet Polonia's
    shade,
Since sight of thee has not undone
My shuddering soul.
    Polonia.   And I have won,
Here in this Babylon delayed,
O'er wrath and rage the victory.
    Luis (*within*). Thy feigned resemblance does not
        frighten me,
Though thou dost take a form
Might tempt my steps astray
And make me turn despairing from my way.
    Polonia.   Thy fear doth badly thee inform,
Poor to be brave and rich to be afraid,
For I Polonia am, and not her shade,
The same that thou didst slay,
But who by God's decree
Restored to life, even in this misery,
Is happier far to-day.
    Luis (*within*). Since I my sinful state
Confess, and feel too well its fearful weight,
Thy wrong, oh, pardon too !
    Polonia.   I give it, and approve of thy design.
    Luis (*within*). My faith, at least, I never will
        resign.
    Polonia.   That grace will be thy safeguard.
    Luis (*within*).   Then, adieu !
    Polonia.   Adieu !
    Luis (*within*).   May God in pity save.
    Polonia. And bring thee back victorious from the
        cave.

SCENE VIII.

THE ENTRANCE OF A CONVENT—AT THE END
THE CAVE OF PATRICK.

Two Canons Regular ; *afterwards* LUIS.

FIRST CANON.   See, the waters of the lake
Move although no breeze doth blow : *
Without doubt to-day some pilgrim
Roweth to this island shore.
SECOND CANON.   Come unto the strand to see
Who can be so brave and bold
As to seek our gloomy dwelling,
Crossing the dark waters o'er.

Enter LUIS.

LUIS.   Here my boat, my coffin, rather,
On the billows I bestow.
Who his sepulchre has ever
Steered, as I, through fire and snow ?
What a pleasant spot is this !
Here has Spring, methinks, invoked
Flowers of high and low degree
To assemble at her court.
But this dismal mountain here,
How unlike the plain below !
Yet they are the better friends
By the contrasts that they show.
There the mournful birds of prey
Hoarsely croak, presaging woe,
Here the warblers in their joy
Charm us with their tuneful notes.
There the torrents leaping headlong

---

* Single *asonante* in the long accented *o*, which is kept up to the
end of the Scene.

Fright us with their frenzied roar,
Here the crystal streamlets gliding
Mirror back the sun's bright gold.
Half way 'twixt that ugliness
And this beauty, I behold
A plain building whose grave front
Fear and love at once provokes.

    FIRST CANON.   Happy wanderer, who here
Hast arrived with heart so bold,
Come unto my arms.

    LUIS.   The ground
That you tread on suits me more.
Oh, for charity conduct me
To the Prior of your fold,
To the Abbot of this convent.

    FIRST CANON.   Though unworthy, you behold
Him in me.   Speak.   What's your wish ?

    LUIS.   Father, if my name I told,
I'm afraid that swiftly flying,
With a terror uncontrolled,
You would leave me : for my works
Are so shocking to unfold,
That to see them not, the sun
Wraps him round in mourning robes.
I am an abyss of crimes,
A wild sea that has no shore ;
I am a broad map of guilt,
And the greatest sinner known.
Yes, in me, to tell it briefly
In one comprehensive word
(Here my breath doth almost fail me),
Luis Enius behold !
I come here this cave to enter,
If for sins so manifold
Aught can ever satisfy,
Let my penance thus atone.

To the Bishop of Hibernia
I've confessed, and am absolved,
Who informed of my intention
With a gracious love consoled
All my fears, and unto thee
Sent these letters I unfold.
    FIRST CANON.   Do not in a single day
Take, my son, a step so bold,
For these things require precaution
More than can at once be told.
Stay here as our guest some days,
Then at leisure we can both
See about it and decide.
    LUIS.   No, my father, no, oh, no !
Never from the ground I'll rise,
Where here prostrate I am thrown,
Till you grant to me this good.
It was God that touched my soul,
And inspired me to come here ;
Not a vain desire to know,
Not ambition to find out
Secrets God, perchance, withholds.
Do not baffle this intention,
For the call is heaven's alone.
Oh, my father ! yield in pity,
With me in my griefs condole,
Give my sorrows consolation,
Heal the anguish of my soul.
    FIRST CANON.   Luis, you have not considered
What you ask of me ; you know
Nothing of the infernal torments
You must bear : to undergo
These your strength is insufficient.
Many are there, more the woe !
Who go in, but few, alas !
Who return.

Luis.   Your threats forebode
Much ; but still they fright not me ;
For I do protest, I go
But to purge away my sins,
Which if numbered are much more
Than the atoms of the sun
And the sands upon the shore.
I will ever have my hope
Firmly fixed upon the Lord,
At whose holy name even hell
Is subdued.
    First Canon.   The fervid glow
Of your words compels me now
To unlock the awful doors.
Luis, you behold the cave :
See !   [*He opens the mouth of the cave.*
    Luis.   Oh, save me, gracious God !
    First Canon.   What ! dismayed ?
    Luis.   No, not dismayed ;
Still it scared me to behold.
    First Canon.   I admonish you again,
For no lesser cause to go,
Than a firm belief that there
For your sins you may atone.
    Luis.   Father, I am in the cave :
Listen to my voice once more,
Men and wild beasts, skies and mountains,
Day and night, and sun and moon,
To you all I here protest,
Ay, a thousand times make known,
That I enter here to suffer
Torments for my sins untold ;
For so great, so dread a penance
Is but little to atone
For such sins as mine, believing
That the cave salvation holds.

First Canon.   Enter then, and in your mouth,
As within your heart's deep core,
Be the name of Jesus.
    Luis.   Be
With me, Lord, O gracious Lord,
For here, armed but with Thy faith,
I am pitted 'gainst my foe
In the open field.   That name
Will my enemy o'erthrow.
Crossing myself many times
I advance.   Oh, save me, God !
                     [*He enters the cave which they close.*
    First Canon.   Of the many who have entered
None has equal courage shown.
Oh, enable him, just Jesus,
To resist the demon host
And their wiles, relying ever
Upon Thee, divinest Lord.   [*Exeunt.*

Scene IX.

Lesbia, Philip, Leogaire, The Captain, *and* Polonia.

    Lesbia.   Before we reach the place,
Whither you wish to lead us, for a space
Let us say why we came
To see you here to-day : a definite aim
All of us here has brought.
    Polonia.   Speak as we go whatever be your thought,
Still following where I lead,
For I a sight that doth all sights exceed
Will bring you here to see.
    Lesbia.   What, then, our wishes were you hear from me.
Polonia, you desired
In this wild mountain waste to live retired,

Making of me the heir,
While living, of your kingdom.   I would share
With you in turn my plans, however small,
And so I hither come to tell you all.
My will is in your hands ;
I ask not counsel, sister, but commands.
A single woman scarce can ever be
Strong through advice, and of necessity
She must be married.
    POLONIA.   Yes ; and if your choice
Has fallen on Philip I may well rejoice,
For then to me you'll owe
Both crown and husband.
    PHILIP.   May you live whilst glow
The sun's bright beams, that orb which dies at night,
And Phœnix of its rays is born with morning's light.
    POLONIA.   Then since you thus have gained
Your wish, ye two, now free and unconstrained,
Listen to what I tell,
And all who hear me listen too, as well.
With all the outward show
Of fervour came a man, whom we all know,
Seeking for Patrick's cave,
To enter there, and so his soul to save.
He entered it, and cometh forth to-day,
And 'tis because my terror and dismay
Are balanced by my wonder, that with me
I bring you to behold this holy prodigy.
I do not tell you who he is lest fear
Should so my heart make craven, that I ne'er
Could reach the end I sought :—
'Tis for this object that you here are brought.
    LESBIA.   It is but only right
That I should mingle terror with delight.
    POLONIA.   If strength from him hath fled,
And he extended in the cave lies dead,

At least 'twill show
His punishment; and if he comes, we'll know
The mystery that is here ;
If safe he comes, who cometh forth, through fear
Perchance he may not speak,
But, flying men, some solitude may seek
To live and die alone.
    LEOGAIRE.   What mighty mysteries lie here unknown.
    CAPTAIN.   The time is opportune that we come here,
For the religious whom we see draw near,
All bathed in tears, now go
To the cave's mouth in solemn, silent row
To throw the gates aside.

SCENE X.

*The procession advances to the cave; the gates are opened
by the* Prior *and his assistants.* LUIS ENIUS *comes
forth, astonished.*—THE SAME.

    PRIOR.   And those of heaven, O Lord, keep open wide
To penitent tears and sighs.
May this poor sinner from these dungeons rise,
This dark and dismal place,
Where never shines the radiance of Thy face.
    POLONIA.   The gate is opened.
    PRIOR.   Oh, what happiness!
    PHILIP.   'Tis Luis!
    LUIS.   Bless me, heaven ! in pity bless !
Ah ! is it possible that I am here
Again on earth after so many a year,
And that once more I see
The light of the sun ?
    CAPTAIN.   How rapt !

LEOGAIRE.   How dazed is he!

PRIOR.   Embrace us all, my son.

LUIS.   My arms were prison chains to every one.
Polonia, since thou'rt here,
Thy pity I may claim without a fear.
And thou, O Philip, know
That thrice an angel saved thee from the blow
Of my sharp sword : two nights I watched for thee
To slay thee ; may my error pardoned be.
Now flying from myself, oh, let me hide,
And in some wilderness abide—
Far from the world in solitude and pain,
For he who saw what I have seen would feign,
So suffering live, so die.

PRIOR.   Then on the part of God, O Enius! I
Command thee what thou hast seen at once to say.

LUIS.   So sacred a command I must obey :—
And that the startled world may now begin
A better course, and man from mortal sin
My words may waken like some midnight wail,
Listen, O grave assembly to my tale.
After all the preparations,
Fit and solemn were effected,*
Which in such a perilous case
Might be needed and expected,
And when I from all around me,
Firm in faith, with courage strengthened,
Tenderly farewell had taken
This dark cavern here to enter,
I my trust reposed in God,
And my lips repeating ever
Those mysterious, mystic words,
At which even the demons tremble,
I then placed me on the threshold,

---

* *Asonante* in *e—e,* which is kept up to the end.

Where, until, as I expected,
They would close the gate, I stood.
It was closed, and I remember
Then I found me in black night,
Whence the light was so ejected,
That I closed on it mine eyes.
(A strange way it seems, but certain
To see better in the dark.)
With my lids thus closed together
On I went, and felt a wall
Which in front of me extended ;
And by following it, and groping
For about the length of twenty
Paces, came upon some rocks,
And perceived through a small crevice
Of this rugged mountain wall
That a doubtful glimmer entered
Of a light that was not light,
As when day the dark disperses,
If 'tis morning, or not morning,
Oft the twilight is uncertain.
With light steps a path pursuing,
By the left-hand side I entered,
When I felt a strange commotion ;
The firm earth began to tremble,
And upheaving 'neath my feet,
Ruin and convulsion threatened.
Stupified I stopped there, when
With a voice which woke my senses
From forgetfulness and fainting,
Loud a thunder-clap re-echoed,
And the ground on which I stood
Bursting open in the centre,
It appeared as if I fell'
To a depth where I lay buried
In the loosened stones and earth

Which had after me descended.
Then I found me in a hall
Built of jasper, where the presence
Of the chisel was made known
By its ornate architecture.
Through a door of bronze twelve men
Then advanced and came directly
Where I stood, who, clothed alike
In unspotted snow-white dresses,
With a courteous air received me,
And too humbly did me reverence.
One, who seemed to be among them
The superior, said : " Remember
That in God you place your faith,
And that you be not dejected
In your battle with the demons ;
For if moved by what they threaten,
Or may promise, you turn back,
You will have to dwell for ever
In the lowest depths of hell
Amid torments most excessive."
Angels were these men for me,
And so greatly was I strengthened
By their counsel and advice
That revived I once more felt me.
On a sudden then the whole
Hall unto mine eyes presented
Nothing but infernal visions,
Fallen angels, the first rebels,
And in forms so horrible,
So disgusting, that resemblance
It would be in vain to look for;
And one said to me : " Demented,
Reckless fool, who here hast wished
Prematurely to present thee
To thy destined punishment,

And the pains that thou deservest ;
If thy sins are so immense,
That thyself must needs condemn them,
Since thou in the eye of God
Never can have hope of mercy,
Why hast thou come here thyself
To endure them?   Back to earth, then,
Go, oh! go, and end thy life ;
And as thou hast lived, so perish.
Then again thou'lt come to see us ;
For hath hell prepared already
That dread seat in which thou must
Sit for ever and for ever."—
I did answer not a word ;
And then giving me some heavy
Blows, my hands and feet they bound,
Tieing them with thongs together,
And then caught and wounded me
With sharp hooks of burning metal,
Dragging me through all the cloisters,
Where they lit a fire and left me
Headlong plunged amid the flames.
I but cried, " O Jesus! help me."
At the words the demons fled,
And the fire went out and ended.
Then they brought me to a plain
Where the blackened earth presented
Fruits of thistles and of thorns,
'Stead of pink and rose sweet scented.
Here a biting wind passed by,
Which with subtle sharpness entered
Even my bones, whose faintest breath
Like the keenest sword-edge cleft me.
Here in the profoundest depths
Sadly, mournfully lamented
Myriad souls, their parents cursing

From whose loins they had descended.
Such despairing shrieks and cries,
Such blaspheming screams were blended,
Such atrocious oaths and curses
So repeated and incessant,
That the very demons shuddered.
I passed on, and in a meadow
Found me next, whose plants and grasses
Were all flames, which waved and bent them,
As when in the burning August
Wave the gold ears all together.
So immense it was, the sight
Never could make out where ended
This red field, and in it lay
An uncountable assemblage
All recumbent in the fire ;
Through their bodies and their members
Burning spikes and nails were driven ;
These with feet and hands extended
Were held nailed upon the ground,
Vipers of red fire the entrails
Gnawed of some ; while others lying,
With their teeth in maniac frenzy
Bit the earth ; and some there were
Piecemeal who themselves dismembered,
And who seemed to die, but only
To revive and die for ever.
There the ministers of death
Flung me from them bound and helpless,
But at the sweet name of Jesus
All their fury fled and left me.
I passed on, and found me where
Some were cured, by a strange method,
Of their cruel wounds and torments;
Lead and burning pitch were melted,
And being poured upon their sores

Made a cautery most dreadful.
Who that hears me will not mourn ?
Who that hears this awful lesson
Will not sigh and will not weep,
Will not fear and will not tremble ?
Then I saw a certain building,
Out of which bright rays extended
From the windows and the doors,
As when conflagration settles
On a house, the flame bursts forth
Where an opening is presented.
" This," they told me, " is the villa
Of delights, the bath of pleasures,
The abode of the luxurious,
Where are punished all those women
Who were in the other life,
From frivolity excessive,
Too much given to scented waters,
Unguents, rouges, baths, and perfumes."—
I went in, and there beheld,
In a tank of cold snow melted,
Many lovely women bathing,
With an upturned look of terror ;
Underneath the water they
Were the prey of snakes and serpents,
For the fishes and the sirens
Of this sea they represented ;
In the clear transparent crystal
Stiff and frozen were their members,
Icy hard their hair was lifted,
Chattering struck their teeth together.
Passing out, the demons brought me
To a mountain so tremendous
In its height, that as it rose
Through the sky its peak dissevered,
If it did not tear and rend,

The vast azure veil celestial ;
In the middle of this peak
A volcano stood, which, belching
Flames, appeared as if to spit them
In the very face of heaven.
From this burning cone, this crater,
Fire at intervals ascended
In which issued many souls,
Who again its womb re-entered,
Oft repeating and renewing
This ascending and descending.
At this time a scorching wind
Caught me when I least expected,
Blowing me from where I stood,
So that instantly it set me
In the depths of that abyss.
I too was shot up : a second
Wind-gust came, that with it brought
Myriad legions, who impelled me
Rudely to another part,
Where it seemed I saw assembled
All the other souls I had seen,
But who here were all collected ;
And though this was the abode
Where the pains were most excessive,
I remarked that all therein
Faces bore of glad expression,
Countenances calm and sweet,
No impatience in their gestures
Or their words ; but with their eyes
Fixed on heaven, as if thus set there
To ask mercy, ever weeping
Tears of tenderness and penance.
That it was the Purgatory
I at once by this detected,
Where the happy souls are purged from

Their more venial offences.
I was not subdued even here,
Though the demons stormed and threatened
Me the more : I rather felt
By the sight renewed and strengthened.
Then they, seeing that they could not
Shake my constancy, presented
To my eyes their greatest torments,
That which is in an especial
Sense called hell; and so they brought me
To a river, all the herbage
Of whose banks was flowers of fire,
And whose stream was sulphur melted ;
The dread monsters of its tide
Were the hydras and the serpents ;
It was very wide, and o'er it
Was a narrow bridge suspended,
Which but seemed a line, no more,
And so delicate and slender
That in my opinion no one
Without breaking it could ever
Pass across.   " Look here," they said,
" By this narrow way 'tis destined
Thou must cross; see thou the means.
And for thy o'erwhelming terror
See how those have fared who tried
Before thee."   And then directly
I saw those who tried to pass
Fall into the stream, where serpents
Tore them in a thousand pieces
With their claws and teeth's sharp edges.
I invoked the name of God,
And could dare with it to venture
To the other side to pass,
Without yielding to the terror
Of the winds and of the waves,

Though they fearfully beset me.
Yes I passed, and in a wood,
So delightful and so fertile,
Found me, that in it I could,
After what had passed, refresh me.
On my way as I advanced,
Cedars, palms, their boughs extended,
Trees of paradise indeed,
As I may with strictness term them ;
All the ground being covered over
With the rose and pink together
Formed a carpet, in whose hues
White and green and red were blended.
There the amorous song-birds sang
Tenderly their sweet distresses,
Keeping, with the thousand fountains
Of the streams, due time and measure.
Then upon my vision broke
A great city, proud and splendid,
Which had even the sun itself
For its towers' and turrets' endings ;
All the gates were of pure gold,
Into which had been inserted
Exquisitely, diamonds, rubies,
Topaz, chrysolite, and emerald.
Ere I reached the gates they opened,
And the saints in long procession
Solemnly advanced to meet me,
Men and women, youths and elders,
Boys and girls and children came,
All so joyful and contented.
Then the seraphim and angels,
In a thousand choirs advancing,
To their golden instruments
Sang the symphonies of heaven ;
After them at last approached

The most glorious and resplendent
Patrick, the great patriarch,
Who his gratulations telling
That I had fulfilled my word
Ere I died, as he expected,
He embraced me ; all displaying
Joy and gladness in my welfare.
Thus encouraged he dismissed me,
Telling me no mortal ever,
While in life, that glorious city
Of the saints could hope to enter ;
That once more unto the world
I should go my days to end there.
Finally my way retracing,
I came back, quite unmolested
By the dark infernal spirits,
And at last the gate of entrance
Having reached, you all came forward
To receive me and attend me.
And since I from so much danger
Have escaped, oh ! deign to let me,
Pious fathers, here remain
Till my life is happily ended.*

———

For with this the history closes,
As it is to us presented
By Dionysius the Carthusian,
With Henricus Salteriensis,
Matthew Paris, Ranulph Higden,
And Cæsarius Heisterbacensis,
Marcus Marulus, Mombritius,
David Rothe, the prudent prelate,
And Vice-Primate of all Ireland,

---

* For the account of St. Patrick's Purgatory, as given by Messingham, see Notes, from p. 354 to p. 368.

Belarminus, Dimas Serpi,
Bede, Jacobus, and Solinus,
Messingham, and to express it
In a word, the Christian faith
And true piety that defend it.
For the play is ended where
Its applause, I hope, commences.*

---

* For an explanation of this list of names, now for the first time
correctly printed, see Note, on "The authorities for the Legend, as
given by Calderon," p. 369.

NOTES.

—◆—

ACT THE FIRST.

SCENE II., p. 247.

> " Patrick is my name, my country
> Ireland, and an humble hamlet
> Scarcely known to men, called *Empthor*,
> Is my place of birth."

The passage in the original is as follows :—

> "Mi propio nombre es Patricio,
> Mi patria Irlanda ò Hibernia,
> Mi pueblo *es Tox*."
>
> Hartzenbusch, t. 1, p. 150.

This is the reading of all the editions, and has been adopted in
the German translation of the drama by Al. Jeitteles (Brünn, 1824).
" *Tox* " looks very unlike the name of a village, and it appears to
me to be simply a misprint. The whole of this speech of St.
Patrick is taken from the *Vida y Purgatorio* of Juan Perez de
Montalvan. The description of St. Patrick's birth-place, as given
by Montalvan, is as follows :—" En cuya jurisdicion ay un Pueblo,
de pocos moradores, llamado *Emptor*. Aqui nació un moço," &c.
(edition of 1664, f. 1.) It is quite plain that "*es Tox*" in Calderon's
play is an easily understood misprint for the "*Emptor*" of Montalvan.

> " Mi patria Irlanda ò Hibernia,
> Mi pueblo *Emptor*,"

even metrically, is a better reading than—

> " Mi patria Irlanda ò Hibernia,
> Mi pueblo *es Tox*."

In the hymn of St. Fiacc, a contemporary of the Apostle, the
birthplace of St. Patrick is said to have been at " Empthor," or

"Nemthur," as it is sometimes printed. The same locality is
assigned to it in the *Tripartite Life of Saint Patrick*, but considerable controversy has arisen as to the exact position of the place. See
The Life of Saint Patrick, by P. Lynch, Dublin, 1828 ; *St. Patrick,
Apostle of Ireland*, by J. H. Todd, D.D. (1864) ; and *The Life of
St. Patrick*, by M. F. Cusack, Kenmare, Co. Kerry (1869), a most
elaborate and very beautiful work.

SCENE II., p. 252.

This long address of Patrick is founded on the following passages
of the story as originally told in Montalvan's *Vida y Purgatorio de
San Patricio*, Madrid, 1627. The translation is made as literal as
possible, to show how closely Calderon followed even the language
of Montalvan.

Chapter I.—" Between the north and west is situated the Island
of Hibernia, or Ireland, as it is at present more usually called. It
was once known as the Island of Saints, because its inhabitants were
ever ready to shed their blood in the lists of martyrdom, which is
the highest proof of courage which the Faithful can give ; since life
being so dear to us, it is a most heroic act for the sake of religion to
offer it to the sacrilegious hands of a tyrant that only lives in seeing
others die.

" In this island there was a village with a few inhabitants, called
Emptor, which the sea, like a cincture of snow, not only encircled
but appeared to bind. Here was born a youth of such virtuous dis-
positions that he seemed to belie the promise of his years, since
virtue and adolescence are not easily reconciled. He gave himself
much to the reading of the Lives of the Saints, of whose exercises
he was a great imitator, very fearful of those snares which lie in the
way of youth, and which, though he escaped, he was not without a
disposition to fall into."   .   .   .   .

[This youth was St. Patrick's father, who married Conchessa, a
French lady, as mentioned by Calderon, who, in the older Lives of
St. Patrick, is said to have been the sister of St. Martin of Tours.
After the birth of Patrick, St. Conchessa, his mother, retired to a
convent, and his father became a priest. The story then continues.]

" Patrick remained in his early years under the tutelage of his
aunt, and God was so desirous of showing to the world the favours
with which He had pre-determined to honour that pure soul, that
He did not wait for the time when Patrick would be of an age to
ask for them ; since before he could speak the words God declared

Himself his friend. For a blind man, Gormas (a neighbour of his in that village), heard one day a voice in the air which said to him, that if he went to Patrick (a child recently baptised), who would with his right hand make the sign of the cross upon his eyes, he would be restored to sight. He did so, and saw : God no doubt to foreshadow by this the great things that he would eventually work through this His servant. And this predestination, as it were, He made more remarkable by another miracle, which, if it was not greater, was more acknowledged and more widely known from the number of persons who were astonished at beholding it. In a certain year, it happened that such a quantity of snow had fallen from heaven, so great was the extent of the thaw when the sun melted it, that the water covered all the ground, and grew to the dimensions of a lake, which, spreading into the village, inundated all the houses, putting even that of Patrick in the greatest danger. But he, being then only ten years old, with a lively and courageous faith made the sign of the cross upon the waters, and in the sight of all compelled them to retire into the bed of the sea, the land remaining as dry and as free from snow as in the height of summer. . . . .

"One morning, being about the age of sixteen years, as he stood by the shore of the sea, reciting the Psalter with some of his companions, certain pirates made a sudden descent upon the coast, and having seized them, re-embarked immediately through fear of being baulked of their prize. Patrick was brought to a remote extremity of Ireland, and, like another Joseph, was sold to a prince of that island, who, thinking him fit for nothing else, gave to him the care of his sheep. This was an occupation very agreeable to Patrick, for as love can avow itself more openly in solitude, he spent all the night and all the day in loving and conversing with God, making altars of the rocks and of the flowers, on which to make to Him the entire sacrifice of his heart.

"The astonishing increase of the flock, which multiplied every day beneath his charge, soon became known to his master, who, being one night asleep, saw among the obscure visions of his dreams his slave Patrick rejoicing and surrounded by a great light, from whose mouth issued a beautiful and resplendent flame, which touching his two daughters, who he thought were by his side, burned them and reduced them to ashes, leaving himself alone untouched by that sweet and amorous flame. Frightened at such an astonishing vision, scarcely had the day come, when he sent for his slave and related to him what had occurred, asking him to explain the mystery of that terrible dream. To which Patrick replied, with great tranquillity, that the flame which he had seen come from his mouth could only be the Faith of the most Holy Trinity, which for a long time he had desired to preach to him and his daughters. And further, that it was because this doctrine would make no impression on his soul the flame refused to touch him, he dying blind in his infidelity. But because his daughters would eventually be convinced of the truth, God permitted them to be burned by the flame of His Faith and His Love, so as to fulfil the end for which they were created. With this Patrick took leave of his master and returned to his flock, leaving him so confused that he did not know whether he should punish him for what he had announced; all which happened in the manner the saint had predicted.

"In this way he lived some years, and our Lord, seeing that the solitude in which His servant passed his life in the fields was very great, sent to him as a companion his guardian angel, Victor, to whom he could communicate his thoughts, and from whom he would receive consolation in his slavery. But one night, being engaged in prayer, and yielding his spirit to a divine ecstasy and rapture, he saw as in a mirror a man of dignified appearance, whose dress gave him to understand that he was of the same country as himself. This personage seemed to be the bearer of a letter, the superscription of which Patrick approaching to read, he saw these words:—*The voice of the Irish people.* And as he hastened to open the letter to see its contents, it seemed that within it were all the inhabitants of Ireland, men, women, and children, even the little infants, all crying out to him and saying, "*Patrick, Patrick, we implore that you will come to us and free us from this slavery.*" The Saint upon this awoke, and consulting his angel, asked him to be released from his captivity, since he had a great desire to return to his country and assist those who had such need of him."—*Vida y Purgatorio de S. Patricio*, per el Doctor Juan Perez de Montalvan. Madrid, 1628, and Madrid, 1664.

[The visit to St. Germain in France is then described: his residence with St. Martin of Tours, the journey to Rome, and all the other events follow in detail, which Montalvan collected from Messingham, Messingham's chief authority being the Life of St. Patrick, by Jocelin. These are all briefly epitomised in the address of the Angel Victor, as given by Calderon at the end of the first act.]

SCENE II., p. 262.

The story of Luis Enius, as given by Calderon in this long address, seems to be entirely the invention of Montalvan. It is told in the sixth chapter of his *Vida y Purgatorio de San Patricio*, and in the edition of 1628 fills over forty pages. Calderon follows the narrative very closely, but in one noticeable incident he greatly improves upon his predecessor. This is in the celebrated skeleton scene of the third act. The corresponding scene in Montalvan's story is puerile enough. In Montalvan Luis Enius has no interview with the skeleton, so powerfully described by Calderon. His conversion is effected by a floating piece of paper which had eluded his grasp for two nights, but which he seized on the third, and examined by a mysterious light at the foot of a cross. On the paper he perceived the representation of a skull, under which is written, *I am Luis Enius*. How utterly ineffective and commonplace this is compared with the fine scene in Calderon need not be pointed out.

The story of the vision of himself at Lerici, as recorded in some of the lives of the poet Shelley, which is almost identical with that in Calderon, was evidently suggested by this scene. Shelley's reference to the *Purgatorio de San Patricio* in a note to *The Cenci* shows the attention with which he read this drama. The "Embozado" which Captain Medwin and others supposed to be the name of one of Calderon's dramas, and which, as might be expected, Washington Irving vainly looked for in Spain, was the "*Hombre embozado*," the "Muffled Figure" of Calderon's *Purgatorio de San Patricio*, act 3, scene i.

A vivid description of this scene by Shelley to one of his friends may have been mistaken for a circumstance that had actually happened to the poet himself.

SCENE VIII., p. 273.

The *Athenæum*, in its elaborate review of the earlier translation of this drama, thus writes :—

" With the prayer of St. Patrick considerable licence has been taken ; but its spirit is well preserved, and the translator's poetry must be admired.

" PATRICK. Thou art of all created things,
O Lord, the essence and the cause—
The source and centre of all bliss ;
What are those veils of woven light,
Where sun and moon and stars unite—
The purple morn, the spangled night—
But curtains which thy mercy draws
Between the heavenly world and this ?
The terrors of the sea and land—
When all the elements conspire,

The earth and water, storm and fire—
Are but the shadows of thy hand ;
Do they not all in countless ways—
The lightning's flash—the howling storm—
The dread volcano's awful blaze—
Proclaim thy glory and thy praise?
Beneath the sunny summer showers
Thy love assumes a milder form,
And writes its angel name in flowers ;
The wind that flies with winged feet
Around the grassy gladdened earth,
Seems but commissioned to repeat
In echo's accents—silvery sweet—
That thou, O Lord, didst give it birth.
There is a tongue in every flame—
There is a tongue in every wave—
To these the bounteous Godhead gave
These organs but to praise his name !
O mighty Lord of boundless space,
Here canst thou be both sought and found—
For here in everything around,
Thy presence and thy power I trace.
With Faith my guide and my defence,
I burn to serve in love and fear ;
If as a slave, Oh, leave me here !
If not, O Lord, remove me hence !"

The *Athenæum*, Oct. 26, 1853.

ACT THE THIRD.

SCENE X., p. 347.

The account of St. Patrick's Purgatory given by Luis Enius in this long narrative is taken immediately from the seventh, eighth, and ninth chapters of Montalvan's *Vida y Purgatorio de San Patricio*, which, as already stated, are themselves a translation from the *Florilegium Insulæ Sanctorum* of Messingham. The following extracts are taken from the tract referred to in the Introduction, the full title of which is as follows :—

"A BRIEF HISTORY OF SAINT PATRICK'S PURGATORY, AND ITS PILGRIMAGE. Collected out of Ancient Historians. Written in *Latin* by the Reverend MR. THOMAS MESSINGHAM, formerly Superior of the *Irish Seminary* in *Paris*. [Paris, 1624.]

"And now made *English* in favour of those who are curious to know the Particulars of that Famous Place and Pilgrimage so much celebrated by Antiquity.

"Printed at *Paris*, 1718."

"CHAPTER IV.

*"Of the Penitent Soldier, his going into this Purgatory, and of the
Messengers sent from God unto him.*

" There was a certain Soldier called *Owen*, who had for many
years served in King *Stephen's* Army.   This Man, having obtained
Licence from the King, came to the *North of Ireland*, his Native
Country, to visit his Parents ; and when he had continued there for
some time, he began to reflect upon the wickedness of the Life he
had led from his Infancy ; upon his Plundering and Burning in the
Army ; and (which grieved him more) upon the many sacrileges he
had been guilty of in Robbing and Spoiling Churches ; together
with many other Enormous hidden Sins. Being then interiorly moved
to repentance, he went to a certain Bishop in that country, and Confess'd all his Sins unto him.   The Bishop severely reproved him,
and let him know how grievously he had provoked God's indigna-
tion.   The Soldier hereupon being exceedingly sorrowful, resolved
to do penance suitable to the greatness of [his] Sins. For the People
of that country have this Naturally, that as they are more prone to
evil thro' Ignorance than Men of other Countries,* so are they more
ready and willing to do penance, when they are made sensible of the
Enormity of their Sins.   When the Bishop wou'd then enjoin him
such penance as he thought reasonable, the Soldier answered : *Since
you say that I have offended God so grievously, I will undergo a penance more grievous than any other whatsoever.   I will go into St.*
Patrick's Purgatory.   The Bishop, to diswade him from so bold an
attempt, related unto him, how many had perished in that Place ;
but the Soldier, who never feared any danger, wou'd not be dis-
waded.   The Bishop advised him to take the Habit of the Canon
Regulars, or that of the *Monks ;* and the Soldier declared he wou'd
do neither till he had first gone into the said *Purgatory.*   Whereupon the Bishop, perceiving he was inflexible and Truely penitent,
wrote by him to the *Prior* of the place and charged him to deal with
the Soldier, as was usually done with those, who desire to enter this
Purgatory.   The *Prior*, upon perusal of the Bishop's Letter, after
that he had observed all the other Formalities required, conducted
the Soldier into the Church, where he passed the accustomed time
of fifteen days in Fast and Prayer. Then the *Prior* having celebrated

---

* It should be mentioned that this unfavourable opinion of the Irish people is
quoted by Messingham from the MS. of Henry of Saltrey, an English monk,
who appears never to have been in Ireland.

Mass gave him the Sacrament, called together his own Brethren, and the Neighbouring Clergy, conducted him to the door of the *Cave*, sprinkled him with *Holy-water*, and made him this speech.— *Behold thou shalt now enter in here, in the Name of our Lord Jesus Christ, and shalt walk thro' the Hollow of this Cave, till thou comest to a Field, where thou shalt find a Hall artificially wrought ; into which when thou hast enter'd thou shalt find Messengers sent from God, who shall tell thee in Order what thou art to do, and to suffer. When these are gone and thou alone in the Hall, Evil Spirits will immediately come to tempt thee ; For so it happen'd to others that went in here before thee, but be thou of Manly courage, and Stedfast in the Faith of* Jesus Christ.

" The Soldier, who fear'd no Colours, was no way frighten'd at what happen'd to others, having often before, Arm'd with Steel, fought against Men, now arm'd with Faith, Hope and Charity, and confiding in God's Mercy, went on boldly to fight against Devils ; so recommending himself to all their Prayers, and making *the Sign of the Cross on his Forehead*, courageously enter'd the Door, which the *Prior* Locked on the outside and Return'd in Procession with his Clergy to the Church.

" The Soldier, being desirous to War a new and an unusual Warfare, marched on boldly through the *Cave*, tho' alone, where the Darkness thickening upon him, he lost all manner of Light. Soon after a little glimmering light appear'd thro' the *Cave*, which led him to the Field and Hall aforesaid. Now there was no more light in this Hall than we usually have in winter after Sun-set. The Hall had no Walls, but was supported by Pillars and Arches on every Side, after the Manner of the Cloyster of a Monastry. Walking awhile in this Hall, and admiring the Beauty of its Structure, he saw the Inclosure, whose Structure he also admired as being more Beautiful. Wherefore having gone into it he sat down, and Casting his Eyes about him to take a full View, he observed fifteen Men clad in white Garments, shorn and dress'd like Monks, coming in, who saluted him in the name of the Lord, and sat down. Then after a short pause, he that seem'd to be their Prior and Chief, spoke to him after this Manner : *Blessed be the Omnipotent God, who put the good purpose into thy Heart of coming into this* Purgatory *for the cleansing of thy sins : But if thou doest not behave thyself Manly, thou shalt perish both Body and Soul. For immediately after we leave this House there will come a multitude of unclean Spirits, who shall inflict great Torments upon thee, and threaten thee with greater : They will promise to lead thee to the Door, by which thou hast enter'd in here, to see if by this means they might deceive thee, and get thee to go out. And if thou be overcome by the violence of their Torments, or frightened by their Threats, or deceiv'd by their Promise, and consent to their Demands, thou shalt be destroy'd both Body and Soul. But if thou be strong in* Faith, *and trust in the Lord, so as not to yield to their Torments, or Threats, or Promise; but despise them with a generous Heart, thou shalt not only be purged of all thy Sins, but shalt also see the Torments which Sinners endure, and the Place of Rest and Bliss which the Just enjoy. Have God then always before thine Eyes, and as often as they Torment thee, call upon our Lord Jesus Christ, and by the Invocation of His Name, thou shalt be deliver'd from whatever Torment thou art in. Lay all these Things up in thy Mind quickly; for we can stay here no longer, but recommend thee to Almighty God.*

" So having given the Soldier their Blessing, they departed."

"CHAPTER V.

" *Of the Coming of the Devils, and of the first Torment which the Soldier endured.*

" The Soldier being thus left alone by the Holy Men, began to exercise himself for a new kind of Warfare, and having put on the Armour of Christ, stoutly waited for him, among the Devils, who shou'd first provoke him to Battle. He put on the Coat of Mail of Justice, girt his Mind, as he wou'd his Head, with the Helmet of the Hope of Victory and of eternal Salvation, cover'd his Breast with the Shield of *Faith*, and armed his Hand with the Sword of the *Spirit*, which is the Word of God, devoutly calling upon *Jesus Christ*, that being defended by this Royal Fortress, his insulting Enemies might not conquer him. Nor did Divine Providence, which always protects those who trust in it, fail him. Being then, as aforesaid, sitting alone in the Inclosure, and with an undaunted Courage waiting for a Battle with the Devils, he heard all of a sudden so great a Noise as if all the Earth had been turn'd upside down : And indeed, if all the Men, and all the living creatures on Earth, in the Sea, and Air, had bellowed out together, it seemed to him, they cou'd not make a greater Noise : so that, had he not been protected by Divine Virtue, and happily instructed by the aforesaid Holy man, he wou'd infallibly have lost his Senses. But Lo, after this horrid Sound, there followed a sight of Devils more horrid; for there appear'd an innumerable multitude of Devils, in ugly frightful shapes ; who saluted him in a fleering manner and said : *Other Men who serve us, do not come to our Habitation till after Death ; but thou art pleased to Honour our Company so much, as that thou wouldst not, like others wait for Death ;*

but hast alive deliver'd both Body and Soul unto us : Thou hast done this, that thou mayst receive the greater Reward from us : Thou shalt then be abundantly rewarded as thou hast deserv'd. Thou art come hither to be tortur'd for thy Sins ; thou shalt then have what thou seekest, that is, Pressures and Grief. Yet for as much as thou hast hitherto served us, if thou wilt follow our Counsel, and return from whence thou camest, we will for thy reward lead thee safe to the Door by which thou hast enter'd in here ; that thou mayest live joyfully in the World, and not lose the sweet things which thy Body is capable to enjoy.

" All these things they said with an intent to deceive him, either with Terror or Flattery. But the stout Soldier of *Jesus Christ* was not shaken by Terror, nor seduced by Flattery ; and therefore contemned with an equal Mind, as well those that wou'd terrifie, as those that wou'd flatter him, in making them no Answer.

" The Devils, perceiving they had been despised by the Soldier, roar'd most horribly, and caused a fire to be kindled in the Hall that cast up a prodigious flame ; and having tyed him Hand and Foot, cast him into the Fire, and with Iron Crooks dragg'd him to and fro, making a most hideous Noise. Then the Soldier having on the Armour of God, and remembering the Documents given him by the Holy Men, neither forgetting the Arms of his Spiritual Warfare, called upon the Name of his pious Redeemer, saying : *Jesus Christ* have pity upon me. Whereupon he was so fully deliver'd from the said Flames, that the least spark of all that great Fire did not appear. The Soldier perceiving this mighty delivery, became more bold, and resolv'd to fear no more those whom he saw so easily overcome by calling for the Assistance of *Jesus Christ.*"

" CHAPTER VI.

" *Of the Four Penal Fields to which the Soldier was Dragged.*

" Then the Devils leaving this *Hall* with an hideous Cry, and an horrid Tumult separated themselves. Some of them dragged the Soldier thro' a vast Region, that was so dark and obscure, that he cou'd see nothing but the Devils. There blew a burning Wind in it, which cou'd scarce be heard, but yet so dry that it seemed to Pierce his Body. From thence they dragged him towards those bounds of the Earth where the Sun rises at *Midsummer*, and being come thither, as unto the end of the World, they turn'd to the right Hand and extended themselves over a large Valley towards that part of the Earth where the *Sun* rises in the Middle of *Winter*. Here the Soldier began to hear, at a distance, the most lamentable Groans and Sighs of a vast Number of People ; and the nearer he drew, the more he heard their doleful Lamentations. Being brought at last by the Devils to an exceeding long and large Field, whose bounds were out of sight, he there discover'd an infinite Number of Men and Women lying naked, flat on their Bellies, with great Iron Spikes red hot fastening their Hands and Feet to the Ground, and Miserably torturing them. Nay and observed them now and then, biteing the Earth for Rage and Pain, crying and bawling out ; *Spare, spare; Pity, pity;* when there was none by, who wou'd *Spare* or *Pity.* On the contrary, the Devils ran over them with great Scourges in their Hands lashing the Wretches, and saying to the Soldier : *Thus shalt thou be tortur'd if thou dost not agree to go back to the Door from whence thou camest, and to which we will conduct thee in Peace.* But the Soldier calling to mind how God had before delivered him, despised their Menaces : Then the Devils cast him down on the Ground, and began to torture him. But upon his invocating the Lord Jesus, they failed in their attempt.

"Leaving then this Field, they drag him to another that was full of great Misery ; for between this and the former, there was this difference, that whereas in the former the wretched People lay flat on their Bellies, here they sat only on their Buttocks, some whereof were surrounded with fiery Dragons, gnawing and biteing them after a lamentable manner. Others had fiery Serpents twisted about their Heads and Necks, fixing their Stings in their Hearts. Others in fine had monstrous big *Vultures* perching upon their shoulders, and sticking their horrid Bills in their Breasts as if they wou'd pull out their Hearts. Besides all this, the Devils went running over them with dreadful Scourges lashing and tormenting them, so as that the poor wretches never ceas'd Crying and Lamenting. All these Torments (say the Devils to the Soldier) shalt thou suffer, except thou consent to return from whence thou camest. The Soldier despised their Threats, and disabled them to do him any harm, by calling upon the Name of *Jesus.*

"Quitting then this place, they led the Soldier to the third Penal Field. This was also full of People of both Sexes, who lay fastened to the ground with so many Iron Spikes on Fire, fix'd thro' them, and so thick set in their Bodies, that from Head to Foot there was scarce any where, the Breadth of a Finger, which had not been pierc'd. These Wretches cou'd indeed form a voice to cry ; but it was such as Men in the Point of death usually do : They were naked also, like the rest, and were tortur'd over and above with a cold and burning Wind, besides what they suffer'd by the Scourges of the

Devils. Now when the Devils wou'd torture the Soldier after this manner, by calling upon the Name of *Jesus* he escaped untouched.

"They drag him along to the fourth penal Field, which was full of great Fires, in which all manner of Torments were to be seen. Some were here hung up in the Air by the Hands with red hot Iron Chains ; others by the Hair ; some by the Arms ; others by the Legs with their Heads downwards, and dipped into boiling Sulphur. Some hung by their Nails, with Iron Crooks fixt in their Eyes, in their Ears, in their Jaws, in their Nostrils, in their Breasts, and in other parts of their Bodies ; others were fry'd in Pans ; and others roasted by the Fire on red hot Spits, which some of the Devils turned, while others basted them with various melted Metals : Nor was the cruel scourging of the Devils wanting, even among the dreadful Cries and Lamentations of these wretched Souls. Here the Soldier saw many of his own companions and knew them ; yea, and saw all manner of Torments that can be imagin'd, neither cou'd any Tongue express the various Cries and Lamentations which he heard. The Devils having then expos'd all these to the Soldier's view, said unto him : These, and a great many more torments shalt thou endure, except thou go back out of the *Cave*. But the Soldier despised their Threats, called upon the Name of *Jesus*, when the Torments began, and so escaped."

"CHAPTER VII.

" *Of the Fiery-Wheel, Smokey-House, High Mountain, and Cold River to which the Devils dragged the Soldier*.

"Then the Devils carry'd away the Soldier to an Iron Wheel, that was red hot, and of a prodigious bigness. The Spokes and Stakes of this Wheel were garnished all round with Iron Crooks set on Fire, and on them hung Men fixed. One half of the Wheel stood above, and the other under ground : the horrid sulphurous Flame which issued from the Earth and surrounded this Wheel, did exceedingly torment the Men that hung on it. The same (say the Devils to the Soldier) that these suffer if thou will not return, shalt thou endure, nay and even see first what it is. Then they fasten'd Iron Bars to the Spokes of the Wheel, and turn'd it about with such Celerity, that not one Man of those that hung upon it cou'd be discern'd from another ; for the whole Wheel appear'd like a Circle of Fire : And when they had fasten'd the Soldier to it and, by turning it about, lift him up in the Air, he called upon the Name of *Jesus*, and came down unhurt.

" From hence they dragged him towards a Certain House of an extraordinary breadth, and so long that the End of it was out of sight. When they drew near this House the Soldier stood still, being afraid to go forward in the excessive Heat that came out of it. Then the Devils said unto him: What thou seest are Baths, and whether thou wilt or no, thou shalt Bath in them, as others do that are there now. Immediately after, there were heard the most dismal Cries and Lamentations imaginable proceeding from thence; and being brought in, he saw a cruel and horrid sight. The Floor of this House was full of round Pits join'd so close together, that no Man cou'd walk between them : and each of these Pits was full of boiling Liquors made of various Mettals, in which were plunged an infinite Number of both Sexes, and of Divers Ages. Some were dipped down over Head ; some to the Eyes only ; Others to the Lips; Some to the Neck ; Others to the Breast; Some to the Navel ; Others to the Thighs ; Some to the Knees ; Others to half the Leg ; Some had one Leg only in ; Others both the Hands : And thus were all these boiling Pits or Cauldrons filled with wretched Sinners, who set forth such dismal Groans and Lamentations as were sufficient to chill the Blood of the most hard-hearted Man. Here (say the Devils to the Soldier) shalt thou Bath, and with that they lifted him up and endeavour'd to cast him into one of the Cauldrons, but upon hearing the Name of *Jesus* they cou'd not prevail. Whereupon they quit this House, and Carry the Soldier to an exceeding high Mountain, where they show him a Number of Men and Women far beyond any of the former. These Wretches sat Stark Naked with their Toes bent, and look'd towards the *North*, as if they expected every minute to expire that way. And while the Soldier stood wondering what they waited for, one of the Devils said unto him: Possibly thou wondrest what these People expect with so much trembling and fear, but if thou agree not to go back, thou shalt soon know to thy cost the cause of their Fear. The Devil had scarce made an end of these Words, when a Whirlwind from the *North* rushed upon them, and blew away the Devils, the Soldier, and all the People, and cast them over the other side of the Mount into a River, that stunk, and was intolerably cold : and as often as any of these wretched people attempted to raise themselves over the Water, the Devils immediately plunged them down. But the Soldier, who had always in mind his Divine Assistant, called upon his Redeemer *Jesus Christ*, and so found himself ashore on the Other Side of the River."

"CHAPTER VIII.

" *Of the Pit that cast up Flames, and of the High Bridge to which the Devils led the Soldier.*

" The Devils were not as yet satisfied with all the injuries they had offer'd to the Soldier of Jesus Christ, and therefore dragged him towards the South, where he saw before him a dreadful Flame of Sulphurous Matter rising out of a Deep Pit, and vomiting up Men red hot like Sparks of Fire, and as the force of the Flames abated, falling down again into the Pit. When they came near this Pit, the Devils said to the Soldier : *This is the entrance to Hell ; this is our Habitation : and for as much as thou hast hitherto carefully served us, here thou shalt for ever continue with us ; for all those who serve us dwell here everlastingly. And when thou shalt once go in, thou shalt eternally perish both Body and Soul. Notwithstanding, if thou wilt obey now, and return to the Door of the Cave into which thou didst enter, thou may'st go safe home to thine own Dwelling.* The Soldier, who had so often experienced God's Assistance before, despised both their Threats and Promises. Whereupon the Devils, enraged to see themselves so often contemned, cast themselves headlong into the Pit, and thrust the Soldier down before them. Who the further he descended, the larger he observed the Pit to grow, and the more sensibly he felt the pain of the Fire : Here the poor Man was put to the extent of his patience ; for the pain was so intolerably acute, that for a while he had quite lost his Senses, and was not able to pronounce the Name of *Jesus !* but Almighty God taking pity of him enabled him at last to utter in some manner that Divine Name : Whereupon the Flame shot him up so as that he fell upon the Brink of the Pit : but so disordered, that for awhile he knew not where he was, neither cou'd he tell whither to turn himself. Then a new and unknown Legion of Devils rushing out of the Pit surrounded him, and asked what he did there? *Our Companions* (say they) *told thee this was the Gate of Hell ; but they told thee a lye, and thou shalt know it is so ; for we are always accustomed to tell lyes, that we may deceive those we cannot by telling the Truth. This is not the Hell, but we will bring thee to it.* And having so said, they dragged the Soldier along to a great and spacious River, that was cover'd all over with a stinking sulphurous Flame, and filled up with Devils and damned Souls. Know thou (*say they unto him*) that under this River lyeth Hell. Now there was a great and lofty Bridge over this River, in which three things appear'd very formidable, and almost impossible to be overcome by those who were to pass over it. The First, that the Surface of the Bridge was so slippery that it was impossible for any Man to fix his foot upon it; the Second, that the passage was so straight and narrow, that no Man cou'd stand or walk on it. The Third, that the Bridge was so high up over the River, as to create a Horror in any that shou'd look down. Thou must (*added the Devils*) go over this Bridge, and we will raise a mighty Wind which shall cast thee down into the River, where our Fellows that are there shall take thee and drown thee in Hell: For we are resolv'd to try how safe thou shalt think it for thee to attempt so dangerous a Thing: However, if thou wilt consent to go back to the Door of the *Cave*, thou shalt escape this Danger, and return safe home to thine own Country.

"The faithful Soldier reflecting within himself, upon the great and many Dangers from which his Pious advocate *Jesus Christ* had deliver'd him, and calling often upon his Name boldly stepped in upon the Bridge, and began to walk forward, feeling nothing slippery under his Foot, but all firm and steady; because he firmly confided in God and steadily adhered to his Promise: Nay the Higher he went up the Bridge the broader he found the Passage; so as that in a short space the way was equal to a Road where several carts may meet and pass. Now the Devils who led the Soldier by the Hands to the Bridge, not being able to walk with him thereon, stood at the Bridge Foot, expecting to see him fall down, but perceiving that he walked on without any Danger, they raised a Cry and Noise so dreadful that it put him into a greater fright than any of the Torments before had done. Yet when he found that the Devils stood still, and did not follow him, he went on securely, relying on the Assistance of his Divine Protector. The Devils also that were in the River under the Bridge, seeing him go on over their heads, ran about the Bridge, and cast their fiery Crooks and Darts at him; but being protected by the Shield of Faith, he felt no harm, and so got clear of all their Ambushes."

"CHAPTER IX.

"Of the Cælestial Glory and Terrestrial Paradise shewn to the Soldier, and of his Conference with the Bishops thereon.

"The invincible Soldier being now deliver'd from the Snares of the unclean Spirits, saw before his Eyes an High Wall raised to the Skies, the Beauty and Structure whereof was beyond Estimation. Its Gate was adorn'd with costly Jewels, and divers precious Mettals, that afforded a most agreeable Prospect. Having approached, as it were within Half a Mile to it, the Gate seem'd to open, and sent forth so sweet a smell, that, as it seem'd to him, if all the Earth had been turn'd into Spice, it could hardly afford so agreeable a perfume, which so refresh'd his tired Limbs and Spirits, that he believed he could with ease undergo again all the Torments he had endured. And looking in at the Gate, he discover'd a Door which excelled the brightness of the *Sun.* As he stood then at a little distance from the Gate, there came out to meet him so beautiful, so great, and so orderly a Procession, as was never to be parallel'd to his thinking in this World, with *Crosses, Wax Tapers, Banners, and Golden Palm Branches* in the Hands of the Men that led this Procession. After these follow'd Men of all Degrees and Orders, some *Archbishops,* some *Bishops, Abbots, Monks, Chanons, Priests,* and *Clerks* of every Degree, all cloathed in the sacred Apparel proper to their Respective Degrees and Orders ; and like in Shape and Colour to those they wore, when they serv'd God here on Earth. Being come up to the Soldier, they all embraced him with unspeakable joy, and conducted him into the Gate with a concert of so Melodious an Harmony, as could not be equalled by any in this World.

" When the Musick ceased, and the Procession ended, two *Archbishops* took the Soldier apart, in order, as was thought, to shew him this new World, and the Glory of it, but first they blessed God, who had strengthen'd his soul with so much constancy, in all the Torments thro' which he passed, and which he so resolutely bore.

" They then conducted him over all the pleasant places of this new World, where his Eyes were so charmed, and all his Senses so ravished that, in his opinion, neither the Tongues of the ablest Orators cou'd explain, nor the Pens of the nimblest Scriveners indite the Glory and Splendor of the Things which he had seen and heard. So great was the light of this happy Region, that as the light of a candle is Eclipsed by that of the *Sun,* so was the light of the *Sun* by the brightness of this. The Night doth never overshade this Land, for the light of a Pure and Serene Sky keeps it constantly bright. All the Land was like a pleasant Green Meadow diversified by various sorts of Flowers, Fruits, Trees and Herbs ; whose very perfumes, saith the Soldier, wou'd keep him alive, were he allowed to dwell always there. The Bounds of the Country he did not see for the greatness of its Extent, only of that part by which he enter'd it ; but discover'd in it so great a multitude of both Sexes as he believes no Man ever saw in his Life, or ever was together in any Age ; of whom some dwelt apart in one Community, and some in another ; yet so as they passed from one society to another, as they pleased. And by this means, it came to pass, that they all enjoy'd one another's company ; and *choirs* joyn'd with *choirs* to sing God's Praise : And as one Star differs from another in brightness ; so was there an agreeable and harmonious variety and difference in the Habits and Countenances of those thrice happy People. For some of them seem'd to be clothed in Golden Vests ; others, in Purple, some in Scarlet ; others in Blew ; some in Green, and others in White. And the Shape and Fashion of each habit was the same as that which they wore in the World ; so that the Soldier cou'd easily discern of what Dignity, Order, and Degree, each of them had been. Some wore Crowns like Kings, others carry'd Golden *Palms* in their Hands. Glorious then and agreeable to the Eye, was the sight of such great Saints ; and no less pleasant, and ravishing to the Ear, the inexpressible Harmony of their Melody, in Singing the Praises of their Lord and Maker. Each of them rejoiced at his own Happiness, and at that of every other. And all of them, who saw the Soldier, Praised God upon his coming among them, and rejoiced at his Deliverance from the Devils. Here was neither Heat nor Cold, nor anything else that cou'd incommode or molest ; but all things peaceable, quiet, still, agreeable. Many more things did the Soldier, see and hear in this happy Region than any Tongue or Pen cou'd express.

" When he had then satiated his Eyes and Ears, the Bishops spoke to him after this manner."

*   *   *   *   *   *

" After this discourse the venerable Prelates took the Soldier up to the Top of a Mountain, commanded him to look up and tell them what colour the Sky over his head appear'd to him to be of. The Soldier answer'd that it appear'd to him to be of the colour of Gold in a fiery Furnace. *That* (say they) *which thou see'st is the Gate of Paradise. By this Gate those that are taken up from us go into Heaven. And you are to know further, that while we continue here, we are constantly fed once a day with Food from Heaven, but that you may know what sort of Food, and how pleasant it is, you shall, God willing, Feel and Taste it with us.*

" These words were no sooner pronounced, when Certain Rays like flames of Fire cover'd the whole Region, and after a while dividing into smaller Rays sat upon the Heads of every one in the Land, and at last enter'd into them. And among the rest, sat upon the Soldier's Head also, and enter'd into him. The Soldier was wrapt up in such extasie at the Sweetness of this Food, that he cou'd not tell whether he was dead or alive, but this soon passed over.

This is the Food (added they) with which God feeds us once a day; but they that are carryed hence from us enjoy it without End. The Soldier wou'd willingly stay there if he were allowed to enjoy the deliciousness of that Food. But instead of so sweet and desirable, mournful things are related unto him.

"*For as much then (beloved Brother continue the Prelates), as thou hast partly seen what thou didst desire to see, namely, the Rest of the Blessed, and the Torments of Sinners; thou must now return by the same Way thou camest hither; and if thou wilt for the future lead a sober and godly Life; thou shalt be secure not only of this Rest; but also of the Heavenly Mansions; but if thou wilt, which God forbid, lead an ill Life and pollute thy Body with Sin; behold thou hast seen the Torments that attend thee. Thou may'st now safely return; for thou need'st not fear any of those Things; wherewith the Devils attempted to frighten thee in thy way hither; because they dare not approach thee any more, being afraid to appear before thee; neither can all the Torments which thou hast seen hurt thee.* The Soldier was astonished at these Words, and began with Tears and Crys humbly to beseech the Bishops, not to oblige him to return again to the Cares of the World from so great a happiness. *I cannot leave this place*, said he, *for I fear I shou'd be intangled in the snares of the World, so as to hinder me to come back here;* It shall not be as thou wouldest, replied the Bishops; but as He who hath made thee and us disposes, so shall it be; for He alone knows what is most expedient for us all."

"CHAPTER X.

"*How the Soldier went out of this Purgatory, made a Pilgrimage to Jerusalem, and how he spent the rest of his days.*

"Then Owen, the Soldier, having received their Blessing, set out, and return'd the same way he came. The Prelates conducted him to the Gate of Paradise, and shut it after him; and being sad and grieved to be obliged to return again to the Miseries of this World, he went back the same way till he came to the Hall, where he was first infested by the Devils. He saw indeed the Devils on the way, but so soon as they saw him, they vanished as if they had been afraid of him. He also passed thro' the Places where he was before tormented; but now they had no Power to hurt him. Being then come to the said Hall, he went in boldly, and Lo the fifteen Men, who had instructed him in the beginning, met him, glorifying God, who had given him so much constancy in his Torments, and, having congratulated him upon his victory, said unto him : *Courage, Brother. We know thou hast overcome the Torments which thou hast so manfully born ; and that thou art purged of all thy Sins. The* Sun *begins now to rise in thy Country : Make haste then up to the Cave : For if the Prior, who when he hath said Mass, shall come to the Door, finds thee not there, he will lock the Door, as Despairing of thy salvation ; and return to the Church.* The Soldier hereupon, having first got their Blessing, hasten'd up to the *Cave*, and at the very Minute that the Prior open'd the Door, the Soldier appear'd. The Prior embraced him, glorified God, and conducted him to the Church, and caused him to continue there fasting and praying for fifteen Days. Then the Soldier put on his Shoulder the mark of the Cross of *Christ* and went with great Devotion to the Holy Land, to visit the Sepulchre of our Lord *Jesus Christ* at Jerusalem, and all the Holy Places round about it. Which when he had Devoutly performed he came back, and went to *Stephen*, King of *England*, to whom he had been before familiarly known, to advise with him, after what Manner he might best for the future, Warfare for the King of Kings, as he had here-tofore carry'd Arms for him.

"It happen'd at the same time, that *Gervasius* Abbot of *Lude*, had got by King *Stephen's* Recommendation a Place in *Ireland* for the building of a Monastry. This Abbot sent one of his Monks, called *Gilbert*, to the King, to be recommended by him to the King of *Ulster*, and then to proceed from thence to *Ireland* in order to erect the said Monastry : who being Kindly received by the King, complained very much that he was a stranger to the *Irish* Language ; I shall find you, by God's help, says the King, an excellent Inter-preter. Then he called Owen, the *Irish* Soldier, commanded him to go with *Gilbert*, and to continue with him in *Ireland*. Owen readily obey'd the King's Orders, adding with all, that he was obliged in gratitude to serve the Monks, whose Charity he had so often and so remarkably experienced. They then went over to *Ireland*, and began to build the Monastry, which they finished in two years and a half. The Monk *Gilbert* took care of the things within the Monastry ; and Owen the Soldier was a trusty Procu-rator, and devout Minister of the Things abroad ; as also a faithful Interpreter : And having taken the Habit of a Monk ; he lived an Holy and Religious Life all the rest of his days, as the said *Gilbert* testifieth. Whenever this *Gilbert* and the Soldier happen'd to be alone ; Gilbert was very inquisitive to know from him the particulars of all the Things he had seen and felt in this *Purgatory* ; and the Soldier who upon pronouncing the word *Purgatory*, used to burst out into Tears, told him all that he had seen and felt, which yet he wou'd willingly have concealed, had he not been persuaded, that it might tend to the Edification, and Amendment of the Lives of many. Nay and affirmed upon his Conscience, that he had seen with his corporal Eyes all the Things which he related. Now it was by the Care and Industry of this Monk, and upon the Testimony and Credit of the Bishops of this part of the Kingdom, who had the account from the Soldier's own Mouth, and that of the other Religious and godly men of those Times that these things were committed to Posterity."

The last chapter, which is "*Of the Examination and Manifold Proofs of this History,*" concludes with the following observations by Messingham himself.

"This History of *Owen* the Soldier, as to that part of it that is related by *Henry Salteriensis*, I borrow'd from an ancient Manuscript of the said Author now extant in the Library of St. *Victor*, and that related by Mathew Paris, I took from his printed History of *England*: But if after all, any Man chuse rather to oppose, than piously to believe the same, let him consult the Holy Fathers, *St. Gregory*, *Venerable Bede*, *Dionysius Carthusianus*, and carefully read the various Revelations, Visions, and Relations not unlike these recorded by them ; to which as to things very probable they themselves were not affraid to give Credit, and which they would not presume to deny."

Calderon was not the only celebrated poet who made the Purgatory of St. Patrick the subject of his song. Four centuries before the great Spanish dramatist was born, a most elaborate and very lengthy poem was written on the same attractive theme by Marie de France, the first woman, as M. de Roquefort says, who ever wrote French verse, the Sappho of her age.* Nor was Marie herself the only minstrel of that early time who yielded to the fascination of this legend. Two anonymous Trouvères of a little later period were unconsciously her rivals in the attempt. M. l'Abbé de la Rue, in his valuable work on Norman and Anglo-Norman Poetry, thus writes :—

"Quoique la célèbre Marie eût, au XIIIe siècle, donné une assez ample histoire du Purgatoire de St.-Patrice, puisqu'elle est de plus de trois mille vers, deux autres Trouvères anglo-normands qui probablement ne connaissaient pas son poème, volurent dans le siècle suivant traiter le même sujet."†

These poems, still unedited, are to be found in the Cottonian and Harleian MSS. The reader is also referred to the very interesting

---

* *Poésies de Marie de France*, par B. De Roquefort. Paris, 1820. t. i., p. 1.

† *Essais Historiques sur les Trouvères*, &c., par M. L' Abbé de la Rue. Caen, 1834. t. iii., p. 245.

and exceedingly rare volume, *Owain Miles* (Edinburgh, 1837), and *The Visions of Tundale* (Edinburgh, 1843), in the Prefaces to both of which, by the late lamented W. B. D. D. Turnbull, much curious information on the subject will be found.

THE AUTHORITIES FOR THE LEGEND,
AS GIVEN BY CALDERON.

ACT III., SCENE X. (the concluding lines.)

The list of authorities at the end of the third act has been, and not without reason, a source of great perplexity. Calderon is blamed even by so thoughtful a critic as Mr. Ticknor for putting into the mouth of Enius himself the names of a number of writers who have in some way alluded to the Purgatory of St. Patrick, all of whom were of periods long subsequent to the time at which he represents himself to have lived, several of them being the very writers who nearly a thousand years later described his own adventures. But this is quite usual on the Spanish stage. There is scarcely a drama of Calderon that does not end in the same way. The last speaker, whoever he may be, and he is frequently the *gracioso*, abandons, for the last few lines of his speech, his assumed character, and addresses the audience as an actor in a brief epilogue. The list of authorities at the end of *El Purgatorio de San Patricio* is nothing more. It is simply an epilogue, perhaps a little longer than usual, which the curious nature of the subject to some extent justifies. The manner in which the names are printed is a different matter. But the reader should recollect that this drama was not printed by Calderon himself, but by his brother Joseph, who certainly in this instance at least considered it no part of his duty as editor to verify the correctness of the poet's references. Some of the confusion certainly is attributable to Calderon himself, as he has separated and transposed names for the purpose of adapting them to his versification. But other mistakes remain behind which we may fairly divide between Don Joseph and the printer.

The original lines, as given in all the editions, that of Hartzen-busch included, are the following :—

> " Para que con esta acabe
> La historia, que nos refiere
> Dionisio el gran Cartusiano,
> Con Enrique Saltarense,

> Cesario, Mateo Rodulfo,
> Domiciano Esturbaquense,
> Membrosio, Marco Marulo,
> David Roto, y el prudente
> Primado de toda Hibernia,
> Belarmino, Beda, Serpi,
> Fray Dimas, Jacob Solino,
> Mensignano, y finalmente
> La piedad y la opinion
> Cristiana, que lo defiende."

Some of these names are obvious enough ; it is with regard to those that are rendered more obscure by the manner in which they are presented that the difficulty arises. The list is taken for the most part from the fourth chapter of Montalvan's *Vida y Purgatorio de San Patricio,* but with the names singularly disconnected and mis-placed. They are turned, too, so completely into Spanish as to be scarcely recognised. Even in Messingham's *Florilegium,* where they are all to be found, though not in one place, they are not always correctly printed. The following attempt at identification, now made for the first time, will be found, it is believed, to be perfectly accurate.

The first name, *"Dionisio el gran Cartusiano,"* scarcely requires any explanation. The work referred to, in an edition of which I have a copy, is as follows :—

"D. Dionysii Carthusiani liber utilissimus de quatuor hominis novissimis, &c.," Parisiis, 1551.

The account *De Purgatorio Sancti Patritii* extends from fol. 235 to fol. 237.

"Enrique Saltarense " is Henry of Saltrey, a Benedictine monk of the Abbey of Saltrey in Huntingdonshire, who about the middle of the twelfth century first reduced to writing the Adventures of Owain, or Enius, in the Purgatory of St. Patrick.

Of him Messingham writes thus. Referring to his authorities, he says :—

" What you shall find under the Letter B, is taken from Henry Salteriensis, an English monk of the Cistercian order, who had been taught most excellent Precepts of a good Life as well as good Letters by Florentianus, an Irish bishop, and Gilbert de Luda [Louth, in Lincolnshire], Abbot of the Cistercian Monks, who also, being him-self well instructed, used to teach others the fear of the Lord as the beginning of wisdom. . . . And hence it is that he wrote unto Henry Abbot of Sartis one Book of the Purgatory of St. Patrick and one Book of the Pains of Purgatory. He flourished in the year of Grace 1140."—*A Brief History of St. Patrick's Purgatory.* Paris, 1718. *Preface.*

" Cesario," which carelessness or the exigency of metre has sepa-
rated from the " Esturbaquense," of the next line is Caesarius of
Heisterbach, a well-known hagiological writer of whom Adrien
Baillet thus speaks :—

" Un religieux Allemand de l'ordre de Citeaux nommé CÉSAIRE
de Heisterbach, qui mourut du tems de l'empereur Frederic II. tra-
vailla aussi à la vie des Saints." He adds in a note :—

" Césaire se fit moine l'an 1198, au Val de Saint de Pierre, dit
autrement Heisterbach, près de la ville de Bonne, dans le diocèse de
Cologne, et ne mourut que près de quarante ans après. Il avoit été
maître des novices dans son couvent, et ensuite prieur de la maison
de Villiers."—*Discours sur l'histoire de la Vie des Saints.* LES VIES
DES SAINTS. Paris, 1739. T. i., p. xlvii.

" Mateo Rodulfo," printed as the names of one author in Calderon, separate into two persons in Messingham and Montalvan.
The first is the well-known Mathew Paris, whose " Relation of the
vision of Owen the Irish Soldier " is expressly referred to in these
words by Messingham, who also alludes to him more fully in his
Preface. " What you shall find under the letter C," says Messingham, " is borrowed from Mathew Paris, an English Benedictine
Monk, who had from his youth consecrated himself to a Monastic
life, and polish'd most excellent talents of nature with exquisite
Arts and Sciences, and adorn'd the same with all Christian virtues ;
being an Handicraft, a Writer, a good Painter, a fine Poet, an acute
Logician, a solid Divine ; and (which is much more valuable) pure
in his Manners, bright in the innocence of his life, simple and
candid. Pitseus, upon the year 1259, in which the said Mathew
died, gives him a great many more encomiums, which for brevity
sake I here omit."

The remaining half of " Mateo *Rodulfo* " turns out to be Ranul-
phus, or Ralph, Higden, the Monk of Chester, whose *Polychronicon*
is quoted both by Messingham and Montalvan. The " Domiciano "
of the next line, which is " Dominicano " in Montalvan, has so completely got rid of the name to which it belongs, that without the aid
of Calderon's authorities, Messingham and Montalvan, it would be
impossible to know who was meant. In Messingham the reference
is to " Jacobus Januensis, the Dominican, in the Life of St. Patrick,"
and in Montalvan to " Jacobo Januense, o Genuense, Dominicano."
The person thus disguised is the famous Jacobus de Voragine, the
Dominican, author of " The Golden Legend," who was Bishop of
Genoa in 1292, and died at a very advanced age in 1298. Of the
Legenda Aurea, the fiftieth chapter is devoted to St. Patrick.

" Membrosio " is called " Mombrisio " in Montalvan, and

" Mombrusius" in Messingham. Correctly it was neither. The writer referred to is *Boninus Mombritius,* a fine copy of whose *Sanctuarium* is in the British Museum. At fol. 188, t. ii., there is a full account of the Purgatory, the name of the adventurous visitor being *Nicolaus.* Of Mombritius, whom he calls Bonin Mombrice, the same writer (Baillet), from whom I have already quoted, says :—

"Cet homme peu connu d'ailleurs étoit Milanois de naissance, conseiller ou fils de conseiller au sénat de Milan ; il vivoit du tems de Galeas Marie, duc de Milan, qui fut tué l'an 1476, et du Pape Sixte IV., qui mourut en 1484. Il s'étoit déjà fait regarder comme grammairien, poëte, orateur et philosophe par divers ouvrages, mais aucun ne lui fit tant d'honneur que son *Sanctuaire,* qui est le titre qu'il donna à son recueil d'actes des Saints dédié à Simonete, secrétaire des ducs de Milan."—*Discours,* p. lvii.

" Marco Marulo " is Marcus Marulus, Cap. xiv., Lib. 6, of whose work, " De religiose vivendi institutione per exempla," is entitled " De revelationibus infernalium pœnarum."—*Apud Sanctam Coloniam.* Anno M.D.XXXI.

In this there is an account of a certain Irish monk, "cui Petro nomen fuit," who appears to have entered the Purgatory in vision. This is probably the passage which Messingham and Montalvan quote, though a different reference is given.

Maurolicus Siculus, who follows next in Messingham and Montalvan, is omitted by Calderon.

" David Roto, y el prudente Primado de toda Hibernia," are one and the same person. This was the famous David Rothe, Bishop of Ossory, so intimately connected in 1642 with the Confederation of Kilkenny, of which an excellent history has been written by the Rev. Charles Meehan, M.R.I.A. The epithet "prudente" seems to have been a happy condensation of the many terms of encomium lavished upon this celebrated man by Messingham. Alluding again to his classification of his authorities under the first four letters of the alphabet, Messingham says :—

" Whatever then you shall find written under the letter A, until you come to the next letter, is taken from the Right Reverend Father David Roth, Lord Bishop of Ossory, and Vice Primate of all Ireland, a Man excellently well read in all parts of literature, an eloquent Rhetorician, a subtle Philosopher, a profound Divine, a celebrated Historian, a zealous chastizer of Vice, a steady Defender of Ecclesiastical Liberty, a constant Assertor of the Privileges of his Country, most devoutly compassionate upon the calamities of his Nation, a diligent Promoter of Peace and Unity among the Clergy, and, for that end, instituted the Congregation commonly called Pacifick, in the year 1620, which has, with no little fruit and advantage to the Clergy, spread itself over all the Kingdom,—a Man, in fine, who has left to Posterity many rare Monuments of his excellent talents, the Catalogue of which I shall not here, for good reasons, insert, but hope for more soon from him."

"Belarmino," "Beda." Cardinal Bellarmin and Venerable Bede are too well known to require any observations.

"Serpi, Fray Dimas," cut into two lines, with the names transposed, mean *Fr. Dimas Serpi*, one of whose works (*Aprodixis Sanctitatis*, &c., Romæ, M.DC.IX.), though not the one referred to by Messingham, is in the British Museum. In Montalvan the marginal note gives, "*Lib. de Purgatorio, cap.* 26," as the reference. The German translator of this drama (Brünn, 1824), misled by the punctuation of the original, treats Dimas Serpi as two persons.

"Jacob Solino," the next authority for the legend, is perhaps the most perplexing in the list. Like twin stars that seem one to the naked eye, but resolve themselves into two beneath the telescope, so the single author of the printed text of Calderon appears distinct persons in the pages of Montalvan. He gives them thus:—"Jacobo," "Solino," with a separate reference to each. Thus to "Jacobo," the marginal reference is, "*In sua historia Orientale;*" and to "Solino," "cap. 35," without the name of the work.

From Messingham we at once learn who the former writer was. He calls him in one place "Jacobus de Vitriaco," and in another more briefly, "Vitriacus." The passage referred to in the marginal note of Montalvan is given thus :—

"Further, *Jacobus de Vitriaco*, in his History of the *East*, chap. 92, writes thus concerning this cave :—*There is a certain Place in* Ireland, call'd *St*. Patrick's Purgatory, *into which whosoever enters, except he be truly penitent and contrite in Heart, is snatched away by Devils, and never returns. But he that with true contrition confesseth his sins, and goes in there, tho' the Devils vex and torture him, by Fire and Water, and many other Torments, yet is he purged of all his sins: Now they that are thus purged, and return, are never more seen to laugh or play ; or to take pleasure in any thing in this World, but constantly weeping and sighing, forget the things that are behind, and stretch forward to the things that are before them."—A Brief History of St. Patrick's Purgatory*, Paris, 1718, pp. 9, 10.

"Solino," who is so strangely united by Calderon's printer to "Jacob," presents some difficulty. In Messingham's list of authorities this name does not appear. The first French translator of Montalvan (Bruxelles, 1637) merely gives the Latin form of the name, "Solinus." The second French translator, Bouillon, in his

Histoire de la vie et du Purgatoire de S. Patrice (Troyes, 1642), turns both names into French, thus, "Jacques *Sotin*, en son Histoire Orientale, chap. 26." This is doubly a mistake. The *Histoire Orientale* is the work of Vitriacus, as already pointed out ; and "chap. 26" refers not to that work, but to some unnamed writing of "Solino."

Of course the first name that suggests itself, as the author alluded to, is that of Caius Julius Solinus. The latest date assigned as the period when this celebrated writer flourished is A.D. 238—that is, about 135 years before the birth of St. Patrick. To quote him as an authority on the subject of St. Patrick's Purgatory would therefore be a more absurd anachronism than any that has been pointed out in this curious list. This difficulty appeared to me so strong, that for a while I was led to believe that "Solino" was but a corrupted Spanish form of "Jocelino," or "Joscelino," as it is sometimes given, whose *Life of St. Patrick*, written in the twelfth century, supplies all the incidents of St. Patrick's early life recorded by Montalvan and Calderon. He is also frequently referred to by Messingham. But further reflection convinces me that the writer alluded to was in reality the celebrated Latin author of the third century already mentioned, Caius Julius Solinus.

Solinus has of course no allusion to St. Patrick's Purgatory ; but in his celebrated work, *Polyhistor*, compiled, it is thought, chiefly from Pliny's Natural History, he has a remarkable chapter on Ireland. Some of his statements are doubtful, and all are very curious; one of them at least depriving St. Patrick, by anticipation, of one of his most famous miracles. This is the banishment of the serpents, which it appears was first mentioned by Jocelin in the twelfth century. It is expressly stated by Solinus, who wrote in the third century, that in Ireland "There are no snakes and few byrdes," to use the language of the old English translator, Arthur Golding. This statement of the previous exemption of Ireland from venomous reptiles was warmly disputed by Dr. David Rothe, the Bishop of Ossory, early in the seventeenth century. It will be remembered that "David Roto" has already been quoted as an authority on the subject of St. Patrick's Purgatory, and it is his collateral controversy with Solinus that probably led Montalvan, and subsequently Calderon, to suppose that Solinus had in some way alluded to that legend. A valuable *Life of St. Patrick*, by P. Lynch (Dublin, 1828), contains many allusions to this subject, of which the following may be given as an example.

"The objections which Doctor Roth raised to the testimony of Solinus have as slender a foundation in reason. For Solinus (saith he) not only mentions this exemption of Ireland from venomous creatures, but says further, that in Ireland there are few birds, and no bees ; and therefore concludes, that as he is mistaken in these latter particulars, so he is not to be believed in the former,"—p. 42.

The author of this Life of St. Patrick goes on to say that Solinus may have been perfectly accurate in these statements. That other writers have alluded to the time when bees were first introduced into Ireland, and that the migration of some birds thither, among others the magpie, took place at a comparatively modern period. He does not add, however, that Solinus states that the very dust of Ireland was so distasteful to the bees, where they are now as much at home as in Hymettus, that if it is scattered about their hives even in another country they abandon their combs. Thus writes quaint Arthur Golding :—

" There is not any Bee among them, and if a man bring of the dust of the stones from thence, and strew them among Bee-hyves, the swarme forsake yᵉ combes."

Another misstatement of Solinus may be pointed out. He says :—

" The sea that is betweene Ireland and Britayne, being full of shallows and rough all the yeere long, cannot be sayled but a few dayes in the summer time."

With the following picturesque passage referring to the warlike training of their children by the Irish, as recorded by a Roman writer in the third century of the Christian era, we take leave of Solinus, who we have no doubt was the author referred to by Montalvan and Calderon under the name of "Solino : "—

" If a woman be delivered of a man childe, she layes his first meate upon her husband's sworde, and putting it softly to his prettie mouth gives him the first hansel of his sworde upon the very point of the weapon, praying (according to the manner of their country) that he may not otherwise come to his death, than in Battel and among weapons."—*The Excellent and Pleasant Worke of Julius Solinus Polyhistor. Translated out of Latin into English by Arthur Golding, Gent.* At London, 1587. p. 105.

The last name in the list of authorities on the subject of St. Patrick's Purgatory is " Mensignano," with the reference in the margin of Montalvan's *Vida y Purgatorio* to his *Florilegium.* This of course is Messingham, out of whose book, aided by his own wild imagination, Perez de Montalvan created the character of Luis Enius, who is presented to us with such dramatic power by Calderon.

Notwithstanding the length of these notes, the following summary, taken with some corrections from the Introduction to the former translation of this drama (1853), may still be useful :—

The curious history of *Luis Enius*, on which the principal interest of the play depends, has been alluded to, and given more or less fully by many ancient authors. The name, though slightly altered by the different persons who have mentioned him, can easily be recognised as the same in all, whether as Owen, Oien, Owain, Eogan, Euenius, or Enius. Perhaps the earliest allusion to him in any printed English work is that contained in Ranulph Higden's "Polychronicon," published at Westminster, by Wynkin de Worde, in 1495 : "In this Steven's tyme, a knyght that hyght Owen wente in to the Purgatory of the second Patrick, abbot, and not byshoppe. He came agayne and dwelled in the abbaye of Ludene of Whyte Monks in Irlonde, and tolde of joye and of paynes that he had seen." The history of *Enius* had, however, existed in MS. for nearly three centuries and a half before the Polychronicon was printed ; it had been written by Henry, the monk of Saltrey in Huntingdonshire, from the account which he had received from Gilbert, a Cistercian monk of the Abbey of the Blessed Virgin Mary of Luden, or Louth, in Lincolnshire (Colgan, *Trias Thaumaturgæ*, p. 281. Ware's *Annals of Ireland*, A.D. 1497). Colgan, after collating this MS. with two others on the same subject which he had seen, printed it nearly in full in his *Trias*, which was published at Louvain, A.D. 1647, where with the notes it fills from the 273rd to the 281st page. Messingham, as we have seen, had printed it earlier from other sources, in 1624. Matthew Paris, however, had before this, in his History of England, under the date 1153, given a full account of the adventures of *Oënus* in the Purgatory, and in the few places that I have compared his account with that given in Colgan, I find both generally agreeing in substance, though not in words. In the folio edition of Mathew Paris, London, 1604, the history of *Oënus* begins at the 72nd and ends at the 77th page. In Montalvan's life of St. Patrick, the adventures of Enius are given much more fully than either in Matthew Paris or Colgan. In their versions of the story the early life of Enius, previous to his undertaking to enter the Purgatory, is passed over with a few general remarks as to its extreme wickedness—while they give in great detail all that he saw and heard therein. Matthew Paris, for instance, opens the story of Enius in these words : "Miles quidam Oënus nomine, qui multis annis sub Rege *Stephano* militaverat—licentia a Rege impetrata, profectus est in Hyberniam ad natale solum, ut parentes visitaret. Qui cùm aliquandiu in regione illa demoratus fuisset cœpit ad mentem reducere vitam suam adeò flagitiosam :

Quod ab ipsis cunābulis, incendiis semper vacaverat et rapinis, et quod magis dolebat, se ecclesiarum fuisse violatorem et rerum ecclesiasticarum invasorem præter multa enormia quæ intrinsecus latebant peccata," &c.—*Mat. Par.*, p. 72. In Henry of Saltrey's account, as given by Messingham in 1624 and Colgan in 1647, this portion of the life of Enius is despatched even with more succinctness, but in Montalvan's *Vida y Purgatorio de San Patricio*, all his early crimes are detailed nearly in the order and almost in the very words that Calderon has used. Sir Walter Scott mentions, in his Border Minstrelsy, that there is a curious MS. Metrical Romance, in the Advocates' Library of Edinburgh, called, "The Legend of Sir Owain," relating his adventures in St. Patrick's Purgatory; he gives some stanzas from it, descriptive of the knight's passage of "The Brig O'Dread;" which, in the legend, is placed between Purgatory and Paradise. This poem is supposed to have been written late in the thirteenth century. It was printed for private distribution in Edinburgh, in 1837, but from the very limited impression, there having been but thirty-two copies struck off, it must always remain extremely scarce. A cognate work, however, "The Visions of Tundale" (Edinburgh, 1843), published by the same lamented scholar (Mr. Turnbull) who edited the former work, though rare, is more accessible.

THE END.